WATCHES III

A CAMPING FIASCO

Rich King

Copyright © 2022, Rich King

All rights reserved.

This book is a work of fiction. Any references to historical events, real people, or real places are used fictionally. Other names, characters, places, and events are products of the author's imagination, and any resemblance to actual events or places or persons, living or dead, is entirely coincidental.

The book contains material protected under International and Federal Copyright Law and Treaties. Any unauthorized report or use of this material is prohibited. No part of this book may be reproduced or transmitted in any form or by any means, electronic or mechanical, including photocopying, recording, or by any information storage and retrieval system without express written permission from the author/publisher.

CONTENTS

Chapter One - *The Roundown (1974)*   1
Chapter Two - *Officer Dawson (1994)*   13
Chapter Three - *Armybrats No More*   19
Chapter Four - *Duffster Dive*   25
Chapter Five - *Joann Dukes*   31
Chapter Six - *Dance Studio Demon*   43
Chapter Seven - *Bloody Bed*   55
Chapter Eight - *Black Cat*   67
Chapter Nine - *Stairwell*   75
Chapter Ten - *Altered Recording*   83
Chapter Eleven - *Broken Bra Strap*   87
Chapter Twelve - *Bratmobile*   99
Chapter Thirteen - *Pete's Struggle*   107
Chapter Fourteen - *Vacuum Velocity*   121
Chapter Fifteen - *Restaurant Masquerade*   135
Chapter Sixteen - *Guitar Strings*   165
Chapter Seventeen - *Wildcat Lanes*   173
Chapter Eighteen - *Black Cat*   207
Chapter Nineteen - *Funeral*   217
Chapter Twenty - *Billy's Decision*   225
Chapter Twenty-One - *Whimsical Moment*   249
Chapter Twenty-Two - *Confession*   253

Chapter Twenty-Three - *Roadblock*	257
Chapter Twenty-Four - *Too Late*	279
Chapter Twenty-Five - *Little Rapids*	285
Chapter Twenty-Six - *The Stairway*	289
Chapter Twenty-Seven - *The Sawmill*	299
Chapter Twenty-Eight - *Discovery*	321

PART III

Oh Armybrats. Oh Armybrats.
Come out, come out, wherever you are.
You can run. You can hide.
But as fast, as fast as, you think you might be,
When you turn around, you'll see me.
Watches, Watches, Watches, haha!

Was it over . . . ?

Unveiled stories from the Armybrats' past had come to light. Submissive about their future, the blue man in the garage, the headless snowman, the devil's doormat on the Fourth of July, the mud man in the stream, gasoline-filled balloons, a science room from hell, barrel-rolling down a hillside, crawling through a minefield, explosions, gunfire, grenades, and blood was the work of the devil himself, Stanley Markesan aka Watches. These were their childhood memories. Even though they posed the very possible presence of Post-Traumatic Stress Disorder, the emotional and physical scars kept the tension.

And the true question, *"Was it over?"* swung like a trapeze wire drilled into their brains. This trapeze hung from deep dark tissues of their minds; below them, a pit of lions waits, veering up, eager for lunch. Pressure tore the tissue from each swing. The hooks ripped at those thoughts separating lymph nodes from their memories—the lions gnawing away at the pieces that fell. Watches had one riddle. One riddle scorned their memories, *"I see a camp where you'll once visit, is where I'll bury your souls, 'n' your cryin' families'll miss it. Puddles of your blood will stain the beaches in splotches."*

They were already at that camp and survived once. Unfortunately, the school conservation trip hasn't happened yet.

Was it over...?

Chapter One

The Rundown (1974)

Granite View had a quaint little bar Stanley Markesan would frequent—other than Gerald and Nadine's establishment. This bar had a reputation for late-night brawls and early morning hangovers. Mostly, it was a breeding ground for thirsty, evening dwellers looking for pleasure, to socialize, or other midnight indiscretions. It was called The Hills Bar and Saloon.

The bartender dropped a pitcher onto the thick polyurethane-coated counter and filled it with a brew. A white towel was slung over his left shoulder. Blemishes within the fabric revealed damp spots from wiping tables. His bowl haircut and fair skin appeared like a mushroom protruding from his white-collared button-up. As he filled the pitcher, he poked at the center of his square spectacles, giving an ogle at the patrons in the dining area.

Stan sat with a young, long-haired, blonde woman. From a corner booth, they laughed mercifully. He had an arm around her neck while drinking from his other hand. She leaned in to give him some lipstick smudges. He rested his mug on a napkin and pinched her chin to help guide the kiss or be in control was more like it.

She smiled. "I have a room upstairs. Would you like to join me?"

In a far booth, Mike cocked his head toward his boss. "That's Stanley Markesan."

"And that's not his wife," his boss replied.

"Tony, I'm sick 'n' tired of sticking my neck out for this guy."

Tony glanced at the restrooms and saw the payphone near the hallway. He suggested, "Well, I know another way you could squelch this thing real quick like."

Mike glanced at the dim-lit phone his boss had noticed. He turned his head at him in agreement. A slight smirk pushed one cheek higher. The intuition spilled out of his boss and splashed across the table. Mike knew what Tony suggested.

The two drunken whippersnappers eased between a few tables on their way to her love dungeon above the bar. Mike turned to watch them stagger out a side door. The young woman ran her hands around his body, making their way toward an exit.

Tony smiled. "They aren't going far. She's got a room above the bar."

Mike took a drink. He lowered the mug, nodded, and headed for the payphone.

Outside, they made their way toward the desolate stairway alongside the locally owned drinking trough. Without haste, Stan found himself rolling across the dirt path in the alleyway. Something rather large bashed him across the back. A man shoved the girl using a steel trashcan lid. She groaned as her head nailed the brick wall. Blood trickled into the concaved granules of brick and mortar. More hung from her chin.

A man stood at the base of the stairway clinging onto the girl. He restrained her from moving. His face was hidden beneath the shadows of a hoodie. Stanley dragged his body through the dry dirt; dust fanned around his legs as he struggled to stand up. The man had used the lid to separate the two of them.

Stan stepped toward him; he grew jumpy, dropped the lid onto the trashcan, and placed a chokehold on the girl. He demanded, "Give me all your money, pal, and I'll let the girl be."

Stanley's one eye blinked. His eyepatch started collecting beads of water from an early evening rain. A fresh cut on his forehead spat blood where it met with rainwater, traveling by surface tension. "Boy, you have no idea who you're messing with. Why don't you go home to mama and forget you ever attempted this?" Not a single expression crossed Stanley's face. No forehead wrinkles, no squinted eye, not even a hint of fear or hostility. He stepped in a clockwise pattern. The man grew antsier.

Rain began; it beat on them. A streetlight created the flicker from the edge of the blade that caught Stan's eye. Seemingly, it appeared from nowhere. Beads of rainwater built upon its jagged edge. It was a combat knife. It was held to her temple. She cried a bit when the sharp tip drew a shadow inward from the pressure; the man's tension on her throat eased the sound of her squawk. He wasn't going home to mama. He wanted Stanley's money. If he didn't get what he wanted, he was planning to take it out on the girl whose body remained twisted in his death squeeze. Her right leg hung over the curb. The man's legs intertwined with hers. The haze of the streetlamp swarmed with moths, yet the rain may have been taking them out one-by-one as their flock dwindled in the blur.

While maintaining discretion and ease, Stanley whispered, "I'm a delivery driver, drinking at this Podunk bar, in this Podunk town. What makes you think I have any money boy?"

"Shut up. Give me your wallet."

"If you knew what was good for you son, you would go."

"What are you going to do about it, one eye?"

A streak of lightning cracked the sky; the buildings lit around them. The man with the knife covered his face and glanced skyward. He cleared rain from his eyes, but when he focused on where Stan had been standing, repetitive lightning displayed an empty path. The boy turned around. The girl was no longer in his tight grip. He approached the side of the building where the trashcan was pressed against the brick wall. He watched the rain beat the lid.

"What the hell?" The man sighed. He stepped onto the sidewalk and turned toward the parking lot near the front of the building. He heard rainwater beating a trellis and peered toward the corner of the foundation where water spat out the angled pipe.

Behind the man, the lid of the trashcan rose, hovering like a silent drone. Rainwater hit the stairwell harder. The man spun around to notice the opened trashcan. He cocked his head in confusion, leaning to peek inside. It was the last place he dropped the lid. Above him, the lid maneuvered vertically, spinning like a saucer—gradually increasing speed.

Within the shadows, Stan had propped himself against the building, one leg cockeyed; the sole of his shoe planted firmly on the foundation wall. In deep concentration, with his only eye shut, he twirled his index finger—in awe of this newly-discovered energy within him. The other man seemed puzzled at first; beads of light twinkled over his head where the saucer hovered, increasing spin velocity. Stan opened his eye and dropped his finger. All at once, the man's face met with wet goop alongside the outer trash bag. The lid had driven him into the plastic when it sliced through dead air, colliding into the backside of his head. The hammer of steel forced him to topple over the trashcans.

Stanley stood over him as he fell to the sidewalk, swallowing trash particles. A thunderous roar filled the alley as the can scraped the concrete. The lid rolled along the brick foundation; each wobble scratched the surface. Stan raised his hand from his side; the trashcan lid lay between him and the building. Sheer anger raged deep within him. A scornful look melded his cheek to his eyeball. The solemn flare in his face presented ill will toward this mugger.

Suddenly, a trail of light launched from his fingers. The light reflected against the lid. Stan hopped off the curb. He held his hand near his face, staring at it awkwardly. His eyeball examined his hand, and he saw the man awakening inside the trashcan. Stan turned his hand toward the lid to test this new force. A light trail shot at it. Stanley seemed to pass energy from his body into the round hunk of steel. Energy lifted the glowing handle at the center and scooted the lid tight against the wall.

More lightning revealed Stan's face, his one eye, and his eye patch above a dimple. His upper lip curled; his one eye held a red tinge. It narrowed. His teeth clenched. With lightning bolts and his electrical surge, Stan's face flickered—his one eye seemingly getting redder amidst the flashes. Light trails dissipated; lightning returned in the sky. Stan was gone.

The man rolled onto his side, coughing; he stared at the few cars in the lot. He spat at the road. He regained his composure, scavenging for his knife, rolling the trashcan away to check underneath. The bright blue lid caught his attention. It almost seemed white, yet it was gray; a faint glow shone in the puddle that surrounded it. He stood up and extended an arm for the handle, his fingertips inches away. With an open shirt sleeve in the water, an electrical discharge flashed. His eyes cast streaks in the dark alley. The hair on his head towered into vicious points like rubber balloons striking static. His entire body rocketed from the wet puddle. He gave a short bellow but winced when the stairway caught his back. A crack echoed through the alleyway from where he had landed. One shoe flipped through the air and bounced off the curb.

He gasped. The rain pelted him hard. He closed his eyes in agony, struggling to lift his shaky hand. Rain tapped his blackened fingers and pelted the shirt sleeve melted to his wrist. Smoke whirled from the darkened material. Focusing on his burnt hand and brownish-red fingernails, one red eye revealed itself in the dark space between steps. A hand shot out and cupped his mouth. His eyes widened. Another arm reached out with his combat knife, jagged edge toward his throat. A muffled scream died in the thunder. But the rainwater, gray from the concrete's surface, transformed into clouds of crimson seen only in the lightning flashes. Blood filled the puddle.

Back inside the bar, Mike glanced up as the door swung open. A middle-aged woman stepped in; she scanned the place until she spotted him. He stood up, waving. She approached him, holding no expression on her face. She glanced at Tony, nodded, and asked, "Where is he?"

Mike glanced at Tony, then at her, and explained, "He's upstairs, but I advise you to take either Tony or myself with you."

"No, this is my problem."

Tony stood up as she turned around, heading for the door. Mike and Tony looked at each other and sat down. Tony shook his head. Mike took another sip of beer. Rosalyn stepped into the alleyway and glanced toward the parking lot as the door shut behind her.

Meanwhile, upstairs, the girl's shredded bloodied shirt hung from her tight body. They were both sopping wet. They both held bruises and scrapes from the altercation. Her body flew to the bed with Stan on top of her, kissing. In an attempt to hold onto him, his strength overwhelmed her; with a casual shove, he forced her backward. Her boobs bounced behind her black bra. She climbed onto her hands and knees; her panties separated from her undercarriage. They flipped beneath her feet, folding across a pillow.

She smiled. "Oh, you animal you. How did you do that?"

Stan never raised a finger to undress her; his mind willed it to happen. She undid his pants. They dropped to his ankles and freed his erect penis. Unbeknownst to him, he was dabbling with an unbroken hymen as the young woman knelt before him with her round, tight butt facing him. His penis separated the teardrop nectar nestled gently at the crest of her labia; his hands grasped onto her hips. He thrust inside her; she moaned. Stan held an evil grin. One hand was on his hip; the other hand clenched tightly to the bloody combat knife.

Rosalyn saw the dim-lit staircase along the side of the bar. She began the climb; halfway up, she dropped to her knees as if a mystical force pulled her down. Grasping onto her ankle, the light above the door at the top of the stairs caught her eye. Eventually, she gained enough courage to pull herself by the railing. She began the climb once again. Underneath the stairs was a bloody mess.

With each thrust, Stanley pulled the girl's hips. The girl spun around and threw her mouth around his penis. His eye rolled toward the ceiling. Rosalyn peeked through the window; all she could see was a kitchen. She pushed the door; it swung open with a creak. Lightning cracked behind her. Her silhouette stained the opening of the doorway for a split second until it returned to darkness. She was already inside the apartment.

The door bounced against a short wall. A ceiling fan in the dinette area gave a constant click. A clock was ticking on the kitchen wall. It was one of those cat clocks where the tail swung with its eyes—like the one in Pete's basement. She crossed through the kitchen. A door was left ajar beyond the fridge; the groans from her husband were growing louder. She eyeballed a broom propped near the refrigerator.

She stood before the bedroom where she could hear them plain as day as she opened the door. A vanity along the farthest wall was the first thing she noticed. She could see her husband in the mirror staring at the ceiling. The girl who knelt before the bed was out of her view. She could see her husband's bare ass. It was almost a ghastly revelation as she readied the broom for the swing.

Now she could see the girl's blonde hair wadded in Stan's firm grip as he yanked on it each time she dipped forward, burying his penis in her wet throat. Rosalyn stood a few feet behind her naked husband and held the broom out to her side. She swung that broom with all her might. The anger, the pure disgust, pushed cold aluminum into his ass. A nice long red welt appeared as his hips thrust forward. The blonde girl was stabbed at the back of her throat and fell over, gagging. Stan lost the knife; it bounced below the bed, leaving traces of blood in its path.

His penis released from her mouth; her face jerked to the side of the bed. Rosalyn hit him a couple more times. The broom handle bent at a weak point as he dropped to the floor—tangled in his pants. He held onto the flaming red bruise developing across his buttocks. Rosalyn released the broom and said, "I will expect you in our family car after you get yourself dressed. Your hussy can sleep alone tonight. Hope you enjoyed choking on that dick, sweetheart."

The young blonde girl was still gagging across the carpet. The force of the broom on Stan's butt had caused the forward motion to ram tonsils into the pharynx, choking on them by peristalsis. She was curled in a ball, trying to catch air. Her mouth chomped on dust bunnies of days past.

Rosalyn stomped her chin; her face nailed the floor; she closed her eyes. Rosalyn exited the apartment. Stanley hustled to get dressed and snatched his wallet from a dresser. He never fully buttoned his shirt, but he never took it completely off. His wife was crossing the parking lot from the bottom of the stairway. He finished stuffing his wallet in his pants and zipped them up, hobbling after her. At one point, he missed his footing, stumbling a few steps. After he regained himself, he headed toward their car.

Before climbing into the passenger seat, he noticed Mike and Tony exit the bar. He realized his archnemesis may have been the culprit who divulged his whereabouts. Mike always drove him home—drunk. He always looked out for him. Tonight was different. Tonight, he wasn't having any part of his drunken sorrows. Stan and his wife drove away from the bar as he glared at Michael Anglekee through the dingy window. Distant lightning took the red glare away from that single eye, seemingly white without an eyeball.

A young girl scampered down the stairway wearing only a robe. Her face was bloody; blood bunched below her nose. She leaned across the railing, trying to maintain her strength. Suddenly, a hand shot from beneath the stairwell, gripping onto her ankle. She glanced at a bloody figure beneath the wooden steps. He gasped, "Help me!" She let out a gut-wrenching, bloodcurdling cry; it was a scream loud enough to bend glass.

Mike glanced at his boss and withdrew a pistol, running toward the alley. Tony followed him. They aimed at the woman on the stairwell. She toppled the last few steps; her robe flipped open as she landed on her back. Her nipples aimed at the bright clouds illuminated by the moon. A patch of pubic hair collected beads of rain; one leg arched over the bottom step; the other lay over the curb.

Tony knelt next to her and helped her sit up. Mike stepped around the stairwell and aimed his gun at the man inside the trashcan; he took his last breath and dropped his head over the curb. The handle of the combat knife sticking out from his neck tapped the wooden stairwell. Mike knelt next to him while he holstered his weapon, feeling for a pulse. He looked at Tony and shook his head.

On the way to their house, Rosalyn and Stan screamed at each other. Rosalyn shouted, "Did you have fun?"

Stanley sighed. "Honey, I'm drunk."

"You have no right to refer to me as honey," Rosalyn snapped.

"But I'm drunk."

"No excuse."

"I'm sorry, Rose."

"When we get home, I'm taking Ron to my mother's."

Stanley glared at her. "To hell you are."

She drove into the driveway and parked the car. Little Ron Markesan's face pressed against the picture window. He couldn't see into their family car; he couldn't see the struggle. Rose slapped Stan in the face while he squeezed her wrist. He gripped her throat and directed her face against the steering wheel. Little Ronnie heard the horn chirp. She threw a punch at him, climbed out of the car, lost her footing, and stumbled on the wet grass.

Stan then jumped out of his side of the vehicle and circled the front of the car. He wadded her hair in a fist. Punching at his groin, she waddled oddly toward the house. Briefly losing his breath, he charged her. He put one arm between her legs and placed his other hand beneath her armpit. He scooped her up and lobbed her through the picture window.

Glass sprinkled across the boy. The family dog whimpered as her body crushed the coffee table. The front door flew open, and the boy's eyes dialed in on his mother's face staring at him from the floor. She mouthed the words, "Run, Ronny, run," but the boy couldn't comprehend, especially when she slid away from his view. Again, she was pulled by her hair and dragged into the kitchen.

Ron crawled off the sofa, easing across the glass. He crawled through the kitchen to care for his mom, lying in the middle of the floor. Climbing onto her stomach, pinching at her cheeks—unresponsive. The boy rested his head between her boobs. Stanley hadn't realized little Ronnie was on top of her. He moved his hand backward; the fridge rocked a bit. He raised his hand and patted his shoulder. The fridge lifted a foot from the linoleum and smashed overtop of them. Ron protected his mom from the crushing blow. Stan wandered through the house, calling for his son.

When the police arrived at the scene, they swarmed the yard. Michael Anglekee and his boss were first to enter the premises; they approached a back room. His boss, Tony, entered a bathroom. He could hear the rings slide on the shower curtain as Tony checked the bathtub. A significant ruffle came from a closet; the door jumped outward slightly. Mike aimed at the closet door, shouting over his shoulder, "Not clear." Tony left the bathroom and entered the room where Michael was. They threw open the door as a black cat ran out. Michael tilted his head toward Tony in anticipation of life, but it was only a cat.

Stanley Markesan was gone. They found a boy strapped to his unconscious mother, Rosalyn. Did Watches kill his son that night? He had been in denial for years. Misconstrued, Michael's dreams of what occurred that night about saving the little boy from that house, never truly happened. He never wanted to imagine the sheer horror and misery little Ronald

Markesan had gone through. Horrendous memories ate at his soul and his mind. And now, the demon was missing.

Chapter Two

Officer Dawson (1994)

Little Rapids nestled in the hills near Wausau, Wisconsin. It was a gorgeous little village. A mayor's cell sat smack dab in the middle of town like a castle amongst peasants' farms. The convenience station held more goods than the grocery store. With farms in the outskirts, beautiful homes gridlocked the town. Anyone would have been lucky to earn more than minimum wage. Back in the day, not too far from the marina, an old sawmill beautified logs; those employees made more than minimum wage. But why were folks driving sports cars and nice trucks? Other luxurious commodities were visible throughout the town, but where was the source of money?

What was hiding in this town? No one knew. What was the catch?

John Dunfri and his sidekick walked a sidewalk. John was the local sheriff; the other guy was one of his veteran cops. They had worked together for years. Their fathers used to work in the old sawmill together. This late evening, they were off duty wearing civilian clothes. Some of the townsfolk would wave to them from their porches. Someone mowing a lawn in the distance threw a gesture at them. Everyone knew everyone else.

John's officer, Jamal Dawson, stopped before a mailbox and withdrew some mail, shaking off the brisk chill from the crisp air. Mr. Dunfri stopped short and asked, "Did your boy get through the basics yet for FBI training?"

He smiled at him. "He sure did."

"Oh, that's great news, Jamal. Splendid! The Force just got stronger."

"It sure did," Jamal said and waved him on as he continued to walk to his house. "I'll catch ya at the office tomorrow."

"Sounds good, Jam." Sheriff Dunfri continued on his way.

Jamal walked up to his front walkway; he climbed the few steps onto his front porch. He stopped and glanced at the sheriff. A UPS truck passed his house and skidded to a stop at the curb next to the sheriff. He watched them for a bit. There seemed to have been an argument; after that, the truck drove ahead and parked in the old sheriff's driveway. Mr. Dawson shook his head and entered his house.

His wife stepped away from the kitchen counter after pouring herself some coffee. She asked, "How was your day, sweetheart?"

He grunted and tossed the bills and junk mail onto a nook. It fanned across it; one letter fell off and landed on the lower counter. He sniffed the air and complimented, "My beautiful darling wife always making me smile brewing the best coffee known to man. And you know what?"

"What?" she asked with a smile as he caressed her midsection.

"It's hot and black like she is."

"Oh, you stop!"

He poured himself a cup and moaned, "Oh, ya wanna know what?"

"What now? You need a little sugar in that hot black coffee?"

"No, I like it hot and black. What I was gonna say was, something goin' on in dis town, and I'm gonna find out what. I'm gonna get to the bottom of it."

She frowned, hesitated, and suggested, "We've known this, Jamal. We've known this for a long time. You think you must do this?"

"Yeah." He took a sip of coffee and stated, "I'm pretty sure I need to."

"Well then, OK, you have my blessing."

"Well, that's a good thing. At least I have that."

* * *

The next day, Officer Dawson drank coffee at the kitchen table. A noise at his door caught him off guard. He approached it, cup in hand, and eased it open; immediately, he glimpsed at a neighbor boy tossing newspapers from his bike. He glanced at his fuzzy slippers to see a bundled paper in a plastic bag through the storm door. "Oh, cool!" As he knelt to retrieve it, coffee split over the lip. "Ouch! Hot!" he grumbled and spilled more as he jostled the newspaper.

He set his cup on the railing. After glancing down the road, he noticed the UPS truck in the sheriff's driveway. His forehead bunched up. His eyebrows dipped; he carefully stepped off his porch like walking a tightrope while tapping the newspaper along his thigh. He withdrew his hand from his robe's pocket; a revolver was in his grip. It was police issued.

He couldn't help but wonder who the sheriff's company was. He had seen the truck there before and thought nothing of it. Since it continued to show up week after week, he grew more and more suspicious. It was time to snoop; decidedly so, his very first investigation was on his boss—go figure. He walked across his front walkway, crossing that same tightrope, approaching the sidewalk. He walked in a small circle to check what was behind him. Further up the road, in the other direction, was another UPS truck. It was parked, facing uphill.

He walked downhill toward the sheriff's house. He waved at a little old lady rocking on her porch. She must have had lousy eyes; there was no acknowledgment. After he approached a T-intersection, a red car turned before him, heading uphill. A dog barked in the distance. He faced the sheriff's driveway; the rear of the UPS truck faced the garage. The garage door was open, but no one was around.

As he approached the driveway, he did another small circle and stopped. He noticed the UPS truck was at the stop sign behind him, facing downhill.

Oddly, no one sat inside; his face swiveled back and forth, from house to house, trying to locate a delivery man. Although peculiar as it seemed for two UPS trucks to be in the area, he shrugged it off. A loud click made him spin around; he continued toward the open garage. The cargo door was open partway. He stopped before the entrance of the garage and inspected inside.

"Oh my God . . . Wesley," he whispered.

Curled in a ball was Gerry Fifer's grandson, in an odd position, unresponsive. Jamal leaned in to check his pulse. When he jerked his head away from the truck to investigate the area, a two-by-four bashed his face. His entire body lifted from the ground; a bullet shot through the two by four. Mr. Dawson managed to squeeze off a round from his folded newspaper; a nice hole shredded the headline. His head nailed the bumper. He hit the concrete floor, out cold.

An eyeball peered through the hole in the lumber. The man moved the piece of lumber away from his face and chuckled, "Watches, Watches, Watches!"

Sheriff Dunfri exited his kitchen into the garage and stood over his body. "Oh Stanley, what did you do?"

"He hates early morning wood."

"Throw him in the truck with Wesley. They'll both have to go to the mill."

Another man exited the house. It was Bonzo, another one of Watches' washed-up rugged-looking fiends. Bonzo cried, "Aww man, we caught another one."

"Yeah, one of my best detectives," the old sheriff sighed and pointed at him. "You better keep this man on a short leash; he's a violent one."

Watches turned toward the sheriff and suggested, "There's plenty of room in that truck, sheriff."

The sheriff held up his hands and smiled. Watches turned toward the officer lying on the ground, his one eye glowing red. His eye patch briefly flipped from a slight breeze revealing an empty eye socket. He snarled, "Get

Billy to join your forces. The son of a cop would be a great addition to your team; don't ya think?" he asked as his head whipped in his direction.

The old sheriff nodded. "He'd be good."

"Bonzo, let's go."

"Yes, boss."

Bonzo worked his way to the driver's side. Watches shouted, "Bonzo, the body." He pointed at the rear of the truck.

"Oh yes, boss."

Watches glanced at the sheriff and tossed him the lumber. He caught it and walked toward his kitchen as Bonzo dumped Mr. Dawson inside the cargo door and shut it. The sheriff stood inside the screen door, watching them drive off. The sheriff closed his eyes and mumbled to himself, "Good Lord, what did I get myself into?"

Further up the road, a lady stepped onto a porch and shouted, "Honey, what did you do—go to work without kissing me goodbye? Jamal, you dedicated fool."

Chapter Three

Armybrats No More

Michael Anglekee's family had undergone many years of torment and threats from a demented deliveryman, aka Stanley "Watches" Markesan. If the cop were to tell the story, he would say the demented deliveryman destroyed his family. From Watches' perspective, Mike intervened for no good reason, and the cop should have been held responsible for dismantling his family. All hell broke loose in 1974 when the demon attacked his wife and kid. Two years after, he drove a UPS truck through the Anglekee's home in Granite View, Wisconsin. It had become very personal at that point.

Michael and his wife, Clarice, were convinced relocating was best for their family. Through a program called WITSEC, they were able to. Although Michael's visit to WITSEC headquarters in Washington had been unsuccessful, their handler, Wayne Richards, may have never recorded the event; he had gone rogue. The story was they relocated to Verona, Wisconsin. There, they raised their two boys. They settled into the new community. Their boys became friends with Duffy Felter, Pete Carson, and Wesley Fifer. They formed a pact known as the Armybrats, trained by a man named, Ralph P. Fallway. The Armybrats had become a band of neighborhood heroes. With Watches on the loose, the Anglekee family remained unsettled at best. They thought he was dead back in the museum in Iowa County. And it was proven untrue. Over a year ago, after the kidnapping, they thought Watches had blown himself up in a boathouse.

If Watches was dead, why was there a missing detective from Little Rapids, a sad (possible) widow, Mrs. Dawson, and a missing Armybrat named Wesley Fifer? The story has it Watches murdered their handler. However, the body never turned up. Some say Wayne Richards had his throat slit. Some said he burned in an office fire. Information on the Anglekees, relocation files, and situational awareness was out the window. All of it was in the hands of the demented deliveryman's son, Ronald Markesan. He was on the prowess; he resurfaced during a training exercise with the cop's sons and their friends; he claimed to be tracking his father. The investigator, Wayne Richards, also claimed to be hunting the same man. But Wayne Richards, aka Ralph P. Fallway was not dead. The spin cycle of terror was on repeat. What the Armybrats did not know was what their father had seen, a smooshed Ronald Markesan beneath a refrigerator. Why was Ronald Markeson helping them through their kidnapping if he was dead?

Wayne Richards lied about his order of business. He too was tracking this demented deliveryman. But why did he kidnap their sons, Billy and Danny? Why did he drug those boys? These questions were left looming in the mind of the old police chief, Michael Anglekee. The same went for the vacant hospital bed where Michael handcuffed him to a bedrail—or so he thought. The true villain in the hospital bed was Watches. All that remained were the handcuffs dangling from the rail. It wasn't Wayne Richards. It wasn't Ron Markesan. The boy Michael thought he saved from the closet was, in fact, dead; it was, however, his father, Watches, lying beneath a body cast that night in the hospital. Mike was so close to the demented deliveryman; he didn't even know it.

Where in the world did Wayne go? Was it Wayne's bloody handprints on the boat named *Wake Menace Part III*? When he kidnapped those boys, Billy, Danny, Duffy, Pete, and Wesley, his intentions were elusive. He pretended they were part of some secret organization called *Kids Can Be Investigators Too*. The boys believed in Ralph (Wayne). They believed in this secret club. Billy had his suspicions, hence the reason he shot him. Mike accused Wayne of using those boys to bait the devil . . . like the big shark he was. He had no idea he was preaching to the devil himself.

Ralph (Wayne) may have gone back to his girlfriend or disappeared in northern Wisconsin, someplace desolate. Stanley Markesan, aka Watches, was nowhere to be found or presumed dead; no one witnessed his fake eyeball pop out; no one heard his cackles through the halls of the hospital; no one overheard him cackling his name three times while picking the lock on his shackles. They remained hanging on a bedrail.

Almost a year had passed since Mark Emerson (the WITSEC-assigned name for Michael Anglekee) discovered the empty hospital bed, mystified at the thought that he had gotten away. The officer outside his hospital room was on the floor with a syringe in his neck. He was out cold but not dead. He removed the empty cuff links and shoved them into a holder on his waist. He shook his head and stared at the bloody bedsheet in disbelief.

His son, Billy, had moved to Little Rapids to pursue his dream of following in his dad's footsteps. He attended classes not too far from there at a well-known Wisconsin State Patrol Academy; it sat in the hills of Tomah. Little Rapids was where he worked for Sheriff Dunfri the past few months, learning to become a police officer. With classes during the day and working part-time for the sheriff on nights and weekends, Billy hadn't had much time to himself, making it tough to date his new girlfriend, Andrea; she worked at the hospital in downtown Madison.

Lately, Billy held frustration with his family. Between police school and work, his social life had cut to the bone. Sheriff Dunfri kept him quite busy. It was easier for Billy to attend the academy and work for the old sheriff; Verona was too far south. Deep down, Billy had a hunch his dad wanted to teach him. In the same breath, his dad did not care for his boss. The skepticism was like trying to weave canvas—hard to stitch and many needle pricks; all that would surface were bloody fingers without a "mend." Yet, the mortality rate in Little Rapids had dramatically reduced. The sheriff calmed Mrs. Dawson on most days. She would be sitting in the main lobby asking for progress on locating her husband. The sheriff lied through his teeth about roving patrols and search parties.

Witness Security was in their past. Billy and Danny's parents, Mark and Mary Emerson (the WITSEC-assigned names of Mike and Clarice) felt switching to their birth names was most prevalent than hiding from their past. One man convinced Mike of that; that one man was Wesley Fifer's grandpa, Gerry. It's been a struggle trying to get used to their real names, Michael and Clarice Anglekee. Michael was now police chief of the Verona Police Department. Consequently, they were indeed the Anglekees once again. No more hiding.

Ever since Danny was born, Clarice quit teaching and enjoyed staying at home, raising the children. Lately, she has been in Danny's business. She threatened to chaperone his upcoming camping trip the school had planned for Upham Woods. Of course, this was the same camp where the boys had survived a ground war. Gerry Fifer, the camp manager, had kept Douglas Malone, the school principal, afloat of all upgrades and renovations. After the camp incident, Wesley moved north to Little Rapids to live with his grandfather; he attended school there. Then he was captured.

Since Danny's mom was a bored homebody, she took over Julie's business at the local dance studio/fitness center (Pete Carson's mom's place of business). She wanted to maintain the business during Julie's extended stay in the Intensive Care Unit (ICU). Thankfully, the dance studio has kept her mind occupied. But the truth was Clarice had been so distraught from her children's kidnapping that she inserted herself in their lives more. Chaperoning the trip to Upham Woods would have been more important to her than maintaining a fitness center; she planned to temporarily close for a few nights due to the upcoming school trip.

Pete's father, Jake Carson, continued being a single parent during Julie's incarceration in the ICU at a Madison, Wisconsin hospital. With no change in her condition, she remained captive in the coma ward; this had taken a toll on Pete; grunge was his new fad. His new friends fit the category. Each new day, the nurse would reassure them of her improving condition. Pete didn't buy it. He knew her patterns; nothing seemed to change. Although he wasn't a doctor, he studied the charts and researched a little; he knew (from speculation) she was as calm as a potato, rotting from the inside out.

He kept to himself and paid more attention to his new friends. Pete was very individualistic. With him separating himself from the Armybrats, no one knew his intentions. No one knew he had been struggling with this issue. No one knew Pete Carson anymore. And other than church, the only time the Armybrats saw each other was visiting his mother at the hospital. Aside from those gatherings, the Armybrats seemed to have been a memory that time forgot.

One boy was about to change that; that boy was Duffy Felter.

Chapter Four

Duffster Dive

The Felters liked to take family vacations. It seemed as though the Felters' home was an easy place for the boys to concoct all the mischief in their younger days. Before their kidnapping experience, they gathered at Duffy's house because his parents were usually out of town. In some kids' eyes, it was a blessing. In others, it was a breeding ground for trouble. Stories like toilet-papering his neighbor's house were one of a few troubles he had gotten in. He didn't like that neighbor. Of course, the high schoolers they egged in the woods for fun were the stories worth telling, but the nature of the beast was them being real deviants . . . unlike what the Armybrats initially stood for.

Robert Felter was still doing construction; his company had branched to other towns. He has done some development in Madison. But he preferred the smaller communities. Barbara was no longer in the floral business; she had continued her schooling and became an RN. She was a registered nurse at the hospital in downtown Madison where Andrea worked. Ever since the explosion in the upper office, she quit the business. Her schooling had paid off.

Robert and Barbara Felter were very liberal with Duffy's upbringing. He could stay up late, eat snacks before bedtime and get whatever he wanted. Yes, Duffy was spoiled. He also knew he had to take on responsibilities in life. Within the last few months, Duffy started a newspaper delivery route; he used any one of his six bicycles and rode around Verona, tossing them to their subscribers.

One day while on his bike route, tossing rolled papers from a basket, he felt vulnerable to an attack, almost as if someone was watching him. When he saw a lady walking her dog in the park, it calmed him for a second. A UPS truck sat in a corner near the park. He didn't think anything of it until it was in a driveway further ahead. Perhaps it was a different UPS truck. Then again, it reappeared near the high school. Scratches in the paint, slight dirt at the fenders, he tried to notice any unordinary markings since the last truck. Nothing stood out.

Something was off. Duffy stopped his bike and noticed a man sitting on the doorstep of the truck smoking a cigarette. He was staring at him. He couldn't make out his face. Duffy tilted his head with confusion and whispered to himself, "What the hell?" Of course, he knew it was a UPS deliveryman by the uniform: crisp, nicely groomed, and shit-brown; although, his shirt was untucked.

Duffy finished his route and passed the high school a second time. The UPS truck was gone. He passed by the park; there it was, on the same corner as earlier, only this time, it was facing the opposite direction with no one inside. He shrugged it off and continued pedaling. Then he stopped his bike. The deliveryman was sitting on the center of the merry-go-round, smoking.

For a moment, he didn't think anything of it other than it was kind of creepy. What was creepier was when the deliveryman waved at him. Duffy waved because it seemed to be the friendly thing to do. An empty swing squeaked its chain and caught Duffy's attention. A teeter-totter rocked without a soul on it, and the merry-go-round started to twirl. It stopped with the man facing the opposite direction, staring off into the woods.

Duffy readjusted his grip on the handlebars and straightened his bike to pedal away; he noticed a single red balloon leave the UPS truck; it floated toward the slide in the park. It reminded him of the day he and his friends were running through those newly constructed houses; they had balloon wars. He remembered when Watches released balloons full of fuel; this balloon didn't go straight into the air, however; it floated directly toward the merry-go-round.

When his eyes shifted to the merry-go-round where the balloon pranced in the center, the deliveryman was gone. His truck was gone. Duffy's heart began to race. Without any wind, without a soul in the park, the merry-go-round spun. He watched the balloon wrap around a handrail. All at once, the merry-go-round stopped, releasing the balloon; it headed straight for him. He glanced over his shoulders and felt a little more relief when he noticed a mailbox with party streamers; only a blue and white balloon remained tied to the post. He figured one had detached itself and was the reason for a single red balloon floating aimlessly.

He pedaled toward his house. When he circled the school forest, he stopped on the hill before his house. A UPS truck rested along the curb in front of his house; Duffy felt his chest cavity punching his shirt, tension in his shoulders. Between the homes, something shimmered. His jaw dropped when he realized what it was. It was the red balloon; it was still coming for him. If he pedaled straight, he would be closer to home yet closer to the UPS truck. He didn't like the option.

Duffy hopped the curb and pedaled through the woods. Unfortunately, he headed toward the school; he wasn't going anywhere near the UPS truck or the balloon. He had no choice. The trail in the woods was the only option. He raced so hard, so fast, he was struggling to keep a balance over ruts. Then there was that damn rock—the same rock that took Wesley's bike out when those high schoolers were chasing them.

His bike tire nailed the sucker so hard; it bent the rim. A spoke sprung outward. The bike flipped. Duffy bounced through shrubbery before a short hill toward a gully of water—collected runoff. Dead branches cracked under his side as his feet tossed leaves through the air until his body wrapped against an oak tree. He lay quietly, staring at the blue sky, trying to understand all this madness. He could see the sun; he could feel the sun. Then it disappeared. It turned black. He lifted his head and realized it was blocked; a single red balloon hovered over him.

It burst.

Liquid splashed his bike and him. It stung his eyes. He tried peeking, but it stung so badly. The liquid rushed down his arms as he lifted his hands. He brought his fingers to his nose. An awful odor created a flashback . . .

The red balloon dropped toward the boys. It briefly suspended in midair, and when it burst, it covered them in a syrup substance. It was red and appeared to be blood. Then the house was bombarded with balloons. The balloons burst open, splashing fuel throughout the framework. The boys ran; they ran for their lives. A lit cigar floated into the house and . . .

Duffy snapped out of his flashback to see his bike burning. More balloons sailed through the woods, popping; the sounds of liquid substances splashed all over the place. The flames wrapped across the trail toward the shrubs he laid behind, encapsulated by fire.

Without hesitation, he tossed himself into the gully of water—rolling down a short decline. Flames grew intense and shriveled dead stuff behind him. In front of him, more balloons bombarded the ground. Duffy's shirt and pants started burning as his body moved flames against the earth until he dropped inside the pond. The UPS truck inched past the woods. From where he lay, he could see the trees engulfed by flames. The entire school forest was on fire. Swelter tightened his skin; chemicals stung his eyes; water popped his ear canals, legs stuck in muck—quietly praying.

Now he could see the sun through the haze. His eyelids narrowed over his eyeballs. He continued to blink, noticing ripples in the water overhead. Heat penetrated the pond. He could see the blue sky, yet the raindrops were splashing all around. What rain? Confusion set in when he couldn't quite breathe. Was it raining? He emerged. Water pelted his face; he closed his eyes and submerged again. He tried opening them; he couldn't see through the disturbed water but knew he had seen movement on the hill.

Firefighters attempted to control the spread of flames, clutching hoses. Fire rippled through the trees; flames flashed across backyards, nearing house siding, dangerously tickling wooden decks and jungle gyms. Men on the ridge sprayed into the gully. They charged through thick smoke and undergrowth; they located the burnt bicycle. Black smoke rose from the rims where the rubber burnt off. Duffy recalled two men standing over him. Arms surrounded him inside the dark hole he was stuck in. Then things became darker with the Armybrats on his brain and a needle pricking his arm.

Chapter Five

Joann Dukes

Any movie portraying a coma victim in hiding usually had the name of John Doe. Rightfully so, this was the name for a male patient in hiding. This lady's chart read Jane Doe. One hospital wing over, Michael Anglekee had investigated the vacant bed a while back, the one that held the cuff links; the escapee was the husband of this Jane Doe. Watches was inside the hospital, staring into an empty hospital room.

At that moment, a flashback arose. It was hazy, yet dark, a man standing in a blurred ring of tannish yellow streaks. It was Michael Anglekee. He heard Mike say, "And your mom, she's here. She's upstairs in a coma. Watches put her here. Hell," Mike laughed, "he put you here too—one big, happy family."

The vision remained the same, but the words continued on and on in his mind: *one big, happy family.* The clouded vision grew fainter. The light seemed to become brighter. The man he spoke to was indeed the tormenter himself.

As this flashback occurred, staff exited the laundry room after tossing towels into a bin. Inside the basket, full of white towels, a hand slapped the frame; a gauze-wrapped villain emerged from the soiled linen. One hole in his head remained dark and empty where there should have been an eyeball. The dark hole in the facial cast opened to a crooked smile. "Watches, Watches . . ." He pressed his gauzed wrapped jaw and groaned. "Ow!" A vibrant echo from inside the chute rattled as his fake eyeball rolled after him. He envisioned the night of his escape. His flashback faded away as he snapped to the present. Watches stood in a hallway dressed in scrubs.

The Armybrats were visiting Duffy, who held minor burns and abrasions. Robert was with their son. Barbara, Duffy's mom, tended to him as his nurse. They stepped into the hallway to talk with Jake (in private) while the boys were left at Duffy's bedside, covered in gauze.

Duffy whispered, "You guys, we need to get the Armybrats together."

Pete shook his head in disagreement and questioned, "Why?"

Duffy took a sip of ice water and said, "He's back."

Pete poked the gauze on the side of Duffy's face. Duffy grimaced and waved him off.

Danny smiled. "Oh, that's silly, Duffy. He blew himself up, remember?"

"You don't understand. There were balloons full of gasoline. And a . . . a . . . UPS truck. The man on the merry-go-round and . . . and . . . a balloon that followed me."

Danny's eyes caught more air as his forehead stretched. He looked at Pete. Pete raised a pill bottle from a bed tray and shook it; tablets shuffled inside, ticking the plastic. Pete smiled. "Look, buddy, you hit your head awfully hard. Do you need me to send for someone? Need a laxative perhaps?"

"A laxative?" Duffy snapped with confusion. *"What?"*

Pete snarled, "Look, Duffster, you need to get the shit out. We all know we were never meant to be secret agents. The Armybrats was a make-believe club name for a make-believe mission from a douchebag who made us believe." The octave of his voice stepped up a level as he continued to say, "We were the Armybrats."

"No, I was attacked. There was the UPS truck. The balloons like when we were younger, 'member the balloon wars, 'member the gasoline in the house?"

"Pull your head out of your ass, Duff; we weren't the Armybrats anymore than we were stupid little ignorant sons-of-bitches." Pete stormed out of the room. "I'm goin' to see m' mom."

Duffy shook his head.

Danny leaned in and whispered, "Don't worry, I believe ya, Duffster!" He glanced at the table near the chairs and noticed brochures to a restaurant in Granite View, Wisconsin. He collected the brochures, reading the specials.

"Thanks, Danny!"

Pete had the roughest time understanding their position in life. His focus was his mother. Visiting Duffy even for a short while was enough to satisfy his play on their friendship. He knew they were friends for life, but he didn't believe in the Armybrats. He didn't want to accept the Armybrats because it was all built on a lie.

Afterward, they planned to visit Pete's mom. Jake Carson had left work early to be with his wife. The recovery room was small; three people were in the room, two coma patients and a nurse. The two patients were both women. One woman seemed very well-lit between her fair skin and linen. Fluorescent lighting cast the intrinsic glow, the gown she wore, and the white bed sheets enveloped her. Julie Carson, aka JC, lay in her hospital bed all beautiful. It wasn't an innocent slip off the edge of the pool. She nearly drowned that day.

The other patient was in a coma for a couple of decades. She was in an identical condition but not any worse off than Pete's mom. Almost three years was long enough without a mother. Imagine what nineteen years would do to a kid whose mother couldn't hold, hug, or beat their bottom blue. To be without a mother in this lifetime would have been unfathomable. Now imagine it being the son of a devil who put her there. Additionally, no one saw Watches toss JC into the pool either. Who's to say she wasn't clumsy?

Anyway, the answer was revealed on the lady's chart next to Pete's mom's bed. The other patient's name was Joann Dukes, aka JD. Pete's jaw dropped. He thought it was a dream. Joann Dukes was in his dream, but her real name was Rosalyn Markesan, Ron's mother. It was Stan's wife, and his dream held some truth. The deliveryman's wife shared a room with his mother. Pete stared at the chart in bewilderment.

Half-pitched around her bed was a curtain. Pete cornered it to see more of her. The curtain blended in with a man's white cape as he stood at the other end with his head down and his white hair covered his face. He was near the woman's monitor next to her head. The machine attached to the monitor bleeped as a green line jerked upward on the black screen. He gracefully moved his head behind the curtain. The other boys could not see the woman.

Oh, and on the other side of the curtain, Joann Dukes, aka JD, decided to rattle the caster wheels on the intravenous pole. JD was usually a quiet roomie. JD and JC pretty much kept to themselves; the irony in this was the machines talking to each other. On most days, synchronized beeps were all that filled the room except JD was tugging at the cord. One man subjected them to a life of darkness. The devil put them there, but Jesus Christ currently had the reigns.

Who was JD hiding from . . . ? She was hiding from someone the boys were trying to understand. The boys hadn't seen her. Emotions accumulated like suds in a tub; they drowned in agony over the JC's dilemma. The boys had no idea who JD was, but she was a bunkmate of JC, not Jesus Christ; even though they had never met, JD was coming to light. Picking up the pace, her monitor bleeped; her eyelids wiggled. The saline drip sloshed in the bag.

Jake held onto Julie's hand and rubbed her smooth skin. Pete paced back and forth at the foot of her bed. He saw her chart hanging at the end; the clipboard held a piece of paper under the clip. It had all sorts of information on it. Most of it was pictorials. The graphs illustrated levels of recorded blood pressures and breathing patterns at intervals throughout the day, recordings based on time. It seemed like a long time ago when they could no longer hear her voice or see her smile. Any reactions from JC were what lines her subconscious decided to draw that day on a machine.

Past recordings demonstrated significant alterations in the sequence of patterns. This Pete could not understand. The nurse behind the desk had informed Jake about more abrupt changes in her condition. The suggested changes could have meant a couple of things: either JC tiptoed across a fine line of returning to reality or slipped further into the point of no return. No matter which ends of the spectrum, it would have resulted in no more coma, which could have been a good thing. A couple of nurses checked on JD; the body language suggested either a bad dream or possibly reviving to a time warp from 1974. JD was not like JC's state of mind, but JC carried the initials of the Lord, the savior. Bedmates of JC and former spouse of the devil were like sharing space with fire and ice.

Jake stood up to leave her bedside, wandering into the hallway to weep some more.

"C-come on, Pete," Danny stuttered as he followed his father toward the doorway. They were leaving, and Pete's attention drew toward the man. Unfortunately, his face remained buried in white hair. The other two were a few beds away, already heading out the door.

Pete stepped away from Rosalyn and glanced at Danny. The nurse looked at them as they left. She smiled at Pete; he waved. He snapped out of his mind wander and followed them out of the room.

After Pete left, the room held its regular beeps. A repetitive clicking sound echoed softly through the room. A clipboard was swinging on the end of Julie's bed; it kept swaying as the nurse tried to write. She couldn't concentrate because it was dragging the chain to the pen. The chain kept clicking the bed frame on its upward swing. She tried to ignore it, but her eyes rolled in its direction. She expected it to stop swaying. But it didn't. Instead, a force flipped it from its hook; it rattled against the tile floor. Either end of the clipboard drummed the tile until it lay flat in silence.

Her head snapped away from her paperwork. The boys were collecting Jake's limber soul in the hallway. On one side of the ICU, she could see them through the windows. Then she glanced at where the clipboard used to rest. If it had fallen off the hook, it should've landed at the foot of the bed, but it wasn't visible. Behind a few ripples in the material of the curtain, a white gown waved; a white-haired man hid from her view.

Between steady beeps, room atmosphere, and a missing clipboard, she felt a sudden shift in room temperature. She stood from the desk and paced toward Julie's bed. "Hello." The curtain divided the two coma patients. She stopped before her bed and viewed the monitor; it steadily bleeped. But the clipboard was nowhere to be found.

She crouched to search beneath Julie's bed. The idea was that the clipboard must have slid beneath it. When she peeked underneath, nothing was there. The white curtain on the other side was erratically flowing. She could see the tile squares on the floor where a shadow emerged and then disappeared behind the ripples of the curtain. The shadow beneath the curtain remained stationary even with the wave.

She backed away from beneath the bed; hearing the scratches, she realized something dragged across the floor. The clipboard had returned. After picking it up, she reviewed the paperwork and hung it on the hook. The curtain was moving, but she was nowhere near it. She couldn't even breathe.

At this point, the only noises in the room were the beeping machines. Snatching the clipboard, the nurse walked around the curtain. Rosalyn Markesan *(Joann Dukes)* lay in her bed with her head turned to one side. Her white hair fanned over her pillow, with a mask piece pressed firmly against wrinkly skin. It was for helping her breathe.

She looked at the clipboard and noticed the documentation belonged to her. It was the wrong paperwork, and Julie's clipboard was still missing. She looked at Rosalyn's bed, and a clipboard swayed back and forth from its hook. She jaunted to it and knelt to compare the charts.

Suddenly, Rosalyn sat up. The nurse glanced at her. Although her long white hair fell against her cheeks, and the mouthpiece that covered half her face fell off, it wasn't her. It was a man; it was Watches. He aimed a gun at her; her eyes widened. Rosalyn was nowhere in sight. The nurse screamed. Watches' one eye widened as he snarled and leaned into the light. "Boo!"

In the car ramps, Pete sat in the passenger seat. His dad was sitting behind the steering wheel. He was about to start the ignition when all muscles seemed to fail him, and he cried. Pete tapped his shoulder. His dad looked away from the steering wheel after dropping his head; they hugged each other for a moment.

Danny sat in the rear seat; a single tear spanned his cheek. He looked out the window. A man walked into the dim light at the far end of the parking garage, closer to the elevators. He lit a cigarette and puffed a brilliant puff. An orange flame flickered as the smoked swooshed upward toward his flop hat. His cigarette lit; he dropped the lighter inside his brown pants pocket. He wore a UPS uniform for the United

Parcel Service; his dark hair remained tied in a ponytail. Danny swore it was Ralph Fallway.

Danny jumped out of the car and walked into the aisle. Mr. Fallway cornered a big brown box truck; he jumped inside. Jake and Pete stopped hugging and were concerned. Danny couldn't see the man through the opened driver's window, but he could tell the door was open; the cigarette smoke poured from it. He could see his black boot and part of his leg. He hollered, "Mr. Fallway!"

The man either refrained from looking at him or couldn't hear him over the motor. Through a side-view mirror, a man rustled inside. Jake and Pete climbed out and stood next to Danny; he stared at the UPS truck. The brake lights flickered, then shut off. Jake stood behind the boys as Pete hounded Danny on what was wrong. Likewise, he had no idea what was going on.

The truck's engine roared; its mirrors vibrated. The brake lights snapped on and then the reverse lights. Jake placed his hands over their shoulders and smiled. "Let's go, boys!" He turned around, and they followed.

By surprise, the squealing caught their attention; they spun around. The UPS truck tore away from its parking stall. It smeared the concrete with black stripes of burnt rubber and headed right for them. They noticed the square roll door enlarge as it drew closer. Everyone scattered. The smell of burnt tires filled the garage. Jake pushed Pete behind another car as Danny rolled beneath a pickup truck.

The UPS truck smashed into the vehicle Danny hid beneath. It bunched the bed of the pickup truck as it rocked on its springs and tapped the concrete wall a few times. The transmission clanked; they could hear the gear lock in the casing. The truck shifted to drive. Jake attempted to hop into the driver's door but fell; he rolled with pieces of plastic from the light cover and slammed into a concrete pillar. The bumper separated from the truck and skidded away from them.

Jake stood with Pete as the UPS truck made for an exit. Jake kicked the bumper across the concrete floor and jumped inside his car. Pete crawled in back. Danny hopped in through the other door. Everyone was inside the car as Jake shifted into reverse and backed out of the parking spot. He whipped the steering wheel in a complete circle and smashed his foot on the brakes. The car skidded sideways out of the stall. Both boys bounced against each other after Danny ricocheted off the door.

"All right, Dad," Pete encouraged.

The UPS truck spun around a pillar at the bottom of the drive. They headed in the same direction. Danny looked out his window and noticed the top of the truck past the underside of the next level below. He pointed around the seat. "There he goes; he's goin' faster!"

Jake mashed his foot against the brake pedal and swung the steering wheel around. The car fishtailed around the corner. They headed down the ramp, nearly sideswiping another vehicle that entered the level they had exited. The UPS truck slipped around the other end, entering the lower level. Danny and Pete were leaning against the front seat, staring out the windshield. Jake concentrated on people walking through the parking garage and vehicles inching from parked stalls.

Pete asked, "Danny, how do you know that was Mr. Fallway?"

"I have a hunch."

Jake asked, "And this is the man that kidnapped you kids?"

Pete justified, "I cannot confirm or deny it was a kidnapping."

Pete's father switched lanes on Regent Street, following the UPS truck. The hospital disappeared in their mirrors as they fled the parking garage. The parking attendant put them a little behind after they paid the fee. But Pete's dad had a keen sense of direction. The state capitol building shined white as they passed by West Washington and then signaled left onto John Nolen Drive.

The boys helped guide Jake as they shouted directions. They could see the UPS truck disappear into an underpass near the Monona Terrace. There were dim incandescent lights throughout the concrete structure; it crossed the road like a tunnel. Almost forty years after the death of its designer Frank Lloyd Wright, the Monona Terrace was newly constructed; he was a well-known architect admired by Alex Jordan. Alex Jordan built the House on the Rock where the Armybrats ended that horrific family vacation a while back; myths had pegged him for hiring drunks and bums from Madison to help build the museum.

They followed suit when they noticed the UPS truck transition lanes through the underpass. Up ahead, the lights turned red; they weren't caught up to the truck yet. The traffic was heavy; vehicles were slowing for the stoplight. Before they could stop, the light turned green. Once they came to a complete halt, the UPS truck cut off another car and took a sharp left onto Wilson toward the capitol building.

When the intersection cleared, Jake had his chance to take a left. The light changed yellow; a car veered into his lane, braking for the stoplight. However, she sped up. Jake nailed his horn at the lady who cut him off. He decided to risk the yellow light and followed her through it. The UPS truck was slipping away. In the moment of strife, the boys' luster seemed tattered. They could see the UPS truck climbing the hill. Then it turned right, out of sight.

One thing was for sure about the square around the capitol building; the traffic only went one direction. The traffic traveled counterclockwise around the capitol building. As soon as the truck turned right, Jake decided to go straight and ride parallel with the square in the same direction to watch for him at the crossroads.

Jake glanced into his passenger's side mirror and his rearview mirror; he noticed cars swiftly approaching in the right lanes. The next light flipped red. He sharply turned the steering wheel. He gave the car the beans as he hammered the pedal to the metal. The car gave a wonderful screech. He flew into the middle of the intersection and breezed through it as the light turned bright green.

The first block would have been only thirty seconds at the speed limit of thirty miles per hour. Jake's top speed of sixty miles per hour got him to East Washington Avenue in about half the time; they glanced at the side street to catch a glimpse of the box truck. It had left the intersection near the square. Jake floored it through the green lights and soared to the next cross street; he turned toward the square.

Sure enough, the UPS truck was at the next stoplight. Danny and Pete noticed the box truck at the same time and pointed at it with anticipation. The man sitting behind the driver's seat turned his head in their direction. He noticed them scream toward the lights. No traffic rolled through; his light was still red. But it didn't matter to him as he punched it and flew through the red light. A bus's horn blared at him.

Up ahead, the bus pulled in front of them and blocked their view. They followed the bus around the capitol. They could see the UPS truck around the corners. On the straightway, the UPS truck was hidden. Abruptly, the bus turned into the right lane. As soon as it pulled off, Jake had to slam on his brakes. Traffic remained at a standstill. Big brown and yellow were nowhere to be seen. They glanced to the right, and the truck was in front of the school bus turning right. Jake signaled with a slight turn, stuck in two lanes waiting for Badger Cab to pass. More vehicles got behind the bus; they blocked traffic wanting to go straight as they waited for the right lane to clear. The longer they waited it seemed like more vehicles had gone right.

Finally, traffic dispersed, and Jake bolted. Before the turn, they could still see the UPS truck. Of course, it was further ahead now; there were more vehicles in its path, but the chase continued to transpire. Danny and Pete were leaning against the headrests trying to locate the truck, but their view had been obstructed by the same Madison Metro bus. What they couldn't see was the intersection. They passed a bank on the corner. Another big white and blue bus in front of them veered left. They headed toward Regent Street where they originally started from.

The UPS truck was gone. They slowed and searched each direction. A block behind them, a bank had cars backed into the street as they waited for the drive-through. On the other end of the drive-through, the UPS truck sat under the awning. He faced the wrong direction, as cars were head-on with him behind the teller window, honking at him.

The man in the driver's seat kept his head low as his brown cap shadowed his face. The rim curved below his nose. His lips curled into a smirk; his eyes rose with his head. He was smoking a cigar, not a cigarette. He smiled at the teller behind the window. She squinted and smirked at him. He waved and glanced at the couple in front of him who were making faces. He tipped his hat at them and reversed out of the drive-through. It was Mr. Fallway.

Chapter Six

Dance Studio Demon

Danny's mom was sitting on a swivel chair in a small office at the dance studio. A water cooler in a corner vibrated and bubbled. She was on the phone, staring out the picture window at a group of girls coordinating a cheer on the drill floor. About fifteen girls were wearing skimpy miniskirts and tight shirts. The outfits represented the school mascot with bright colors; the shirts had "VAHS!" across the chest. The letters were orange and curled over their breasts. They were doing facing movements. The fancy routines were not only well-coordinated, but each girl seemed physically fit with their washboard stomachs; they thrust their buttocks backward and forward without a wiggle. They spun around with their backs facing the office. The back of their shirts spelled out: "Wildcats." And a silhouette of a tiger outlined in orange.

Clarice cradled the phone to her ear. "Yes honey, I know. How late will you be working tonight?" While Michael talked in her ear, she clicked on a link to a drug bust in Northern Wisconsin. The picture of a two-story restaurant bar popped onto her screen. "Oh honey, do you remember that bar you took me to on the hill up near Wausau with the beautiful deck?" She scrolled through webpage scripture; an ad popped up about Yahoo Chat Rooms. She closed the ad. "Yeah, that's it!" The Webpage read The Hills Bar and Saloon. "Yeah, they caught some young kids storing drugs in the kitchen. Yup, that's the one, it was condemned in the late eighties. Oh, you want to take me there. Something tells me they aren't serving any food, sweetie." She chuckled, "That isn't fine dining anymore! OK, I'll see you tonight. Love you!"

No sooner had she hung up than the phone rang out. "Hello, yes, I am booked all afternoon. But I will be happy to hold the floor for you on Saturday. No, I understand that. No, she has a medical condition that keeps her from this job. Nope, she's alive but in a coma—in a coma. She fell onto a pool cover and nearly drowned. Yup, she nearly drowned," Clarice screamed into the phone as if the person on the other end were hard of hearing. "I am taking care of the studio in her absence. Yes! We won't be open that week due to a conservation trip to Upham Woods. OK, so Saturday will work for you?" She typed on her keyboard while staring at the computer monitor—a big old box screen. It consumed half the desk. "All right, Mrs. Kurimoto. I am logging you in right now. Saturday, ten in the morning, the floor is yours. Yes. No. These girls . . . ? Yeah, they are from the local high school. They are practicing cheer for the homecoming game. They're cheerleaders, the cheer squad for Monday night's game. Yes, I realize that. But there was a basketball game, and they had no floor space, so I offered the dance studio. OK then. Thank you. See ya Saturday. Yup. Uh-huh. Bye now."

She dropped the phone into the cradle and finished writing the schedule in the appropriate square on the calendar. The girls were seniors in high school anywhere from seventeen to eighteen years of age. Their bodies were spinning and twirling around the floor. Some girls skidded across the smooth floor. Squeaks wailed around the gymnasium as they flailed across the floor and through the air. When they dipped forward, a reflection in the mirrored walls showed a man standing in the corridor. He stared at Mrs. Anglekee. Then the girls covered her view of him.

They danced about the floor. Clarice emerged from behind the desk catching glimpses like a terrible film reel of memories. His body returned to the mirror. Each time a girl jumped in his way, the vision of the dreadful soul from her past vanished. When the girls jumped on top of each other, they blocked his reflection. When they crouched, he reappeared. In the mirror, it was a depiction of Stanley Markesan.

She paced around her desk, carefully scanning all mirrors. She swiped her hands across the desk. Folders, papers, and racks toppled, scattering across the floor. She scooted the chair out of her way to escape the tight cubby she was in; Clarice stepped on paperwork without care for the mess she created. She headed for the door to the office; her arm seemed like a rusted mechanical dilemma. She did manage to work the door open. Stanley disappeared. The door bumped away from the water cooler; it eased shut at a similar pace.

The girls separated from each other and stood in three rows. In the mirror, Stan magically reappeared as if he was in the middle of their routine, but he wasn't physically present. Although the reflection showed him standing behind the girls, he may have been inside the mirrors, but he wasn't on the gym floor. If he were, he would've been standing in front of Clarice in her stone-walled daze. She couldn't see her reflection; she could only see him.

He raised his hand and made a motion. Behind Clarice, the office door flipped open. It bumped the water cooler, tossing it from its pedestal. The door swung shut, office windows shattered. The cooler flipped over the desk; the plastic cracked; water dispersed. Water spit across the desk, beneath the desk, and across the wall. Some water splashed a power strip; sparks shot across the wet floor. Flames ripped the interior, shattering the computer.

She glanced at the office and spun around, screaming and running. The girls separated, surrounding her. As Clarice ran, she noticed the reflection of flames in the office behind her. From her perspective, Stan was in front of her. He stood between her and the mirrors. It was the reason she couldn't see herself in the reflection; he blocked her view. At one point, she reappeared—as if she had passed through his body. He stood behind her like a silhouette before the flames. His back faced her. She screamed, "Nooooooo!" Stan slid his foot across the floor with a squeak from his rubber sole.

All the gymnasium walls had mirrors; weight equipment sat in one section. At the center was a boxing arena. On the other end of the arena were punching bags hanging from rafters. Windows at the top corners of the walls brought in fair amounts of light. Sunlight cast over the rafters. The mirrors helped spread the light. The ventilation had done a poor job at sucking in the smoke as the fire consumed the office. The water jug ignited. Perhaps it wasn't water.

The girls screamed. They latched onto one another. Clarice had heard the horror stories about her sons; it bothered her immensely. She was dwelling over the past. While the past was doing Hula-Hoops around her mind, she saw the UPS man in the mirrors. She meant to attack him, but Watches planted a foot somehow and drove her body forward. When she passed through Watches' illusion, he used a concussive force at her back. Her body arched and blew through the mirrors. Glass shattered to the floor. She landed on the hardwood as pieces of the mirrors rained all around.

A couple girls crouched alongside her. They sat on their heels; their skirts bunched up their legs. Pantyhose of different colors surrounded Clarice's bloody face. One of them jogged to a red emergency phone mounted on a support pole. Stan stood over the two girls who knelt next to her. He watched one of the girls bundle a towel, dabbing it beneath the bloodiest cut across her forehead. Another girl propped her head.

A girl screamed, "We need to get help!" Smoke poured into the gymnasium. Crackling flames continued to chew at the office.

Some girls coughed. Some girls fled from the gymnasium as the fire expanded to the neighboring office. Blood fused through the white fuzzy towel. Cuts in Clarice's arms and legs bled across the floor. She lay unconscious. A few girls surrounded her. Stan was in the center. He lowered his head and closed his one eye. The sunlight expanded across his face, spanning his neck as his face aimed toward the ceiling. His eye snapped open; he smiled devilishly.

None of the girls acknowledged his existence. He walked backward. A boy stood near the punching bags. Stan spun around and clobbered the bag. The chain link snapped; the bag flew at the boy and flattened him through another mirror on the other end of the gym. All at once, Stan was gone. A girl screamed as blood and glass sprinkled across the weight equipment. Flames ripped the corner offices.

"It's getting hot in here," one girl said.

Two boys leaped off the weights to tend to the crushed boy bleeding across the mat. Another guy threw a towel around his shoulder as he ran to them and observed his flattened face. One boy's name was Samuel Baxter and the other's name was Shawn Pace. They were known as the high school bullies in Verona. They put the word "hell" in freshmen *hell* week. Shawn punched Sam's shoulder. "Whoa, dude! Did you see that? That was crazy!"

Clarice moaned and turned her head to cough. The girls were trying to pick her up.

Sam crouched near the boy who impelled the mirrors and joked, "Yo man, you all right? Did you see your reflection?"

One girl shrieked, "Shut up, Sam. Do something useful for a change and help him!"

Shawn raised his fingers from the flat-faced kid's neck. "No need; he's dead."

Another girl walked toward them from the locker room and stated, "Help is on the way."

One of the girls walked at him, holding onto a bloody towel from Clarice, bumping Shawn aside with her hip. "Why do you got to be such a jerk?" She let go of the bloody towel. Shawn held onto it for a few seconds until he realized wet red streaks across his hand and dropped it. It slapped the floor like sloppy red gelatin.

Clarice glanced at the fire shooting out of the office; smoke billowed toward the ceiling. "Everyone get out," she coughed.

Sam hollered, "Clarissa, can I make it up to you? Come on. Sex, my place . . . ? Anytime . . ."

Another girl pushed Sam aside and followed Clarissa toward the locker rooms. Sam bumped into his buddy, and he turned to look at her. His buddy stepped forward and asked, "What Vic? You mad at me too?"

Clarissa entered the locker room. Victoria stopped following her. She turned around and approached him. She stopped a foot from his face. He stepped away from the evil glare. She whispered, "Yes, I am."

"Why, you're still mad at me because of Kort? I was only talking to her."

"You weren't just talking to her."

"Yes, it was a friendly conversation!"

"It looked very friendly while you rubbed her shoulders."

"She had a kink."

Vicki had her arms crossed. She kneed him in the groin. "There, now you got a kink!"

He fell to the floor, groaning. His hands cupped his genitals.

Clarice coughed. "Everyone get out of here, now."

Students made their way toward the exit. Vicki encouraged Clarissa to hurry along; her scream echoed inside the locker room. The two guys hoisted Clarice onto their shoulders. After Clarissa returned from the locker room, Vicki spun around to head inside. Shawn lunged at her and grasped her arm. "Where are you going?"

She pulled from him and grimaced from the squeeze. She rolled her eyes in his direction. "Ow," she sighed.

"Hey!" he hollered at her. "Fine, forget you then!" She grasped onto her arm, rubbed it, and continued into the locker room.

Sam resituated his grasp of Clarice after Shawn jumped in to help. "Let's go, Shawn. These bitches suck."

One girl said, "Hey!"

He pushed her out of his way as they plowed through them and walked out of the gym. When the two boys exited the gym, cops surrounded them. Paramedics stopped them. The paramedics were the same two guys who aided Wesley during the bridge mishaps. It was the same bridge when Watches made his dramatic appearance. Also, they were the same two paramedics at the poolside tending to Pete's mom when she almost drowned. Now they were tending to Clarice. The boys helped them place Clarice onto a gurney. Her face held glass freckles mixed with blood.

Before the cop could ask questions, the doors swung open, and girls were running through them. Sam looked at him and claimed, "Those girls kicked the shit out of that poor woman. They shoved her into a mirror and everything."

Shawn's head whipped in his direction.

"You boys step across the street, please."

"OK," Sam snickered.

Shawn gave his shoulder a nudge. "Why did you say that, huh? I don't want Clarissa in trouble!"

Fire trucks stormed in, sirens blaring. The boys jogged across the street. The paramedics wheeled Mrs. Anglekee into the ambulance. She acted as if she hyperventilated but tore the mask off. "There's a boy still inside," she gasped. The paramedics attempted to calm her down, reattaching the oxygen supply. The cops heard her and dashed inside the burning studio.

Sam asked, "Hey, what sort of trouble could they possibly get into, huh? All I did is make their day a little longer. They may have to sit through more questioning but that's on them. Oh well, it'll teach them for treating us like they did."

They walked the sidewalk along the park; Sam was joking about the girls losing their cool. Shawn laughed wholeheartedly at the situation. A wind flipped a lid away from a trashcan and nailed Shawn square in the face. He fell and rolled onto the sidewalk. Sam turned around, raising an eyebrow at him. Shawn was cursing while coddling a bloody nose. Sam handed him the towel he had around his shoulder. Sam chuckled. "Whoa man, you, all right? That trashcan took you out."

"No, I am not all right. That damn lid just kicked my ass, man!"

"What was that all about?"

Shawn unraveled his body, hollering at the sky. "Oh, God's probably mad at me for lying to the cops!"

He retrieved the lid and winged it at the trashcan; it nailed the side, dented it, and rolled into the road. They walked away and cut through the park. A shadow encompassed the trashcan; someone stood behind it. The person spat inside the trashcan and cackled. "How come God always gets the credit?"

Shawn was following Sam past the merry-go-round. A whistling gust of wind tossed the trashcan lid into the backside of Shawn's head once again. He toppled over the merry-go-round and rubbed his face after it struck one of the metal bars. The trashcan lid slid across the merry-go-round with a loud scrape, rattling between the handrails. Sam ran to him and stared at the trashcan lid. Then he glanced back at the trashcan near the sidewalk. Beyond the trashcan, the road remained empty. It was the same lid.

A knocking sound drew their attention in the other direction. Watches was dribbling a basketball on the court in the distance. He stopped and tossed the ball into the air. When it dropped over his extended forefinger, it spun like crazy. The merry-go-round began twirling. Shawn tried to stand, but the speed increased, uncontrollably spinning.

Watches walked across the court as he spun the ball on one finger. As the ball increased speed, so had the merry-go-round. Sam was between him and the merry-go-round. He kept glancing at Shawn as he was cussing, struggling to hang onto the rails since the saucer spun like a Frisbee. Watches stopped about ten feet from Sam with the basketball still spinning on his finger with an awkward smile. He tossed the ball to Sam. "Catch!"

Without haste, Sam caught the ball and flew backward. His body wound through the spinning merry-go-round; the handrails violently batted his body as he struggled to maintain possession of the ball. All at once, it stopped. Handrails caught Sam's body from the sudden stop. His head whipped around, and he puked over the other side. Watches waved his hand; the basketball stripped from Sam's hands, curved through the grass, and hopped his toe right into Watches' hands. The merry-go-round put Shawn flat on his back, between a couple of the metal bars. He stared at the sky and closed his eyes as the sky continued to whirl around in his mind.

Both boys played with the devil; they didn't even know it. Sam splayed out with injured arms and shoulders; half his body was still lying over the edge of the merry-go-round. Watches tossed the basketball upward and caught it. He played catch with himself as he giggled; the two boys were lying in misery.

Sam rolled onto his back and stared at him. Shawn was staring at Watches. Sam cried, "Who are you, man?"

Watches cackled. "Well, I ain't God; that's for sure!"

Shawn was swaying back and forth, his head slightly wiggling. He pointed at Watches and stuttered, "You do this?"

"Turn your head now," Watches directed.

Shawn did just that. As he faced the ground, he vomited again. His head turned like a heavy door hinging open and asked, "So . . . like . . . who are you, man?"

Sam rolled his eyes at him and asked, "Yeah, what are you, some kind of devil?"

"I guess you could say that. I am not just your worst nightmare. But I have a message for you two."

"A message . . . ?" Sam groaned.

"You've seen my display in the dance studio. You saw what I could do with just a trashcan lid and a basketball. You puked after I said you would. I spun the merry-go-round without effort. Why do you think Clarice Anglekee ran through that mirror? Oh, and what do you think happened to your buddy who crashed into the other mirror?"

Shawn's eyes lit up. "Because of you?"

"Well, it wasn't God." Watches laughed. "So now I come to you with a little secret about what the future holds. I see candlelit tables, your girls, and fine dining. A restaurant is where they'll be."

Sam rolled onto his side as he seemed to become engaged in his little story. Shawn looked at him in wonderment.

"I see two guys, your girls, some beer, and some pearls. Your girls are lovely, and everyone knows it. The candlelight swirls. And then the guys kiss your girls."

Sam got onto his knees and hollered, "What the fuck are you talking about, mister?"

"You both know these rats, for they call themselves the Armybrats. Who knows what they plan? If anyone could stop them, I know you two can."

Shawn coughed. "Which two are they? There are about five of those little cunts."

Watches suggested, "I've told you more than you need to know. Something must be done about these boys."

Shawn threw up his fingers. "Yeah, we're gonna kill 'em."

Watches stepped away and walked around the merry-go-round. Sam worked his way to his feet. Shawn was still pointing at the sky. He dropped his arms at his sides and looked at Sam and sarcastically asked, "What?"

"Where is he?"

Shawn looked around the park. "Hey, where did bitch-ho go?" He continued to search for Watches with no sign of him. He glanced at Sam.

Sam was squinting. His lips curled. His eyes glowed, and he snarled, "Those fuckin' Armybrats. I should've known."

Chapter Seven

Bloody Bed

Police officers surrounded Pete's mom's hospital bed; a lady lay cockeyed over the messy, crimson-spackled bedsheets.

Flashbulbs brightened the spackles. Ralph Fallway stood at the head of the bed and looked at the young kid with his eyes strapped to a viewfinder on a Kodak camera. Mr. Fallway asked him to leave.

The photographer complained, "But I am taking pictures for the paper."

Mr. Fallway snatched the camera and opened the back. "Not anymore, you're not. Now shoo."

"You exposed my film," he whined.

"Yeah, I did."

"Now it's ruined."

"Aren't you a genius journalist? Leave."

The photographer snatched his camera and sluggishly walked away. He extracted another Polaroid, struggling to hold each camera, and snapped off shots. He spun around and took a few more quick snapshots of the cops standing around the hospital bed. The blue light flashed across walls and steel handrails on the bed frame.

Mr. Fallway's cheeks shined blue for a second; he snapped his face toward him and hollered, "Wanna see mine flash?" He withdrew a pistol and aimed at the kid; the kid continued to run and bumped into a couple of media personnel standing in the hallway. A camerawoman almost fell; she regained her footing and straightened herself out. Mr. Fallway walked toward her.

She assumed he was a cop and politely asked, "Excuse me, officer, may I have a few words?"

He peered into the lens. "Yeah, you may; suck it, CBS," he proclaimed. He peeked around the side of the camera and tapped a button. The side tray popped open; he withdrew a cassette.

She pulled away and screamed, "Hey!"

He pulled the tape from the cassette and tossed it through the doorway to the hallway; it nailed a wall and pieces scattered across the floor. From a bag slung over his shoulder, another man pulled another cassette out and handed it to her. She slid it inside the side compartment and shut it. Mr. Fallway walked toward the room and shook his head; he threw his hands into the air and spun around.

"You people never quit, do ya?" He lifted the camera away from her shoulders and turned it around. He filmed the news crew and questioned, "Do you guys like interfering in official business?"

They nodded and shook their heads.

"And who am I speaking with?"

The photographer waved into the lens. "I'm Jason Bradley."

He turned the camera to the female, and she exclaimed, "Hi, I'm a reporter for the Channel 3 news crew. My name is Linda Andrews!"

He turned the camera and faced the other guy who handed her the last cassette. He smiled. "John Scott," he sighed. "Film crew advisor."

He ejected the tray, popping out the cassette. He slid it into his trench coat pocket and handed the camcorder to Linda. "OK, now I have all your names on file. Thank you. And don't make me ask you twice.

Leave the premises." He withdrew a pistol, cocked the slide, and hesitated before saying at the last minute, "Or don't."

John Scott shook his head. Jason backed away with his hands slightly hanging over his head. He had his other camera in one hand and hid it. Mr. Fallway glared at him as they walked backward. "Oh, and by the way, Jason Connor Bradley?"

He stopped pacing backward, baffled by him using his full name, and smiled innocently. "Yeah?"

"Those last pictures you managed to squeeze off, I won't see those published, will I?"

"Umm . . ."

"'Cuz if they do get published, 332 Willshire Road is where I'll be coming next." He shook his gun at him.

"Damn." Jason gritted his teeth at Ralph stating his home of record.

* * *

Jake Carson parked in his driveway; Pete jumped out and ran inside. Jake climbed out. Danny followed and smiled at him. He looked down his driveway; the newspaper was lying in a puddle on his lawn. He shut the door and shook his head. The delivery boy always seemed to always aim for water; sprinklers watering the lawn had turned it to mush. Of course, it was Duffy who delivered it.

Danny smirked and waved. "Well, I better get home, Mr. Carson. Pete's going to see his friend Jackson tonight, and I don't want to get in their way."

"Thanks, Danny. Hey, don't be a stranger. You know you're welcomed anytime."

"Thanks, Mr. Carson." Danny smiled and turned to walk away.

"You need a lift?"

Danny shrugged. "No, thanks. I'll walk."

"Come on, let me give ya a ride."

"No, it's all right, Mr. Carson. Thank you for taking me. It was nice to see Mrs. Carson."

"You're welcome."

Danny walked down the sidewalk with his hands in his pockets, staring at the ground. Mr. Carson said, "I'm sorry, Danny."

Danny stopped and turned around. "You have nothing to be sorry about, sir."

"I am a terrible father without Pete's mother around. I can't seem to tie my own shoes anymore. It's my fault Pete hasn't hung out with you kids."

Danny looked at Jake's shoes; he was wearing penny loafers. "You don't have anything to tie, sir!"

"Exactly. Do you think I dress up for my own health? My son is driving me up the wall." He smacked the roof of his car. "I'm a lousy failure!"

Danny stepped forward and held up his hand. "No, you're not. All you need to do is sit down and talk with your son."

Mr. Carson couldn't even face Danny. Here he was a psychologist and Danny was giving him advice. "I can't, because every time I do, I sound like a damn psychologist. I'm bringing my work home with me. I get under his skin," he complained.

Danny stopped short of making any more suggestions and immediately thought about his father. His father was the same way. He was nothing but a cop. He dealt with some of life's lowest people and then came home trying to be a father. "But that's what you do, sir," Danny stated the obvious.

A squad car tore up the road and braked behind Danny. He spun around. Lights were flashing without sirens. His father sprung over the roof and hollered, "Hey, Danny. Your mom was brought to the hospital fifteen minutes ago. She got hurt at the dance studio."

Danny acknowledged what he said and jumped inside the squad car. Mr. Carson spun around, "Hold on, Mike. I'm coming along!"

"OK."

Mr. Carson ran toward the house. When he burst through the front door, he heard clicking noises, footsteps scrambling across the kitchen floor. He entered the kitchen and looked at his son who was nervously sitting on a stool. "What's going on, son?"

Pete was sweating, staring out the patio door toward the pool. "Nothing, dad."

"Son, you're coming with us."

Pete snapped, "Where?"

"Back to the hospital . . ."

"Huh?"

"Look, I don't have time to explain, but apparently Danny's mom was injured today. His dad's out front in the squad car waiting on us."

"Well, hell. What are we waiting for? Let me grab a Mountain Dew before we go."

"Why don't you grab four of 'em." He smiled and walked away.

Pete lifted a stack of newspapers away from his arm. Underneath the newspapers, he was holding onto a pistol. Pete approached a cookie jar on the counter and placed the weapon inside. He stuffed newspaper inside to conceal the gun and secured the lid. A gun hidden inside the cookie jar was a brilliant place since no one was baking cookies.

Pete scampered to the fridge, collecting four Mountain Dews from the middle shelf. He ran through the hall and out the front door, darting across the lawn and through a puddle. He looked at his soaked pant leg and ignored it, continuing to run. As soon as his butt hit the seat next to Danny, the car sped off.

The newspaper swirled in circles in the titanic puddle. Ripples followed the ball of stories as a sudden movement carried water away from the edges. A hand shot out of the water, squishing the newspaper, suffocating the words. The hand wrung the paper, twisting ink and letters into the mud. Then, a body emerged. Water shed away from his muddy face and clothing. One eye glowed red; the other hidden by an eye patch; it was Watches. He crouched low as the squad car sped around the pine trees at the end of the road.

"You go, Mikey! You go!" he cackled and laughed.

Eventually, they were flying down highway twelve toward Park Street, which led into the heart of Madison. Meriter Hospital was on Park Street, a couple blocks south of University Avenue. Park Street crossed University Avenue and ended at the University of Wisconsin, the college in Madison. There were quite a few universities throughout the state; (it was called the UW system).

They passed college students heading toward the football stadium; the Badgers were playing. University housing spanned either side of the road. They drove off Park Street toward the entrance to the hospital.

They could see it. The sign out front drew closer. Mike had his flashers on the entire way; his sirens were going. Blue signs flashed from the squad's lights with the letter *H*, representing a hospital straight ahead.

Mike whipped into the parking structure and entered with caution; he looked at the beams overhead. Pebbles clicked below the timid tires. A car door shut in the distance; the bang echoed through the ramps. His foot let off the clutch, killing the car. His mind went into reverse.

Danny looked out the rear window as the gate guard jumped out of the shack. Not only did Mike's mind go into reverse, so did the car. Mike watched the girders split apart from an explosion. His mind recreated the whole scenario between him and Stanley Markesan almost twenty years ago. The structure collapsed around him; the squad car headed toward the gate guard's little shack. Mike appeared to be in a daze. Danny yanked on his dad's shoulder. The gate guard fell on his butt as the brake lights shined on the concrete walls. Mike stopped two feet from the shack.

He gripped the steering wheel and looked at the concrete structure of the parking garage. Everything was intact. Nothing was falling apart, and the ramps weren't collapsing. He glanced at the boys and Mr. Carson; they all sat with silly little grins. He smiled. "Sorry." The painful memory of being in a car ramp when this villain tossed a hand grenade into a concrete pillar was sheer torture. An explosion started a chain reaction of concrete sections collapsing all around him. Even though he walked away from it unscathed, he hadn't felt the same in any parking garage since.

Jake sensed the pain from his past. But he had no idea how much his mind had been dwelling over it. Jake knew something in his old memory banks had wrinkled his perception. He stared into his eyes. "Uh-huh, we need to talk later."

"What is there to talk about?"

"Your mind, big fella . . ."

Mike nodded.

The blood was flowing through Pete and his father. They were at the hospital not even an hour ago. Now they were back. Mike had parked the car, and they were all walking through the hallways. Mike outpaced the rest of them. Danny was struggling to keep up. They approached the information desk.

Mike stuttered, "M-m-my wife was brought through here probably thirty-five minutes ago. Her name's Clarice Anglekee. Would you happen to know what floor she's on?"

The girl behind the desk knew who he was. She even knew Clarice was his wife.

Pete was staring into the hallway; a black cat exited an elevator. He looked at the young girl behind the information desk as she plugged away at her computer. As if he would get information quicker, Mike leaned over the counter. Her name was Andrea; Danny's brother was dating her. She peaked around the fat monitor.

She looked at Mike. "Oh hi, Mr. Anglekee. Where's Billy this evening?"

"Andrea?" Mike ignored her question. "Sorry, Andrea. Hi . . . my wife?"

She looked at her monitor. "What happened to Mrs. Anglekee?"

Pete was staring into never-never land, trying to figure out where the black cat had gone. Before he realized the cat was even there, his attention was on the clerk behind the desk. When he whipped his head in the cat's direction, it was nowhere in sight. The cat had vanished. The black cat made Pete think about Watches the night he nearly killed him on Slamming Drive when he was younger. They were having a balloon war in those newly constructed homes when Watches made his dramatic appearance, beating his body against studs. Pete looked at his father. "I'm going to check on mom, Dad."

"Wait, Son!" He held up his arm as Pete scurried away. They were primarily there to visit Clarice. Pete sensed trouble, and his father was distraught at his selfishness. Mr. Carson smiled at Mr. Anglekee. "I have no idea what's going through that boy's head."

Mike rattled, "Coming from a head shrink, that's an understatement."

They both gave it a good laugh.

Andrea rattled off a room number; Mike was already halfway through the hall before she finished trying to explain her rest hours. She stood from her computer and watched them run through the hallway. When she glanced away from them, she smiled at the same black cat Pete had seen. "Here, kitty, kitty. How did you get in here, huh?"

In the lobby, the cat sat on a black leather chair. It licked its chops, staring at Andrea. She wore a headset over her head. Being a receptionist, she had to deal with visitors and answer phones; apparently, she also tended to stray fury stragglers. She shook a bottle of cat treats and moved around the counter to see the cat. "I have something you might like." She stopped herself short and removed the headgear after it tugged her head.

All of a sudden, the automatic doors slid across the tracks; she glanced at them. Billy entered. He raced to the desk and stopped short when he realized Andrea wasn't there. He turned to see her near the waiting area. She jogged to him, throwing herself into his arms. He gave her a midsection a tight squeeze while picking her up. Andrea was slung over his shoulder as the cat licked its paws. Billy twirled her around. She noticed the cat hissing. On another spin, the cat was gone.

He was still wearing his uniform from the academy. After classes let out early on Friday, he stopped into the Little Rapids office to work for Sheriff Dunfri. His dad called the sheriff to inform him of Clarice's accident. Immediately, the sheriff released Billy.

Their passions were true, yet his mind was on his mother. She glanced at the leather chair in the waiting area as they separated. Sure enough, the cat had vanished. She looked down both halls. No little lost fur ball anywhere. A few older gentlemen played cards at a table in the lobby.

Billy held onto her shoulders. "Why are you in the waiting room, anyway?"

"I saw a cat, and I was going to feed it treats," she smiled, "but it's gone."

Billy dropped her. White blemishes appeared as the pigmentation in his cheeks seemed to suck the life out of him; his eyes lit up. He stepped away and asked, "A black cat?"

She smiled. "Yeah, how did you know?"

Billy shook his head and blinked his eyes rapidly.

She smiled and reached between his legs. "You know, with your busy schedule lately . . ." Billy jerked his body away, looking in all directions for this so-called cat. "I do have a fifteen-minute break, and I know where there's an empty room."

Billy's eyes widened, and he mumbled, "Fifteen minutes? Is that all?" Billy itched at his forearm.

Andrea asked, "What's wrong with your arm?"

"Nothing."

Upstairs, Pete swiftly moved toward the ICU. He stopped when he noticed cops. Yellow caution ribbon quarantined the entire section; he ducked underneath it to get to the coma patients' wing. Pete approached the picture window that brightened the room. Just beyond the police officers and doctors, he could see the foot of his mom's bed. A couple cops noticed him and pointed at him.

Inside the room, a few people stepped aside; the bright red blood gleamed in Pete's eyes. He stepped toward the doorway but felt the room pulling away from him. The bed appeared like the cavity of a tiger's meal. Then he noticed a body lying in the red. He squinted, trying to make out the facial features. Then he screamed, "Mommmm!" He turned and ran toward the doorway. Two cops grabbed him and wrestled him backward. "Nooooooo!" he screamed. "That's my mom."

He ducked and pulled each officer's arms so that they smacked into each other. He ran through the doorway. The cops struggled to stand after bashing into one another. They ran toward him and missed him as he entered the room.

He ran to the body and glanced at the face, but it was not his mom. It was a dead nurse in his mother's bed. She had been shot once in the chest and once in the head. Pete kicked and screamed, retained by burly arms. It was that moment when he realized Joann Dukes was missing as well. Cops were holding clipboards, reviewing them. There was so much blood.

"Where's my mom?" he shouted.

Mr. Fallway was nowhere in sight; he wasn't in the room. Cops and doctors swarmed the hall. They had a dead nurse in the hospital bed and two missing coma patients. Pete wasn't about to walk away until he heard some answers. Cops were trying to remove him from the room; he pushed back.

Chapter Eight

Black Cat

Pete demanded answers while being dragged through the hall toward the double doors at the end. Wailing his arms toward the block walls, the cops continued to extract him from the ICU wing. All at once, he shut up. A black cat had stepped out of a dark, empty room and stood in the hallway between them and his mother's hospital room. It shook its head and wiggled its entire body as it yawned. It looked at him; one eye glowed yellow. Although it seemed there wasn't a second eye, the cat pranced past them and disappeared into another dark room.

"The one-eyed cat . . ."

"What?" one cop asked.

Pete's head turned toward the doorway. As the cops tugged him past the room, he turned his head to look inside the darkroom. He couldn't see anything but felt a slight pressure on his calves. Inside, he could see nicely made beds with clean, fresh linen. Equipment sat in one corner, but he didn't notice any cats. The cops threw him through the doors at the end of the hallway. The double doors slammed against walls, and a cop snickered, "Now stay the hell out of our crime scene, kid."

Three other people were sitting on the steps. It was the camera crew. They looked at him as he rolled into a railing. Pete hadn't noticed them sitting behind him, but he screamed and slapped the rail.

"Where's my mom?" He sat on his butt against the wall. He cried. "Why won't you guys fuckin' talk to me?"

One of the camera crew filmed him. Pete stood up; he released a knife from a sheath; it slipped between the door latch before the door completed its swing. He peered through the square window and noticed the two cops had already returned to the ICU wing. Pete's eyes followed the doorways; the lobby seemed empty. With the urge to locate the cat, he rocked the knife against the steel door handle; the door popped open, releasing the bone-handled dagger into his palm. He slipped inside.

Andrea turned to John. "Did you see the way he stopped that door from locking?"

"I filmed it. Quick, catch the door."

The news crew peered through the door window behind Pete. Andrea was still filming. The darkroom he wanted to snoop in was fifteen feet to his right. Pete hugged the wall and wove his body toward the coma wing entrance. No one noticed him except the news crew; he slithered through the doorway.

One bed at the end of the room had white sheets. In the dark, the sheets were the only noticeable objects in the room. At the end of the room, something appeared to have been sitting on top of the sheet. It was nothing but a black blob. As Pete drew closer, a cat lifted its head. The cat licked its chops and glared at him. He stopped and heard a noise behind him. He spun around and glanced at the light pouring through the doorway from the hall.

A picture on the wall between the door and a bathroom represented a henchman holding onto a sword. On a backward glance, the cat was gone. Over his shoulder, the henchman rose from the frame like a Venus flytrap spotting food. A shimmer of light glistened over the wedged tip of the sword, which the henchman wound like a baseball bat. Pete spun around; two metals clanked together as Pete averted the sword using his bone-handled knife. The swordsman twirled the sword around his blade and jabbed upward. Pete lunged backward, blocking the swing again.

He stood far enough away from the picture and said, "Holy hologram hell, what are you?" The swordsman withdrew inside the frame. Pete chucked the bone-handled knife; it stabbed through the forehead of the henchman.

"Hello," Pete shouted at the picture. A flame lit over his shoulder in the door window's reflection. Watches was on the end of a bed, behind him, smoking a cigar. The cat was gone. Watches sat in its place.

Pete's eyes sparkled in the dark. He charged the door as an IV pole bashed him tight to the wall; it wheeled past him and wound through the door handle. Pete held onto his face where something sharp cut his cheek. He watched the metal IV pole continue to wrap itself through the handles. Pete no longer felt the pain in his cheek; instead, it was the fear in his gut. Watches leaped off the bed and clamped onto his neck; he lifted Pete's entire body from the floor. Pete grasped onto his hairy arm and stared into his eye. He took another drag of his cigar with his free hand. He growled, "Peter."

Pete's foot shot outward and nailed him in the groin. Watches released his neck. Pete retrieved his knife from the henchman's face as he fell to the ground. He sliced downward and landed on both feet with the knife held to his side. Sparks fanned across the floor as Watches dropped to his knees with a hand over his genitals. His flop hat tilted over his ears partially cut. A thin red line spanned the length of Watches' face, yet he somehow managed to maintain possession of the cigar in his fat lips. He pulled his cigar out to ash, carved in half, sending more sparks.

Pete ran to the metal IV pole and wiggled on it. He dropped to his knees, gagging. Unable to breathe, he slid backward and spun around, facing Watches.

"Watches," Pete choked.

Watches smirked and chuckled. "Miss me, Peter Cottontail?"

Watches wasn't physically holding Pete. Pete's body hoisted against the wall once again. Watches stood up. Pete's eyes opened wider as if his lids were about to lose their eyeballs. Fresh blood oozed from Watches' forehead and slit nostril. Even though Watches stepped away from him, his body remained suspended, mid-air. A mythical grip retained his chest cavity; his eyes could move; his legs could wiggle. His arms could wail, but he was stuck and felt the veins in his neck jostle under tension.

A cart curved out of his way as Watches spun around to peel him from the wall like loose wallpaper. Carrying him by the neck, he tossed him onto the bed. The next thing Pete knew, Watches crawled over the top of him. He lifted an arm to his throat. Pete could feel a cold, sharp blade dig into his skin, wriggling his Adam's apple. Of course, it was Pete's knife. Watches somehow retrieved it. Outside the room, Linda Andrews filmed through the window. Pete and Watches were going at it; her hand shook behind the Velcro strap.

Watches grumbled, "Have you given any thought about our deal, Peter?"

Pete stared at him and couldn't speak. All he could think about was the blade digging in his neck. He rolled his eyes and finally replied, "What do you mean? I owe you nothing."

Watches smirked. "Oh cool, there's a bedpan down there; it can catch your head once it's through." The blade placed more pressure at his Adam's apple.

Pete's eyes were lost inside his forehead; from his position, he could not see the bedpan. Watches flicked some ashes into the pan, and then dropped the cigar inside; it tapped it with a clank. A new odor of burning ash arose. He placed another hand over the blade preparing to chop.

"OK," Pete conceded.

Watches withdrew the knife. He snickered. "Good answer, Peter."

He slipped the knife into a sheath at his waist; a small flaming object burned Pete's face and his eyeball. The cigar had left the pan and returned to his hand. Pete rolled over, holding onto his eyeball. He curled against the bedrail and opened his one eye to look at him. Watches removed the cigar from his mouth and sat on the end of the bed. Pete held onto his throat with his other hand, coughing. Watches stated, "Trust me when I say this, but you can only fight half as good as me, Peter."

"Well that's the only half you can see."

Watches' eyebrow rose over his eye patch. "I need you to deliver a car to me."

"What car?" Pete snarled.

He blew smoke at him and smiled. "The Armybrats' car."

"What? We don't have a car."

"You will."

"We don't have such a car!"

"You will, Peter, you will!"

"You're making no sense. Where's my mom, Watches?"

"Not sure. I think Mr. Fallway got her. I think he may have taken your mother." He held no expression while taking another hit from his cigar.

"If I bring this car, you will deliver my mom—alive!"

"You trying to negotiate, Peter?"

Pete nodded.

"I like your style. Just so you know, you don't deliver, and your mom will come back to you—in pieces."

Pete coughed. "How will I know where to find this car?"

"Ohhhh," Watches grumbled, "you'll know. *Once you see it, you'll know.*"

Both of them snapped their heads toward Linda Andrews. The door creaked; she was stretched over the square window when the camcorder focus knob tapped the pane. Watches stood away from the bed. Pete leaned forward but couldn't see her behind the short wall. She pulled away from the viewfinder and looked around the other side to see Watches holding a cigar in one hand. She removed the videotape, holding it behind her back. Watches raised his arm; he drew his hand backward; the camcorder hurled through the glass in the door; it shattered against a wall at the opposite end of the room. She unhinged herself from the doorway, charging through the ICU.

Watches turned toward Pete. He snickered. "Don't forget my offer. Here, have a smoke on me." He handed him his cigar and vacated the room.

Pete looked at the cigar; it remained lit. He lifted it to his nose. The lump of rolled tobacco flamed. The smoke burned his eyes; he pulled away. The cigar transformed into a ball of fire. Pete pushed it away. The direction he shoved it had forced it to sail across the room. The fire trail annihilated a television like something out of a video game. A hissing fireball dropped to the floor and dissipated. Meanwhile, he patted a fire on the bedsheet.

A light flicked on. A physician shouted, "Hey, what are you doing in here?"

Pete ran around him. He heard his father yelling at a couple of cops. Then he heard his dad say, "Hey, Mr. Fallway . . ." A significant moment of hesitation had occurred. Pete briefly paused in the hall; then he heard a loud smack. Someone punched someone.

He bolted into the entry, hearing all kinds of commotion. His father was screaming. His father wanted what Pete wanted—*answers*. Pete stood in the middle of the lobby. He opened his mouth but couldn't speak; instead, he blew smoke into the air. All arguments stopped; the cops stared at him. He froze for a moment. Mr. Fallway stood up, holding onto his jaw.

"Hey, there's no smoking in here, kid," a cop stated.

Pete was offended; more smoke poured from his mouth when he tried to talk.

His dad spun around. "Son."

Pete stared at Mr. Fallway, almost in a trance.

His dad shrugged, "What, you're smokin' now?"

Pete gasped, "Where's mom?" A plume of smoke made his view of Mr. Fallway hazy.

"Yeah son, so I just found out; and no one's giving me answers."

Pete fainted and fell over chairs. A cop ran over and tried to catch his limp body. His father ran toward him, knocking chairs away; his body collapsed onto the hard tile floor with a thud. Jake held onto his son and hugged him. As Pete went down, he noticed a mangled policeman's body behind the desk in the lobby. The cops stood over them as Jake rocked his son back and forth on the floor.

Jake glared at the cops. "What's going on at this hospital? Where's my wife? Someone bring a doctor! Help me!"

Chapter Nine

Stairwell

Somewhere, on the first floor of the hospital, Andrea lay on a hospital bed with her feet in the air held by stirrups. Her vulva glistened in the dim lighting from a nearby bathroom. She had one arm around her head and her other hand over one breast rubbing a nipple. Her hand dipped into her vagina and repeated the offense to the opposite nipple, leaving wet traces over the areola. "Oh Billy," she called for him and spread more juices over each nipple without flexing their stiffness. "I'm so wet for you."

He shut off the sink and slid out of the bathroom wearing a hospital gown. The opening remained in the front. The tie was loosely dangling but looped around his erect penis. He casually strolled to the end of the hospital bed and tipped his police cap, wiping his hands in a towel. He sighed. "Uh oh, you're crowning, miss." His eyes affixed her vulva.

She pointed at him and gestured her index finger toward her thumb, signaling him to come closer. She grasped onto his penis and ran her hand upward. "What's this doctor? You got your member stuck in your tie."

Billy dropped his chin to his chest. "Oh dear Lord, I did it again."

He slid one hand down her thigh, fingertips gently pressing the top of her vulva. Pink-toned skin curled with circular motions. Two of his fingers disappeared past the joints as they slid inside. She rolled onto her side, with her feet clung to the stirrups, "Closer, doctor. I must untie your knot." Wetness oozed over his shaft when her mouth enclosed over it; the tie seemed to cinch tighter as Billy's erection was lost inside a dentist's daydream, feeling teeth and tongue. Billy nearly fell over from the kink of the tie, using an IV support pole to keep him on his feet. All muscles seemed to go limber—dead weight.

"Oh, dear Lord . . ." he glanced to see her teeth carry the tie away from his erection. Her eyes rolled upward. She smiled; her teeth clenching the fabric. Billy's other hand nestled over the back of her head when she spit the tie out and continued her dental exam.

In the stairwell, the news crew ran in circles. Watches stood at the very top and leaned over a railing. He could see the three of them through the center; briefly, they paused when they heard him chuckle. He held up his hand and pointed. "Listen, Linda. Linda, listen. I want that tape."

Linda's eyes widened. She never met him. Perhaps he had seen one of her broadcasts. After all, she was a journalist. Jason and John took off running. She screamed and followed them. Watches shook his head when they ignored his demand. He waved his hands before his face; the entire stairwell transformed into an orchestra of chimes; the noise was like that of a construction site. The railings separated and blew apart, scraping at block walls and concrete. Railings clamored steps, walls, and windows; one railing clipped the wall before Jason and John. John spat teeth from the strike. Jason hurdled the rail, clung onto another busted railing which bent outward, and hung in the center. He was swaying over dead space. Several floors below him lay the bottom concrete floor. That's where the last stairwell led into a dead man's drop.

He reached for John and screamed, "Pull me up!"

More railings blew apart as Watches willed them to detach from their supports. Railings were bunching over one another and rolling across the steps behind Linda. The railing Jason held onto rocked a bit and screeched as it bent and snapped. His body wound across a wall, one floor down. Watches held his hand toward Linda.

"The cassette, Linda . . ."

She fell against the wall and shook her head. John glanced at her. "For Christ sakes, Linda, give him the tape." She pushed him out of her way and continued running. Watches' face glowed red; he dropped his hand. The pole snapped and Jason's body fell. His back cracked over a railing before Linda; he gasped, "Linda, help me."

Due to his snapped spinal column, all he could do was plead one final cry. Linda stood before a doorway, shaking her head, crying. She walked toward him; his body slipped backward. Railings mushroomed into the center. John was sitting on the stairwell cowering against the wall. Railings were bouncing all around. He could hear the clanking noises as they continued to rain through the stairwell. She screamed when a railing speared the floor in front of her and bounced against a wall. Railings cracked over Jason's head as they showered him. One pierced his leg as he screamed her name and detached from the railing. He fell backward into the square abyss.

John reached over the edge screaming for him. One railing rolled into his lap; he grasped onto it as it lay across his legs. He rocked on the floor with the pole in fear of his life. Linda watched railings fall from above. She paced away from the ledge. Linda listened to the vibrations echoing through the stairwell. Then she noticed one particular railing; it was still intact on the other side of the stairwell. A railing swooped across it, wiggled it a bit, streaming right for her. She noticed the sharp broken edge, gleaming in the sunlight from an upper window. She spun around.

The double doors were a few steps away. The railing hummed as it vibrated and sprung off the other railing like a flying serpentine prepared to strike. It scorched her back and blew out her stomach. The railing poked into the door handle; the door blasted into the hall. Her body hung through the doorway as she remained staked by the pole like a barbeque gone wrong, and she was the shish kebab. Blood splashed across the white tile floor; some splattered across the wall at the opposite end. The door swung against her and clamped her to the center frame.

Billy and Andrea exited a room as the blood blew across the hall. Andrea's hair was a mess. Billy's uniform was left partially undone. They were taken by surprise as Linda's body dangled between doors. Andrea screamed. Speckles of blood wrapped around Linda's cheek, across her forehead, and matted her dark hair. In her right hand, tightly clenched, was a videocassette. Billy stood before her. Andrea cupped her mouth, sheltering a cry.

Linda gasped, "Take it." Those were the last words of the well-known journalist before her head hung loosely over the pole. The tape fell into Billy's outstretched hand.

Doctors and nurses bombarded the doorway, propping it open to collect her limp body. Her head bobbed against the door before they gently lowered her to the floor. Streaks of blood engrained the wooden pattern behind her. Billy looked through the doorway at the waterfall of railings in the stairwell. The noise was treacherous. He sighed. "Stairway to hell!"

Andrea stopped screaming. Instead, she couldn't look away from all the blood. Behind the tears, she stared in awe. She panted, "What is happening, Billy?"

Billy asked, "You remember that black cat you saw?"

"Yes."

"It's him. But it can't be. Can you make a recording?" She nodded. He handed the cassette to her and pointed two fingers in the other direction. "Take this. Go now."

She hugged the cassette. Those puppy dog eyes rolled upward. "What are you doing?"

"Never mind, just go . . ."

"Oh no, you are coming with me, William," she demanded; her voice sputtered like cry-talk.

Billy was on edge; he wanted to go into that stairwell. He wanted to know the ugly truth. His mind kept asking, *Was it Watches?* It was too hard to believe that he was still alive. Without a resolution of the devil from his past, Billy stepped toward the stairwell; she tugged at his arm.

"Billy, if you love me, you won't go in there."

Billy looked at Linda's bloodied body lying on the floor. He turned around. His father approached him. "Billy?"

"Dad?"

"Billy, what's going on?"

"Ah . . ." Billy stepped aside and let him see Linda's body.

Mike was about to head toward her. Billy stopped him. "Dad, don't go in there. Trust me, there's a devil in the stairwell."

"Son, get out of here. Now. Take Danny with you. Go out to the car and wait for me."

"No, dad, you don't understand," Billy hollered.

"Go, Billy."

Mike approached Linda. One door propped open against her body while the other door was accessible. He heard railings clanking. He peeked into the stairwell and then through the center. Stanley Markesan sat over the edge of a step, swinging his legs like a big kid on a jungle gym. He couldn't see Mike as he swung his arm around and shot him in the shoulder. The doctors and nurses dispersed from the doorway after the gunshot. Watches dropped backward and crawled to the edge. No more railings hugged the stairwell. They all piled in the basement somewhere, still bouncing. All at once, the chiming stopped. Mike had sent two more rounds skyward; the gunshots rang through the stairwell.

Mike peered around the edge without any sign of Watches. Watches noticed him as he was peeking around a fire hydrant attached to a wall. His one eye grew large; he whispered, "Mikey boy." He drew back, returning to a shadow.

Mike slid and hugged a wall. He never noticed Watches peering at him. Mike heard the devil somewhere inside. He was about to jump out when a bloody body fell before him. It was John Scott. John rolled over and winced; he looked at him. Mike lowered his weapon. "Who are you?"

"Ow!"

Mike reeled him away from the stairwell by the arm.

"I'm John Scott. Don't shoot. I'm just a reporter."

"What are you doing here?"

"Trailing the story on a coma victim who was murdered earlier today, but those jokers upstairs wouldn't let us film."

"Coma victim," Mike angrily snapped. At that moment, he feared for Julie Carson's life; he was unaware of what happened. "OK, get out of here."

"But I can't."

"Why not?"

He cried, "Both my legs are broken—I think!"

Mike blindly shot two more rounds through the stairway and dragged the victim into the hallway. A blood trail followed one leg.

Mike returned to the stairwell. More gunshots rang out as the nurses tended to John Scott.

Chapter Ten

Altered Recording

VCRs, otherwise known as Video Cassette Recorders, were popular, but the 4-head VCRs were the next best thing. High definition or True Def wasn't even a thing. There were only 2-head and 4-head VCRs. Billy and Danny have heard their own father toying with the acronym because he called them *Very Crummy Radios*. If he heard FM radio playing on any stereo, he would refer to it as *Funky Music*. Of course, he never listened to FM broadcasts. He always listened to AM talk radio or newscasts; he called it "Awesome Music." He never liked the music the boys listened to; they never remembered him listening to music at all, not even a single day in their childhood. Perhaps music was not the thing in the fifties, or maybe he didn't know what good music was.

The hospital had VCRs in all the lounge areas. Billy followed Andrea to her reception desk. A few older men still played cards near the window; they laughed and remained focused on the card game; they didn't notice Andrea switching the TV input to *Very Crummy Radio*. The television was a monstrous tube-style TV; it rested in the corner.

The VCR swallowed the cassette whole as it popped inside; the white noise switched to a hospital floor where someone had been running with the camcorder; clicks echoed from their footwear hitting the hallway floor. The phone rang. Andrea ran to the counter, remote in hand; she extended over the counter, trying to reach her headset. She failed to retrieve it and wandered around the partition wall to answer the phone call.

She answered, "Thank you for calling Meriter. How may I direct your call?"

A humble voice laughed in her ear. "Ha. This is the best part sweetheart; you don't want to miss this. Watches, Watches, Watches!"

"Who is this?" she demanded.

"Um, gee lady. I just told you like three times!" And he hung up.

The camera on the television lifted to a hospital room window and the image flickered. The picture zoomed in on Billy's white ass as he had his arms wrapped over bed rails. Andrea's feet were desperately struggling to maintain their position in the stirrups. This was a recording of them having sex. The camcorder moved through the door as if the door was irrelevant. Billy hopped toward a coffee table, throwing magazines left and right trying to find the remote.

One old man's jaw fell, and a toothpick dropped from his dried, cracked lips.

Another elderly man shouted, "Hey, you gonna deal or what? You waiting on my colonoscopy to happen, Frank?"

"Screw your colonoscopy, Lloyd. Check out that colonoscopy." He pointed at the TV.

"Whoa," said the third old man, sitting at the table. He dropped his hand; cards scattered across the table.

"That sure is a pretty young number."

Andrea stood behind the counter, tapping the Power button. Nothing was responding; she ran around the counter. Billy unplugged the television. She dropped the remote on the table and slumped into a chair. They looked at the three men; they were sitting there, jaws dropped, drooling over themselves. "Hey, we were watching that," Lloyd stated, breaking the silence.

"Play your cards, Lloyd," Andrea scorned. "What was that, Billy? Are you playing a sick joke on me?"

Billy reached for her hand. "Come on, we have to get out of here."

Andrea said, "Oh no, we have to take that tape first."

Billy replied, "You're right."

Moaning and groaning were heard. The TV turned on. It was them continuing with bad doctor, naughty patient. She freaked out, pulling at her hair as Billy stood up. On the screen, jumbled pixels with poor quality, Andrea jumped off Billy's erect penis and shouted, "I want it." Billy was a foot away from her face stroking his penis.

Lloyd shouted, "Here it comes—the money shot boys."

A splash of cum drilled Andrea's left eye, which had become a hole in the television screen. There were glass particles, plastic pieces, and sparks falling to the floor. Everyone jumped afoot. Smoke encompassed the sparks across the wall and curled into the ceiling. Billy lowered his handgun after shooting the television. A few grumbles came from the elderly still playing their hand at cards. Billy ejected the tape; they scrambled away from the lounge.

As they ran through the hall, Andrea asked, "How come you unplugged the TV and it still turned on?"

Billy shouted, "I cannot explain it right now."

Lloyd mumbled, "That dame looked like Andrea."

Another man grunted, "What?"

"Turn up your aides, Walter."

Chapter Eleven

Broken Bra Strap

Andrea hugged Billy as they sat in the rear seat of the squad car. Danny was sitting next to his brother. They were frantically watching the doorway near the elevators, waiting for their father. The doors hinged outward; they perked up as flocks of people stormed through the corridor. After the herd split apart, the doors shut without any sign of him.

Billy whispered, "I shouldn't have let dad go alone."

Danny defended, "He'll be all right."

"You should have seen that stairwell, Dan."

The doors reopened; an older couple exited with a few kids. The dad was jogging with a daughter over his shoulder. The mom was pushing a stroller. More wheeled devices followed them; it was a procession of wheelchairs. Billy opened the car door after noticing Pete and his father. They were stumbling toward them. Billy glared at his brother as Danny exited the car. More people walked off the elevator behind them. Finally, Mike and their mother limped outside. Clarice had bandages around her forehead, some on her neck; both of them hobbled toward the car. Mike had fresh scars. New blood was at his waistline, seeping from his shirt.

All at once, three Lincolns swarmed them. There were several cop cars closely following the SUVs. Andrea followed Billy out of the car and leaned into him. A few men climbed out of the other cop cars, greeting Mike and his wife.

Mike slid his gun into his belt. "OK, take my wife and kids home. Also, I want you to escort Pete and his father. The rest of you are coming with me. Lockdown all exits; comb through every doctors' lounge, nurses' lounge, closets, and dining facility. Interview all staff. He's wearing scrubs. He's still inside this building."

Billy stepped forward and asked, "Dad, is it him?"

"I got your mother released because I don't trust what's going on here. Son, watch Danny and your mother for me, OK?"

He climbed into a squad car. Pete followed his father inside one of the Lincolns. The cops returned to their squad cars and prepared to follow Mr. Anglekee. Other cops separated doctors and nurses pouring from the doors at the end of the parking garage. Billy and Danny stood by the squad car as their mom tried telling them to get inside one of the Lincolns. Danny obeyed her request; Andrea followed Danny. Billy was more curious, however. He leaned through the passenger window and asked, "Dad, was it him?"

"Billy, go with mom now." He backed out of the stall.

Billy followed alongside his car. He screamed, "All I want is a damn answer, dad!"

Billy backed away from the squad car. Andrea poked halfway out of the Lincoln door and hollered for him to get in. His father tore out of the parking lot; the other squad cars blew past them to follow Mike. Madison police raided the hospital after more squad cars surrounded the perimeter. Billy eased toward the Lincoln. He felt he hadn't tried hard enough to stop his father; Billy had a hunch where he was headed but wasn't a hundred percent.

Billy leaned inside the Lincoln and looked at his brother. "Danny, who did you guys see earlier today? I overheard Jake talking to dad on the phone, but I couldn't understand what he was talking about."

"We thought we saw Mr. Fallway."

"By any chance, do you remember where he lives?"

"Of course."

Billy ordered, "Tell the driver, Danny."

"Driver, take us toward the Oscar Meyer plant."

Billy's mom whined, "Billy?"

The driver turned around in his seat after glancing in the rearview mirror. Billy withdrew a handgun and tapped his thigh with it. "My brother gave a simple instruction, driver."

The driver admitted, "I am under direct orders by your father to take you guys straight home."

Clarice mumbled Billy's name.

Billy sarcastically remarked, "Look, driver. Look at my gun. I don't care what my dad or mom says."

The driver held up his hands and glared at their mom. "OK, OK." The driver turned around.

"Thank you!"

His mom glared at him as he climbed inside the car. "This isn't how we raised you, young man!"

"Mom, I don't want to hear it."

"Billy?" Andrea said his name with a grumble.

Danny sarcastically sang the Oscar Meyer Wiener song.

"Shut up, Danny," Billy hollered. "You know what's on my mind?"

Danny agreed. "Yeah, I know what's on your mind."

"Well, I don't think dad should go at it alone."

"Well, I agree. Fallway is a psycho and can't be trusted."

"He's a delusional son-of-a-bitch is what he is."

Their mother sat there and listened to her boys. Their discussion seemed full of rubbish. Andrea had no clue what they were blabbing over. Although their father had told them to go home, they completely disobeyed his orders. Mike was a professional who loved his job. The boys felt compelled to assist him in dealing with his next bust. But the boys sensed where their father was going. They weren't about to let him go at it alone.

Lately, Billy had been taking classes at a tech college. He was taking police science, among other things. Billy worked part-time at his father's police station as well. That's why he asked to tag along in Mike's squad. When he rejected his son's offer, Billy felt insubordinate for giving him pushback. At that moment, his father acted as a father figure to him. He disliked that more than sushi.

One Lincoln peeled away from the group. Pete turned away from peering out the rear window and sighed. "Wonder where they're going." Pete and his father were in the Lincoln that headed toward Verona. The other Lincoln drove past the Badger bus station. They circled the capitol on the square and veered east toward East Washington. First Street brought them to East Johnson, which turned into Packers Avenue. The building on the left was a well-known factory. It was the Oscar Meyer plant.

The Dane County Regional Airport wasn't too far from there. There were more residential homes near Oscar Meyer. It was about sixteen hundred hours. Employees were struggling to turn left onto Huxley Street, leaving work. Employees of the Oscar Meyer plant scattered across the sidewalks. From the overpass, they could see squad cars propelling down the ramps. The cops zipped through the congested traffic. People and vehicles dodged them as they headed into the residential area across the street from the plant.

A car, with a beige cover wrapped over it, sat in the driveway of a small gray house. The cops blocked the driveway and surrounded the property. Mike's squad car slid to a halt on the front lawn. He bolted from the driver's seat while other vehicles surrounded the house. The brothers watched their father run through the yard, kick through the front door, and disappear inside.

Danny sighed. "Mr. Fallway's house."

A woman sat on a couch wearing a bra and eating crackers while watching Judge Judy. Mike cornered a wall and noticed a television flashing to different scenes; another cop eased in and stood alongside him. Other agents ran along each side of the house toward the backyard. Mike aimed Mr. Steely at the woman who stood from the couch and dropped crackers onto the coffee table. The shiny inscription of Mr. Steely was his personalized pistol.

She jumped to her feet and screamed with her hands waving in the air.

"Where's Ralph?" Mike hollered.

She bumped the coffee table with her knees. A glass of tea tipped over and splashed across a few magazines. A newspaper soaked most of it up. The crackers turned to mush. Tea dripped off the opposite end of the table. She shrieked, "Not again, Michael."

The cop next to Mike advanced toward her. She fell backward with a shriek and landed on the couch. He handed her a piece of paper; it was a search warrant, Ralph Fallway's last known place of occupancy. She slumped into the couch cushion and sighed. "Who is this?"

Billy walked in and stood in the doorway. Mike looked at him and shook his head. He lowered his weapon and asked, "Where is he now, Rachel?"

"I have no idea!" she claimed. "He's a deadbeat anyway. I don't care."

"Is that not your address on that sheet of paper?"

Cops swarmed the hallway and through individual rooms. A drinking glass shattered after a rifle barrel knocked it off the kitchen island.

"Hey!" she shouted. "That is my address, but that person does not live here. My fiancé moved out about a year ago, something about a camp as if that camp were more important than me."

"Is that not his car out front?" Mike asked.

"He left it there," she proclaimed. "Oh yeah, he told me that someday a cop would come looking for him. He told me to tell you that the car belongs to your sons, so by all means, take it."

Billy looked at his dad and shrugged. Mike glared at him and then looked at Rachel. He carefully avoided the coffee table; he snatched an electronic ankle bracelet from an end table.

She exclaimed, "My fiancé never paid the bills! He claimed he was an investigator; he was a deadbeat is what he was. This is my parent's home. They retired from Oscar Meyer years ago. They left it to me when they passed."

Mike took a step backward and held the ankle bracelet for her to see; he meant business. "Where is Ralph Fallway right now, Rachel?"

"Look, I already told you, Mike. I have no idea. And take that friggin' car off my property. I'm sick of looking at it. I'm tired of driving around it to get into my garage. Oh, and he also mentioned that you would have a problem with accepting the car, so he left a note for you. I'll go get it." She dropped the search warrant on the couch and moved toward the kitchen.

One cop who handed her the search warrant grew a bit edgy; he aimed his gun at her, following her. Mike raised his weapon in unison.

The cop stated, "Hold on, ma'am. No sudden movements. Where are you going?"

She put her hands in the air and innocently smiled. "I'm just going into the kitchen."

"Famous last words, lady," the one cop threatened.

"I'm going to get the note," she declared and swiftly breezed past the kitchen island.

Mike and the cop followed her. She hustled through the kitchen. The one cop was growing extremely nervous. He moved around a kitchen table; the lady was no longer within arm's reach from him. She whisked toward the cupboards and opened a drawer near the sink.

The cop's voice grew more hostile. "All right, lady. That's enough. Step away from the drawer. Move away from the counter immediately."

Mike glanced at him from the kitchen doorway. He rested against the doorframe and lowered his weapon. He recommended, "OK, Vince. Calm down."

Vince lowered his gun and looked at Mike. The lady took an object out of the drawer; she stood over the sink and flipped on the garbage disposal. Vince heard the noise. He shouted, turned to face her, and shot her in the shoulder.

The bullet separated her bra strap. Blood sprayed across the window over the sink as the bullet shattered the pane. Mike raised his gun when Rachel screamed and nailed the counter. She dropped the object in the sink. It rolled into the garbage disposal with a clatter. She dropped to her knees and held onto the counter with one arm, gripping onto her tattered shoulder with the other. She rolled away from the cupboards. One of her breasts escaped the fabric cup.

Two other officers moved in on her. Specks of blood dribbled on the white bra which hung across her left breast, dangling from one arm. She clenched tightly to the torn shoulder above it. Vince ogled her breasts, blinking to clear his mind. Two more cops hovered over her body. She was breathing heavily, gripping the wound. She looked at him and cried, "Why did you do that?"

"We told you no sudden moves, lady."

"I was his fiancé. What has he done that's so bad?" She struggled from the clutches of an officer who held both of her arms behind her back. One breast bounced before Mike.

Mike shut the disposal off. He took a quick peek in the sink to notice the black box erected from the drain hole. He tucked his gun into his pants. Inside the left sink were a couple of forks, a steak knife, a couple of plates, a couple of cups, and white powder across the basin. More traces of the white substance were on the black plastic flaps in the drain hole. The black box protruded from the center. Rubber drain flaps held it in place. Even if forced, it wouldn't have fit inside the drain hole. He reached inside the sink and withdrew the black box. He asked, "What is this?"

"A black box!"

He proceeded, "Why did you run the garbage disposal?"

She cringed, "I had a mess in the sink, food everywhere, and I didn't want you guys to see it." She watched a stream of blood trickle over her nipple. "Ow, I can't believe you shot me."

He hinged the lid open; it was chopped on one corner and empty. There were more traces of the white powder inside the box. "Yeah, well, I know you don't keep flour in this." He noticed the two forks, two cups, and two plates. "OK, if you broke up with your so-called fiancé, why are there enough dishes for two?"

"Two nights buildup, ass. Now, will one of you take me to the hospital? I'm bleeding all over my fuckin' floor." She snarled, "He did leave me, asshole. The Charger is yours, so get it off of my fuckin' property."

"Whoa, aren't we hostile tonight?"

"Well, you bust into my house, prosecute me, shoot me, and accuse me of lying. You are also making a mess in here. You broke my door, broke a drinking glass, broke my favorite bra." She juggled her blood-striped boob in Mike's face.

"Miss Waters, you are in a lot of trouble concealing drugs, harboring a felon, and disobeying a lawful order."

"That's flour."

"He kidnapped my sons a few years ago. And I'm guessing he introduced you to your excessive use of flour," Mike explained and tossed the black box across a counter. It smashed through a microwave door; pieces fell to the floor. Bags of white powder fell out of the microwave. Mike shouted, "Well, what do we have here? That isn't a Hungry-Man dinner. Look at that, fellas—more flour."

Inside the partially opened drawer, where she withdrew the black box, a handgun lay on top of a phonebook. The other cop looped a pencil through the trigger guard. He extracted the gun from the drawer, "And look-y what we have here; this is why we ask for no sudden movements. People get shot over a lot less."

Outside, Danny stood next to his mother in the road. She appeared worried when she asked, "Danny, how did you boys know where this terrible man lived?"

"Terrible man? I don't know about terrible, mom."

"He is a criminal, Daniel. He's been convicted before. And after he got bailed out, there were more deaths in Little Rapids. So, I ask you, why do you defend this man? Did he do things to you?" She was suggesting sexual misconduct.

"What? No, mom!"

Billy jumped out the front door of the gray house. His father smoothly guided Rachel out the door before him. He paced along the front stoop and allowed her to take her time down the concrete steps. Her shoulder was bleeding through the flannel button-up shirt. A pair of handcuffs draped across the humps in her jogging pants. The chain links bounced off the stretched material on her rear end. Michael held onto papers.

Billy walked straight to the car under the burlap. Danny watched his brother work the tarp around the bumpers to unravel it. His dad hollered at him not to open any doors. Her name was Rachel Waters. Her boyfriend, wherever he was, remained at large. Since Jake warned Mike of the UPS truck, his next step was to contact the local United Parcel Service. The real questions were: *Who's missing a vehicle from their inventory? And if they weren't missing any trucks, was Ralph P. Fallway or Wayne Richards employed there?*

The note read:

Watches is presumed alive. The general order of execution has already begun. We intercepted this transmission:

> Family members and friends of the Armybrats are to be terminated immediately. Non-essentials will be removed or killed first. The remaining will be held captive at my discretion. Spare no one, destroy their families, end the seed of the Anglekee's legacy at the pit of their desperation.

This was intercepted by intelligence agencies in WashingtoN between Watches and a member of his faction. This message is of sincere regret to inform you of your family's grave danger. The EXTraction of family members and friends has Already begun. Their whereabouTs are unknown. After the House on the RoCK incident and the CAMP fiasco, Watches has recruited more GangsteRs. He has reached OUt to locals in the area to terminate your lives with payouts to anyone who completes their mission. There also have been narcotics involved in some exchanges to eliminate you and your family. Please advise I am still your WITSEC haNDler. There is a possible connection between Mr. MarkeSan and loCal law enforcement. I am going to disappear for a wHile. I will bring dOwn this villain, even if it ends me. And I'm truly sorry abOut what happened at camp. In no way did I willingly endanger the Lives of your children. I hope you find This note in confidence. My fiancé was not any paRt of thIs. PleAse excuse her from any wrongdoIngs. I felt I endangeRed her life. I had to get out of this Situation. I heard aboUt Possible activity NEar the HousE on the Rock. I will be investigating in Dodgeville.

Sincerely,
Wayne Richards aka Ralph

Mike shoved the note into his pocket and then reviewed a car title transferring ownership to Billy Anglekee.

Danny walked away from his mother. He passed by Rachel as an officer tucked here inside a squad car. He noticed his brother had half the burlap peeled away. The car was more beautiful than ever. It almost seemed as if it was freshly painted and waxed. The chrome wheels shined bright. Things seemed different with the vehicle. On the side, a word appeared. It was still half-covered, but it read *ARM*. Billy continued to unveil the rest. More of the word had become visible. And letters were inscribed in the metal, fancy-like; the *R*'s had sharp points on them as well as the first "*A*." And the *S* had an arrow drawn at the bottom of it as it partially curled under the word: *ARMYBRATS, routed into the doors.*

It was wicked pretty; the letters were stylish. The car was astounding, dedicated to their honor; it was a personal gift from Mr. Fallway. After Mike read Rachel her rights, he locked her inside his partner's squad car. He lumbered toward his sons, who were in awe over this fantastic gift. He stood between them and wrapped his arms over their shoulders. Danny stepped away and ran his fingers along the letters in the door of the Dodge Charger.

Billy looked at his brother and in unison replied, "Wow!"

Mike shook his head.

Danny cried, "Oh why not? This is way cool, dad. This is our club name!"

Mike argued, "That's what he wants you to believe, that you're in some kind of stupid club. He's a crook, and this car was probably bought with drug money, so the answer is N-O, NO. Absolutely not! I am going to impound this hunk of junk first thing in the morning!"

Chapter Twelve

Bratmobile

After Danny retrieved the keys from his dad's desk drawer in the den, he snuck out. Duffy picked him up in his parent's old minivan; they drove into the school forest. Deep in the woods, Danny followed him out, driving an old beat-up Dodge Charger from Rowley's junkyard. It was the greatest $150 scandal of a lifetime. They had driven to the east side of Madison. Duffy parked the minivan in the Oscar Meyer parking lot; they drove the old beat-up Dodge into the driveway next to the black Dodge wrapped in burlap.

Duffy helped Danny roll it off the car. They covered the rusted Dodge Charger with the canvas and carried their attention toward the more beautiful one. Duffy was astonished.

"Now that's the more *beautiful-er* one!" Duffy whispered.

"Looks like the batmobile," Danny suggested.

"More like *Bratmobile*," Duffy exclaimed, pointing at the lettering on the door.

They sat inside with the headlights off and discovered all sorts of whistles and widgets. The dashboard was like sitting behind a pump player piano. Except there were no ivory keys, just buttons, and of course, pedals.

The car wasn't any plain old Dodge Charger; there seemed to have been some variations with different components both inside and outside. Danny slid the key into the ignition. The dashboard glowed blue, and everything lit up. There were LEDs across the entire front of the dashboard. There were computer screens inside the dashboard and console with all sorts of buttons.

Duffy played with some of the buttons. Different things happened. Like one button turned on backlighting behind their club's name along the doors. "ARMYBRATS" lit along the doors and cast the name backward across the ground on either side of the car. Duffy tried a few other buttons with no outcome. But certain buttons required a series of other buttons to be pressed to initiate some sort of response.

A red button on one of the consoles read *Ready Front Weapon.* Another one read *Ready Rear Weapon.* Duffy hit the front button one. Their curiosities ran wild. After the button was pushed, a monitor turned on. A weapon lowered from behind the bumper. It swung forward; optics mounted to it transmitted the signal to a monitor. It was a fully automatic weapon system mounted to a hydraulic extension where it was housed inside the front bumper near the grill. Their eyes lit up.

Crosshairs at the center of the screen targeted the neighbor's trashcan across the road. The images were darker green, like night vision. They were cold colors: black, green with shades of gray. But another button was flashing on the console. In the middle of the white button, there were red letters which spelled the word *Fire*.

"Umm, we shouldn't." Danny sighed.

"We should!" Duffy iterated and pressed the button.

An amazing phosphorus glow lit the driveway as rounds buried themselves through a trashcan on the other side of the road. The can folded in half, shredded apart; it tossed trash clear across the lawn, onto the sidewalk, and to their front door. Every fourth round or so was a tracer; a streak of red flared through the trash bags inside. The tracers appeared to bounce over the houses toward the Oscar Meyer plant. A small fire burned inside.

Duffy let go of the button.

They ducked as porch lights flickered on. The weapon mechanically rotated and wound back inside the grill. Duffy shut the Armybrats' door lights off. Danny pulled the key from the ignition; the monitors on the dash faded as well as all the other lighting. After a few seconds, all instrumentation fizzled into darkness. Danny and Duffy peaked over the dashboard. The owner of the house with half a glowing trashcan crawled across his porch wielding a shotgun. He snatched some of the trash, held it in his hands for a bit with a puzzled expression on his face, and headed for the front lawn. He realized his trashcan was glowing orange. He paced towards it, glancing in all directions. Even an owl hooting in the distance threw his body into a dizzy little ballerina spritz while swinging the shotgun.

A third of the steel trashcan protruded from a storm drain. The other bits and pieces of steel were in his driveway, in his yard, and the neighbor's yard. Some trash was even on top of his roof. The trash bags were obliterated, with trash scattered in every direction. Some clung to his trellis. The man walked in circles trying to figure things out. *Someone must have done a drive-by*, he thought.

Suddenly, a dog jumped on the driver's window. Its paws hit it with a thud; its nails clicked the glass. Danny and Duffy screamed. The man holding his shotgun noticed his dog viciously charge the car. He raised the double-barreled gun to his right shoulder. He tucked the butt of the gun tightly to it and hollered, "Who's over there?"

Danny and Duffy looked at each other. They had nowhere to go. They were trapped inside the car with a drooling mutt biting at the glass and a shotgun ready to remove them from life. When he squeezed off a round, the boys' hearts both sank into the pits of their stomachs. They felt the blood rush straight to their heads and their toes.

Supposedly, the blood was going in every direction with an overwhelming ring in their ears. The shotgun was aimed at the windshield; neither one of the boys ducked. Instead, they covered their heads as if it would have protected them. The shell casings flattened against the windshield as they watched the smoke puff outward from the small sparks upon impact. The BBs inside the shell casings scattered outward and fanned across the windshield, bounced into the air vent, and rolled across the hood. The dog yelped and backed away only to return barking more vigorously.

Duffy turned toward Danny. He smiled. "Friggin' bulletproof windows, man."

The dog barked some more. The man noticed his shells had done nothing to the windshield. He grew upset and stomped across the road, screaming, "OK, I know I'll get you with this next shot, you little punks."

By the time he was in the driveway, they noticed him slurring his words a little. He was fairly drunk. He was stumbling around and could barely hold the shotgun up. He blasted away at the driver's window. Just like earlier, nothing happened; the window deflected BB's and casings. The man's dog had run off. He lowered the weapon and tilted his head at his hairy arms where BBs embedded his skin. He hopped around in agony for a second, twirling his shoulder cannon, and wiggling his arms. Duffy frantically reached for the armrest on his door and clicked a button; the automatic door locks slammed downward as the man threw his gun. He was ready to whoop asses.

Danny was viewing the console when he found a button that read *Intruder Buzzer*. Unsure of its feature, he pressed it. It flashed for a moment and then remained lit. One monitor at the center outlined a bird's eye view of the Charger with a bright white line. The button was no longer blue; it turned red. The dog scurried around a bush. Once again, it jumped at the driver's door, barking. Amazing blue trails of zigzags wrapped around the mirror and across the door, throwing sparks over the roof. An electrical surge enveloped the dog. The dog turned into a frizzy puffball of frenzy cries and flew through the same bush.

The dog's owner watched it disappear; the dog yelped and scampered toward the house with its tail between its legs, smoke swirling away from its hindquarters. The owner cried, "Aww, Rexxy! Why, you bastards?" He scowled at Duffy who was sitting in the passenger seat. "You fried the piss out of my poor little Rex, you little mother . . ."

He leaned forward and extended for the door handle. Duffy's face lit behind the pane; he was shaking his head trying to warn the man to not grab the handle. The little *Intruder Buzzer* button was still glowing bright red. The man couldn't finish his sentence when his mouth froze crooked. He got a shock of electricity, sending neurons through blood cells. A foot planted firmly in the grass. His head tilted to its side; the dark holes of his nostrils glowed as if his brain turned into a lightbulb. Light trails wound around his arm and his right side. His hair stood on end; the voltage was spitting sensory commands to all extremities like a hard rocker on speed.

The endoskeleton of the man flashed before the boys. They jerked away from the bright light. Even though the man's feet were grounded, the force blew his body upward, and he landed on the windshield. His robe burned; his buttocks glowed at them as his bare ass mushed against the glass. The man's arm was awkwardly wrapped over the fender, still clinging to the door handle. The boys screamed. Unsure of what to do, Danny cranked the ignition. The car shook the shrubbery along the walk. He shifted into drive and mashed his foot over the gas pedal.

One awful fact about electricity was its hold over anyone. However, the man let go of some excrement as a brown substance blasted across the windshield. Duffy groaned, "Oh man, he shit himself. Get him off the car; he's poopin' on our car, man."

Danny shouted, "Hit the red button!"

Duffy hit it. Danny braked. The man detached from the hood before shuttling into his mailbox. He folded around the pole and it broke. He lay in his driveway, glowing while pieces of the robe burned around his body. Even the pubes around his genitalia were singed, outlining his reddened tallywhacker.

The boys fled from the neighborhood. Danny ran the windshield washer fluid trying to remove poo streaks while maintaining steady driving. They crossed Huxley Street and headed for the minivan. As soon as the car slid to a stop, Duffy ran out laughing.

"How about you drive this one? I wanna drive."

"Later. Let's go."

Duffy jumped inside the minivan and cranked the engine; he followed Danny toward Verona. They hid the Dodge in the gully in the school forest. They covered it with some undergrowth, camouflaging it in shrubs.

The mobile weapon Mr. Fallway had left them almost immediately refastened any corals between them. Danny's father was going to have it impounded the next morning; now they were in a pool of trouble—almost neck deep. If Pete had seen it, his interests would have peeked. Perhaps it would fuse him back with the group as well. But his mother's disappearance drove him mad. All Danny wanted to do was show it to him.

They needed to show the car's significance to Billy and Pete. Of course, none of the boys had any idea of the total firepower it possessed; they just admired Chrysler products. Ultimately, Mr. Fallway expected them to complete a mission. It was obvious; the mission was to terminate one hell of a devil. If they needed a tank to do it, this was it. This could—quite possibly—restore the Armybrats.

Danny and Duffy had experienced fifteen percent of the capabilities of one of the most powerful mobile weapons known to man. The Armybrats rose out of the clutches of extinction; they seemed to have been separated and segregated. Danny and Duffy were still very close friends. Billy was never around anymore; he hung around Andrea or in Little Rapids every day and night.

Now the old beater, the Dodge Charger Danny and Duffy swapped for $150, was left in Rachel Waters' driveway. The old Dodge's keys were placed inside Danny's father's desk drawer. The misconception of any old Dodge Charger being crushed was what the boys concocted; their precious baby was for sure theirs.

Chapter Thirteen

Pete's Struggle

It was Saturday; Pete walked downstairs from his bedroom. His door swung shut behind him. It muffled the blaring music from the room. The bass from the stereo rattled the picture frames as he trotted the steps. His father clutched his arm before he stepped into the kitchen for breakfast. He spun him around and applied pressure over his forearm. "Look, son. I don't know what has gotten into that little brain of yours lately, but you used to pull good grades. I received a letter yesterday concerning your academics. What happened to you, Peter? And can you go back upstairs and shut that devil music off right now?"

He pulled away from his dad to retrieve a Pop-Tart out of the cupboard. He slid it into the toaster and snarled at him, "It ain't devil music, dad. It's called—"

"Hey, I got a call from one of your teachers this morning. She said that she would be expecting you during your first hour period on Monday. Have you been skipping out on English, son?"

"She's an anal bitch, dad. Who cares what she wants?" The toaster clicked; the aroma of Frosted Watermelon filled the kitchen from the warmed breaded pastry. Sweetened frost snapped at the breaded edge as half the tart had gone into his mouth from one bite. He leaned into the counter staring at his father. He gave a quick glance at the cookie jar.

"Hey, son. I need you to stop ignoring me," he shrieked and latched onto his arm once again.

Pete could feel his muscles roll over his fingers when he squeezed. Without thinking, he pushed inward on the inside of the elbow joint. His dad folded and uncontrollably stepped forward as Pete pulled away. His dad's face smashed into the overhead cupboards above the counter. His dad turned away, coddling a nosebleed. Pete stood there in awe from his reflex. The self-defense tactics were like a natural reaction, all taught by one man named, Ralph. He stepped away, staring at his hands, then looked at his dad; Mr. Carson sat at the kitchen table with his head tilted back, pinching his nose.

Pete approached him and swallowed, "Dad, are you OK?"

His dad held up a hand and didn't want to discuss any further.

Pete's mind backtracked to when he was on his school bus with Beaner and Greg. They always treated him like a percussion instrument (beating on him) and stole his lunch money. His mind wandered to the days he avoided those bus rides. He snuck bagged lunches to school. He kept lunch money to pay those clowns for freedom. He kept visualizing all the bad things in life; all those things made him who he was today. He kicked his dad's ass with slight effort. He wasn't the little nerd everyone used to think he was. He wasn't the little wimp with thick-rimmed glasses anymore. Nope, he lived to please no one. Plus, he wore contacts now.

"You want to know what happened to me, dad. I will tell you. I got selfish." Tears formed in his eyes. He was still shocked that he had done that to his father. "That's it, dad. I got selfish, and I don't care about anything else or anyone else for that matter." He backed away from his father. He whispered, "I'm losing it, dad."

His dad overheard that comment. By the time he glanced at the doorway, blood stinging his right eye, Pete was no longer in it. He ran, holding onto a cookie jar; he had swiped it from the counter. Jake stood from the table. He screamed for him to stop. Jake let go of his nose and ran toward the hall. When he cornered the wall, the front door swung shut.

Jake stomped through the hall. When he opened the front door, he saw Pete running for his car. Jake watched him climb inside his four-door sedan. A pile of porcelain rolled across the driveway where the front tire pivoted and smashed the cookie jar some more. "Wait, son," he hollered. He was a psychologist, and he knew behaviors real well. He knew his son's state of mind was fragile; he may have pushed him to the brink.

Pete's head spun around; his eyes stared through the opened driver's door window. He looked into his father's eyes and shook his head with a smirk while backing out of the driveway. Then he spun the tires and painted streaks on the concrete. He squealed halfway down the block, and it kicked in high gear.

His dad's shoulders dropped. His son watched him in the rearview mirror. His dad was too disgusted to cry, wishing for his wife to be home; he would have gone inside to collapse in her arms. He would have pouted with disgrace. He removed his glasses, rubbed the bridge of his nose, and leaned against the door. Perhaps none of this would have been happening if his wife was actually there.

He ran inside to fetch the phone. He dialed the police station. An operator responded, "Verona Police Department."

"Michael James Anglekee, please?"

"Please hold."

"Verona police department, Chief Anglekee speaking."

"Mike!"

"Jake?"

"Pete just ran off on me. I think he may do something foolish."

"OK, Jake, get a hold of yourself—calm down. I want you to go into your living room, grab a scotch, and relax. Watch some television. I will personally patrol the neighborhood. Cool?"

"Find my boy, Mike. Please."

"Don't worry, Jake. Now relax."

"OK, thanks, Mike."

They hung up with each other. Mike threw his pencil and released the lever in the receiver's cradle to dial a few numbers. "Yes, hi, this is Chief Anglekee with the Verona Police. There is a vehicle at 314 Sycamore Lane near Oscar Meyer I would like impounded. It is a Dodge Charger. Yes, I will hold."

* * *

Meanwhile, Danny and Duffy cruised around the countryside. They were driving the country roads with the Bratmobile. Duffy laughed as the music blared over the stereo system inside the car. Guns N' Roses blared over the Bose speakers. Danny took a risk and headed through a cornfield. They ripped through the field and stopped in the center of the cornstalks. Up ahead, they faced a mound of dirt.

Danny shifted into park. "This is too cool. Why should I let you drive?"

Duffy replied, "It's my turn," and undid his seatbelt.

Danny climbed out of the driver's side door and walked around the car. Duffy crawled over the console in the center. His knees tapped a few buttons. There were three significant bleeps. One bleep, armed laser-guided rockets somewhere on the vehicle. The next was the *Ready* switch and two compartments along the front fenders slid apart. Small footlong arrowhead rockets positioned themselves and were set for engagement. The third beep dropped Danny flat against the earth as rockets whizzed over his back.

Danny rolled to the side away from the thrust of the rockets torching the ground and the green ears on the stalks. Danny covered his head as the rockets released and whistled away from the tubes. A red laser speckled the mound of dirt just ahead. Duffy ducked as the mound of dirt mushroomed into the sky. Flames cut cornstalks in half alongside the car. Stalks flipped out of the soil and shot upward like lawn darts escaping the dirt.

Further in the field, a farmer jumped off his tractor; he stood in front of it. His forehead was sweating from the sun beating on him all morning. In the distance, a portion of his feed flew with clouds of dirt falling toward the earth. He crossed his hand over his heart as the Catholic religion within him blessed his Savior. He gulped, "Mother of Mary, what in tarnation was that?"

Danny leaned over the trunk and screamed as dirt caked to his hair; the trunk rattled vibrantly. He rolled beneath the car as stalks speared the ground around him. Duffy stared out the window. It was hazy from the dirt settling. He was confused for a moment. But the mound of dirt wiped off the earth, leaving an empty plot of land. Danny jumped inside; they stared at each other for a moment. Danny snapped, "You shot a rocket at me."

"Oops!" Duffy nodded and smiled; they tore out of the field.

The farmer was driving the tractor toward the explosion. He neared the opening, jumped off his tractor, and killed the engine. The rocky hill where he never planted corn was gone. He walked around the crater, staring at the sky. In all actuality, the boys opened another fifteen square yards of land for cultivating. His eyes were the size of melons. Where the heaped earth disappeared, he knelt to retrieve a charred metal casing. It was one of the explosive's casings. He smelled the tube and oddly stared through it.

At Rachel Water's house, a towing company called Mike's Towing hitched to the Dodge Charger. The Madison Company was doing exactly what officer Anglekee had instructed. Of course, Rachel Waters was in jail; the Dodge was from Rowley's junkyard. It was there to misconstrue Mike's wishes, and his wishes were to have the Bratmobile impounded.

"I still can't believe what you did back there!"

Duffy laughed. "I didn't mean to. I just crawled across the console. How was I to know that I would blow shit up?"

Danny smiled and turned toward him. "Do you think that old beater Dodge was a good decoy?"

"Of course, it was my idea!"

"I don't know . . . I feel like I'm cheating my father's wishes."

Duffy laughed. "You are."

The boys drove the main road and passed the schools. The buildings remained quiet over the weekend. In the high school parking lot, Pete's four-door sedan sat in the far corner. Thoughts accumulated in his head. They festered. His mind was like an old basketball losing threaded beads as the internal pressure ripped them apart, one thread at a time. It was just a matter of how long he would last before he imploded.

He remembered Watches bribing him to deliver a car. Watches had gotten under his skin. His father was in his mind, scolding him. His father was on his nerves. His mom was missing. What more could possibly go wrong? He was on the edge of an internal meltdown. His father was upset over his wife's disappearance and the family was being ripped apart. He felt as though his dad was taking it out on him. His grades were slipping in school.

He shut off the car. He slipped the keys from the ignition and sat there for a while. He wore a trench coat, blue jeans, and a denim shirt underneath. As he opened the door, a gun clanked across the pavement when it fell from his lap.

Across the street, a kid sitting in a tree near the church noticed him scrambling for the gun. To him, it appeared to be a camera or an odd-shaped flashlight, but he couldn't quite figure it out.

Pete retrieved it and slid it inside his trench coat pocket. He swung his car door shut and crossed the street to find another place to think for a while. He turned toward the church and walked inside. The boy in the tree lifted his paperback book and began reading.

Pete's love of church and God were still holy and pure. He slid the gun out and placed it over an ivory bucket holding holy water in a beautifully sculpted dish, like a bird feeder. He dipped his hand in the water and walked toward the back of the church. He respected his religion and never believed anyone should bring a weapon inside God's house. An arrangement of candles was surrounded by flowers.

The bouquets sprouted from the base of the brass sculpture of the cross. There were characters depicted from the bible within the sculpture across the wall. Concrete moldings whirled around the sculptures, more flowers nestled along the concrete moldings. Stairs led to the arrangement. At the center of the stage, a podium stood before the mural. The pastor preached from there. He read his sermons from that podium. Pete walked past and knelt before the cross.

"God, please forgive me. I can't imagine living a life full of misconception. And this anxiety hanging over me is far too painful to carry. All around me, I see people laughing, smiling, with their bright smiles and happy thoughts. I have none. They make it through life simply because they love their jobs, their home, and their families. Me, I'm a lost soul with an opaque attitude about finishing school or ever finding a career suitable enough for me. And there is no way I could do this without mom. How could I heal people if I need healing, God? That's why I cry on your carpet today.

"God, why did you take my mom from me?" he cried at this point. "I see me as an old man with no friends, no family who cares, and a childhood of double-crossing my friends, and all for what? Money, greed, selfishness? My memories are poisoning me, Lord. I've decided enough is enough with this life that you've provided me. Before I go, I want to thank you, God, for everything you have given me—all the pleasures which are probably sins, the highlights, and the precious moments in life. I'm sorry I plan to vacate it now, but I hope you accept me after this."

He jogged across the red rug, swiped the gun, burst out the church's oak doors, and ran through the park. The kid reading his book noticed him run beneath the tree branch. Pete briefly paused underneath because he dropped the gun again. It rolled in front of him. The boy in the tree perked up when he noticed it. Pete bent over and retrieved it. It wasn't a camera. It wasn't even a flashlight. The kid in the tree knew exactly what it was. Pete turned to look toward the slide in the park and ran toward it.

The boy still had the book in his hand, but he was no longer reading. He couldn't breathe. He froze with his back tightly pressed to the trunk. His legs were locked straight. He watched Pete climb into the shelter at the top of the slide. He looked at his book and decided he could no longer continue with the story until he figured out Pete's madness.

Pete sat inside the shelter and cocked the slide hammer until a round entered the chamber. He spun the gun around to investigate the barrel. He kept his eyes closed as he placed tension over the trigger. Pete Carson, after seventeen years, wanted to take the easy route out of this life. Perhaps Watches had driven him into a blustering fool. First, he took his mother, then his self-worth, and next would have been his life.

The boy in the tree noticed young boys run around their mother as she walked a black lab puppy on a leash. The puppy stopped for a second as he shook his head and pranced before the kids who were distracted by a butterfly, pulling their mother's arm upward. She halted the puppy. The boy continued reading the book.

"Our Father who art in heaven, hallowed be thy name. Thy Kingdom come, thy will be done, on earth as it is in heaven . . . forgive me of this sin, my final sin. I love you, Father, as I love those who raised me and loved me."

Pete's self-esteem was as present as his mother's. With her being gone, his grades dwindled; his bad attitude heightened; his outlook on life had gone down the toilet. The new crowds he hung with at school had no morals, no respect for others, and no clue as to what they were supposedly doing in life. Thus, the real reason why Pete was even considering ending his own was over a stupid question*: why am I here?*

He reopened his eyes when he smelled a sweet tinge of tobacco. Smoke was flowing past his face. A voice ranted, "Pull it, Peter. Go ahead, pull the trigger, Peter." He looked beyond the clouds to see Watches lying flat on the slide staring at him with one eye. A couple strings hung from a fray at the corner of his patch. Pete backed away. "Wake up on the wrong side of the bed this morning, Peter?"

Pete shrieked, "Ahhh!" He aimed the gun at him. Watches pushed his aim higher. A round penetrated the shelter above the slide. A stream of smoke followed upward from the new hole.

The black lab puppy perked its head; the mom rushed her children away from the park fighting against the dog's leash. The kid in the tree worked through the limbs like an arborist. He couldn't put the book down. He held onto it, even when he scaled the trunk. He stared at the slide for a moment. His sunglasses reflected the sun until he lowered his head to see the mom scurrying away with her boys and the puppy.

In the shelter of the slide, Pete and Watches looked away from a fresh hole in the plastic. "Pete, I'm tellin' ya, it's about time you kill yourself."

"Yeah, you're right," Pete agreed.

Watches puffed at his stogy and curled his lip. "I figured—" He puffed some more. "—you'd end up screwing me over, eventually. I just didn't think it would be sooner than later."

Pete pulled away. "What are you talking about, Watches?"

The kid heard the puppy bark; the bark seemed to ricochet off the school. He glanced at the slide. Pete's voice had him convinced he was on a cellphone. Then the boy thought about the gun he had dropped. He shoved the book inside his backpack. He slung the bag over his shoulders and walked toward the slide. He thought the gun was a toy; that shot heard across the schoolyard made him realize it wasn't. He jogged toward the slide. He couldn't see inside the shelter. It was tall and angled funny. Half of the slide was an enclosed tube. The other half shined bright orange under the sun.

Watches snarled, "You are about to betray me, Pete."

Pete asked, "How's that?"

"You promised to bring that car. If you kill yourself, then you'll fail me!"

"I guess so." He smiled and held the gun to his temple.

"You couldn't do it anyway, you ungrateful little turd."

"Oh yeah?"

Watches smiled devilishly and scowled. "Yeah."

Pete breathed heavily and pushed the barrel tightly to his head.

"Do it or I will end you myself."

Pete glared at him.

"What are you, some kind of pussy, Peter?" Watches crawled up the slide and pressed into his face and groaned, "Pull the trigger, Peter."

He smelled ashtray-lips drowned in alcohol fumes. "Ready?"

"Yeah, I'm ready, you little baby. You cry to your daddy every day because you miss your little mommy. They spoiled you rotten, and now you miss it. Do it."

Pete thought about that statement and took it to heart. "Oh yeah?"

"Yeah, you ain't nothing but a wussy. Your mom's gone. Your dad beats you more. Your grades have gone to hell. What do you got to lose, Peter?"

Pete shook his head with the barrel pressed to his temple. "Nothing!" Pete turned the gun toward Watches and pulled the trigger. The hammer slid forward and struck the charge. The round blasted out the end and went through Watches' head. Watches' entire body cracked like the porcelain cookie jar piled in his driveway. Pieces sprinkled into the tire pit off the slide. Particles of Watches' body scraped the plastic as fragments of him scattered in different directions. Of course, Watches may have been a figment of his own imagination at that point. The way he shattered was unrealistic as he oddly watched the pieces slide away from him.

The kid charged the steps to enter the slide. When the shot rang out, he let go of the rails and flew on top of him. Both boys sailed down the slide; the gun released from his hand. It buried itself in the shredded tires. The kid sat up and adjusted his sunglasses. A lens had fallen out of the frame. He looked at Pete who was still trying to understand what had happened. The kid slid his glasses off the bridge of his nose. Pete scrambled for the gun. He was glowing with anger. The boy drove his head through Pete's face. He turned around and noticed Pete had let go of the pistol. It drove tire pieces away from it as it landed below the slide.

Pete wiggled his head and noticed who he was. "Jerome."

"Pete." Jerome punched him in the face. Pete flew backward, nailed his head over the hard-plastic slide. He gave a few grunts and went for the gun. Pete was kicked in his face. He stepped backward while this kid looked at him. Jerome was hanging from the edge of the slide, upside down. He smiled, dumbly.

Somehow, he had retrieved Pete's weapon. Jerome flipped backward off the slide and landed on his feet and twirled it with his index finger inside the trigger guard. He turned the handle, so it faced him for him to take. "You know who I am?"

"A dead man," Pete exclaimed.

"Wrong," Jerome smiled.

Jerome squeezed the gun. He smiled at Pete. Pete looked at his black fingers wrapped snuggly over the barrel. His eyes widened. Jerome swung the handle of the gun across his face. Pete caught the hard steel blow and rolled through the shredded tires. His head bobbed around. Tire pieces shot from underneath him. Jerome pistol-whipped him so hard; the color of the backside of his eyelids was all he could see while stars twinkled in the moonlight.

His name was Jerome Dawson. He was his high school classmate. Jerome recently moved to the neighborhood and knew no one. Over a week ago, he attended the Verona school for the first time and talked to nobody. Pete happened to be in his English class. The one he skipped out on recently. They sat in opposite corners of the classroom; he knew of him but did not know him. With little recollection, they barely knew each other. He was in a couple different classes with him. Jerome loved reading and writing. He knew different languages such as Arabic, French, German, Russian, and Spanish. He was smart, skeptical, clean-cut, and focused. He knew Pete wasn't about to listen to him, so he knocked him out to allow him to ponder that thought. It may have kept Pete alive a little longer

.

Chapter Fourteen

Vacuum Velocity

The next morning, at the Anglekee house, Danny was in bed when his mother stepped in. "Get up, you're going to church!" Danny wrapped his pillow over his head and rolled. This was a recurring Sunday ritual of waking the boys and getting them ready for church. The hen continued to squawk, but Danny was ignoring it until the rooster started in.

Church service was about to be in session. Clarice, Mike, and Billy were ready for church, but Danny was not. It was an early Sunday morning tradition to harp on Danny to get out of bed. Danny didn't want to rejoice. This was the first morning where he stood firm on the argument. He did not want to go to church. Then he heard his father.

"Danny, your brother, and your mom have already eaten breakfast. Be downstairs in ten minutes," he ordered.

"No, thank you!"

"Danny, get dressed immediately—ten minutes!"

His dad hollered from the bottom of the staircase. Danny tucked his head deeper into his head's fluff nest. The intercom snapped on and crackled. His father's voice returned, "Get up, boy!"

Danny realized the hold button was left on. He could hear Billy and his father conversing. He scooted to the foot of his bed and yawned. A sock rolled off the end of his bed and splayed across the floor. Dishes rattled, he assumed his mom was doing something with plates and bowls. Obviously, they were in the kitchen.

Danny squinted. He acquired one shoe from the floor and walked to the intercom. "See ya when you get home." He swung his shoe into the plastic box near his door. Pieces fell to the floor. He locked the door and dropped into his bed.

Billy and his father turned to look at the intercom. It continued to squawk. Mike stood up and scurried to the plastic box in the wall. He pushed all the buttons; nothing fixed the squelch. It continued to buzz. Mike scratched his head and wondered why it was acting up. Finally, he shut it off.

Several minutes had gone by. Mike knocked for a while and shook his doorknob. "OK, if this is how it's going to be, you better consider your punishment. You're grounded."

A half-hour went by. Danny was feeling far from God. Pete was truly in a world of hurt as well. Perhaps, the boys needed a good reminder of where they stood in life. The little secret cult they escaped from was in the past. Lately, they had seen a lot of death and awful stuff happen, but overall, Pete losing his mother killed him. Danny's parent's dishonesty (about their real names) devastated him. The attack on Duffy in the woods crushed him. Billy had his own demons working for someone he couldn't trust—Sheriff Dunfri. However, Billy was still joining them for church.

Danny's eyes snapped open. He couldn't sleep. All he could think about was his past misdemeanors. He remembered that with every punishment, there were always special chores. He had to take out the trash, clean the dishes, and clean both bathrooms; he also had to mop the hard floors and vacuum the basement.

He threw off his bedsheets, deciding to begin basement chores. The first thing he noticed in the basement was a bundle of blankets piled over the couch; the TV flashed to a commercial. When he stepped around the couch, he rubbed his arms, feeling the goosebumps grow.

Their house had an exposed basement, and when he glanced left, he realized the basement door was open a crack. Why the door was left open, he had no clue. He walked toward it, stubbed his foot on a rocking chair, and fell over; he held onto his throbbing toe. He was very quiet about it, yet he grimaced, revealing all teeth. Throbbing to the beat of his heart, he felt his toe and then pressed it into the carpet struggling not to scream.

He crawled to the door and shut it. He sat against the door for a while; the cold tile floor in front of the patio door soothed the throb. He pressed his toe over its coolness. He then listened to the TV; it had become annoying. He stood up and fell from the pain. Then he hobbled to the entertainment center. He shut it off. When he looked at the ruffled blankets sprawled across the couch, he frowned upon the thought of cleaning that heap. Then he noticed a vacuum next to the couch.

He unraveled the cord, carrying the plug end to an outlet near the television. As soon as he plugged it in, a body fell out of the bundle of blankets and tackled the vacuum cleaner until whoever it was found the on/off switch. They killed the motor and brushed the blanket away from their face.

"Oh, Pete. I didn't see ya there. Go ahead, beat up my vacuum, ya big dumb bully," he sarcastically whined. "I mean, what did it ever do to you, huh? I know it sucks."

Pete was sprawled over the vacuum and turned to look at him. His eye was black and purple, the type of shiner kids would cover with hats, makeup, or sunglasses and then sulk, avoiding their parents so that they wouldn't notice. That was all Danny could see—a blackish welt across his eyeball and forehead. Danny unraveled from his crouched position. He had fallen over when Pete screamed; it startled him.

"Damn, that vacuum cleaner must have kicked your ass."

"What?" Pete asked.

"Pete, why are you in my basement?" Danny asked. "And what's with the shiner, man?"

"What shiner?" he asked.

A glass china hutch rested in a corner with a mirror inside; Pete crawled to the hutch. He pulled himself onto his feet as blankets followed his legs. He played with the purple skin around his right eye. "Holy shit." He spun around and angrily snapped, "I'm gonna kick that black kid's scrawny little ass." He walked toward the basement door, retrieving his trench coat slung over a coffee table.

Danny wandered after him and latched onto him to conquer his boastfulness. He stopped him. "Whoa, nelly. You sort of answered one of my questions. I now know that some kid beat you up, but how did you end up here? What's wrong, Pete?"

"Some black kid jumped me and stole my gun," he brushed against Danny; Danny countered his weight and held him back. Pete shouted as if he had just recalled a memory. "He pistol-whipped me."

"Talk to me, buddy?"

"Just let me go so I can go find this asshole."

"Are you doing drugs?"

"What?"

"It's a perfectly legitimate question, Pete. Are you involved in any illegal activities? I mean, you can't seem to explain how you ended up here. You have a shiner and a missing gun."

"No, Danny. I'm not doing drugs."

"Drug deal gone bad?" Danny suggested.

"What? Just because I had a run-in with some black guy, you automatically pull the racial card. What are you, a racist?"

"No, that's not what I was implying." Danny cringed. "I'm concerned is all; you're crashing in my basement with no recollection of how you even got here. Your words are slurred."

"OK, I will tell you what happened but not now."

Danny was a little disappointed that he couldn't spill the beans right then and there. But he accepted it and stepped aside. He proclaimed, "The other day, my dad went to arrest Mr. Fallway. He no longer lives in that house on the east side."

"Oh really?"

"Yeah, but he left us something, and I think you should see it. Duffy and I have it hidden."

"What is it?"

"It's a car. You just have to see it for yourself. It's our calling, Pete."

Pete hesitated with his hand on the doorknob of the exposed basement door. A brief thought had placed him back inside that hospital bed with a burnt eye, cut on his neck. Watches straddled him breathing cigar smoke in his face. Pete could see the scar deep in his cheek where he had tossed a rock in his face when he was younger. Then he noticed his eyebrow rise over his eye patch. He remembered Watches' demand: *I need you to deliver a car to me.*

"OK, meet me in the school parking lot on Monday after school."

"All right." Danny nodded. Before Pete ran off, he sighed. "Oh, and Pete, be careful because you really have to see this."

"I will." He nodded and stormed out the basement door.

The boys were drawn into a world of violence. Parenting had gone out the window. Danny was still managing good grades, yet he did cut classes a lot. Pete cut entire school days. He never did his homework. Of course, he doesn't even take any home with him anymore. One thing was for sure, the boys needed to find sanctity before they wreck themselves.

On the bus, when Pete was younger, the lunch money scandal was enough to drive any kid insane. Brackstin tried calming Greg; it wasn't enough; he didn't listen and almost got killed over it. Brackstin did recover. His speech was slurred now due to the incisions in his neck; the bus's glass window tickled an artery; he has since graduated from high school. Pete visited Greg once when he was in the hospital. It was then that he apologized to him for what he had done. Greg promised that he would pay him some year. Pete thought that wasn't necessary, but he insisted that it was.

Danny shook his head. He threw the blankets on the couch and tipped the vacuum cleaner upright. He flipped the switch; it roared while filling its little dirtbag. He vacuumed around the couch and coffee table.

Oddly, it shut off; the motor died down. He looked at the outlet; it was still plugged in. He figured that he might have tripped the toggle switch on accident, so he repetitively flipped it between positions. Nothing happened. He unplugged it. He checked the prongs. They seemed fine. He bent them a little to make sure they made contact with the conductors inside the outlet. He plugged it in.

No reaction. He snapped the switch—nothing. He walked to the plug and pulled it. He looked at the television and turned it on. It turned on, so he knew there was still power. He couldn't understand it. Apparently, the motor was fried. It was the only logical explanation.

His assumption was flushed down the deepest darkest drain when the vacuum screamed at him. The little dirtbag whined like a buzz saw. The vacuum was fully functional. Its roaring motor took him on by surprise.

Without hesitation, he flipped into the air. The velocity of the vacuum soared at him. The cord tightened over a leg on the coffee table. The table flipped. The glass shattered and sprinkled into the carpet.

He twirled through the air and rolled onto his back. The vacuum drove itself through the drywall. The lower plastic mold concealing the motor exploded into tiny pieces. The pieces cut the wall; a small electrical fire blackened the outlet. The handle flew forward and buried itself into the wall. The vacuum bag burst open; black dust pelted the wall and bubbled into the ceiling. The dust cloud curled away; lint and trash particles splashed to the floor and across Danny's lap, face, and hair.

He scooted against the part of the wall that was still intact. Strangely, white paint chips fell into his lap. The chips hit the lint and puffed in the air. He glanced upward; more paint chips fell over his face. Some stung his right eye. He flinched and whipped his head toward the ground, picking at it. White dust streaked away from his hair.

A green glass pendant lamp hung from a black steel hook above his head. This monstrosity hanging above him looked like a giant hourglass with a fancy brass top and a brass bottom with a sharp brass nipple pointing at his face. It seemed antique. But it also weighed about fifty pounds. A yellow power cord ran to it.

A brass chain link wrapped around the power cord; the cord was plugged into the same outlet next to his head. He could hear the chain wiggling. More paint chips fell over him. As he listened to the wiggle of the chain, he realized it wasn't swaying back and forth; it was folding up. It was curling around his neck. The lamp had torn away from the ceiling and fell at him. More white dust fell into his hair; he rolled onto his side. The light pierced the floor and compressed into a pile of brass and glass. It pierced the subfloor, remaining upright and protruding from the carpet.

Danny finished unraveling the cord from his neck. A black cat screeched and jumped over his butt as he lay there looking at the mess that almost killed him. The black cat walked toward the basement door. He heard a peal of faint laughter; he rolled over to notice everything in his basement, including the cat. The cat walked through the glass. The laughter died off. But he knew whose laugh it was. He tucked his knees into his chest and stiffened to the wall.

A flame flickered in the corner of his eye; the vacuum bag burnt to ash. Faint laughter returned. Danny watched pieces of the bag drip onto the floor as the fire separated it. Danny eased away from the wall, listening to his joints popping; the laughter stopped. He dragged the entire vacuum contents outside. He tossed it from the patio; it smashed through the wooden well his mom built. Then he noticed the black cat. It seemed to be missing an eyeball. Searching for the cat through the puff of vacuum dust, his jaw dropped; it didn't drop because of the cat, but the mere thought of his mom actually killing him after smashing her yard décor.

He pointed at the cat and said, "You don't scare me, Watches, ya one-eyed pansy-ass freak. You hear me? Better count your blessings 'cuz your days are numbered, pal. The countdown has already started. The Armybrats will come for you, and you will die. Ya friggin sick little pussy. Get out of my yard, you stupid cat," he hollered. He went ballistic, waving his hands in the air and stomping the ground after the cat. He even retracted into the basement and chucked a chunk of drywall in its direction. The cat ran behind the pile of busted yard décor.

A neighbor was watering some flowers. Astounded by Danny's vulgarity, she let the water go wherever as she witnessed an insane little boy prancing about. Danny scowled in the direction the cat had disappeared. He walked toward the basement door. An explosion pounded the ground after a hiss of flames torched the wooden well.

Bricks along the base scattered across the grass. Danny had flown to the block patio, returning to his feet with bloodied knees. Watches was standing in the flames—at the center of a fire pit.

He cackled. "Ha ha, ha." He tilted his head downward and snickered. "We'll see about that Daniel Anglekee."

Danny rolled to his side behind a grill. A jagged bolt of current popped grizzle from the drip pan and charcoal ash across his face as the grill shoved into him; the loudest pop was when the surge of electricity snapped the backside of the grill. The force was powerful enough to shatter the glass patio door before it shoved Danny through it. The grill hung on the door frame sending Danny inside the coffee table as the pile of blankets collapsed over him. All at once, the flames dissipated. Watches was gone. The neighbor lady never saw the devil; however, she witnessed a grill bury the neighbor boy through a doorway of busted glass. She blinked a few times. Her jaw scraped her neck; it was seemingly impossible to close her mouth.

* * *

Danny opened his eyes. Darkness was all around him. *Well, I guess I'm dead,* he thought. A stream of daylight caught his eye within the fabric. He shoved the blankets aside. He rolled onto his shoulder and coughed. His eyes adjusted. He leaned forward, attempted to stand up, using the couch for support. He coughed and glared through the broken doorframes. Dirt mounds in the yard had carved earth away from the devil's playground.

He wandered up the steps into the kitchen. The beer choice was home-brewed from New Glarus, Wisconsin. His father drank it. A Spotted Cow inside was calling for him. The cold bottle chilled his palms and his temple. He tipped it back and swallowed some bubbly.

He sat in a dining room chair. He kept his foot on the table and stared at the china hutch as he enjoyed the beer.

Before he knew it, the garage door motor vibrated his rump. He didn't move. He was in a daze. His brother entered the kitchen and noticed him drinking beer in the dining room. He tried to warn him dad was coming. But his dad beat his warning as he strolled in behind him. Billy stopped waving.

Mike nonchalantly asked, "So Danny, did you do your chores?"

Danny's mind was lost. He hadn't seen his mom opening the basement door. Danny ignored everyone. He continued to enjoy some more alcohol, leaning in the chair, in a trance. A scream bellowed out. Their mother had already gone downstairs; her shriek may have tilted a plate in the china hutch. She called for their father by his full name. Mike ran toward the basement door.

"You OK? What is it, honey?" he asked.

"I think you need to come down here, Michael Anglekee."

Whenever she was in a good mood, she called them by their first name. Whenever the mercury tipped the scale, she used their full names. Sometimes she would intermix names like Danny would become B'Danny and Billy might become D'Billy. Either way, none of this was damn silly. He trotted the steps. Billy jumped into the dining room.

"Now's your chance, man. Dump the bottle, bro."

Danny looked at his brother. "Watches."

Billy's eyebrows rose. The look in his brother's eyes was the same one he had seen before. They once had their heart-to-heart talk; it was the time Billy told him the story of Ricky Palmer—the boy who was murdered in the park years ago. He remembered how Danny sort of melted into a pile of brotherly goo desperately clinging to hope.

Danny nodded. "He was in our house. He was a pussycat."

From the basement, Mike hollered, "Danny, get your little ass down here."

Danny swiped the bottle of beer and headed toward the basement door. Billy snatched the bottle from his hand as he passed by. "I'll take that. Trust me, I just saved you from another ass chewing."

Danny hobbled the steps. Pressure from his toe made him wince. He entered the basement; his parents were standing between the busted lamp, the hole in the wall, and the missing patio door. His father was keeping his hips up with both hands. His mother was walking out the basement door. Danny noticed his mom stepping outside. He ran after her. "No wait, Mom." It was a sporadic outburst to call for her because all he could think about was the smashed well and Watches standing over it.

His father jogged toward him as he wandered outside. His mom was staring at her demolished well. She bought the wood kit from a hobby craft store. The well design was a model from a book; she followed the instructions and built the entire thing from scratch. It was for showcase, a yard decal. Now the wood sat in a pile and was charred. The entire well was burned to the ground, bricks laying everywhere.

His father glared at him. "Is that our vacuum cleaner?"

Danny looked at him and replied, "Yes."

"You mind explaining?"

"The vacuum had a short, so I unplugged it, but it started up again. I dodged it. But it came at me. It busted through the wall and started on fire. That green lamp you bought at the garage sale, Mom, it fell at me. I threw the burning vacuum out here so it wouldn't burn the house down. I'm sorry I smashed your well. Then Watches light beamed my ass like Raiden in Mortal Kombat right through dad's grill and the patio door."

Mike's eyebrows tilted toward his hairline. "Danny, I . . . ahh . . . um . . . I-I'm not buying this story."

"Of course, you wouldn't, dad!"

"You unplugged the vacuum. It was still running. I'm sorry. I don't buy that."

"You live in a shell, dad. Then again, weren't you attacked by gloves with kitchen knives and a freezer cord?"

Mike hesitated. He lowered his head and turned toward him. Danny saw the sky over his shoulders. His face was a silhouette; the sun was directly behind his head. After his father had struck him across the face, Danny noticed grass flash before his eyes as if they were going to explode from their sockets. It was a backhanded brain-cleanse; it left his cheek throbbing; the sting seemed to pinch at his ears.

"I am telling you the truth, Dad. Watches did this, not me. And in no way did I intentionally destroy Mom's well. Look at your grill." Danny clenched a wad of grass in pain while wiggling his jawline.

Mike looked at Clarice and sighed. "You expect us to believe that story?"

Danny screamed, "Yes."

"What did you do, throw my grill off the roof?" Mike muttered.

"No, Dad. I didn't do that."

"I'm tired of your stories about Watches," his dad snapped.

"They're true, and you can't handle the truth."

"Have you been drinking?"

Danny hesitated, "Yes." He told the truth.

His father wound for another smack. Danny stepped back as the swing carried through. Danny guided his arm and forced his father into a clothesline pole. His father flew away from the pole and cupped his nose as Danny swept his legs from underneath him. The bright red blood seeped through his fingers; Clarice screamed and crouched beside her husband.

She scowled at her son. "Oh my goodness, what did you do, B'Danny? What were you thinking?"

Danny stepped away from them and stared at his hands. Billy ran out the basement door and stopped dead in his tracks. He noticed his father on his back and glanced at his brother. Danny was without expression. Billy asked, "What did you do?"

Danny mumbled and cried, "H-he wouldn't believe me. He wouldn't listen."

"So you beat him up?" Billy asked.

Danny stared at his brother dumbfounded. He shook his head. His father sat up. Danny charged out the backyard gate. He ran in the middle of the road. He could hear his mother screaming his name. Mike grasped her arm and reeled her close. A hand remained cupped over his nose. Blood gushed from his nostrils.

"Let him go, Clarice."

"But he's scared."

"If you believe that, there's something wrong with you, honey."

Billy asked, "Dad, you all right? Danny's a killer, ya know?"

Mike turned to look at his son. "I want to know something, son."

Billy swallowed, "Yeah, dad."

Mike's facial pigmentation held redder blemishes. He dropped his hand from his nose with blood all over his cheeks; he asked, "Are you kids into drugs? And are you drinking my beer?"

Billy glanced at Danny's Spotted Cow. He raised his hands and dropped the bottle. "No, dad." The bottle hammered the ground with a thud. The darkened malt of New Glarus brew foamed around its neck. "This was Danny's. I mean . . ."

"What did this Fallway character teach you kids? I'm starting to think there's more behind this Kids Can Be Investigators Too, BS."

Billy nodded. "Yes, sir. We've been taught a lot."

Chapter Fifteen

Restaurant Masquerade

Danny was grounded. Earlier on, Duffy and he decided to go on a double date with a couple of high school sweethearts. Of course, Danny had to sneak out of the house. He had become his own fugitive for a night out. He bunched all kinds of stuff under his blankets; the garage roof led him from his bedroom window closer to the deck; he released his grip from the trellis, dropping to the railing.

The lucky ladies of the evening were two gorgeous classmates. Clarissa was a dark-haired, levelheaded girl. Victoria was blonde and evasive with smiles that were seemingly too good to be true. Her personality was very chipper. These were the same two girls Danny, Duffy, and Pete rescued from the parking lot during a football game a few years ago; it was nearly a date rape. Unfortunately, the girls still dated those jockey jerks. *Why they were special in their eyes was beyond reason.*

Danny liked Clarissa all through high school; she was always in a sick and twisted relationship with Sam. Sam's best friend was another douchebag, Shawn. He dated the smiley blonde. Perhaps that's why Duffy felt she was so special since she always presented herself in happy-go-lucky spirits. This double date was against all odds. Sam and Shawn despised the Armybrats throughout middle school and high school. They bullied their girls and others. Maybe it was a popularity contest. Who knows? So for them to court the girls, this night was a bittersweet juvenile affair.

The boys tried to play it smart by asking them to meet in the high school forest in front of Duffy's house. Both girls were standing there whispering amongst themselves. A slight breeze forced the trees to sway back and forth before the dark sky. The moon was hidden, so the night was exceptionally dark; this brought the conception of new goosebumps.

The girls wore dressy outfits. Clarissa had a red dress on with white stockings and sleeves. Around her tight stomach was a white sash. The dress itself was short enough to show more than her upper thighs. Vicki wore a black dress with a mesh white top, and it almost appeared metallic when clouds let loose from the moon. She wore a white ribbon in her hair and white boots. They stood there in the middle of the dark forest covering their breasts as the breeze climbed their legs. The cool air tickled tender spots; they hugged to keep warm.

"Where are they?" Vicki asked.

"I don't like this," Clarissa stated. "I feel wrong."

"Why? Because of our boyfriends?" Vicki snarled. "Forget 'em. I am so pissed at Shawn right now, it's not even funny."

"Well, Sam isn't exactly bursting my bubble lately either."

"Oh, they hate Danny and Duffy though," Vicki testified. "And they acted so immature at the gym on Friday."

"Oh, I know. Could you imagine them knowing about tonight? Wow, I think their whole world would come crashing down."

"Good, and I hope it burns to the ground."

"Why did they ask us to wear something white?" she asked.

Vicki laughed. "I have no idea."

"Well, I couldn't find anything white."

"Neither could I. They said as long as there was some white in our outfits," she added.

"Umm, OK. Yeah, I don't get it."

"There has to be a reason." She crazily smiled.

"Hey, do you hear music?"

She hesitated. "Yeah."

A faint thumping was heard as a song was quietly played in the distance. It was a quiet electrical guitar rhythm. It was the song "Today" by the Smashing Pumpkins. The opening strum of the guitar was peaceful and quiet. But as soon as the drumbeat kicked in, the forest came alive.

Lights turned on. It was the Bratmobile. The lights were deep purple along the undercarriage and the headlamps. The car sat on the trail before them. The lights emulated the whole scene. The music was coordinated with their light show. The word *Armybrats* was lit along the doors. The black lighting cast a marvelous glow through the forest.

Both girls shined bright. The white portions of their dresses sparkled like whitecaps on a moonlit ocean. Clarissa was nothing but arms, legs, and stomach. The white parts illuminated with a beautiful fluorescent glow. Vicki was speckled where the details of her dress were white mesh. Her boots added a little flavor to her body. The ribbon in her hair was eye-straining. The boys sat inside the car staring at them through the windshield.

Rocket launchers angled away from the fenders. When Billy Corgan sang how great today was, the thrusters blasted with thunderous sparks. The tubes weren't empty; they were jam-packed with white confetti and packaging peanuts. The boosters shot them out; emeralds showered the girls. The glittering garb and glowing strands of paper rained around them like a sparkling rainstorm in the moonlight. The black lighting and music from the car set the mood. Already, the girls were astonished in their own glow.

A fantastic flash took them by surprise as a built-in camera captured the moment. The music blared through a pair of loudspeakers transferred by a megaphone inside. The melody seemed too perfect to the girls as they stared into the night sky of shimmering lights twinkling around them. Intrinsically, the glow of energy started the date with a memory worth cherishing.

Danny spoke into the megaphone, "Tonight is your night, ladies."

Duffy swiped the megaphone from him and added, "So we thought we would make it rain jewels from the heavens. You deserve it."

The picture taken of them under the black lighting was transmitted to the windshield. The girls could see themselves in the glass. It was a picture of white streaks bombarding them with an array of flashy sparkles. The glow of their cheeks and smiles represented true thrills. The picture disappeared and a picture of Danny reappeared on the window. Then he left the scene and was replaced by a picture of Duffy.

Duffy asked, "Will you girls accept this date with these two fine gentlemen?"

They smiled and glanced at each other. Their jaws dropped as they faced each other. They nodded at Danny and Duffy inside the car. The windshield was used as a digital display. Fireworks shot across the windshield after they answered them. Gray smoke burst from the undercarriage. When the smoke cleared, the boys were standing in front of the car in tuxedos.

They approached the girls each holding onto single white roses. The rose petals stained the air with bright streaks. The car's black lighting synchronized. It flashed in sections as more charges went off and more confetti shot into the air from separate boosters.

Danny glanced at the car. "Did you change out the flame throwers?"

"No, I thought you did."

Danny tackled everyone. They fell to the ground. The girls gave short wails. Two balls of flames burst from two tubes inside the grill. The confetti falling to the ground caught on fire and small fires burned out as they floated to the ground, pelting the forest floor in ashes. Danny looked at the car. Smoke poured from the tubes sticking out of the grill. He panted, "Whoa."

Duffy replied, "That wasn't mood lighting."

Danny nodded. "No, Duff. That was a sloppy mess."

"Overlooked that one, I guess."

Later, they drove around the country roads, laughing, singing, and listening to music. At one point, Duffy hit a switch labeled: Night Vision. The headlights automatically shut off when the night vision came on. All the windows were night vision. The ground turned bright green with splashes of gray where the trees were. The sky was still black, but everything else they could see. They could see everything as different shades—no color.

When the boys stopped the car along the road, they climbed out to look at the car from the outside. It was so dark they couldn't even see the car on the road. "Armybrats" was lit up in blue along the doors—almost a dark purple. They ended up near a restaurant in the Town of Texas.

An empty pole towered in the sky. At the base of the pole, a dingy billboard lay between the pole and the road. It was broken and cracked. It promoted the restaurant The Hills Bar and Saloon. The restaurant was set in the trees on the outskirts of Wausau. A faded strip of paint wrapped the front of the billboard. What they couldn't see as the car breezed past, debris blew off the billboard and revealed: Permanently Closed. Below the banner, it read Granite View.

Danny drove a narrow trail deep in the woods. About a mile or so, a two-story family restaurant/bar nestled within a group of trees. A huge wooden patio wrapped around the entire front side of the building. It was gorgeous. A staircase loomed on the left side of the building. Luckily, very few patrons were at the place. The parking lot remained mostly empty, with the exception of a dumpster along a fence and a couple of cars parked out back. They shut off the night vision and parked in a stall in front of the main entrance. The boys stepped out and opened the doors for the girls. They stepped out with smiles as the boys treated them cordially. They jogged up the porch hand-in-hand.

Awkwardly, the building was where this story had begun. In the middle of a lightning storm, a devil served the hand of a mugger. A bloodied body was left in the wet alleyway where the mugger was stabbed through the head. This was the same place Mike and his boss, Tony, called in the devil's wife to collect her drunken husband. Back in the seventies, this place may have been hopping. Within the walls were hidden secrets the boys didn't know about. The idea to eat here was given to Duffy from a brochure left in the hospital on his bed tray. Those were the same brochures Danny had noticed. They advertised great food at this place.

When they entered the front door, the setting seemed cozy. A woman with straggly black hair, dressed in a black suit, walked them to a table. There were glasses set upside down on the tables. There were napkins folded into neat triangles and tucked along the plates with shiny silverware. The restaurant seemed ritzy. The waiters and waitresses were even dressed up, even though the place reeked of must. Certain things were caked in dust. After all, it was a log cabin in the middle of the woods with a fireplace roaring. According to the brochure, it has been in business for years.

Inside, it was dimly lit. There were booths along the walls. Tables lined evenly at the center. They chose a booth in the nonsmoking section as a waitress handed out menus, explaining the soup of the evening, and walked away allowing them time to decide on menu options. Dishes rattled in the kitchen as the doors swung open and another waitress immediately came out to take their order. None of them knew what they wanted, so they asked for more time. Oddly, the service was abrupt; she took their drink orders and asked if they wanted appetizers. The girls each ordered Crystal Pepsis, the boys ordered regular. They settled with some sort of fried onion snack.

Modestly, the waitress smiled and excused herself to allow more time for their dinner decisions. There were lights hanging from the ceiling, but they were on their dimmest setting. Candles burned on every table. The candlelight lit the white placemats on the maroon tablecloths. Arrays of shadows danced near napkin dispensers, sugar, and saltshakers. Small puffs of smoke rose directly out the top.

"I'm not really that hungry." Vicki smiled.

"Screw you!" Clarissa closed her menu. "Yes, she is. She didn't eat lunch."

Duffy turned to Vicki and suggested, "In that case, am I going to have to order for you?"

"No," she snapped.

"Uh-huh," Duffy sarcastically accepted.

"OK, I pretty much know what I want." Danny closed his menu and added, "Everything."

When the waitress returned, she knew they were ready; everyone had their menu closed. Duffy ordered a New York strip. Danny ordered the beer-battered cod fillet (lightly buttered). Clarissa ordered a turkey club sandwich. Vicki ordered a chicken Caesar salad. Before the waitress could take the menus from everyone, Duffy stopped her.

"Yeah, one more thing, please." He smiled. "We would like to add The Sampler appetizer with a side order of your Grizzly Taters." Vicki glared at him. He knew she ordered the smallest entrée; he really wanted to stuff that little tummy with more than salad.

Outside, a box truck pulled into the parking lot. Beams of light shone across the restaurant as it entered the lot. There were two people inside. The driver lit a cigar and snickered. "We're here." He parked alongside a dumpster. "Welcome to my old stomping grounds."

He tipped his top hat and revealed his scarred face; it was Watches. In the passenger seat, his buddy Bonzo glanced into the cargo bay. Balled in a corner were two boys with ski masks over their heads. Watches tipped the rearview mirror downward and blew smoke into it. Smoke dissipated toward the plastic mold around the mirror; the vision of the ugly beast reappeared in its reflection.

"OK, this is it, boys. Your women are here. But they have no idea you guys are coming. That's why I asked you two to look sharp. The suits really do look nice, fellas." Watches looked at Bonzo and nodded. He smirked and brought the cigar to his lips.

He climbed out and walked around to the cargo door. Bonzo opened it from the inside. The hinge gave a squawk. The boys climbed out. Bonzo ripped their ski masks off. Sam spit on the ground. Shawn tugged at his necktie.

"This is where they are?" Sam asked.

Bonzo replied, "Yup."

Sam said, "I've never even heard of this place."

Shawn walked toward the restaurant and proclaimed, "Who cares? Let's get some pussy, Sam."

Watches stopped him dead short from hopping the curb to run up the steps. He snarled, "If you go inside with that attitude, you lose. Both of you gather around."

Shawn exclaimed, "That is my attitude. How do you expect me to act?"

"Smooth, ya nitwit." Watches thumped him on the head. "You both must remain calm. Pretend as if you had no idea they were here. Sam, has Clarissa ever met either of your uncles?"

"No. Why?"

"OK, Bonzo will be your uncle tonight—on your dad's side of the family. Uncle Bernard! He will guide you in as your uncle treating you guys out to dinner." Watches slapped his shoulder. "Uncle Bernard here owns some land outside of Wausau, and he invited you two to his house for the weekend. How does that sound?"

"Damn good," Sam smiled.

"Yeah, I suppose that does sound . . . pretty gay," Shawn disagreed sarcastically.

"What? You don't like that idea? Too bad. Suck it up, buttercup."

"I've never heard of this restaurant before. I've been up here several times with my father. We've gone hunting in these parts, but I have never seen this place. You would have thought that I would have at least heard of this place."

"You wouldn't have." Watches stepped toward the patio and puffed away at his cigar. He withdrew it from his lips and stated, "It doesn't exist."

In a shallow puddle, Watches saw a reflection of his younger self. His flashback brought him back to when this bar was lit up. The parking lot held New Yorkers, Caprices, an AMC Pacer, a Ford Mustang II, and a Porsche 914. Lightning lit the sky. A car pulled in behind him. He spun around to see Rosalyn slam the door and scurry toward the front entrance. She disappeared inside. Watches crossed the parking lot toward the alleyway. He caught a glimpse of his fancywork from the past of the man he stuffed in a trashcan below the stairway.

Watches was remembering this past as if he were there; although, in the same breath, he seemed to have traveled through time. He seemed to have inserted his future self in that very moment the mugger attacked him in the alleyway. Breaking his concentration, a side door opened on the bar. Rosalyn stepped out and glanced into the parking lot; the door shut behind her. She turned and looked at the stairway. For a moment, Watches felt she could see his future self. He watched her take a breath. She headed up the dark stairway; Watches reached through the steps and clasped onto her ankle. She immediately fell forward but caught herself on the railing. She had no idea why she tripped.

Watches snapped out of his flashback when Shawn piped up.

"Huh." Shawn sighed. "It's right there. What do you mean it doesn't exist?"

Watches rolled his eyes at him and smirked. "Here, you might need this." Watches handed Sam a pistol. Sam's eyes grew a size. His eyebrows rose as he nodded at the wicked man and tucked the gun away.

Sam and Shawn followed Bonzo toward the front door. Watches smirked; evil festered. He puffed away at his brown fatty and walked to the rear of the restaurant. He passed the windows below the dining area directly underneath Danny and Duffy. Inside, they were still waiting for the appetizers. Danny excused himself to use the restroom. Then Duffy followed his lead. The girls remained seated in the booth. They discussed the black lighting effects from earlier. The evening was full of enjoyment; they appreciated everything thus far.

The bell rang as the front door swung open and brushed into it. Both girls glanced at the front section of the restaurant but noticed no one. A short wall divided them from the entrance. Sam and Shawn followed Bonzo through the kitchen. There were tons of people chilling on counters. A few were smoking cigarettes and leaning against empty shelving units. Others were rattling pots and drink glasses every few seconds. Strangely, the stoves were gutted. No one was cooking. Bonzo smirked at a few of them; they returned glances. They exited the kitchen at the rear entrance. They snuck past an empty salad bar and walked toward the non-smoking section, opposite the girls.

Danny entered the bathroom and walked into the furthest stall. There were three stalls. The middle stall was occupied. Duffy walked in and immediately washed his hands. Rust-colored water spurted from the faucet, as the pipes seemed to flush themselves from rarely being used. He gave it an odd glance and then watched the stall door shut as Danny propped the toilet lid; a spider ran out of the lip of the toilet bowl. Danny jolted away. Smoke rose from the second stall. The man inside was smoking; the tone of his cough seemed raspy.

Duffy explained, "Could you imagine what would happen if Sam and Shawn found out?"

The man in the middle stall chuckled.

Duffy was washing his face when he noticed the smoke. He noticed the smell. It wasn't cigarette smoke. It was cigar smoke. "I'm not so sure what to do after this. Perhaps a movie or drive around."

Danny was finishing when a newspaper slid under the stall and folded against his foot. He saw someone's foot easing it into his. He glanced at it. The title of the article read "Indian Boy Murdered, Grandfather Denies Accusations." Danny bent over and flushed the toilet. He swiped the ad from the floor. He eased the stall door open, reading through the article. As he walked out, he stopped and fell between the hand dryers mounted to the wall.

Duffy dried his face with paper towels and spun around to see him in a daze. He tapped his shoulder. "What's wrong, man?"

"Wesley Fifer."

"What about him?"

Danny held the article next to the towel dispenser. "He's dead."

Duffy swiped the ad from his hands. "What?" he asked and read through it.

A squeak echoed within the tile walls; the middle stall opened. A man stepped out. He cocked his head to his left and avoided eye contact. His ponytail swung over his right shoulder and rolled into the arch of his back. He wore a black trench coat, smoking a cigar. He tucked a Wisconsin State Journal under his arm and turned the corner, exiting the bathroom. "Last supper, boyssss," he chanted as he exited the bathroom. Cigar smoke trailed his flowing trench coat.

Duffy dropped the article. It floated like a feather to the tile floor. The bathroom door sprung shut. Danny snapped toward him. Danny asked, "Did he just say . . . ?"

Duffy gritted, "I think we need to leave this place."

They jumped into the hallway. They stared into the dining room. A door shut behind them; they both spun around. A familiar kid strutted through the hall and swiftly approached them. Danny and Duffy glanced at each other. The boy wore a gray trench coat. It was Jerome Dawson. A female waitress exited the girl's restroom. She noticed the boys, then Jerome, and whipped hair spikes at him. Jerome avoided the sharp daggers. He placed a hand on each side of her head and spun her neck; he casually lowered her body before them. He pressed into the boys' shoulders and pinned them to the wall.

"OK, don't ask me any questions." He hesitated, "You are inside a trap."

"I knew it! Fine dining, it said! Eat at deathly low prices! Ribs you'll die for!" Duffy exclaimed. "Who are you, again?"

Jerome abruptly snapped, "I said, don't ask questions."

They each nodded.

"Watches is here. The kitchen is full of his men. This restaurant was condemned several years ago. We don't have much time. So I can't explain a whole helluva lot. But Watches also brought some confusion for you two on top of more confusion."

Danny asked, "Confusion?"

Jerome smiled. "No, no, you need to getch ya ladies outta here. Tell ya what, allow me. You two wait here. Better yet, go out that door and wait outside."

"What if they catch you?"

"They have no idea who I am. Here, hold dis." Jerome removed his trench coat and handed it to Duffy. He noticed blood on the sleeve. Underneath his coat, he wore cook whites. He removed the vest from the dead lady on the floor. The newspaper slid away from his arm; his hand clutched onto a pistol. He opened the revolver, spun it, and then closed it. He slid it inside the elastic at his waist. "I already had a run-in with one of Watches' cooks. He's out back, suckin' on a spigot. I stole his uniform. In dat kitchen, no cooks in there, man . . . just a bunch of his mercenaries like her. They're fixin' to kill ya."

Danny pushed Duffy along as they moved toward the restroom. Jerome nonchalantly paced through the hallway. He walked straight toward the girls' booth. Duffy stopped Danny. He suggested, "No, no, wait. Do you trust him?"

Danny glanced into the empty dining room where Jerome disappeared. "Well, if he's telling the truth, then we're in the lion's den, dude."

They moved toward the end of the hall. Sam and Shawn were sitting a couple booths away from the girls. They could see them in the candlelight. The confusion Jerome mentioned was the girls' boyfriends. Jerome smiled at Sam and Shawn; he disregarded Bonzo. "I'll be right with you." They nodded as he stopped at the girls' table and tilted his head at them. "Good evening, ladies."

They smiled at him.

147

Jerome whispered, "Hello, ladies. Your dates asked me to have you join them at the bonfire. Duffy asked me to kindly ask you two to join them. They are out that side door." When the two girls gave each other odd stares, Jerome continued, almost desperately, "Ladies, please hurry. They're waiting for ya." He pointed at the hall.

Bonzo lifted a walkie-talkie; it buzzed from the click of his thumb. A cigarette hung from his lips as he stated, "Boss, the waiter's here."

Watches indulged in a puff of nicotine, carrying the walkie-talkie over the steering wheel. He pushed in the button and asked, "What waiter?"

Bonzo whispered, "Some black waiter."

Watches dipped his head and growled, "We don't have a black waiter, Sherlock."

"I see. I'll give him my order then."

"Oh, waiter!" Bonzo hollered.

Watches carried the walkie-talkie to his face. "Everyone go, now."

Jerome closed his eyes and whispered, "Shit." He bobbed his head forward in disbelief that he had been caught. "I'll be right with you, sir." He twitched his head to influence the girls to leave. They got the hint and exited the booth. They moved past him as he turned to face Bonzo. Sam and Shawn watched Bonzo struggling in the tight booth.

He jumped out holding a gun on Jerome. The girls breezed past him toward the main entrance. Jerome watched them head the wrong way. Duffy crouched low in the hallway; he whistled to gain their attention. They noticed him as he waved them over. They spun around and bumped into each other, whimpering.

Sam slapped Shawn's shoulder. "It's the girls."

The girls glanced at their boyfriends stepping out of a booth.

Shawn asked, "What?"

"They're leaving. Come on," he shouted as he noticed them run out of sight.

Duffy ran through the hall with the girls. Sam and Shawn ran after them. "Hey," Sam hollered. "Where do you think you're going, Duff?"

Duffy ignored him; they ran out the door at the end of the hall. Sam shot at them as he drew the pistol Watches had given him and squeezed the trigger a few times. Cooks, waiters, and waitresses poured out of the kitchen. Jerome was surrounded. He looked at them. "Damn."

Sam and Shawn bolted through the hall. Out from behind a water fountain, Danny slithered upward and pinched Sam's arm. As he shoved him backward and spun him around, he used his body to knock Shawn over. He cracked his arm through the wall. With the gun in that hand, he wedged it toward the wall so he couldn't use it. He glanced at Shawn who dropped his jaw toward the dead lady on the floor.

"Hi," Danny said.

Before they could respond with any violence, Danny elbowed him in the neck and turned Sam toward the wall. He thrust his arm forward and used his free hand to guide his face into the wall. Blood splattered across the rustic boards as he broke his nose and passed out. Danny spun around as Shawn knelt in front of the water fountain. He kneed him in the side of his head while he held onto his throat. From the force into the side of the water fountain, he rendered him unconscious. The casing around the bubbler jumped away from the wall with a wrinkle in the aluminum.

Danny straightened himself out and glanced into the dining room. It was full of Watches' men. He squinted and glared at the group of people surrounding Jerome. Each wielded automatic weapons. Jerome was trapped. Even though Danny had absolutely zero knowledge of who he was, he decided to vacate the hallway. He ran out the door and jumped the steps. Immediately, he noticed the Dodge parked in front of the exit. He ran around the car and opened the driver's door. Duffy was in the driver's seat. The girls were in the back.

Danny exclaimed, "We have to get that kid out of there!"

"Are you nuts?" Duffy asked.

"It's the right thing to do, Duff."

Danny made him slide across the console to the other side. A bullet skimmed the window; he jolted his head and noticed Watches. Inside a box truck parked near the dumpsters, Watches hung out the opened door with a pistol hanging over the mirror—taking potshots at him.

"What?" Duffy asked, "I am not going back in there, and oh my God, Watches is shooting at the car." He stared out the rear window. The girls dropped to the floor as sparks skipped along the trunk and trickled across the window.

"Yes, you are. All of us are going back inside."

"Are you crazy?" Duffy asked.

"A little," Danny smiled.

The tires spun on the pavement. Gray smoke shot from underneath the shaved rubber. The girls screamed as hot lead crumbled across the rear window. He dropped the shifter into reverse and backed up several feet. The brakes clamped the wheels; the car skidded sideways until its front end faced the parking entrance. Watches continued firing upon them. None of his rounds penetrated the car or the glass.

Watches tossed his pistol into the truck and walked into the center of the parking lot. Duffy watched him standing in the dull light. He couldn't see his face or his eyeball. Danny searched the console. His mind was focused on saving the kid inside the restaurant. Duffy was tapping his shoulder. The girls were staring at this creepy man wearing what appeared to be a brown robe; it looked like a cloak straight from the cowboy days. Watches lifted his head. A single red eyeball sat inside the dark shadow of his face.

Duffy sighed. "Ahhh, Danny."

"Not now. I'm looking for options."

Watches raised both hands. The brown cloak hung from his wrists. In the shadows of the fabric, a significant glow accumulated the darkness. Duffy tugged at Danny's shoulder. "Danny, look . . ."

Danny glanced at two streams of light arch away from Watches' hands. The entire car lit up. The girls shrieked. "Is he electrocuting the car?"

Duffy glanced at the Intruder Buzzer and pressed it. An amazing counterattack of electricity arched away from the Bratmobile. The demon's one eye was no longer red as an electrical force built up around the car. The two streams of white light collided. A brilliant glow shone through the windshield. The girls braced each other in the backseat. The parking lot appeared like a blue pond. Two tractor beams swelled in the center.

Watches repositioned his legs after the force dragged gravel beneath his soles. The heels of his boots dug deep. Danny cocked his head toward Duffy. A brilliant flash exploded at the swell of light. The pavement tore through the center; a lamp post buckled. It fell into the crook of a tree. Watches' body flipped past the box truck, bent the side mirror, and clobbered a dumpster, leaving a dent in its green face. The Bratmobile slid backward into the front decking. Wood peeled away from the frame.

Danny commanded, "Duffy, The Muffin Grenades."

Duffy searched the panels for the appropriate button. "Oh boy." He found it and crammed his forefinger over a raised lit square tile. The girls leaned over the seat and watched two canisters launch from tubes beneath the rear end of the Dodge. The grenades arched onto the patio and exploded. The entire porch waved away from the foundation; the restaurant walls folded inward. An awning collapsed. Watches removed his top hat and stared at the destruction as he sat on the ground. His illuminated body was smoking.

"Damn you, Armybrats," Watches muttered. "That's supposed to be my car."

Danny backed into the restaurant smashing through the salad bar. A surge of electrical energy transferred into the metal salad bins; a man fried over the top of the empty trays. The empty salad bar slid off its podium and crushed two of Watches' men against another wall as they fired upon the car. Blood patterns spotted the wall. Danny and Duffy watched Jerome inside a ring of Watches' men. Bonzo turned around and ran through the dining room.

Danny reached across the console and hit a few buttons. He armed the Uzi at the front of the car. The monitor turned on; he shot at Bonzo. Booths tore open as bullets ripped them apart. Tables flipped. Duffy operated a joystick and shot a canister out another tube mounted inside the front grill. The canister nailed one of Watches' men in the chest. It tossed him into a booth, crushed his chest cavity, and popped smoke. He blinded everyone from Jerome.

Smoke fluffed over tables as Duffy lobbed more smoke canisters at other people. Jerome unleashed his own little renegade of fury on four men. Duffy managed to take out the fifth guy with another smoke canister, decreasing Jerome's opponents. Although Jerome seemed to manage just fine. Danny watched as he leaped into the air and took out two guys with a roundhouse kick. He spun around with a combined thrust. He punched one guy in the face and brought his other arm back; his elbow crammed into the man's genitalia. The man dropped to his knees caressing his danglers.

Jerome clamped onto his head. As he spun around, cracking the man's neck, he twirled over his back and kicked another man. The man flew backward and landed on a table. The candle flipped into the air and smashed over the floorboards. Oil from the bottle fanned out across the floor and began burning.

Another man stood up after being kicked. Jerome punched him in the face and gut at the same time. He grasped a hold of his tie and whipped him around, so he bumped into another guy. Watches' men on the other side of the car were working their way around the front. Danny noticed them. They were shooting at the car. One round ricocheted and shot his buddy next to him. He oddly stared at his weapon.

He turned to Duffy. They both had a new name for the plan of attack on them. They both rattled the phrase "Mood Lighting" at the same time.

Duffy hit a few buttons. Black lights snapped on. "Look at those cook whites glowing."

The headlights, taillights, and their club's name transitioned to black lighting. *Armybrats* reflected in purplish letters across the wooden floors and walls. Unbearably blinding, cook whites became a fancy bright, outlining the enemy for Jerome to wallop.

Danny glanced at Jerome. He could see Jerome prancing through the black lights. Jerome ditched his cook whites to evade his glowing enemies. His chest glistened from sweat. That and his teeth shone from grinning ear to ear in a combative pose. Danny was hoping he would hurry up; but at the same time, he was admiring his fancy footwork. Jerome clung onto one of the men's neckties. He spun it around another man and choked him as he repetitively kneed the one guy.

Duffy rotated a heavy gun that retracted from the roof of the Charger and riddled Watches' box truck with holes like anti-aircraft shells spotting the skies during War World II. Every fourth round traced through the truck. Watches rolled sideways, scurrying behind the dumpster screaming, "Armybrats!" With limited space, his evasive maneuvers barely escaped the hot lead. After he dropped behind the dumpster, he raised his holy trench coat. His one eye peeked through a section of missing material. He shook his head in disappointment.

Jerome was still holding onto the tie as he danced around the other guy on the floor and choked him with the other man's tie. He let go of the tie; they both were gasping for air. He stood over their lower backs and lifted on the tie between their necks. He brought each of them swiftly backward, folding them over his boots, and cracked their spines. When he released them, they rolled onto the floor, lifeless.

Danny watched Jerome raise one of their weapons over one knee, making sure the coast was clear. He glanced at him. Danny motioned for him to get moving. While darting toward the car, he dropped the pistol as his body flew into a table. Bonzo jumped out of nowhere and caught him off guard, punching him in the face. Danny perked up and noticed Bonzo retrieve his weapon and aimed it at him.

Bonzo muttered, "You're done, kid!"

Bonzo disappeared through the salad bar after Danny launched a smoke grenade into his head. Jerome sat up and shook himself off. Vicki threw open the backdoor; he dove inside. Watches' men were crouched in booths throughout the restaurant.

Two whirls of fiery flames shot out the tailpipes. Tables lit on fire; two men chasing Jerome became droopy marshmallows. The restaurant floor was now burning as well as booths. Flames shot across the walls and burned the curtains draped over the windows. The wooden base of the empty salad bar caught on fire and two bloody-faced men were still hung over the backside of it, crushed to death.

The Uzi barrel glowed red as it worked double time. Duffy shot men in booths as they drove through the dining room, crushing chairs. He continued spraying bullets through the restaurant. The car drove through the kitchen tossing shelving, wood, and appliances out another wall. They drove across a steep deck and busted through the railings.

Before they plummeted thirty feet, a series of lights flashed on the dashboard with beeping clangors. Duffy noticed them as Danny tensed his grip on the steering wheel, "What's happening, Duffster?"

"How the hell do I know? You're the one driving us off a deck."

Jerome and the girls screamed as they neared the ground. A three-second beep was followed by five flashing buttons. One button remained lit. It read Hover. The wheels folded upward and moved outward. They slid back into the wheel wells and jet thrusters flared downward. The car sensed no hard surface. It never landed. Thrusters burned for a second as the car swooped across the hillside. After it dropped a second time, they sprayed a fantastic blue flame like Bunsen burners in the science room. The car floated across the grass. It had become a sky car.

"Holy crap! This car can fly too!" Duffy shouted. "Oh, I'm definitely flying next."

Danny flew past a stairwell alongside the restaurant and into the parking lot. The thrusters torched one of Watches' female mercenaries who kept firing at them in rapid succession. The thrusters pancaked her to the ground. The woman's face blackened, singed hair and her cook whites burned, melting her in place.

Danny braked to avoid a tree. Nothing happened. He screamed and leaned back, tugging at the steering column. They hovered for a second realizing how close they had come to crashing in midflight. Danny looked at the shifter and then the steering wheel. He pulled backward on the steering column; the car whipped backward. The change in force tossed the female mercenary underneath a pickup truck. She folded around the rear tire. Her burning whites sent flames over the fuel tank. The bed folded away from the frame. The windows popped outward. Balls of fire rolled across the lot. Watches stumbled from behind the dumpster; the explosion sent him into orbit. Yet again, he nailed the side of the dumpster.

Duffy asked, "What are you doing?"

"Sending a message to Watches."

The awning over the porch burned as flames ripped through shingles and lit more mercenaries on fire from the thrusters. Danny slammed the steering column forward; they flew off.

Jerome spun around in the backseat. He noticed Watches' men prancing about like little dancing lanterns. He pulled out a remote detonator and clicked the lever forward. An enormous flash lit the entire parking lot. Duffy operated another Uzi at the rear of the Dodge. He fired upon Watches' box truck and the dumpsters. The truck sank over the flattened wheels. Duffy released the firing call and duct as the restaurant exploded. Their faces lit up. The force shook the Armybrats' car across the night sky.

Watches sat behind the dumpster with Bonzo. Bonzo held onto a reddish welt spanning from his jawline above his left ear, "Boss, my head really hurts." Sam and Shawn peeked around the corner.

Danny looked in his mirrors and watched the restaurant burning behind them, "Holy shit."

Jerome smiled. "I rigged this entire lot. See that dumpster?"

Duffy sighed. "Yeah."

Jerome smiled. "Watch this."

Watches, Bonzo, and the two girls' boyfriends sat against the dumpster listening to beeping noises. Watches waved his hand to shut them up. He crouched below the dumpster to discover C-4 plastics stuck underneath with a red light shining on a small device, protruding from the putty. "Ohhh," Watches gritted his teeth.

Bonzo's eyes widened. He agreed, "Ohhh."

They unleashed themselves from the dumpster and dove behind a berm; Sam and Shawn toppled down the hill after them. The red light switched to green. The dumpster flipped through the air as an explosion, powerful enough to reroute a river, tore up the lot. Pieces of the dumpster shifted the box truck; the wreckage was still burning. The vehicle sliced in half. Watches and Bonzo both noticed the cargo door drop at them. They crawled away as it pierced the hillside behind them. They screamed, and the steel corner edges scooped up grass and weeds. A spare tire drove Bonzo's body into the woods like a stone skipping across water. The dumpster slammed into the ground, caging Watches.

Watches patted around in the dark and kicked at the sidewall. "Get me out of here," he hollered. Bonzo's face was mushed in a mudhole. Tread marks outlined his cheeks and forehead. Firelight from the restaurant burning to the ground shined across his face.

"Awesome," Duffy erupted.

Vicki was crying, and Clarissa held onto her. Clarissa said, "I was so looking forward to my turkey club." A stutter in her voice had shown a slight presence of fear. She was aggressive yet scared at the same time.

Danny focused on the trees as he flew toward highway 12 and headed home. He almost missed his turn as he sideswiped a billboard. He was trying to get used to the fact he wasn't on four tires. Duffy cocked his head toward him.

"Did you just signal?"

Danny glanced at him, "Well, yeah. I took that turn."

"Good choice. Don't wanna confuse birds."

Danny stared at him.

Jerome's extended a hand in front of Clarissa's face and held another detonator. "Would you care to do the honors?"

"Depends?" Clarissa questioned.

"Push this little red button for me," he smirked and pointed at the red button.

She pushed it. Rolling flames scattered across the entrance, digging through the dirt, carving new trenches. She screamed and ducked forward, holding tighter onto Vicki. Duffy stared out the passenger window at the flames chewing up ten different fat trees. The trees fell over and barricaded the entrance to the burning restaurant. Flames shot across the road and burned up the billboard Danny had bumped.

Duffy turned his head toward Jerome. He stuttered, "You are who?"

Jerome shook his hand. "Jerome—that's who I am."

Danny nodded at him in the rearview mirror. "We're indebted to you, Jerome."

"No, you're not." His boyish charm produced squinty eyes and a bright smile.

Clarissa's eyes widened as the boys conversed.

"Explain yourself."

"There's plenty of time for that. Trust me. Let's just keep," his eyebrows arched with a bit of confusion, "flying."

Clarissa gasped, "Danny."

Danny looked away from the steering wheel and stared at the console. Meanwhile, both girls were shrieking in the backseat. A semitrailer was storming at them. A smokestack chewed through the night's darkness; a horn blared, catching them off guard. Danny sharply turned the steering column, avoiding the smokestack by inches. The big old trailer nearly yanked them out of the sky; they drove across the top of the trailer. The thruster rippled it like melted butter.

Duffy glanced down and cried, "You're driving on a truck!"

Danny turned to Duffy and asked, "How do I stop this bitch from floatin'?"

"I have no clue," Duffy stated.

He screamed as Duffy frantically searched the panel. The car floated off the backend and over a cornfield. Duffy finally decided to hit the Hover button. The vehicle lowered toward the ground as the flames withered away. Thrusters in the undercarriage kicked on; it counterbalanced the weight. Before touchdown, the momentum stalled as the wheels folded outward, lowering to the appropriate height. They dropped inside the stalks; the thrusters shut off. Danny stomped on the brake pedal.

Behind them, a trail of fire blazed in their direction. The grassy meadow was burning in its path. The thrusters had torched the entire field, where the flames dug the soil, except for the thirty-foot skid when the tires finally made contact with the ground. Hooting and hollering remained muffled inside the enclosure while they scraped through dried cornstalks. A few feet from a drop-off, the car stopped. They were parked sideways alongside a ridge; a rock cliff cut the earth straight to the bone. The Wisconsin River flowed far below.

Danny jumped over the seat. "We have plenty of the night left, so explain yourself, Jerome."

"All right," he smiled. "I grew up in Little Rapids. Wesley Fifer was a good friend of mine. He taught me a lot: how to fight, nunchucks, lassoing, karate—things I could never imagine. He was a very good friend," Jerome cried, "until I found him slaughtered. The cops pinned the crime on his grandfather. He hollered 'Conspiracy!' when they dragged him into the Little Rapids jails. I moved to Verona with my moms."

"Where on earth did you get a hold of all those explosives?" Duffy asked.

"Wesley told me about a man named Ralph. He is the one who hid this shack full of artillery and explosives up near da Upham Woods

Campground. Dat's where I got all that neat stuff. Neat, huh?" Jerome smiled, revealing a bright set of teeth.

"Well, you found two of his best friends," Duffy said.

Jerome cleared his throat. He cried, "I knew it. I finally found the famous Armybrats."

Duffy joked, "Yeah, that's us, but what do ya think about the car?"

Jerome laughed. "Man, that was one helluva flight, my brotha."

They laughed.

"Yeah well, you were awesome back there." Danny nodded. "What made ya come here?"

"I've been following you two ever since Wesley's death."

"Why?" Duffy asked.

Jerome stared at Duffy with a blank look. He had no clue what to say. Jerome stepped out of the car and peeked over the ledge. Along the shore were rocks of all shapes and sizes. Danny and Duffy stepped out and slammed their doors. One door remained ajar; the girls listened in on their conversation.

Jerome brought his hands to his hips. "The entire police force was restructuring, and the whole town seems possessed. Watches' men are infesting Wisconsin, man. He killed my father. He was a cop."

He cried, and Duffy wrapped his arm around his shoulders. "It's gonna be OK. We hear you. We feel your pain."

"No, you don't. No one does. What brought you two to this masquerade anyway?" Duffy held up two coupons. Jerome snatched them from his hands and read them. "One free entrée with the purchase of an entrée limited one coupon per guest," Jerome smirked. "Man, they were phishing. And they got you two cheapskates good." He laughed.

"Hey!" Duffy snatched the coupons from him.

"I'm the brotha who gave your friend Pete a black eye."

Danny walked along the ridge and stared at the river below. Although Jerome risked his neck to save them, he did not see Danny dive at him. Duffy spun around and screamed. Danny tackled Jerome; they sailed off the cliff.

Without haste, Duffy hopped into the driver's seat. He demanded the girls buckle up as he reversed the car. He smirked and drove over the cliff while shutting the door. The girls hugged onto each other and bellowed out glass-shattering screams. They had no idea their date would voluntarily drive them off a cliff.

The Dodge Charger's Hover light snapped on. They floated past the two bodies. Duffy watched the river approaching his windshield. He scanned the console and tried to understand the best plan to save the two idiots. Duffy angled the rearview mirror to see the two bodies hovering over the trunk. Then he noticed a Parachute button. The thrusters kicked on; Duffy knew the car had come close to the side of the cliff. He hit the button. A colossal parachute released from the tail; it swallowed Jerome and Danny; briefly, it forced them upwards. The webbing tangled the two boys. Duffy swerved the car as he mashed on the brakes—even though the brakes were useless in midflight. The red taillights made the white parachute pink while two boys were neck in neck inside the woven ripstop nylon. The thrusters shifted the car sideways. The momentum flung the parachute, tossing the two of them into the river.

Danny swam to Jerome and punched him in the face. Jerome shoved him underwater. "Man, what's up brotha? Either you're savin' m' ass or you're beating on me! What's up with that?" Danny clobbered him a few more times and attempted to choke him with the parachute cord. Duffy dropped out of the driver's door and pushed Danny underwater. Jerome treaded until Duffy dragged him toward the river's edge.

Clarissa opened the backdoor and leaned out as the thrusters pushed water in her face. The car hovered over the river.

Danny swam through the raging water. He struggled to meet up with the other two lying on the sand. The two girls were screaming. No one was in the car to fly it.

Danny asked, "Why did you do that to Pete?"

"He tried killing himself."

Danny glanced at Duffy and dropped his head onto the sand, trying to regain his breath.

"I can't bear to grieve over my moms trying to support me, let alone herself. You guys really do mean well. You stick together with pride. Wesley told me about that; he said that you guys went up against Watches before. And I have a proposal." He hesitated and suggested, "I want to join the Armybrats."

They sat in silence; it was difficult to fathom the new revelation that Pete had attempted suicide. They knew their buddy was off a little but not that far off.

Duffy piped in and broke the silence. "You have proven to be a valuable asset, Rome."

"What you did back there was Da bomb. But look man, you can't join the Armybrats because of hatred or revengeful thoughts you may have. You need to trust yourself before you can become part of the Armybrats. Do you understand that?" Danny asked. "We aren't about revenge."

Jerome sighed. "I know. After Pete tried offing himself at the park in Verona, I followed him to your house. I saw you guys with the girls, so I hid in your trunk."

Danny glanced at Duffy; Duffy nodded. Danny acknowledged his nod in return with another one. "Yeah, of course, you can join us. We're down a man. We sort of fell apart for three years."

"We still are," Duffy added.

Jerome smirked.

They sat on the sand as the thrusters spat water at them. They were dumbfounded. The car still hovered over the river. The parachute was still hanging and wrapped around an uprooted tree along the shoreline. The Bratmobile swayed over the river like a black kite. The girls shrieked as the lines tightened and turned the car slightly.

The boys sat in silence until Danny broke the awkward quietness. "How do you propose we get the car down?"

Duffy looked at the girls crying in the backseat. "We could climb the chute."

After a struggle, Danny returned the car to the sandy front. The other two boys climbed inside. Danny shifted into drive; the Dodge raced alongside the river. After experimental attempts at speed, Duffy found one button that plastered everyone to their seats. A jet engine propelled off the rear bumper; sand ripped up rock walls; trees swayed. Their bodies compressed seat springs.

Clarissa's cheek muscles struggled with a question., "So where's the second date?"

They laughed. Vicki did not, however. She wrestled an extended hand before her face; the propulsion helped guide her hand backward. The echo of the slap pounded the windows with a vibrant force. She must not have enjoyed the first date.

Again, Clarissa had a hard time repenting. "Ow, bitch!" Her arm wiggled to reach for her and gripped onto her hair, yanking on it.

"No more dates. The Armybrats are crazy," Vicki screamed as Clarissa tugged at the roots of a group of hair.

Jerome laughed, "Those coupons worth it?"

Danny and Duffy rolled their eyes at him. In the rearview mirror, Jerome's cheeks wiggled, forming into a wide grin in the dark.

Chapter Sixteen

Guitar Strings

Jerome and Danny walked a couple of blocks from Duffy's house after hiding the car in the school forest. The next day was Monday; school was back in session. Jerome spent the night in Danny's basement. Of course, he had to sneak him in since he was still grounded.

The place Danny and Duffy visited was Pete's first period study hall. The teacher told them he hadn't shown in over a week. No matter what, they waited for a good fifteen minutes. His second period class was English. Jerome arrived at the door to the class and smiled at them. They nodded.

"Hey, brats." Jerome asked, "Still can't find Pete?"

Further down the hall, Pete was weaving in and out of flocks of students carrying a guitar case. A buddy approached him, a kid named Jackson—another social outcast; this guy was a real winner. His hairdo harbored grease in about ten different spikes; he wore black eyeliner. He enjoyed listening to Scandinavian music. He patted Pete's shoulder. Without asking nicely, he proclaimed, "I left one of my homework assignments at home, and I need to get it before the next hour begins. Can I get your car keys?"

"Yeah, it's been parked out near the flagpole. I haven't driven it since Friday." Pete dug through his trench coat pocket and located the tiny ring with the jagged toothed lock openers. "All right, here ya go. No scratches."

"Thanks, buddy. I owe ya one."

"Hey, I walked to school this morning. My car's been sitting out there all weekend, so pump the gas a bit."

"All right," Jackson replied and squeezed the ring of keys tightly in his hand.

Pete noticed a ceramic sculpture of a dog tucked under his arm. He asked, "What's with the dog?"

"It's Scooby-Doo, man." He held up the dog, "Scooby Ruby Roo." It was painted brown and spotted with black splotches. Its tongue hung out of its jaw.

"OK, Shaggy."

"I'm taking Scooby home. I figured I might as well take him home now."

Pete raised his eyebrows and continued walking toward his English class. Suddenly, he stopped dead in his tracks. Danny and Duffy stood next to Jerome. Jerome was blabbing about the night before. At that moment, Pete wasn't sure what he was mad over. The look on his face suggested sheer anger with Jerome for clocking him a good one Saturday night. Danny and Duffy were joking around with his infamous foe. Part of his anger was geared toward friendship and the true meaning of *friendship* while the other Armybrats laughed at Jerome's jokes.

Pete bolted toward him. Danny and Duffy backed away. Jerome spun around as Pete swung the guitar case into his side. Jerome flew through the doorway, knocking a teacher into a crowd of students. Students flushed into desks. Desk legs skid across the tile. Students clogged the hall. Danny and Duffy stopped Pete from peeling people away from the doorway to attack the core of his anger.

"Whoa, big guy," Danny hollered.

Duffy smiled. "He strummed a good chord with that guitar solo."

Jerome stood up. He dipped his head real low and charged Pete. The entire class jumped from their desks and watched as he bulldozed through Danny and Duffy knocking Pete into the hallway. Students toppled to the floor. Danny and Duffy fell over.

Danny sighed. "Here we go."

They charged after them as the two boys stood up to brawl. Danny grasped onto Jerome's waist and pulled him back. Duffy ran to Pete and missed his arm as Pete swung at Jerome. Jerome ducked; Danny got sucker slapped. He flew backward and crushed the door on a locker. Duffy jumped around him, clutching Pete's fist before he punched Jerome a second time. At the same time, he caught Pete's fist he kicked Jerome's knee. He fell to the floor.

"Pete, you don't want to do this to an Armybrat," Duffy warned.

"Don't stand in my way, Duff. I will hit you too, army...*what?*"

"No, you won't."

Pete struck Duffy across the face. He smashed into the wall and clasped onto his jaw. "I can't believe you did that." Pete lunged at Jerome clenching his neck. Jerome squeezed his neck; they strangled each other.

Duffy latched onto Pete's guitar. He walked toward the rear entrance to the hallway which led to the parking lot. Pete glanced at him from the corner of his eyes. People gathered around them. Pete let go of Jerome and spun around. "Hey, where are you going with my guitar?"

Duffy walked backward holding it in the air. He threatened, "I'm gonna throw it off the balcony."

Pete paced toward him. "Oh no, you're not."

Jerome followed behind him and asked, "Hey, are we through or what?"

Pete stopped. He pointed at him and exclaimed, "Hold one; I got to see about my guitar first."

Danny and Jerome followed Pete. Duffy exited the doors and hung over the wall along the stairwell. He held the guitar case over the ledge and unlatched the first latch. Far below, a sidewalk ran along the brick wall; it was about a fifty-foot drop. Pete punched the glass doors out of his way as he burst through them. Duffy unlatched the second latch and then the third. Pete ran out the last set of doors and tackled Duffy.

Duffy struggled to stand up. He still held onto the guitar case. Pete threw a punch. Duffy moved the case to block it. The case inverted and strummed the guitar. Pete dropped to his knees when Duffy threw his case. Danny and Jerome walked out the doors. Pete abducted his guitar from the case and hugged it. He inspected every square inch of his baby and stood up, glaring at Duffy.

"How dare you threaten my property?"

Duffy remained calm. "Take a good look at yourself, Pete. Take a good hard look. You tell me what has become of you. We were always good friends, Pete. Danny, Billy, Wesley, you, and I were good friends. So now what, Pete? You gonna stand there and tell me how much more valuable that guitar is compared to our fuckin' friendship?"

Pete held the guitar in front of him. He was staring at Duffy but was lost for words. Duffy's vulgar outburst was strong. Pete was helpless in his defense. He turned around and looked at Danny standing next to Jerome. Beyond them, the principal was standing before a crowd of students who watched the entire act. The teacher he had knocked down was practically pushing the principal in their direction.

Pete approached a half wall. He sat on top and pulled out a pack of smokes. He tapped it; a cigarette popped up. He slipped it between his lips and placed the pack inside his trench coat pocket. In the same hand, he carried a lighter to his mouth, lighting the cigarette. Placing the lighter inside his pocket, he strummed a tune on his guitar. He began tuning it.

Duffy shook his head. "Ignorance is bliss." He walked towards Pete.

Pete played his guitar and stared at him. A car attempted to turn the engine over. Everyone could hear Pete's car trying to start. Scooby-Doo sat in the passenger seat. Jackson looked at the ceramic dog and mocked Shaggy, "How 'bout some Scooby snacks, Scoob?"

Pete stopped strumming and lowered his cigarette. With one blink, he tilted his head ever so slightly to his right and noticed Jackson in his car. He was correct about the cold start. Jackson was cranking away at the ignition. He smiled at the ceramic dog in the passenger seat with its tongue hanging out. Finally, the car's engine roared out. When he crammed the shifter into second and the gears gave a hard grind, Pete cringed. Jackson noticed him sitting on the wall. He smiled, waving with two fingers.

A fiery ball of flames reflected in the windows of the school, the doors, and Pete's sunglasses. The last thing Pete could see was Jackson's two-fingered salute before the flash that consumed him. The windows on the face of the school rattled. A few blew out. Danny and Jerome flew backward. Danny smashed through a glass window. Jerome's body twisted around a metal frame through part of the window. Glass rained over them. A young girl fell on the stairwell behind Duffy and harshly nailed the metal railing in the center. She remained unconscious, lying against it.

The ceramic dog had blown out the windshield. The dog cracked through the glass on the school doors and landed on top of the principal. As the ceramic dog sat on his chest, its black paws burned through his shirt.

Duffy uncontrollably wobbled in Pete's direction. The force of the explosion caused Duffy to slam into the wall Pete sat on. The three-foot wall stopped him from toppling over. Pete was already rolling backward. He fell from the ledge. Duffy let out a howl as the wall crushed his gut. At the same time, he extended his arm and latched onto the neck of the guitar. Pete flipped downward with one hand inside the acoustics hole at the center of the guitar.

Duffy crammed into the wall from his weight. The guitar swung against the brick and Pete squeezed the C- and G-string inside the hole. The guitar smashed into tiny pieces. Pete slid down the strings as Duffy held him by the neck of the guitar. The pieces fell below as Pete glanced skyward. He swung freely from the balcony under Duffy's control.

Danny stepped out of the busted window and noticed the unconscious girl lying on the stairwell. A second explosion flipped him over Jerome. Both of them fell onto the rough concrete stoop as Jerome latched onto him before he went sailing through another glass window. Students were crowding each other as they grouped before the entryway. Pete's car flipped through the air; its grill bent the railing as its tail end flipped up the steps.

Danny stood up and ran toward the girl. Jerome followed suit. Duffy fished Pete up the wall like an amateur fisherman wrestling a king mackerel. His guitar was in shambles. Pete's hands were bleeding from the strings slicing his palms. He could barely hold on. He let go and latched onto the concrete blocks jutting from the base of the brick. He hung there. Duffy flew backward from the released tension. He casually looked at the guitar's neck in his tight grip in fear of losing his buddy to a fifty-foot death drop.

The railing twisted and squeaked as Danny and Jerome carried the girl away from the steps. Danny sighed when the car seemed at ease. Awkwardly, it rested on the railing; people gasped when it rocked a bit.

Together they saved the girl, especially when Pete's trunk hinged open and a dual wooden subwoofer busted over the staircase where she had lain unconscious. Flames shot out of the trunk and burned the subwoofer as it lay smashed on the steps. The flames wrapped up the staircase like a wave of lava.

Pete removed his trench coat, rolled it, and flung it over the ledge. Duffy let go of the guitar neck, reaching for his coat. Sweat ran off Pete's brow. Duffy stared into his eyes. Pete broke eye contact and looked beyond his feet. He closed his eyes; at the moment, he thought of letting go. Instead, he gripped the ledge. Duffy lunged at the wall and latched onto his back. Both of them fell onto the concrete. Pete plopped his rear end next to him as they sat panting.

Pete looked at his car. The railing wrapped around one of the doors, stuck through a window, and out the roof. Flames engulfed his car. Somewhere inside, Jackson's flesh-torn body bounced around with raging blazes eating at his endoskeleton. The car slid forward, bearing more weight on the railing; the entire railing folded. The car's roof smashed the steps; it caved inward.

Chapter Seventeen

Wildcat Lanes

The phone cord stretched around the refrigerator as Mike reached for a bag of pretzels on the other side. He questioned, "What do you mean there was an explosion?"

The officer on the other end was Derek Darcy. "The high school is on fire; faculty and students are evacuating now."

Mike dropped the bag of pretzels on the floor. The plastic bag clip, holding the bag shut, cracked and separated. Pretzels scattered across the tile. A jingle sounded when pretzels hit the floor vent. A couple of pieces disappeared through it. He asked, "Derek, where did the bomb go off?"

"Possible front entrance detonation, sir," he explained. "There are fires along the front face, the shrubbery along the eastern corner, the western corner, there are broken windows, and sections of the eaves came down on a few students. About twelve injuries: minor abrasions, cuts, scrapes, and the principal has second-degree burns on the chest and hands from a hot Scooby-Doo. That's all that has been reported at this time."

"Scooby-Doo?"

"Apparently, a ceramic Scooby-Doo landed on him."

"Where are the students now?"

"As of right now, the entire body of students is in the east parking lot, sir."

Mike punched a cupboard door above the kitchen sink. "I'm on my way; I'll be there in two minutes. Find Duffy Felter or my son. Perhaps they know what's going on." Mike crammed the receiver into the phone's base. "Damn it!" He wandered into the living room and shouted, "The high school is on fire!"

His wife who sat on the sofa shrieked, "What? What do you mean on fire?"

"Possible bomb threat."

"Oh my God!"

"Our sons are in trouble. I just know it."

Clarice tossed a book onto the coffee table. Her face held some scars from the broken mirrors; she was healing nicely, still in partial bandages and gauze.

Mike strapped on his gun belt and asked, "Honey, what are you doing?"

"The last time I stayed home alone like this, you went running off chasing assholes, and I was raped by one. Our boys are in trouble, and I'm going too."

Clarice and Mike climbed into the family car; she watched the garage door swinging upward in the mirror. It stopped.

Mike said, "Damn it!"

"Seriously," she stated, glancing over her shoulder and then in the rearview. Out of the corner of her eye, she noticed Mike's finger on the opener mounted to the visor.

He smirked. "Just kidding, honey."

She gave him the look. The look was simply that—*the look*. It divided a fine line between humorous or nearly slapped. Clarice and

Mike spun out of the driveway and headed into town. The smoke from the fire at the high school was far above the school forest. They could see the thick clouds. His instinct preceded him.

A fire roared across the face of the school; mangled metals lie crushed on the concrete staircase. Students were released early from school. The elementary school and middle school let out early as well. The bomb squad from Madison had to flush out the buildings to make sure there were no more devices.

Clarice focused on the flames. Even though the school was in the background, the car window reflected a memory from her past. She watched as her house burned down. Firefighters whittled away at the flickering flames; it was still burning. Mike appeared before the window. No sooner had he hopped the curb, he stopped short. He noticed her daze. Memories flourished in her mind, the terror of Stanley Markesan driving that truck through their home. The image replayed in her mind; she saw it in the windowpane, but it disappeared from view when Mike opened the door.

Crowds of people surrounded the stairway quarantined by caution bands. There were a few officers at the bottom of the staircase discussing things. Principal Malone had two blackened paw prints on his chest. Chest hairs were wrinkled to the red skin. Red welts sat behind the designer button up. Singed fabric hung outward. A paramedic was rubbing ointment over his hairless scorched pectorals.

Mike ran to him and questioned, "Talk to me." He gave an awkward glance at the paw prints. "You OK, Principal Malone?"

"Oh, this?" He pointed at his chest. "I got this from a hot dog."

"You should switch to cold sub sandwiches."

The principal's eyebrows rose across his brow.

Two cops approached: it was Darcy and Penski. Penski smiled. "Hey boss, ya don't wanna know whose car that was."

Clarice watched the firefighters flip the car upright. They had Jaws of Life with them. Mike's head whipped toward the car. The rear license plate was still intact. Reading the personalized plate, it spelled: RAVER. He flinched and knew whom it belonged to. His head snapped in the direction of students in the parking lot.

"Is that Pete Carson's?" Clarice asked, pointing at the car.

"Without an autopsy, there's no way of telling, sir. That dude in there is toast."

Clarice asked, "How many were inside?"

Darcy stated, "One, ma'am."

Mike snapped at the principal, "Where's my son?"

"Everyone's been released."

"He didn't come home." Mike jerked his head in anger and walked in circles.

Clarice watched her husband pacing. She sighed. "Perhaps he's with Duffy. Let's check that out before we blow things out of proportion."

Mike sarcastically added, "Oh like nothing's blown out of proportion already. That was Pete Carson's car. If he's dead in that car, Jake will probably end up in an insane asylum. And let's not forget the time he ended up in detox where you two ass clowns once put him," he snapped at Darcy and Penski.

"Yeah, yeah, we're sorry about that."

Mike walked away with his wife. "We need to find Danny." He walked backward. He delegated, "Can you two handle this?"

They nodded as Mike turned to walk away.

Outside the bowling alley on the edge of town, a mile north of the school, the Bratmobile pulled into the parking lot. It parked along a fence in an alleyway. Pete was sitting in the passenger seat. Jerome and

Duffy were sitting in the back. Danny was driving. A sign out front read Wildcat Lanes.

Pete was reviewing the dashboard—the buttons and doodads.

"Why are you parking way over here?" Jerome asked.

"Well, someone wanted this car impounded, and Duffy and I sort of, well, stole it back."

"Oh boy." Jerome sighed.

Pete cupped his mouth; his eyes wetted his cheeks. "That was meant for me." Oddly, it seemed as though he just realized his dead friend died in his own car.

Danny looked at Duffy.

Pete rolled his head toward Danny. "It's my birthday today, and I was supposed to die."

"But you didn't, so let's cherish the day together. Shall we?"

Pete pinched the bridge of his nose. He looked at the bowling alley and shook his head.

Duffy asked, "So, Pete, what do you think about the car?"

"You got a pretty slick car, Duffster," Pete implied.

Duffy narrowed his eyes and spoke with assertiveness as he lectured, "Wrong, I don't have a slick car. We have a slick car. We started this, and together, we will finish it. We are the Armybrats. You're an Armybrat. I'm an Armybrat. You can't hide from the facts, Pete."

Inside the car, the interior held in dead silence. Jerome was staring at Duffy. Danny glanced in the rearview. Then he monitored Pete who stared at the bowling alley, sniveling. Pete turned around to look at Duffy. He smirked, "Yeah, the Armybrats. Sorry, Jerome."

Danny objected, "On the contrary, he saved our lives last night. He's definitely an Armybrat, Pete."

Pete scowled at him and suggested, "A true hero. Let's go bowling, huh."

They climbed out of the Dodge. Pete ran his hand along the roof and trunk. He knelt and inspected the rocket tubes. Impressed was hardly the word for it. It was far from the average daily driver. Even though it seemed as simple as a Dodge Charger hot off the assembly line, it was a tank. It was a weapon, and it was theirs.

Pete lit a cigarette as he ran his fingers across the (lighted) lettering on the doors. A blue haze shone in the whites of his eyes; the backlighting of the embedded letters captured his gaze. He stood up, crossed the lot, and stood between a couple of empty slots on a bike rack next to the front doors. Duffy and Jerome walked inside the building as Danny broke away and approached Pete. He stood directly in front of him—for several quiet seconds. Pete blew smoke over his right shoulder, squinted at him, but never broke eye contact.

Danny gripped his collar and shoved him against the wall. The cigarette fell from his hand. Danny stomped on it, smearing ash on the asphalt. He continued to press into him, snarling at him.

Pete groaned, "What's your fucking problem, Danny?"

Danny screamed, "What's my friggin' problem? What's your friggin' problem?"

Pete panted, "I don't have any problems." He pulled away from him and straightened his trench coat.

Danny whispered, "Our conversation isn't over."

Pete continued walking inside the bowling alley and replied, "Fine, I prefer talking inside anyway."

Danny blurted, "Pete." He hesitated and then said, "Fuck!"

Danny placed his hands over his hips and dropped his head. He kicked at a pebble on the ground. Pete was at the counter ordering bowling shoes. Duffy and Jerome were already on lanes nine and ten.

There were other families and friends bowling. On lanes one and two there were small children throwing granny balls—with blue rubber tubing inside the gutters; bumper bowling, they called it. Some students had the same idea after the dismissal. They were bowling on lanes five through eight. There were sixteen lanes. A few at the end were vacant. All ten pins sat in the display cages at the end of the alleys.

Pete sat on the chair alongside the ball return. Rows of chairs, back-to-back, faced each scoring terminal. Duffy was keying their names into the computer for who was bowling on which lane. Pete had begun undoing his shoelaces. He removed his shoes and put on the bowling shoes. He couldn't finish tying the laces. His hands cupped his forehead as he leaned over his knees. Emotions struck him hard. Thoughts of Jackson dying were on spin cycle in his brain.

Danny sat one chair from him. Staring at him for a second, he decided to put on his bowling shoes as well. Pete then finished tying his laces. Danny asked, "Pete, I thought you and Jackson weren't on the best of terms?"

Pete tightened the bowtie and eased into the seat. "Yeah."

"Why was he driving your car? I'm just trying to understand why your car was left at the school all weekend."

"Just what are you implying, Danny?" Pete snapped and jumped from the seat. "Are you..." He swallowed. "Are you suggesting that I murdered my friend?"

Danny stood from the chair as Pete hung over him. He was two inches from his face. Danny glared. "No, Pete. I'm just..."

Pete filled his mouth with words. "You're just blaming me for his death, that's all."

"No," Danny disagreed.

"Fuck you, Danny," Pete whispered and shoved him. He flipped over the chairs and landed near a computer terminal for lanes eleven and twelve. A group of girls caught his body.

Both Duffy and Jerome stood up from their chairs, concerned for Danny. Pete stepped backward, easing around the seats. Danny stood up. Girls helped him to his feet. Brushing himself off, he maintained a visual on Pete. Duffy was stunned.

Pete turned around and headed toward the restrooms.

Danny glanced at the other two and suggested, "Duffy, you really shouldn't have busted his guitar like that, man."

Jerome sighed. "Look, there's more to his anger than you two know."

Danny turned toward Jerome. He explained, "Hey, Pete's mom was abducted. His father is constantly getting wasted, and his best friend just died. Intrigue me! Tell me what more I don't know."

"OK, someone got to yo boy. Watches gots him, bin mind-fuckin' 'im for a couple weeks now."

Danny nudged Jerome. "What are you talking about, Rome?"

Pete strolled through a hallway and into a bathroom. He whistled as he strolled up to a urinal. A man stood at another urinal; he was parked kitty-corner between the dividers and wore a baseball cap low to his eyes. He wore a black trench coat. Pete whipped the last trickle and raised his hand off his zipper; after he flushed, he unsnapped loops around two individual knives at his waist. Inconspicuous people had been entering their lives lately. Things seemed on edge. He did not know the other man pretending to piss without a single stream on the white porcelain wall.

As he stood at the sink, he caught a glimpse of the man at the urinal. It seemed wrong, he was peeing when he entered the bathroom, and he was still standing there. Something was off. Either this guy had a late night with amber and ale or early morning with coffee bliss. Pete prolonged his handwashing to keep a keen eye on the stranger. Unfortunately, the towel rack was tucked behind another wall, out of sight from the man. Pete ran his wet fingers through his hair and decided to brave it.

He left the sink. The man was still at the urinal when Pete approached the towel rack. Before he could turn a fresh towel downward, he was pinned by pointy elbows. The man forced him around. When Pete faced him, he had both knives to the man's throat. Of course, it was a close friend of his—a young man he knew quite well; it was Billy. Somehow, he managed to bond Pete's wrists in shiny shackles before Pete could even react.

Billy stepped away from the knife blades. Pete stood there for a second. He was more confused about the handcuffs. Billy lifted his head and revealed his eyes. As the rim of his cap lifted, the shadow across his face dissipated. The bathroom lighting hit his face and shimmered across the cufflinks. They cast a bright glow across Pete's cheeks. Billy's next statement made Pete lower his hands in shock. The knives angled toward the floor.

"You're under arrest, Pete Carson."

"Arrest?"

"You are under arrest for the murder of Wesley Fifer."

"Birthday prank." Pete smiled.

Pete pushed Billy backward; the knife tips scratched at his neck. Billy spun around and elbowed him in the gut. Pete crawled toward a bathroom stall and sat up. Billy knelt in front of him. He explained, "You know, I wouldn't have believed it. But I was at the hospital and a reporter handed me a videotape before she died. I reviewed the tape, Peter. You wouldn't believe the shit I saw. You were in bed with the devil." Billy swallowed and glared at him. Pete was shaking his head. Billy asked, "How could you, Pete?" Billy screamed.

On lane ten, Jerome itched at his skullcap. His mind was performing Hula-Hoops over a god-awful truth. He revealed it to them. "Duffy, Danny, what I'm 'bout to say may change things a bit, but I ain't mean no disrespect for any of you. Yo birthday buddy was forced to murder a good friend."

Duffy asked, "What?"

"You killed the boy!" Billy's echo crawled into the hallway.

Billy kneed Pete in the gut. Pete gave a wretched bellow. Billy hoisted him off the floor and dragged him out of the bathroom. He carried him through the hallway toward a side door that led into the alleyway along the bowling alley. He kicked it open and tossed Pete down a short flight of stairs.

Billy screamed, "What has gotten into your head, Pete? Have you gone completely mad?"

Pete looked at Billy and held back tears. He said, "I didn't want to do it."

Billy kicked him in the stomach. Pete flipped over and rolled. "Then why did you, huh?"

"I didn't do it," Pete cried.

Billy knelt on his neck and used his weight to crush him. He pulled a pistol out of his belt. He wore his uniform underneath a topcoat. With a flick of a wrist, he loaded the 9mm. The gun barrel tapped Pete's temple. Billy asked, "Give me one good reason why I shouldn't shoot you in your own sick, twisted, fucking piece of shit head, Pete."

Pete lifted his head from the pavement. Blood ran down his cheek; he cried, "Watches has my mom." Tears mixed with blood. Rain began hammering them. Rapidly, eyelids shed away the rain and tears.

Billy stood up allowing the pigmentation to return in his head, the ring dissipated where the barrel had been pressed. Sliding the gun into his holster, he was caught in the temptation of torment. Pete was crying, gasping for air. Rain pounded Billy's cap. Wesley Fifer was murdered. Pete Carson was prime suspect number one. While trying to defend his actions, Billy stammered with accusation, ripped his chest apart from the inside out, bit by bit. A birthday he would never forget was this day—the day he lost his best friend, Jackson. It was the day Billy laid down the law.

Pete rocked gently onto his knees; his head tucked deep to his chest. He explained, "Watches kidnapped my mom. I knew he had her. So, one night I drove to the camp. I stole a canoe. I went to where that old sawmill is."

Billy sighed. "I know, Pete."

The rain created an alley of clicks and splashes. The loudest clicks were the ones tapping the lids on the nearby dumpsters; bold white letters spelled out *Pellitterri* on the hunter green paint. The name was one of their good acquaintants, the son of the owner; he owned the local waste management company.

Pete glanced at him and explained, "Watches coaxed me there." Pete cried some more. "They captured me and brought me to the mill. He had Wesley." He was barely breathing but still crying as he explained, "He was in a wooden box. There was a conveyer belt." Billy scowled at him, even though Pete hadn't noticed behind the tears, the fog, and the mist. "There was a huge blade."

Billy stepped back and lowered his head.

"You know the kind that cuts huge ass trees." A moment of hesitation before Pete screamed, "Then they turned it on. That god-awful sound— oh I can remember that grinding. Someone was pounding—inside one of the boxes."

"We found blood all over the place, Pete. A message written on the wall said, 'You can thank Pete Carson for this.' We had it analyzed,

Pete. DNA traces, the true lineage of an American Indian, a good boy, Wesley Fifer, all over that sawmill floor and the walls."

Pete whispered in a questioning tone, "Wesley was in that box?" The intensity grew like the vein across his brow. "I tried to stop it, and he did. But then he told me I had to bring him something, and he would free them all."

"Bring what? Free who, Peter?"

"I told him he could pound salt."

"Yeah."

Pete cried as a smirk lifted the corner of his lips. "He didn't like that too much." Pete's neck veins pushed at his collar. "And then he started the sawblade again."

Billy cringed. "Did you know Wesley was in that box?"

Pete hesitated and shook his head. Rain splashed off his face.

"Did you know he was in that box?" Billy asked louder.

"I swear, Billy. I didn't know. Then the blades, the blades dug into the wood. The conveyer belt stopped again. That's when I heard Wesley screaming. I put up a fight. I killed one, I killed one guy, then another; they were Watches' minions. You know me. I killed two guys, but it was just me. I couldn't fight them all."

Billy asked, "Then what?"

"Then, I was in a box."

"And . . ."

Pete relaxed and whispered, "For a brief moment, I smelled my mom's perfume." His eyes narrowed; he turned toward Billy. "I think she was in that box."

"What happened?" Billy asked.

"Watches asked if we had a deal."

"What deal, Pete? You're telling me jack shit, man."

"And I told him sure, that we did." Pete cried and was talking faster than before. "He said, *'OK, but since you just killed two of my men, listen to this!'* and the conveyer belt started . . . and the saw," he wailed through the rain while expressing what happened with his hands in the air and slapped the pavement with fear. Rain splashed outward. "I couldn't see anything. But I heard the screams. I heard the screaming."

"You traded Wesley's life for your own."

Pete blinked his eyes as rain pelted him. His cheeks wiggled. Rain sparkled after it sprinkled away from his chin. "No, I just never carried it out. I have no clue what he meant." Pete's eyes narrowed as he glanced over his shoulder at the Armybrats' car. "He's gonna kill me. He's gonna kill them if I don't follow through with the deal."

Billy sighed. "He's been attacking all of us, Pete. It's not just you."

Billy knelt beside him and placed a hand on his shoulder. He sat him up, latched onto each shoulder, and stared into his sorrow-filled eyes. He witnessed two best friends getting slaughtered. No one has a mindset to recover easily from something like that. Not even the most mean-spirited animal in the world could recover from killing a fellow predator.

Suddenly, Billy received a blow to the back as a kid nailed him with a three-foot piece of conduit. Billy fell forward, his body hammered the pavement. Pete rolled and groaned as two guys kicked the daylights out of him. Billy stood until he felt another whack from the bar. He flipped into the air and landed on his back.

"Where's your brother, Billy?" Sam asked.

When he pulled out his pistol, the other kid stepped on his wrist. Billy squeezed off a round. The bullet sparked the caster wheel under a dumpster. Danny and Duffy heard the shot as they exited the bathroom in search of Pete who had been gone a while. They charged toward the side door of the bowling alley. As soon as they stepped out the door, they noticed Shawn repetitively smacking Billy across the face with brass knuckles. They were taking turns as Sam continued beating him with the conduit. Pete laid in a puddle, facedown, half the cufflinks buried in water along his waist.

At first, it was a shock to see their classmates kicking the living daylights out of Danny's brother and their friend. They figured those two died in the restaurant with some of Watches' men. Here they were stealing what sense of mobility Billy and Pete had left in them. Pete had been trying to defend himself even though his wrists had been bound.

Danny bolted across the pavement. Before the two bullies could turn around, Danny was in the air on a downward spiral. Both feet shaped new imprints on their cheeks as they flew away from Billy's limp body. Danny dropped to the ground, water kicking up from his bowling shoes as they slapped into the puddles. He straddled his brother after relieving him from pure torture. Duffy casually approached Shawn and lifted him with one arm. He walked him headfirst into a dumpster.

Shawn's brass knuckles were lying next to Billy's head. Danny retrieved one and slid it over his right hand. Sam stood up and lifted the conduit bar. He persuaded Danny to attack. Danny wouldn't budge; he stood over his brother—in full protection mode. He maintained a human presence, shielding his brother from any more attacks.

Instead, Sam charged him. He sliced the air with the conduit. He swung at Danny. Danny held up his fist. The conduit clanked the brass knuckle. Danny threw an uppercut through his jaw and nose. Sam flew backward and returned to his feet. Blood trickled from each nostril. An evil glare revealed itself from trapped aggression. He lunged at Danny, swinging the conduit bar left and right. Danny simply adjusted the brass knuckles to connect with each blow. Until he grew tired of blocking, he stepped away from his brother to swing upward through Sam's face using the brass knuckles this time.

Sam arched into the air as he flung backward and landed on his left shoulder. The conduit rolled away from him when his shoulder impacted the blacktop. A snap traveled through the alleyway, and the bowling alley reflected the sound.

Duffy kept walking Shawn's head into a dumpster. The repetitive motion created an immense rhythm in the alley. He smiled. "The more I keep this up buddy, the more stupid you become. Man, I should stop, but I love the beat of this drum." Pete sat up; he watched Duffy toss Shawn inside the dumpster.

Jerome quietly sat behind the computer and noticed a pin drop at the end of his lane. No one was with him. Everyone else was a bit preoccupied. Of course, he had no clue about the fight in the alley. He was the only one left watching the pins drop. They haven't started any matches yet.

Pin by pin, more continued to knock over, one lane at a time. He stood up from behind the computer and walked onto the boarded floor. Each lane broadened as he drew closer. His white basketball shoes reflected in the floor's oily surface. He never changed into bowling shoes. The pins continued to drop, and all he could do was wonder why, just like everyone else trying to bowl. People grumbled and complained, holding onto balls and watching pins drop.

Walking beyond the ball return, he stood directly in front of lucky lane number nine. The number nine was his favorite number. It was a good number. He always appreciated number nine, until one pin flung out of the terminal and bashed into his gut; he flew backward, crushing the ball return. Cracks soared through the casing. Some of the plastic bunched up and knocked a ball off the ball tray. Number nine wasn't so lucky anymore.

All the monitors flickered. Watches' face took over the displays. The name "Watches" rang three times through the bowling alley. It was an eerie echo that would make any kid cry—some sniffling did come from the bumper bowling lanes. A few mothers gathered the children. Numbers scrambled across the television screens and then switched back to the scores.

A head poked out the end of the alley. It was Watches. He snickered and cackled, hanging upside down. Oddly, he dropped like a metamorphosis. The alley gave birth to a pinhead. Knocking more pins out of his way, he crawled out of the pin compartment. He stood at the end of the lane juggling bowling pins. He wore a flop hat and a brown trench coat. His face was as sickening as ever, with one dark eyepatch, one red eye. Jerome reached behind his shirttail and stroked the handle of his revolver, staring at the devilish fiend.

"Watches, Watches, Watches!"

Pete scooted across the pavement and undid the cuffs with the key hanging from Billy's belt. He withdrew Billy's pistol and turned toward the backdoor of the bowling alley. Danny was carrying Sam over his head and threw him inside the same dumpster as Shawn. Pete wandered inside the bowling alley while Danny and Duffy aided Billy. They picked him up and hung his arms over their shoulders. They walked him toward the Bratmobile.

Through the torrential rain, at the end of the parking lot, several men stood in a line. In each hand was a fully automatic weapon. Strangely wet hair covering their boney faces; mostly, they appeared hopped on steroids—inhumane beasts. They blocked the entrance to the alley with no way out. A fence ran alongside them on the north end and behind the boys where it met the corner of the building. They could see Watches' men. The Bratmobile was a couple of steps away. They struggled with Billy's limp body. Danny turned his head toward Duffy.

Danny asked, "Now what?"

Inside, Pete walked through the hallway and crossed the carpeted walkway toward the bowling lanes. People were gathered in the center; a couple of younger girls were helping Jerome stand up from the ball return. Pete looked toward the end of lane nine. There were pins everywhere: wedged in gutters, others in doors, pins in the drywall. One pin sweep couldn't drop to clear pins; the machine's clank echoed through the bowling alley. Pete could see Jerome stand up. At the end of the lane, he noticed Watches holding onto a couple of pins. Everything seemed slow motion. Pete's trench coat waved away from his body as he continued walking to the upper floor.

Suddenly, the conveyer belt rotated. At the end of the lane, Pete could see through the plastic window. He was in line with lane nine. A ball was being returned up the conveyer belt toward Jerome. Jerome squinted at Watches who appeared motionless almost like a manikin and whispered, "I didn't send any balls." As this round black object shot out of the ball return, sparks danced from an eight-inch wick. It was a bomb. Watches had lit a bomb and placed it in the ball return.

Without hesitation, Pete fired the pistol at the evil manikin. Watches came alive; he twirled the bowling pins before his face, deflecting rounds. Jerome hugged the bomb with the burning wick. Like the kids' bumper bowling, Jerome carried the ball to the lane ignoring the sparks burning at the flesh on his upper arms. Using both hands, he rolled it down the lane at Watches. It continued to roll over the sparking wick, burning the threads into a smaller nub. Pete looked at the kids running around and at the girls surrounding Jerome.

He stepped forward and hollered, "There's a bomb!"

With Billy being dragged by Danny and Duffy, they carried him behind the dumpsters. Watches' men were shooting at them. Bullets ricocheted off the steel. Danny and Duffy hovered over Billy. Danny reached around Billy's waist to find an empty holster. He glanced at Duffy and questioned, "Where's his gun?"

"Again, you think I always have all the friggin' answers? I have no clue, Dan the Man."

Lead nailed the dumpsters, echoing across the alley and splashing into puddles. Danny slouched. His wet strange hair slapped his forehead. He screamed, "This sucks!"

"Yes. Yes, it does," Duffy agreed. He covered his ears.

Jerome glanced at Pete. He ordered people to vacate the premises. A couple of kids ran in the other direction toward lanes one and two. Watches' men were shooting the entranceway. A lady had been shot; they were digging in deeper. Jerome watched people scatter away from the exit as glass shattered from the frame. A lady crawled across the carpeting, dragging a bloody leg through shards of glass.

Two children were still running around bowling racks, charging the other direction past Jerome. Jerome's eyes grew a few sizes. Watches watched his bomb rolling at him. Even his one eye seemed bigger than his eye patch. He dropped to the floor and tried blowing the wick out. Pete continued to fire rounds. Watches rolled into the pin return and climbed into the ceiling behind lane nine. A new set of pins dropped after his legs vanished.

Jerome tugged on Pete's shoulder to direct his attention toward the children. Pete maintained his site picture where Watches had disappeared. All at once, Jerome and Pete dispersed, grabbing children aimlessly wandering through the ball returns. The bomb rolled over its burning wick, clicking its way across the lane, and stopped before the lead pin. Pins tumbled one at a time. Pete pulled a few kids behind the counter where the ball racks were. Jerome sailed across the alley and sacked the two other children who were crying. They fell to the ground as the last pin fell in lane number nine. The gutters tore open beyond

Jerome's feet; the force shoved them down the lane. Flames roared over them. The ball return separated from the floor.

A couple of bowling balls burst through a trophy case on the back wall near the cash register. Pete tucked the kids' heads. Light fixtures fell from the ceiling. Some broke tabletops. Others fanned across the carpeting. More bowling balls flew off the ball return. Wood splinters and balls blew over their backs as they launched through the counter above. Pete stood up. He let go of the boy who ran for the hallway. People inside the bar were still dining. Chaos unfolded around them, yet they continued to drink and eat. Some kids were standing near the arcade machines, frozen solid.

Lights flickered. Electrical surges made power intermittent. Jerome brushed himself after helping the kids out of a pile of pins. Ordering them to head straight for the door, he picked up two bowling balls and stood in the center of the lane. Sprinklers placed beads of water across his high fade hairdo. Water from the smoke detection system hit his brow. Cautiously, he glanced at each dark lane, searching for Watches.

Pete squinted, trying to notice movement through the haze. He leaned to his left as Watches appeared in lane seven. Lights flickered a few times; he was gone. Between light flickers, Jerome saw Watches waving at him from lane twelve. Lights blinked within seconds, and Watches disappeared yet again. Reflections on the oily wet surface bent the illusions of where Watches appeared next.

Suddenly, a pin shot out of nowhere. Jerome blocked it with one of the balls. The force made him slide backward; his back arched over a ball return. His fancy basketball shoes spread water away. He dodged another pin and blocked a third. He dropped one ball onto the floor but managed to hold onto the other one. Squeaks chirped from his spin move around the ball return, he retrieved another ball from the machine, scanning the lanes for evil.

Pete heard a few clanks. Jerome was blocking maple wood missiles launched from different lanes. Brilliantly, Jerome spun through water-crushing pins, surrounded by white glistening slivers piecing around him. Pete was amazed by his skills. More clanks were heard. Watches' men were shattering glass at the front entrance. The clanks weren't coming from the entrance, however. They came from behind.

He spun around. Bowling balls were falling from shelving units. Pete watched as they continued dumping across the tile floors as if some force ripped them from their stored locations. The balls migrated and seemed to line up like a pack of vicious cannonballs aboard a pirate vessel for rapid reload.

Pete paced backward as the balls continued to fall from shelves. He stopped when more clanks were heard from the other end. He spun around to realize balls were swarming the tile floors like a hot riverbed of mosquitos after a cool rain, surrounding him.

Without haste, he threw himself across a row of chairs as two balls collided over his back; they shattered in a colorful array of resins; his shirt wiggled from the force. All the balls targeted Pete. When he sat up, a ball connected with the chair at his left. He tilted his head as two more balls pancaked next to his ear. Ringing set in like a bad case of tinnitus; chards ripped his cheeks and neck. He tossed his body over the seatbacks. Balls blasted through computers, monitors, and ball ejection ports. Pete braced himself on the metal supports between two rows of chairs as balls nailed the seats on either side of him. He screamed through the thunderous roar.

Jerome cowered near a ball return watching the balls peg the seats behind him. A shadow emerged alongside him. Watches slithered out the ball return. A new shadow sprouted. Jerome kept a keen eye at the balls exploding near Pete. Pete was in the middle buried by the coverstock shedding particles, plastic, and urethane. Pete tilted his head to avoid reactive resin carving out his eyeballs. Fresh blood warmed his neck. With whatever strength he had left in his arms, he maintained his position between the metal supports. He peeked at balls exploding below him. He felt a couple of balls land on his back. Pieces sliced him. Muscles protruded from his neck, turning his head with a wretched scream.

Watches stood over Jerome with two pins in his fists. He swung them together like a cymbal-banging monkey toy. Jerome held both balls beside his face like a boxer on guard when he noticed movement across the shiny floor. He brilliantly danced across the lanes to avoid the blows as Watches swung; Jerome helped guide his swing by spinning around one arm; he hopped onto the edge of the ball return and leaped into the air, three fingers gripping a ball; with a wide arm swing, he crushed Watches' jawline, sending his body into a pile of ball debris. It was an eerie yet celebratory moment considering the devastation, wetness, and smoke.

Jerome continued his spin on one leg and lost Watches in the mess behind him. Out of the corner of his eye, he noticed the devil's red-eye glaring at him from a computer terminal. Jerome spun behind the front side of the ball return as Watches threw his arms forward. All the shrapnel around Pete left the floor and annihilated the ball return. Jerome held the balls over his head to avoid being clocked by all the pieces spreading up lane seven.

When the footsteps of the devil's prancing grew louder than the pieces sliding across the wet oil slick, he lunged upward through two pins flashing before his eyeballs. Jerome blocked them on an upward hop. He continued to block the pins as Watches slid past him and spun around, acting like a windmill in a crazy storm. Watches swung the pins at him as he blocked each blow. It was a rhythmic clocking of ticks. Pete could hear the knocking sounds of fat pins to balls, but he wasn't sure if the balls were still piling into the seats around him.

Jerome went for a strike as he pushed the bowling ball straight for his face. Watches used the pin to block the ball. Watches swung the pins inward toward his head like a pair of scissors. Jerome held the balls at the side of his head and stopped the pins short from sandwiching the ear canals inside his brain cavity. Jerome tried to bash his gut in from both sides. Watches twirled the pins in his hands and tucked them alongside his gut. The balls contacted the pins at his sides. Swinging upward toward Jerome's groin, another ball was held in front of him; the oily floor seemed slicker as he lost his footing.

Watches missed his groin since he had fallen. He backhanded to block Jerome's swing and swung downward at him. Jerome held a ball and blocked the swing. Parts of the ball cracked and sprinkled over him. Watches swung his other arm around to bash his face. Jerome blocked another swing using the ball. More of the ball cracked apart. He kicked upward and bashed Watches in the side of the head with his foot. One pin rolled out of his hand and tapped Jerome's forehead. Watches tripped on the gutter between lanes nine and ten. He slid across lane ten but rose from the oily floor. Emerging from the bowling lane, Watches' one eye shone red in the oil.

Pete's arms wiggled. Fatigue set in. Finally, he collapsed over the stack of rubble below him—bowling ball pieces. He glanced through the seat supports and broken balls. Watches' back faced them. He could see Jerome passed out on the floor. Watches withdrew a handgun. Pete glanced at a pile of rubble to his left and noticed his firearm laying cockeyed underneath. The barrel gleamed in the emergency lighting. Carefully, he dug through the remains of bowling ball pieces, scattered waist-high. The alleys were quite dark. In the darkness, Watches' red eye loomed as his head rotated backward, facing Jerome's direction. The handgun aimed at Jerome's head.

Pete fired rounds at larva-face with one red eye. Watches flew forward. Pete rolled from under the chairs, firing away at the bowling alley beast. He worked his way toward Jerome, shooting around the sizzling ball return. Watches rolled across the lanes trying to avoid hot lead and Pete's anger. Watches returned fire through the smoke and rounds cracked a plastic ball return. Pete dragged Jerome's unconscious body away from the middle. All at once, the noise dissipated, yet the water droplets gave constant pitter-patter.

Watches screamed somewhere in the smoke. "Come out, come out, wherever you are."

Balls burrowed into his back and gut. Watches shot the ground. Bowling balls flew at him. Watches dropped his gun and leaned forward, trying to retrieve it. Another ball pinched his fingers on the oily floor. He withdrew his arm and coddled his pink digits like a schoolboy discovering an electric fence for the first time. One ball nailed his hand; he slapped his own face and fell. More and more bowling balls bashed into him. Jerome was behind a ball storage unit, out for the count. Pete was winging balls from the lobby, protecting his wounded companion.

By the time Watches turned around, Pete's foot concaved his face. Flying backward through the air, Watches bumped his handgun; it rattled inside a gutter. Before he could sit up, Pete was standing over him wielding two bowling pins. Watches attempted to sit up. In Pete's best baseball player's stance, like Boston Red Sox's Ted Williams, he was fully prepared to bust clouds. Both pins sliced through the smoky abyss and clobbered Watches. Blood sprayed sideways from each nostril. Watches flew down the lane. His body slid into the pins and knocked all ten down. Pete recovered his bone-handled knife when he withdrew it from Watches' sheath and sliced his arm.

Pete snarled, "Strike."

He scrambled across the oily floor, recovering Watches' pistol from the gutter and firing upside down as he ran.

Watches coddled his ears at each ping from bullets cracking pins and metal. He sat and laughed. "Bring me that car, Peter, or they die. They alllllll dieee." Blood spat from his lips. It was the ugliest smile in the darkness.

Pete lunged over the ball return and said, "You can take your offer and shove it up your ass, Watches. I ain't catering to you."

Pete struck the Reset button on the machine. He watched the mechanical arm bash Watches' legs and wipe him away. His body disappeared in the dark.

"Peterrrrrrrrrrrrrrr!" he growled as the mechanical arm swept his chest backward. Watches' red eye was the last thing Pete could see.

Pete took a prone position over his knee, aiming into flickering alleyways and clouds of smoke. Light shimmered off the steel arm. More pins lowered in place. Watches was gone. The arm slithered back into the ceiling; it was nearly dead silent after the machinery set a new target for bowling. Pete's target was missing. Water sprayed from above. The hissing sound was all that was heard. Then a faint cackle arose. "Watches, Watches, Watches, ha!" Jerome winced and titled his head. Wrinkles formed across his brow as he coughed.

Suddenly, each lane sent black balls with little sparklers on one end. One by one, each ball return was sparking through the peep windows at the end of the lanes. Lane one exploded. Pete turned his head and ducked at the same time.

Jerome said, "Pete."

Pete fell across gutters, holding onto Watches' pistol. When he looked at lane one, pins of fire torched the plastic chairs and the computer system. A pin smashed a water fountain mounted to a wall near the arcades. Another pin took out the pinball machine. Glass and sparks shot up the walls. The kids from the arcade machines dispersed.

Jerome suggested, "Let's go, man."

Lane two's ball return exploded. Blue goo dripped from the ceiling tiles overhead as a fluffy gutter bumper melted through the air. The balls shot out of the holder. Balls took apart the ceiling tiles and light fixtures. Another ball busted through the wooden empty shelving. Balls flipped the melted plastic chairs and rolled across the tile floor. More pins fell and rolled across the lanes. Flames roared down the oily floor engulfing chairs, computers, and wooden racks. Television monitors detached from the ceiling and crashed over the tile.

Right after the TVs smashed the floor, lane three's ball return ripped apart. Both monitors smashed the computer system. Daylight poured inside the bowling alley from outside. Ceiling tiles dropped from their brackets and insulation flopped outward. Pete watched the explosions working their way toward them. He squinted at an elderly man sipping whiskey at the counter before a cash register. It seemed as if the old man didn't have a care in the world. More sparking balls continued to drop through each ball return. Shortly after realizing the pattern, lane four gave a brilliant orange glow. He could feel the heat.

Jerome latched onto his shoulder, tugging him out of the daze he was in. Pete tucked the gun inside his trench coat pocket. They wrapped their arms around each other, limping across the wet oily lanes. Lane five streaked behind them in a fiery flash. Junk splashed across the arcade machines. They spun around to see lane six rip to shreds. Lanes seven and eight were almost instantaneous. They jumped lane ten as an inferno of terror flashed across lane nine. They felt the heat on their backsides.

Flames whirled through the gutters on lane ten. An expensive disco ball for lighting effects snapped the rotating bar that held it and smashed through the glass counter near the cash register. The cash drawer rang. Blood dripped from broken glass cabinets. It also took out the shoe racks in a back hall. Shoes spilled across the smashed counter and jumped across the carpeting. It was then that Pete realized the elderly man was crushed.

More lanes were exploding behind them; they kept running. The high-tech lighting across the entire bowling alley's ceiling came crashing to the floor. They ran up the steps past the last lane, lane sixteen. They darted across the main hall. On a backward glance, Pete noticed remaining ball returns seem to grow teeth as they chomped through the flooring in their direction. He shook his head in disbelief while scurrying toward the exit.

Mike and Clarice drove alongside the bike rack. A couple of men were shooting at the entrance; when the shooters spun around, Mike shot each guy from his driver's side window. He parked out front of the doors and walked around his car as Jerome and Pete burst through the busted glass. He let go of Jerome. Mike caught his flailing body. Flames scooped up the awning as the force shoved Pete into his car. Mike flipped backward onto the hood as the awning crashed to the ground and flames blast out the doors and torched the awning. He held tightly onto Jerome. The bowling alley lit up. Clarice rolled to the opposite side of the front seat; the flames brightened her face and cooked her inside.

Mike ran with Jerome to avoid his squad car. Pete had disappeared. Clarice screamed as the car flipped onto its side and slid into other parked cars behind Mike and Jerome. After the explosion receded from the parking lot, Mike ran to his car. With a backward swipe of his nightstick, he destroyed the windshield to help his wife out after the firestorm, seated sideways.

Danny and Duffy felt the tremors in the alleyway. They were surrounded by Watches' men. They were pinned in. Billy rested against the dumpster out of sight. His head hung over his left shoulder as blood ran down his cheeks and dribbled off his chin, soaking the collar of his overcoat. Danny made a break for the Dodge. Bullets snipped at the chicken wire fence as hot rounds followed him. He fell to the ground and rolled toward the Dodge.

All he had to do was open the driver's side door. A few more bullets skipped across the pavement near Duffy; he backed behind the dumpster, waiting for Danny to make his next move. In his mind, he prayed quietly. Billy was coming around as Duffy welcomed him back to reality. Billy slid his pant leg upward as sparks danced around them from bullets. He slid a pistol from an ankle pouch and shot a man jumping around the side of the dumpster. The man fell backward shooting the mesh-wired fence as he died against it.

Duffy's chin dropped a few inches. "Oh, thank God."

Billy nodded. "You're welcome, Duff."

"You had a gun on you this whole time?"

"I have five more."

Once inside the Dodge, Danny knew he would have been in control. Duffy gave a backward glance to notice him struggling for the door handle; rounds sparked across the hood. Duffy squinted, anticipating Danny being shot. White threads tapped Duffy's shoulder where it draped downward from the lip of the dumpster; he tugged on it and more rope unwound from the receptacle. It appeared to have been one continuous length of rope. These ropes were part of the bumper bowling. They were attached to the rubber. When a shredded end popped out the side, he realized it had been trashed due to frays. Otherwise, it was a perfectly good rope.

Danny dropped to the ground as a man standing near the hood ordered him to do so. He told him to lie down and place his hands over his head. Two more men were shooting at Mike and Clarice as they took cover behind cars. Another man lifted his aim toward the dumpster. Danny surrendered. He knelt before the driver's door. There were no other options staring down the smoking barrels. One man demanded, "You. Out from behind the dumpster or your friend here gets it." He swung the weapon, aiming at Danny's head.

A spiraling line flew from behind the dumpster. The loop wrapped around his muzzle. It tightened against the stock, leaving zero slack; Duffy yanked his weapon from his hands. With a moment of disbelief, he stood with his fingers webbed outward. Danny peeked out of the corner of his eyes; the man's weapon bounced toward the dumpster.

Another lasso whirled out and wrapped the other two guy's waists. It cinched them; they sandwiched together. The rope whipped backward; both of them flung into the side of the dumpster. The impact bumped Billy's body forward. Danny looked at the man who stood over him. He twirled around and tripped him. Another twirl allowed him to kick the man's face after he lifted his head from the pavement. The man held onto his face and backed away as Danny flipped onto his feet.

When the man sat up, Duffy used the other end of the rope to lasso him with. Danny jumped inside the Dodge as a few men shot at him from the other end of the fence line. Lead bullets flattened over the bulletproofing. The car's engine fired a fantastic roar. The Uzi's under the grills rotated and shot back. Although instead of killing them, Danny used the pinpoint accuracy of the targeting system on the monitor, he shot the weapons out of their hands. With the crosshairs, he took out each man with shots to their legs and shoulders.

Duffy felt confident about Danny's control over the situation and stepped out from behind the dumpster. He ran and twisted one man's body around, giving each end of the rope a good tug. The two men tied to the other end flipped sideways. Duffy sprinted between them; he released the rope around the driver's mirror on the Dodge.

Danny revved the engine and reversed into a few men. They folded across the trunk; a blue light flashed on their bodies as the intruder prevention system kicked in. The men were glued to the car as the electrical waves held them in place.

The solo dude tied in a noose stood up; Duffy spun around, stepped on the slack hanging from the mirror; it yanked him forward. The man flew toward Duffy. He kneed his face. With quick loops, he wrapped the loose rope around his neck a couple of times and pulled the rope tightly to choke him. The fibrous rope gouged into his neck; he punched him in the face until his body went limber. He wrapped the slack around his shoulder and yanked on it; he pulled the man over his back; the rope unraveled from his neck as the man dropped to the pavement.

The other two guys (lassoed together) stood up, working at the rope tight around their waists. They struggled to break free from the noose. Duffy noticed them. He wrapped more slack around the driver's side mirror.

Danny spun the rear tires on the pavement as the car drove forward. The two men shared a quick glance at one another before they skidded across the pavement and collided with the solo dude who was trying to stand. The intrusion detection system shut off. Danny mashed the brakes. The guys held by the electrical current flipped over the windshield, soared across the hood, and crashed into the fence.

He brought the shifter into drive and turned the steering wheel. He floored the gas pedal, driving around a small group of men. The rope on the mirror stretched as the guys slid several feet across the pavement. Danny drove around the group once more; the stretched rope kinked their stomachs and dropped everyone to the ground.

A few guys crawled in circles. The driver's side door swung open and bashed one man in the forehead. Duffy charged a couple of other guys as they tried to stand from the pile of men. Danny jumped out of the car and kicked the guy he hit with the door. His foot jammed his jaw, his teeth sprinkling to the pavement; he flipped over another man. Danny tugged the thighs of his next victim and flipped him backward. His head bashed into the side of the Bratmobile. Duffy jumped Danny and kicked two men in the face as they tried to stand.

One man bear-hugged Duffy and squeezed; Duffy's feet left the pavement as the man leaned back. Duffy kicked at his kneecaps. They both collapsed to the ground, but the man continued restraining Duffy's body. He reached over his head and tugged at the rope that kinked under the car's tires. It wrapped around the man's neck and released it. The rope snapped over his jaw and choked him as he lay beneath the car. The man's tongue hung out as he grasped the rope around his neck. Duffy punched his reddening face.

Bullets streamed through the alley; one man retrieved a weapon and shot at them. He shot a couple of his men in the process but missed Danny and Duffy. They dropped behind the Dodge. A couple of bullets were fired from the dumpster and seized the man's chest. He fell and bounced across the ground. Danny and Duffy stood behind the car. Another man lifted a weapon from the pavement and Mike shot him around the corner of the bowling alley. He strode around the building with the barrel of his pistol smoking.

"Danny? Duffy? What the hell is this?"

Duffy smiled. "Hi, Mr. Anglekee."

Billy panted for air, falling against the dumpster with a grunt. Mike held his handgun out and approached them. He stopped when he realized a bunch of men tied up. Watches' men were defeated. He tucked his gun into his holster. A few cops charged into the alley, plucking Watches' men away from the Dodge. Mike ordered other cops to secure the perimeter.

"This car was impounded," Mike shouted while pointing at the Dodge.

"No, Dad."

Duffy smiled. "The car you had impounded was very similar, sir."

Mike strode to it as cops carried a few men out of the alley. He sighed. "No, I'm pretty sure this is the car."

Billy screamed, "Where's Pete Carson?"

Mike snapped his head toward the dumpsters and squinted when he noticed his other son. He wondered, "Billy?"

"Dad, we need to talk. It's about Jake Carson."

"What are you doing here?"

Danny and Duffy followed Billy as he headed farther into the parking lot. "Dad, we really need to talk."

From inside a squad car, Clarice heard shouting. The smoke was thick. She had no idea her sons were involved in this fiasco. Her eyes lurched across the dash. Suddenly, a hand clamped her throat. Her head was yanked back, tightly to the headrest; a muffled scream trapped inside the car. Watches sat in the rear seat, holding her throat. He smiled. "Your whole family's falling apart, Mrs. Anglekee."

In the rearview mirror, she saw him lean forward from the shadows. Her eyes widened when she noticed it was her old postman. Of course, she knew who he was. He released her neck as his other hand-wound her hair inside his balled fist, maintaining pressure to keep her head tight to the headrest. A knife blade gently slid across her neck. Watches watched Danny and Duffy walk out of the alleyway. Firefighters sprayed the bowling alley, and smoke billowed between parked cars. Smoke filled the entire parking lot, drastically reducing visibility.

Danny proclaimed, "Dad, I can explain."

Mike completely ignored him. He turned around; his two sons disappeared in the smoke. The dark clouds hid them from view. Billy threw Danny against a car in the parking lot. He screamed, "Where's Pete?"

"Why?"

"He made a deal with the devil and killed Wesley."

"Calm down, bro," Danny sighed. "You need to chill, man."

Billy lifted a pistol; he aimed at his brother. Danny's eyes widened. Billy exclaimed, "Watches is around here and you're telling me to chill. Pete accepted his bribe; I need to take him in. He's not anyone's friend anymore, Danny—unless you're in on it too? I won't hesitate to take you either."

Danny jumped off the hood of the vehicle and screamed, "Oh what, are you gonna shoot me now? Your own brother!"

Mike told Penski to hold back as he jogged toward his sons' voices. The argument grew louder as he moved through the smoke. Billy heard a car door slam. Bodies moved past the vehicle. Watches dragged their mother as she screamed. Mike hollered for her. Danny noticed his mother trailing Watches by a handful of hair.

"Mommmm," Danny screamed.

Billy leaned over his brother and shot his mother's shoulder. The bullet had gone through Clarice and buried into Watches calf. She cried out in anguish. Watches slit Clarice's chin as he fell into the thick smoke, releasing her. Mike screamed. Clarice rolled into a bike rack. Danny dropped to the ground and wrapped his arms around his mom. She was bleeding from her shoulder.

Skeptic about his son's shot, Mike knelt next to his wife; Watches was nowhere to be seen, but what was seen was his wife, bleeding out. Danny stood behind her. Billy gazed at them in a trance; he had shot his own mother. Danny kept staring at his brother; the questions inside seemed to scorch his soul. What Billy had done was saved his mother from being taken by a devil.

Billy hollered, "Come out, Watches. Face me, you one-eyed freak."

Watches' whisper returned like a sassy schoolgirl, "You're in trouble."

Mike inspected the shoulder wound. "Danny, take your mother to that car, now." He ordered him. Duffy joined him as they walked his mother to the squad car.

Mike stripped the gun from Billy's firm grip. He disassembled it and placed the different pieces in different pockets on Billy's overcoat. He dumped the extra rounds, placing the empty clip into his palm. "As for you, I wouldn't go very far. You're on a slippery slope, boy."

Billy's eyes narrowed. He glanced at Danny and Duffy helping his mother inside the car. He asked, "You disowning me, dad?"

"Why you're down here is beyond me, son. Go back to Little Rapids, Billy. This isn't your district. You aren't here under my authority so what are you doing here? Whatever spell you're under, Sheriff Dunfri has you brainwashed. You have no good intentions for being here, boy."

"Dad, we need to talk about Jake and Pete Carson."

"You just shot your own mother," Mike stated and then screamed, "My wife! And you aimed your gun at your brother!"

Billy's eyes widened; his jaw dropped. He remembered the last time his dad yelled at him on the sandy shores of Upham Woods.

"You have separated yourself from this family; I don't even know you anymore."

"But dad?"

Mike was about to walk away when he snarled, "No son of mine dares to point any weapon at any member of this family. Have you got that?"

"Dad . . ."

"Have you got that?"

He sighed. "Yeah, yeah, I've got that! I've gotten your bullshit my whole life. Danny and I have tried to tell you so much, but you never listen. That's your problem."

Mike ignored him and walked away. He climbed inside the driver's seat. The window dropped down; he leaned out, "Go find yourself first, Billy. Then maybe I will listen. Keep mindful around Sheriff Dunfri—you hear me? Be mindful of Little Rapids and what's going on there. This is why I inserted you into that town."

Billy squinted; it was true. His father talked him into joining Sheriff Dunfri's unit. Billy stepped forward to pound on the glass after his father rolled up the window. Mike drove away. Billy was left standing alone, confused, in smoke.

Chapter Eighteen

The Talk

Another vehicle's engine roared. Smoke kept it hidden from view until it zipped alongside Billy. Billy shook his head. The smoke cleared. He pulled yet another pistol out of a sling over his shoulders. He aimed at the driver through the passenger's side window. It was Pete. During the commotion, he retrieved the Bratmobile. He cranked the window down and asked, "Could you please just hear me out, Billy?"

"Why should I, Pete? I know what you and your dad were offered."

"Get in, Billy," Pete sighed.

Billy didn't take his aim away from him. He opened the door and sat inside the car. Pete lit a cigarette. The Armybrats' car quietly breezed away from the scene. Pete blew smoke so it guided out the window.

"You don't mind if I smoke, do you?"

"No."

"Want one?" he asked, holding the pack.

Billy shook his head. He questioned, "OK, Pete. You brought me here to talk, so let's talk. What's the bribe?"

Pete flicked ash out the window. He asked, "Billy, do you trust me?"

"I'm not so sure anymore, Pete. There was a time when I thought I did."

"Well, you have to trust me on this one. I would never hurt a friend."

"OK, then explain Wesley. You sold him out, didn't you?" Billy snapped, "You son of a bitch!"

Pete drove into the school forest and parked in the gully. It was the same gully where they built their hut a long time ago. Trust wasn't an issue. Communication seemed to be a bigger problem. They were older; the pressures were on. Watches had his claws in everyone. Who knew who could have been trusted? Pete jumped out of the car pacing in circles.

Billy shook his head and climbed out. He said, "Explain, Pete."

"I loved Wesley."

"Then why's he dead?"

"I loved him like a brother. And he will always be one of my friends, just like the rest of the Armybrats."

"Why's he dead, Peter?"

"Billy, I think you should think really hard about where you live."

"Don't change the subject."

"No, we'll get to that, but right now, I want you to explain something to me. If you can't explain it, then I want you to think really hard about it. In Little Rapids, what do you see?"

"What do you mean?"

"What I mean is, in Verona, people are driving station wagons and cutting food coupons to feed their families."

Billy shook his head with confusion. "OK? What's your point? What's with the rhetorical questions, man?"

"What do you see in Little Rapids that you don't see in Verona?"

"I don't know—railroads, bus stops, grocery stores in gas stations. I am not understanding where you're going with this, Pete."

"Well, those aren't gas stations. Those are convenience stores. You're too involved with the actuality of it all."

Billy stopped holding his weapon toward Pete. He lowered it and turned around as a few squirrels ran in circles and wound up a tree trunk. Words are nothing without meaning. Pete had meaning behind his words; he wanted to hear it from Billy. Although Billy may have been speechless and stuck in a rut since he hadn't moved an inch. He whispered, "There are a lot of nice cars."

"Yes, nice cars—Mercedes, Jaguars, and sports cars." He rolled his eyes toward Billy and sighed. "Oh my."

Billy whispered, "And a lot of newer homes."

"Newer homes," Pete smiled. "$380,000, $400,000. How much was your home, Billy?"

Billy glanced at him. He sighed. "I don't know; it was given to me."

"Are you hearing yourself right now?"

"OK, Pete." Billy sighed. "Enough, I think I get it."

"Try half a mill on up. Ah, and the closest jobs around there pay on average what would you say per hour?"

"OK, Pete."

"I swear, man. That entire town is in on it."

Billy nodded. He tilted the handgun he was holding and noticed the inscription on the side. The manufacturer was a well-known gun designer. Dressed in an expensive leather vest and a gun belt with weaponry the police force in Verona could only wish for, he could sense Pete's truth behind his words. The truth was Little Rapids was built on lies and distrust. There were drugs in town on almost every street corner. Someone was in control of the town; it sure wasn't the mayor. Who was in control? Billy was in the hierarchy of the chain, but in the mix with none other than Watches' men.

Pete proclaimed, "Now, the real reason why you're after me is because of Sheriff Dunfri. He ordered you to arrest me based on . . . evidence . . . which either he or his lackeys concocted."

Billy nodded and sighed. "He did."

Pete smiled.

"All right, Pete. It's my turn to question."

"Shoot!"

"What happened between you and Wesley?"

Pete cried, "You don't want to know."

"I wouldn't have questioned you if I didn't want to know. So, are you going to make me restate the question?"

"No, Billy. Why can't you just trust me?"

"You are a witness. You can tell me."

"I need your help, Billy. I am going to leave you the keys for the Armybrats' car; there is something I have to take care of. But you two have to give me time. I know about your partner. You guys stay off my back."

"What do you mean? What partner?"

"Don't play coy."

"They arrested Mr. Fifer and threw him in jail under suspicion for his grandson's murder."

"That's a ploy. They're weeding us out because they told you to come after me."

"Don't put words in my mouth, Pete."

"It's true though, isn't it?"

"Pete, I am the one asking you questions."

"Who investigated the scene—you or the sheriff?"

"Pete, answer my question first."

"Fine, I was there when he was killed all right. I accepted a bribe to keep my mom from dying," Pete cried. "I made a deal with the devil."

"The deal was to bring him this car, wasn't it?"

"But I'm not. The keys are in the ignition. I'm leaving it with you. It has a job to do."

Billy squinted.

"The deal was to bring him this car. At the time, I had no idea what the Armybrats' car even was."

"You sold out Wesley."

"Billy, we have been through this. I had no idea he was in that box."

Billy stared at him.

"His dad is being held hostage."

"Who is?" Billy sighed.

"Mr. Fifer is locked up in one of those steel carts on wheels and you know what they're doing to him."

"What? No, he's in jail."

"No, Billy." Pete smiled. "They're breaking him down, Billy. He's got his riches buried in the hills and only he knows where the pot of gold is. He's not in jail, Billy. Check on the school; the conservation trip was never canceled. Mr. Fifer is reporting to Principal Malone that the camp is all clear. It's a trap."

"What happened, Pete?"

"Sheriff Dunfri was beating Mr. Fifer."

"No!" Billy hollered. "No way! Sheriff Dunfri?" He walked closer to the tree line and stood with his hands on his hips, staring into the sky. He pointed at him and said, "I will not listen to this."

"Believe it, Billy. The whole town has a secret."

He whispered, "Fuck you, Pete!"

"You too," Pete replied sarcastically.

"I'm in it, so why can't I see it?"

"Cuz they only let you see what they want you to see."

"Oh, come on . . ."

"And your crooked boss's best friend," Pete said, "is Watches."

"Oh, hell no . . ."

"Hell yeah."

"So, your dad talked to the sheriff?"

"Yes, we were looking for mom."

"What happened?"

"I'm not sure, Billy. I thought you already knew what happened."

"If I had known this prior to going into work last week, I would have been more stressed out than I already am. What happened?"

"You'd have to ask my dad. John Dunfri pulled him into some office in the mill and had a talk with him. I haven't seen Mr. Fifer since our last visit which was that particular day that dad was harassed." Pete lit another cigarette, and his hand violently shook. "Dad barged from that room, dragged me away, and told me I wasn't to go back. The next thing I knew, we were out of there. Dad told me not to discuss this with anyone."

"What happened?"

"I can't say, Billy. I don't know."

Billy yanked Pete by the shirt collar and threw him against the Armybrats' car. A cool circular muzzle pressed Pete's nose upward. Billy wanted answers. Buts, ands, ifs, or I don't know weren't gonna cut it. The conversation needed meaning behind the words. Pete was either too afraid to tell, or the bribe given to him from Watches was still in effect; he didn't want to give away his secret at the risk of his own mother's death.

Pete snarled, "Go ahead. Shoot."

Billy held a look of disgust, contemplating what he had to do.

Pete clenched Billy's arm and spun him around. He slammed his wrist onto the roof of the car just above the opened driver's side window. Continuing to slam his wrist, he freed the weapon; it slid across the hood and fell on the opposite side of the car. He squeezed Billy's neck and sighed. "Don't forget to check the trunk." He tossed Billy's head, so his face collided with the door frame. Billy fell backward, unconscious. Pete cried, "Damn it, Billy. Why do you got to be so stubborn, huh?" He threw his arms in the air, walking away.

* * *

Billy walked a sidewalk through downtown Verona. He could hear the ruffles from the creases in his dress pants. The police uniform he wore was crisp. Even though his dad warned him to stay away from Verona, he couldn't. He did the exact opposite. He hung around more often. A little old woman was whistling and screaming from behind, "Excuse me, officer? Officer! Excuse me?"

As he walked toward the church, he turned around to notice a little elderly woman with gray hair. He noticed Father O'Brien standing on the front stoop. He stopped and asked, "How may I serve you, miss?"

The elderly woman griped, "Yes, I've gotten this package in the mail. This will be the third time now. I've written the company, but I've gotten no response. It said it was a free gift, but I really don't want it. It's not mine to keep."

"What is it?"

"A cuckoo clock," she moaned. "A gift from the clock manufacturing company called Watches."

Billy dropped his smile altogether. He placed his hands on her shoulders and asked, "Where is this cuckoo clock right now, ma'am?"

"Well, it's in my house." She smiled. "Everyone's been getting 'em. My neighbors, Douglas and Francine, they got one. My daughter, Maria, got one. The handsome couple across the street, Todd and Shirley, got one too. My neighbors out back, Jim and—"

"OK, OK, I get the picture. I must see this clock," Billy advised.

"Oh sure, it's right this way, Officer."

They walked toward her house. He put his arm around her shoulders as they walked. She was shorter so her hand ended up on his butt. Billy dipped his head with a goofy gesture. He glanced at her and smiled. "So, who delivered these packages?"

"The UPS man delivered the clocks," she stated and pointed. "See." Her voice changed when she pointed at a UPS truck driving away. Her voice had a low tone. He spun around; she was now holding onto his arm. Her grip was tighter; her face was different. She ripped off a wig and sunglasses. One eye had a patch covering it; it was Watches. He cackled.

Billy struggled, but the hold was too tight. Watches whipped Billy around until he was on his knees. He cackled and laughed. "Ticktock, it's all about the clock. The time is near; there's someone on the pier. Can you feel the heat? Tied up, thrown down, the world will rock all around. When the world will rock, it will be because of a clock, poor boy on the dock."

"What have you done, Watches?"

"Watches, Watches, Watches."

Billy screamed and tugged from his firm grip. "Let me go. Let me out of here."

One by one, the houses along the block exploded. Every home with a free cuckoo clock pieced through the sky. Some packages were left on porches, some were near garages, and others were mounted on the walls of the homes that blazed in the sky. With cuckoo clocks in cars, the explosions shredded driveways. The charges detonated; the clocks annihilated homes. Whatever time it was, wherever the packages were, Watches made sure everyone was on his time.

"Let me out of here. Let me go, Watches. Let me out of here."

* * *

Billy groaned, balled a fist, and squished a clump of dirt. He crawled out of his little nightmare during his unconsciousness.

"Let me out of here," a muffled voice rattled.

Billy snapped out of it. He was in a chaotic trance from the exploding cuckoo clocks. The bomb threats were his day nightmare. He rolled onto his butt from the forest floor. Twigs stuck to his shirt as he glanced at the Armybrats' car. It shook a little as someone continued to scream. Repetitively, the person asked to be let out followed by a series of banging. Billy tried to stand and held onto his head. A migraine had set in.

He leaned through the driver's side window. Sure enough, the keys were in the ignition like Pete had said. He pulled them out and headed toward the rear of the car. The pounding noise grew louder; whoever was pounding was locked inside the trunk. Billy unlocked it; Jerome lunged at him. Billy shrieked and jumped away.

Billy smiled. "How did you get in there, partner?"

"Why don't ya ask Pete, Partner?" He smiled. "He's out there, brotha, like Looney Tunes out there."

"He figured you out."

Jerome nodded.

"He said the conservation trip is still happening."

"It is. He's telling the truth."

"Stay in it."

Jerome nodded.

Chapter Nineteen

Funeral

Families were grieving next to the rectangular slice from the earth. Danny stood near the priest. Words of life, love, and the lord spilled out through the power of prayer. The procession ended near the church. The pallbearers wore sunglasses, standing on either side of the casket, perfect rows of men in gray suits. One girl, Jackson's sister, comforted their mom.

"No sign of Pete." Jerome tugged at his lapel, speaking into it.

Billy stood in the opposite end behind the priest. He was closer to the church, standing at the edge of the parking lot. Verona police controlled traffic for the procession. Their flashers were still flickering in people's sunglasses, yet no sirens. They had finally let the traffic continue. Winds hit the trees but the solemn voice that echoed came from the priest, Father O'Brien. An apprentice stood on his left, wearing a brown robe; a hood shadowed his face. A silver chain hung from his neck bearing the cross.

"Jerome, there's no way he would miss Jackson's funeral. His dad's even here."

"I know. I got eyes on him."

"Just keep an eye on that tree line; I'm watching the main road and the lot. If you wanna sweep the trees one more time, go for it."

Jerome glanced over his shoulder; squirrels gave chase up a tree. He repositioned himself near the trunk; squirrels chirped and jumped away. Jerome noticed a man standing solo at the other end; the man wore a trench coat, blocked by the many trees. He weaved through them, advancing toward him.

Billy watched a car enter the lot. He monitored the windshield, waiting for the glare to clear as the car neared him. Billy said, "You got anything?"

"I'm not sure yet," Jerome responded from the north side, thirty feet from the solo man whose trench waved in the winds. He darted inside the south edge of the tree line; the man wasn't visible. He looped around the other end to find no one. It appeared as though the man had passed through a tree.

The priest was finalizing a prayer. A moment of silence from the gravesite, filled with cries and sniffles as the casket began its descent into its final resting spot. The priest's apprentice traced the cross over his chest. A man clung to his wife as she nearly fell inside the hole, collapsing to her knees.

Jake Carson turned toward the parking lot; other folks were already leaving. Others remained at the gravesite. Father O'Brien's reflection was in the car window. He stood directly behind Billy. Billy noticed the driver in the car was a female and spun around to see the priest was nowhere behind him. He lost sight of Jerome through the crowd. He pranced sideways to catch glimpses between moving bodies.

Jerome stopped short of the last tree and glanced in the other direction at what appeared to be a floating gravestone. He squinted and lowered his sunglasses. Instead of a floating headstone, a cat prominently itched its back near the base. He smirked after realizing it was only a cat. The cat perked up; its tail sharply arched backward. The cat snarled. It almost seemed to be hissing, but he couldn't hear it. Jerome figured the crowds spooked the cat.

A body was on the ground near the church parking lot, and a girl continued to shriek. Jerome glanced away to notice a scuffle in the distance. After whipping his head back in the direction of the cat, he watched the cat dart headfirst into the headstone.

"What the . . ." Jerome witnessed an oddity and felt compelled to investigate.

Behind him, Mr. Crendal, Jackson's father, had punched Jake; he had fallen to the ground. Jake wiped grass from his suitcoat; he stared at him in bewilderment. Mrs. Crendal was tugging at her husband's sleeve.

"Tim," Jake said.

"Where's your boy, Jake?"

The priest and his apprentice passed Billy. Billy watched the priest pass by without eye contact. He moved around the priest to watch Tim Crendal encroach upon Jake. The tension was real! Jerome continued stepping through the gravesite with caution.

"I beg your pardon, Tim."

"What? He's too good for my boy's funeral?" Tim asked, "It was your son's car, wasn't it?"

Mike Anglekee helped Jake up and said, "OK, this is a time for mourning and not accusation, Tim."

"It was Peter Carson's car that killed our boy."

Mr. Anglekee stared into his bloodshot eyes. His words were a bit slurred.

Jerome knelt before the stone and gave it a good thump with his knuckle. It was one solid piece of granite. The cat was nowhere; it wasn't behind it. No mysterious hole in the ground swallowed the cat.

A quarrel broke out in a pile of undergrowth; two critters tussled, crinkling leaves. Jerome withdrew his pistol. From afar, Billy witnessed him flaunt his gun. Perhaps he found Pete. W*hy the gun?* He thought. All hope yielded after the scornful glare from his father.

The priest headed toward the church while his apprentice stopped midway through the parking lot. His hands were steepled. Still, Billy couldn't see his face, but his main concern was his partner. Mrs. Anglekee placed a hand on Mike's shoulder; her other arm remained in a cast. Danny stood to her right. Tim threw a punch in Danny's father's direction; Danny jump kicked his arm. Tim fell, pulling his wife with him. Jake continued to walk toward the parking lot.

Once again, Tim scrambled to his feet and darted after Jake. His foot drew back. Jake was in tears; the blame was falling on his boy. It was his son's car that killed Jackson. Tim's foot connected with Jake's gut. He flipped onto the pavement. The priest's apprentice remained in the parking lot; his head was low, facial features were unrecognizable. Father O'Brien stood at the base of the steps leading to a rear entrance, befuddled.

Tim was positioning for another strike on poor Jake Carson. Suddenly, his leg swept away as Danny performed a sliding maneuver that dropped Mr. Crendal. He flipped backward and rolled away from the lot. Out of nowhere, two pallbearers charged Danny. Danny kicked outward and dropped each man by kicking their legs as they approached him. They both hit the ground next to him; he chopped at their throats and rolled away from them. Duffy dropped two more pallbearers enclosing on Danny; he followed Danny to the parking lot. Billy noticed Father O'Brien's body seemed to disappear from the corner of his eyes. Billy glanced toward a few pines near the rear entrance of the church. His eyes shifted in search of the priest. He cocked his head in confusion.

Jerome approached two dead squirrels. He glanced upward as a twig fell before his face. Prowling over a limb, the cat reappeared; it arched its back. It only had one eye. Jerome stepped about to get a better view of the cat, aiming skyward. A smaller headstone tripped him. His head nailed another marker where the cat walked into earlier. His pistol bounced away from him. He winced, holding onto his head and scattered leaves to locate his gun. Dirty toes were before his nose. When he rolled onto his back, he found himself staring into his pistol.

Jerome sighed, "Father."

"Such a primitive weapon for a funeral, son. What were you gonna shoot with it—the dead?" Father O'Brien stood before him, holding onto his pistol.

"No, father." Jerome smiled and crawled to his knees.

Jerome heard tension on the trigger. His eyes jumped a bit. The priest articulated. "I do not know you."

Danny defended himself from Jackson's relatives. His father stood on the sidelines, attempting to stop the violence.

Out of nowhere, Mr. Crendal tackled Jake to the pavement. He pointed at him and condemned, "That bomb was meant for your boy, not ours." Then he stood up and kicked Jake's gut.

Danny ran around the Armybrats' car and hollered at a pallbearer, "Whoa, Steve. Back off!" Both boys approached the Armybrats' car, rubbing at their necks.

Duffy opened the passenger door as Danny climbed into the driver's side.

Jake looked at Mr. Crendal. "It was a bomb, Tim. It's nobody's fault except the one who planted it."

Mike and Jake stood on the pavement.

Dust waved around Jake as the Armybrats' car shook pebbles. A fancy glow wrapped around the base. Pallbearers lunged at the doors; the electrical current guarded the Armybrats like an angel. They sparked from the surges. The car roared like mad and lifted from the pavement. Mike backed away; Clarice tightened her grip on his shoulder, noticing its capabilities for the first time.

Jake smiled. "Isn't that slick, Mike?"

"What the hell is it?" Mike sighed.

Billy tilted his head in amazement. The electrical current held the pallbearers in place. Billy struggled to stand as flames curled from the boosters beneath the car. The Bratmobile climbed about ten feet above the funeral-goers; the families scattered to avoid debris and heat from the thrusters. They flew along the berm past Jake and Mike.

Mr. Crendal ignored what everyone else was admiring. Danny flew backward and released the Intrusion Detector. All pallbearers detached from the car and crushed Tim Crendal through a pine tree. The entire Crendal family stared at the car with intrigue. The family of the deceased victim stared skyward. "Armybrats" lit up along the doors. Tingles bore down in the deepest places people never wanted to discuss. Danny flew toward highway sixty-nine and shut off the hyper-glide system. The wheels retracted; they landed on the road.

Mike pointed at Billy. "Follow me."

The apprentice lifted his head in amazement. His fingers remained steeped. The reflection of the intrusion detection system was flashing in his sunglasses. The man lifted the cloak and squinted. It wasn't an apprentice after all; it was Pete. He watched the Bratmobile leave the lot and turned toward the Crendal family. He was as amazed as they were at the Armybrats' car.

Billy nodded and ran after his father. His squad car was on the end of the lot. The funeral was over, but the preaching was about to begin;

Mike wanted that car. He jumped inside the driver's seat. Billy climbed into the passenger seat. Flashers twirled, and lights made headstones scenic glares. Danny kept a keen eye at the rearview mirror; he noticed the squad car streaming out of the church lot. His head whipped around.

Mike exclaimed, "Shoot the rear tire!"

Billy cranked the window, wrapped an arm out, and shot the tire. Naturally, the tire blew. Uncontrollably, Danny swerved. A light was flashing over the dash; it appeared to be a picture of a tire. Duffy tapped it. Danny jerked the car away from almost self-correcting into a ditch, the rear tire auto inflated. The vehicle caught the hardtop; the chase carried on.

Billy retracted through the window and glanced at his dad. "I shot it."

Mike nodded and shifted gears, peeling highway debris from the surface along with tire particles. Jerome ran to his car and tore out of the church's parking lot. He followed them. Mike drove over the hill and swerved to the side of the road. Jerome stopped behind them.

Mike stared at the empty highway ahead. "Where the hell did they go?"

Billy's eyes rolled upward. He was scanning the sky. "I'm not sure, dad. But that car is pretty cool."

"Cool or not, we have no idea what that car is capable of. I need it impounded. If you get to them first, I want to be the first to know about it."

Jerome stepped out of his car and leaned against his door. Billy nodded at his father when he noticed Jerome. "OK, dad. I'll bring the car in." He jumped out of the squad car.

"OK, Billy. Take it immediately to the impound lot and have it crushed into a tiny little cube. Got it? Let me know when it's done so that I can inform your boss. He actually has been on my case about getting this tank destroyed once and for all."

His dad implied Sheriff Dunfri wanted the Armybrats' car demolished. Billy nodded. He squinted as his dad's squad car whipped a shitty and headed into town. He glanced in Jerome's direction.

"Why would our boss want the Armybrats' car destroyed?"

Between houses, the Bratmobile hovered. Duffy glanced out the passenger window as a woman spilled a coffee cup across her deck. A little girl carrying a doll waved at him. Duffy gave an odd smile and waved back. The girl's mother seemed to be in a trance of sorts.

Chapter Twenty

Billy's Decision

The following morning, the senior class grouped in the high school gymnasium. Wooden bleachers hugged the walls; they remained collapsed. Taped to the backside of the bleachers were papers with alphabetical lettering. Students gathered in their appropriate stations. All they had to do was look for the first letter in their last names, letters *A* through *F* on the left and *G* through L. On the other side were *M* through *R,* and the remaining *S* through *Z* was hanging beyond that. Of course, one kid in school held the last name of Zimmerman.

Students stood in gaggles before the signs, their bags scattered at their feet. Two adults stood within each group. They were the chaperones. Naturally, Mrs. Anglekee was involved in the school function. She was in charge of *S* through *Z*. All Danny could think was thank goodness for that.

School buses lined up at 6:30 a.m. The school was not in session, but the entire senior class assembled for their conservation trip. By 7:15 a.m., the buses were leaving, scheduled for Upham Woods Campground. Whether one hundred percent of the seniors were there or not, if people weren't there for the count, then they simply weren't included in the three-day adventure. Of course, there would have been repercussions for missing the event. Classes for those who stayed behind would carry on.

Sam Baxter and Shawn Baker kept to themselves ever since being stuffed into dumpsters. Their moms were there. Sam's mom was a chaperone of A through F. Shawn's mom chaperoned M through Z with Danny's mom. Sam and Shawn had a taste of the devil's plea. Their grudges with the Armybrats were enabled by their true tormentor, Watches; they were in the same group as the Armybrats. Of course, there was only Danny and Duffy. Billy had graduated, and Pete was absent without leave. Jerome stood in a corner.

"He's not here," Jerome whispered into a headset.

Duffy asked Danny, "Where's Pete?"

Danny shrugged, "I have no idea. But I think giving my brother the Armybrats' car was a huge mistake."

Meanwhile, on the outskirts of Verona was a little junkyard called Rowley's. Billy listened to cars thrashed in a compactor. A heavyset man dressed in dirty blue overalls approached him. He stopped within a foot from him, almost bumping into him with his belly. "I'll give ya fifty dollars for her."

Billy was in his own world. The junkyard dealer wanted the Dodge. Of course, Billy thought about what Pete told him the other night. And he thought of what his dad said yesterday. His preserved thoughts ate at him; his cell phone buzzed. The heavyset man was pressing the issue about purchasing the Bratmobile. Billy spun away to listen to his phone. "I thought that trip was canceled."

He hung up and walked away from the junkyard dealer. The man pointed at him and hollered, "Hey, what about the sale, man?"

Billy looked at him. He hesitated for a moment, looked at his phone, and then at the junkyard dealer. "I'm sorry, mister, but this car isn't worth the piss stains in your shorts."

"Hey, seventy-five dollars then . . ."

Billy opened the door and stood over the hood. "The car's not for sale. I think it has one more job to do yet." Billy felt a strange kink in his forearm and rubbed at it. He itched for a bit.

"Who said I was buying?" The big man smirked. "Huh boy?" He mashed a red button on a gray box hung from a yellow pole near the trailer entrance. Beeping sounded through the compound. Billy snapped his head toward the gate while itching at his forearm; the chain-link fence closed. The man snapped his fingers at a crane operator named Frank.

The mechanical boom started hissing as the magnet swung from a chain. Three guys approached Billy. He spun around. "What are you going to do—jack my car?"

"Get in the car, son." One of the men demanded.

Billy stepped around the opened door and approached him. He asked, "And if I don't?"

"Either way, the car's getting crushed—with you in it."

Billy's eyes widened. Without a blink, he wrapped his arm around his neck and threw him face-first into the car. The other two guys sandwiched Billy in their burly arms. Outweighed by at least six times his weight, Billy was refrained from moving. As one man stood up, he noticed blood trickling across the windowpane; he could see Billy in the reflection between the webs of blood as the other two men restrained him. Knuckles rolled his liver around. All stomach components shifted as this man punched the daylights out of him. His wallet fell from his pocket; his badge flipped open. One man picked it up.

"Oh look, boss. We got ourselves a pig."

"Hey, let's do this quickly and quietly. Sheriff Dunfri wants no evidence."

Billy heard it but could not believe it. They dragged him to the Dodge and tossed him inside. Slamming the door, they stepped away as the boom magnetized to the roof of the car. Billy rolled off the seat as the car lifted from the ground, gasping for air. The heavyset owner of the junkyard directed the boom operator. The other three men walked alongside the machine to watch; they laughed as the car carried toward the compactor.

The rear window rolled down. Billy stuck his head out and shot at the boom operator. The operator ducked. Their heavyset boss screamed at him, "Drop that little bastard!" The car was swaying above the compactor as the boom operator bumped the lever a little (avoiding gunfire). The car was still idling. Billy shot the boss. He flopped onto his back and landed on a pile of automobile doors. The boom operator leaned out the side drawing a shotgun to his shoulder. Billy hopped the seat as the blast nailed the rear window. Nothing penetrated the vehicle, but the car rocked outward, still suspended from a stretched chain.

Billy threw his seatbelt on, reviewing the dashboard for anything useful. The Intrusion Detection button was glowing; he glanced at the boom operator, reloading the shotgun. Billy pressed the button. Electricity took the path of least resistance; given a minute of current, the crane operator was on fire. He was violently shaking against the door. The men on the ground were hollering for the guy to drop Billy into the compactor. One guy ran to the boom to assist the operator; he got caught in a lightning storm as electricity flashed across the side of the crane. While latched onto the side, his body wiggled next to the wheel hub.

Billy glanced upward at the glowing chain. The electrical field had generated so much heat the magnet was glowing red. It had fed the fire near the operator. Before Billy realized it, the car had commenced a circular rotation. The tires adjusted horizontally as the thrusters kicked on; the car entered hover mode. The amount of force Billy bestowed upon the chain crippled the magnetic field, causing the colossal magnet to detach from the roof. Swinging upward, the chain snapped at its reddest point followed by sparks; the glowing magnet soared into their boss. Metal crinkled below him; glass shattered upon bloody impact. The lava magnet melted through his body and the doors.

Billy glanced out the window as the compactor flashed before the windshield. Other men ran from a trailer; they watched the car dive toward the compactor. When a few buttons lit up along the dash, Billy realized the car self-corrected based on the surrounding terrain. Billy was thrown back across the seat. All the junkyard guys were ogling the car suspended over the compactor.

An elderly man dropped his cigar and glared at Billy. He glanced at the gooey boss man oozing through the junk doors. "Get the guns, boys!" he shouted.

He yanked a man closer to him and shouted, "Should've offered more than seventy-five dollars for Christ's sake."

Billy popped out of the driver-side window; he attempted to shift into reverse, accidentally discovering the steering column was his flight control when he pulled back on it. The thrusters torched two men; their burning bodies drooped into the junk cars. He flew around the compactor and shot a dart at the crane operator. The dart busted through the glass and pierced him in his blackened gut. The crispy critter gasped for air before the dart exploded. The crane separated and flung over piles of vehicles. Several men scattered. A majority of the crane piled into the compactor. Flames blew upward as the compactor directed the blast straight for the clouds.

Billy brushed their heads with fire and tread; they fell to the ground, avoiding the thrusters which seared paint jobs on scrapped vehicles. One of the vehicles held fuel cans inside the truck bed. The windows popped outward; the cans ignited. Flames wrapped around the Dodge

Charger as it whizzed past them and dove behind a pile of scrap. The thrusters shot vehicle carcasses in all directions; a hood from one scrapped vehicle flipped upward. Hinges creaked. A snap echoed; the hood raked through a few junkyard bullies and disappeared through a trailer.

"I knew we shouldn't have messed with that guy," Another round-bellied, bearded man hollered. He was running as more explosions rocked piles of vehicles stacked behind him. He tripped and fell as an engine block buried through the dirt next to him. Rocks and debris turned his face into a giant dust ball.

A man walked up to him and extended a hand. "That was close, huh?"

The round-bellied man peeked around him as a Ford F-250 grated his buddy through the radiator. The truck tires skinned his nose as he laid flat to the ground. The truck impelled his buddy through the same trailer as the hood. Edges of the trailer tore inward as the Ford pickup truck teetered inside. The trailer rocked on its axis. The fat man closed his eyes, trying to catch his breath. Noises churned his eardrums as the trailer slid a few feet. The man rolled onto his side as he heard more explosions and gunfire. The trailer rocked backward, releasing the hunk of metal. The fat man sighed, in a single stretch of relief, just before the F-250 squashed him; blood fanned outward like slapping a wall with a doused paintbrush.

More artillery rounds fired at the junkyard men. Molten lead spotted the junkyard; junk blew over the top of them. They tried to run away, but Billy sprayed more ammunition into the heaping piles. The materials crushed men, burying them. Billy dialed his cell phone; he called Sheriff Dunfri.

"Yeah, listen, I'm at the junkyard in Verona called Rowley's. I'm stuck in the compactor. They're fixing to crush me."

"Billy, I'd advise you to wait. I will send help immediately."

Billy's heart sank; the mere thought of his boss wanting him dead was enough to crush his soul. Yes, he was not always by the book, but the many get-togethers, luncheons, and training him for the police academy should have been enough to earn his trust. He was Billy's role model. "Sheriff Dunfri, I found out that the school conservation trip is still going to take place today. I was under the impression that it was canceled."

"It wasn't canceled, Billy. It was delayed. It was put off a week."

"You told me it was canceled."

"I did?" Sheriff Dunfri conspicuously asked. "Listen, hang tight, Billy. Help is on the way." He glanced at the phone. An evil smirk arose, and he hung up.

Billy remembered Pete's conversation about Little Rapids being under the influence of Watches' control. For good measure, Billy cut the main office building with some bullets. The main office split apart and exploded. Another shell dug beneath the soil under the fence; the entrance gate shredded away from the chain links. The control box sparked. The motorized gears exploded, sending more sparks. Each end of the fence wiggled vibrantly. The fence bent, folded and rippled from the earth. He drove the car away from the junkyard, shooting the remaining men who fired back.

He flew over the fence and landed on the road after the thrusters shut off; the car scooted left and right a bit. The Dodge screamed away from the junkyard. Billy laid his clip across the seat, reloading it as he drove. Nerves kicked in full speed; the jitters didn't stop him from packing more bullets into his empty clips.

Back at the school, the chaperones gathered the troops. They introduced themselves. Kids who were goofing around immediately were placed on the chaperones' hit lists. Some were assigned baggage detail. Others were assigned bus monitors.

Jerome rejoined the group after talking on the cell phone. Over his head was a bulky pair of headphones. The chaperone taking attendance called out, "Pete Carson!" There was a moment of silence until the chaperone repeated his name.

Danny nudged Duffy, "Wonder where Pete is?"

Duffy whispered, "No clue."

"I promise you there's plenty of time later to strap those things to your head and listen to whatever rave music you were listening to." A bulky, muscle-bound chaperone stood before Jerome.

Duffy tapped Jerome. Jerome looked at him with dead silence.

"Jerome." Duffy shrugged.

Jerome noticed the chaperone glaring at him. He removed his headphones.

The chaperone explained, "Now, my name is Larry Schwabenhaus, and I will be your chaperone. My co-partner in crime," he wrapped his arms around a woman; he was enormous, "is Malory Georgeson."

Duffy automatically snapped his head toward Victoria in the next group. Her full name was Victoria Lynn Georgeson. Vicki's mother was their chaperone. Now he knew where her beauty had come from. Mr. Schwabenhaus seemed a bit sterner than her. His appearance alone was intimidating.

Mr. Schwabenhaus exclaimed, "Hi, kids!" He had no expression, no smile—just serious scorn. "Victoria and I used to be on a bowling league together. We know each other from way back. I am from Little Rapids. All I have to say is keep the noise decibels down, and we'll get along fine. I have a couple Pit Bulls chained in separate corners out back not too far from the campground. If they bark, I'll know you were too loud. So, don't make my dogs bark."

Danny whispered, "Creepy." That was his reaction to his profound German accent. Of course, his last name was a dead giveaway about his ancestry. His parents must have eaten one too many dumplings back in the day because their boy was threateningly tall.

He hovered over them. His shadow blanketed them. Gymnasium lighting remained hidden from the round-bellied zeppelin. He threatened, "A couple short whistles from me," he whistled two quick, loud whistles which echoed through the gymnasium and down the hall. He explained, "And my dogs will find you? They might eat ya."

Danny swallowed. Jerome raised his eyebrows and stared at him.

Larry spun around and proclaimed, "But hey, we're here to have fun, so grab your bags and let's move out. We'll be on lucky bus number neun, ja. Sehr Glücklich."

Jerome tensed his shoulders. Number *nine* must have been the number of the week. They were on bowling lane number nine as well. It was where he almost got his head bashed in with bowling pins. Now he was ready to ride bus number nine for ninety-nine miles. The number nine appeared yet again. With hope, number *nine* was still his lucky number.

Kids exited the gymnasium. Jerome dialed his cell phone and held it to his ear. Danny walked beside him and nodded at him. Someone answered on the other end. Jerome smiled at him. "I'll have to call ya back."

Danny asked, "Who was that?"

"Mom wanted to know when we were leaving."

"I thought you ran away from home."

"Well, I ran away from my dad's home. I am, however, living with mom."

"Oh."

Danny gave Duffy a funny look. Jerome wandered toward the bus. One of the chaperones tried to confiscate Jerome's bag to throw into the underneath compartment; he shook his head and told her he had munchies and music to listen to. She couldn't argue with that.

Engines in the buses were firing up. They roared like mad. Billy lit a cigarette; music blared in the Armybrats' car. He sat inside the Dodge on the wooden bridge near the stream on highway twelve outside of town. The orange flames expanded across the chips of dried greens inside the roll of paper. The end ignited, and Billy puffed away at it. Smoke flushed through the bristles of the fabric on the roof of the car. A beep was heard and compartments in the roof material opened up like an intake manifold, sucking up the secondhand smoke. Billy ogled the mysterious console.

After a few minutes of waiting, the big hand struck quarter past and the buses pulled away from the redbrick, alma mater, Billy's former high school. He opened the window a crack and flicked ashes. Everything spun around in circles. While the next three minutes passed by, Billy envisioned several years of hell. Thoughts flourished; his mind cascaded every horrifying moment with Watches.

He continued thinking. He saw Ron Markesan, Mr. Fallway, and Watches. The more he reflected on the little details of his past, the more it felt like he was reliving the moments. Sweat flushed from his pores, his face dabbled with specks. Then he saw his father standing in the parking lot of the bowling alley. He was screaming at him. This time his father aimed a gun at him. Although things were out of sequence, they still had meaning. More sweat pumped from his forehead.

The second bus pulled away from the parking lot. Billy's mind was out of whack; anything taking place in his mind was far from reality. Then he saw Sheriff Dunfri, his own boss. After his father told him that he had separated from commitment, family, and love, he could sense the anger. In his heart, he could feel the true frustration. Stanley, the demented deliveryman, was the true frustration. He survived the boathouse's explosion. It couldn't have been possible. Although he did survive the grenade Pete launched at him in the House on the Rock so maybe it was regrettably true.

Late one night, Billy stayed late after Wesley's murder. He remembered the visions of Wesley; then he saw visions of the old sawmill. Sheriff Dunfri was the other officer in the station that night. The sheriff's office was the largest room in the building. He talked to him about the murder and the old sawmill. Billy described it in graphic detail and tried to pin the blame on a supernatural being otherwise known as Watches. Sheriff Dunfri grew angry with him. He didn't want to hear it. Their stakeout was a bust; Wesley's body wasn't found. He wanted to forget about it—swept it under the rug by laying the blame on Wesley's grandfather.

He opened a lower desk drawer and removed a square metal box. He extracted a baggy full of powder. Billy's mind was on the case, but Dunfri's mind was on altering his thoughts to keep his mind pure. The drugs were there to keep him sidetracked. The ugly truth was precisely that—*Dunfri's plea bargain was the acceptance of drugs to protect Watches.* He was in on it. Billy was too thickheaded to believe Pete's words.

What was Dunfri hiding? The real question was what was Gerry Fifer hiding? Everyone seemed to want a little portion of it. Was it money, gold, more drugs? Was it treasures? Billy's mind was on a rampage, but answers were trickling in like a leaky faucet filling a dirty bowl. He remembered Mr. Fifer rowing them to the campground after twirling around in blue drums. He remembered the junkyard man saying, *Let's do this quickly and quietly. Sheriff Dunfri wants no evidence!*

The argument Ron Markesan had with Watches on the hillside seemed too quick and too short. He remembered seeing Ron Markesan shooting up the hillside—*at nothing*. When he was inside the blue drum, he remembered seeing Ron Markesan's legs flash past the bullet holes in the plastic. He never saw Watches. Ron was tied at the bottom of the hill. The argument was strong. He heard Ron Markesan arguing with Watches. The voices were concise as a bell in his head. He heard the bell; oh wait, he heard his cellphone dying.

Billy snapped out of it. He drove away from the old bridge outside of town. A hand wrapped around the wooden post near the roadside. A man eased around it wearing a flop hat. An evil smirk stretched the corners of his mouth. The eye patch bunched from a raised cheek. One eye narrowed. It was Watches.

Billy passed the rubble of Wildcat Lanes. He blinked to clear his mind as he drove by. The visions made goosebumps nervous. The A&W restaurant was dead ahead. The school buses exited the lot before the church. By the time he cornered the road near the school parking lot, the buses had already cleared the hill going northbound. Billy could see the flagpole before the school entrance. It was closer to 7:35 a.m.

The tires screeched the pavement while Billy shut the door; he bolted inside the school. He ran toward the senior classrooms. They were mostly empty. He circled through the library; no one was around. He rushed into the main office. The principal stood from his desk. He opened his door and stuck his head out. It was Douglas Malone. He asked, "May I help you, Billy Emerson?"

"Don't you mean Billy Anglekee?"

"Huh?" he asked for clarification and stepped out of his office.

"Where's the senior class?"

"They've just left. They're headed to Upham Woods Campground for their conservation trip."

"No, they're not," Billy disagreed. "They're heading to their own gravesites."

"What?"

Billy grabbed a receiver from its base on the secretary's desk. She adjusted her spectacles to see Billy dialing the rotary. "You know they have push-button phones now, right?"

"Did you go to the junkyard yet, Billy?"

Billy looked away from the secretary, his eyes shifted toward the principal. He asked, "What was that?"

"Billy, there's no reason to be irrational here."

Billy extracted a handgun and aimed it at him. He hollered, "Give me a goddamn rational one then!"

The secretary shrieked and covered her face. She kicked her chair backward and knocked a few file racks onto the floor after her chair slammed into a credenza, papers scattered beneath. She nervously spun the chair away from Billy.

Billy asked, "What's the extension for an outside line?"

"Billy, weapons aren't allowed on school grounds."

"What's the extension for an outside line?" Bill repeated, staring at the mysterious principal.

"Nine," she shrieked.

"Thank you, ma'am." Billy smiled but kept his focus on Douglas Malone. "See, how hard was that, huh Doug?"

The principal shook his head and sank back inside his office.

Billy hollered into the phone, "Hello, I need to speak with Jake Carson in the human services department. Yoo-hoo, Dougy, what are ya doing?"

"I'm sorry, sir, but Jake took the day off," a lady's voice replied.

"Shit!" Billy staggered and crammed the phone into the cradle. "We're not done talking, Mr. Malone." He dialed another number. He watched the principal lean over his desk to open a top drawer. It was ringing.

Back on bus number nine, Danny watched Jerome with a keen eye. He had one foot on his bag, partially stuffed below his seat. His phone rang. He pulled it out to answer.

Billy asked, "Are you on the bus?"

"Don't worry. The bread is in the oven, brotha."

"Jerome, cut the undercover crap! Are you able to see the highway behind you?"

Jerome spun around and looked out the back door. Their bus was sandwiched between two other buses on the highway. He replied, "No, not really."

"Where's my brother? Where's Duffy?"

"On this bus with me. Why?"

"Be prepared for hostile takeover."

"Hostile? Takeover? Like taken to a Packer game or taken to a Jimmy Buffett concert? Man, we're in for one helluva trip, isn't we?"

Ironically, the principal retrieved a gun from his desk drawer and spun around. Billy, who had been keeping a keen eye on him while talking on the phone, felt a single bullet whiz past his eyelashes and bury through the bulletin board behind him. He raised his gun and pulled the trigger. Blood trailed off Principal Malone's hair waving away from a tattered hole. At the same time, the window behind his collapsing body shattered. The secretary shrieked. Billy spun around and aimed at her.

"Yeah, we all are. Watch your back. Trust no one."

Jerome chuckled. "Well, don't keep me in this shit for too long. You know how I don't like long parties."

"Uh-huh." Billy sighed, still optimistic about shooting his old principal, Douglas Arthur Malone.

"All right, brotha. See ya soon."

Billy handed the phone to the secretary and thanked her. He walked into the principal's office and scoped through his belongings. Doug Malone had a cellphone charging on a corner table. Billy inspected the flip phone. He scrolled through the incoming calls. The latest outgoing call seconds prior to Billy's arrival had been a call from Little Rapids. He knew the number and dialed it. While holding the phone to his ear, he listened to the ring. Someone answered, breathing heavily. Billy hesitated.

Sheriff Dunfri asked, "Did Billy leave?"

Billy couldn't believe the voice on the other end. It was almost too surreal. This was becoming a pandemic. First, he was targeted in the impound yard. Second, he was almost killed by his old principal.

"I'll see ya soon," Billy said.

He hung up on the old sheriff and yanked the cellphone charger from the phone and the wall. He tossed the phone; when it struck a wall, it crawled across the block with tiny plastic pieces and buttons.

He bolted out of the office and shouted at the secretary, "He was going to kill me. I had no choice. Call the police. Tell them everything." He jumped the burnt concrete steps outside and charged toward the Dodge. He slid across the hood and jumped behind the steering wheel. Hopping the curbs, he drove across the street toward the church.

He squealed through the parking lot and halted before the church. He hopped out of the driver's seat and headed inside. He knew exactly what he had to do. Of course, he had to find his father and Jake Carson. The day was still young, so he had plenty of time. Three buses streamed up highway twelve toward the dragon's mouth. Time was cut short, especially when Watches could strike at any moment.

He entered the church and slipped two pistols from holsters near his rear. Holsters also hung from suspenders at slanted angles beneath his armpits. From the pouches at his chest, he pulled out a couple more pistols. He laid his weapons in a uniform fashion around the white porcelain edge of the Holy water. With the barrels facing inward, the last weapon he placed on the dish accidentally slid in, splashing Holy water over the edge. He fumbled a bit, scooped it out, and placed it on the edge.

Water splashed on him. He crossed his fingers over his chest, performing Holy Trinity. Emotions struck him hard; mixed thoughts garbled the truths. The confession booth was on the left side near the pews. He crossed through them, lunging inside the very first booth.

Tapping the window, he gained attention from a man in cloth, Father O'Brien. The steel plate slid away from the mesh wire enclosure. Father O'Brien sat inside, positioning himself for comfort. Billy sighed. "Bless me, Father, for I have sinned."

"William."

"Yes, Father."

A few moments of confession took Father O'Brien by surprise. His description of Watches matched closely to the Scripture that well-defined the devil. It amazed him how much Watches' description matched the devil. Billy even quoted the devil. He discussed drug use and sinning; the pleasures buried him from genuine truths. Sheriff Dunfri had him so wound up—he was about to spin his top.

Billy knew what Pete was up to; he knew everything about Pete. Pete was either going to endanger the Armybrats' lives or die trying to save his mother. The only way to do it was secretive.

He jumped to his feet to leave. Hoping for guidance from Father O'Brien, he discovered his mind was on a different track from reality. He avoided his dad the past few years. The Father suggested he talk to him. Billy had to find him first, hoping his lapse in judgment would not be a mistake. He paced toward his weapons on the Holy tray.

At the high school, the secretary hung up with the local police. The word was out. Billy was on a rampage; he needed to find Jake. Trouble was brewing. There were things he needed answers to, and Jake may have had those answers. He had to pull out of the past. It was time to bring his mind up to speed. He needed his dad; he could not beat this thing by leaving his dad in the dark any longer. He had learned the hard way plenty of times. His common sense had to cooperate with his morals without backing down. There were dead bodies in a junkyard, a dead body in the high school, and Billy left breadcrumbs throughout Verona.

Strolling through the rows of pews, he went for his weapons. The Holy Trinity rested over a hand-carved porcelain tub, beautiful and hand-painted like a glorified bird feeder. With a mission, Father O'Brien soared from the confession kiosk. His robe flowed past the red-cushioned seats. Billy nodded with a smile, wiggling his guns in the air. The Father paused when he noticed the firearms. His eyes widened. "Go with God, son," He placed a hand over his heart. One eyeball shifted, a mismatched direction from the other.

Billy burst out the church doors, ran down the steps, and stood before the Armybrats' car. When he glanced up, cops leaned over squad cars, aiming guns at him. Penski hollered into a megaphone, "Freeze, Billy Anglekee." The word "freeze" seemed to echo. "Please take five steps backward and turn around while placing your hands over the back of your head."

Billy scanned the crowd of cops. His dad was nowhere to be seen. He glanced to his left as police evasively crossed the road. He had nowhere to run. It was at that very moment when he realized he had called in to his boss to report each incident. However, the Verona police weren't about to back down.

"Officer Penski, this is a mistake," he screamed.

"If you cooperate with us, there will be a chance to speak with your father."

Billy watched the other end of the road as two more officers moved up the sidewalk.

"Hold your fire. Nobody shoot."

Billy held his hands over the roof of the Charger. His eyes continued to scan the cops. He hollered, "You have this all wrong!"

"Take five steps back and place your hands over your head."

"I can clear this whole thing up if you call my dad."

"Take five steps back and place your hands over your head."

Billy glanced at the Armybrats' car; the door remained ajar. He saw the cops on either side of the sidewalk. At that moment, his heart had no beats as he dropped inside the car. Police fired upon the tank. Billy dove across the console, his knee clipping the Hover button. As he reached to shut the door, one bullet grazed his arm. Officer Penski tried stopping them from firing at the chief's son.

As Penski continued to holler at the police not to fire, a few cops walked further up the sidewalk to view the other side of the Dodge. Billy had already seated himself inside the driver's seat. The cops leaned over the squad cars, gunning for Billy. They had no idea the vehicle was bulletproof. Even Billy wasn't too keen on the vehicle's armor or full potential.

The Armybrats' floated before the entrance of the church. Billy cranked the engine. Gripping the steering wheel tightly, he knew where he had to go. The cops lowered their sights and stared at the flames shooting from the thrusters. Billy flew toward one of the squad cars and floated over it. The paint blackened from the flame. The sirens cracked and popped out of the mount with sparks. Of course, it was Penski's car. He blurted cusswords at Billy as he torched it. He tossed the megaphone at the Armybrats' trunk. It nailed it and squelched at the same time.

The word "Armybrats" lit along the doors. He floated across the street and headed toward Pete's side of town. He tore the Carson's lawn and floated to the house. As he parked the car, it settled on the driveway. He shifted into park. He bumped the console, and a monitor flipped on. There were five blips on the monitor. Billy glanced at the screen in confusion. As he zoomed in on three blinking lights, they appeared to inch along Highway twelve. He zoomed out and noticed a fourth blinking light in Little Rapids at the campground in Upham Woods. He zoomed out to trace the fifth blinking light. Miraculously, it happened to be in East View Heights, Verona, Wisconsin—exactly where he was.

Billy glanced at his arm and itched at a particular spot, running his fingers over it. He whipped out a knife. He glanced at the windshield as he held the knife to his arm. Clamping his eyes shut while dug the tip into his flesh. He slowly cut the tissue to reveal a small black object embedded under his skin. Wiggling the blade back and forth, he extracted a cylindrical device. "What the fuck?" He sighed and noticed a soda can in a cup holder. He dropped the doodad inside the half-drunk soda. On the screen, the fifth flashing light disappeared. He whispered to himself, "A tracker."

He darted up the steps to Jake Carson's front door. He ran through the house, hollering for him. When he jogged into the kitchen, he noticed a little red light blinking on the answering machine. He hit the Play button. After ranting credit collectors, Billy's dad's voice arose.

"Listen, Jake, this may be a long shot, but I may have a lead into your wife's disappearance. If you would like, we can meet at A&W over a coffee."

He jogged toward the Dodge. In the distance, he could hear sirens from squad cars. He ran faster. A whisper breezed past him and crept into his ears; the whisper plain as day; it said his name. It was quiet, but he heard it clear as mud.

A shop vacuum on wheels rolled out of the garage. Spinning around, he whipped out a pistol, firing at it. The Shop-Vac transformed into a dust cloud. Suddenly, the garage flashed; the flashes came from the trusses in the framework. Watches lie across the beams; the flashes lit his face as he shot him. Billy wailed and landed on a short hill along the driveway.

Watches flipped from the rafters; he landed on the concrete, hopping out of the garage. He kicked the dusty vacuum. It tipped; dirt fanned outward. Cop cars squealed up the road; houses reflected lights and sounds. Watches approached Billy—folded like a newborn. Billy lifted his head from the grass; a few strands clung to his hair. He stared at him. The sunlight at his back blocked his facial features.

"You're dead, Watches," he spat blood onto his bottom lip.

Watches' raised his left arm from his hip. Billy didn't see the gun; he saw the muzzle flash. A round buried in his upper chest. Watches yanked the trigger to the trigger guard; the hammer sparked the casing of another shell. Another round surged through Billy's chest. He flattened against the hill and slid into the ditch. A stream of blood ran over his bottom lip. Watches snarled, "That's funny. I don't feel dead, William. You, on the other hand . . ."

Watches lit a cigar, watching authorities turn into the driveway. They blocked it. He looked at the Dodge Charger and noticed Armybrats inscribed across the doors. He snarled, "Armybrats." The driver's door remained ajar. Leaning over the doorframe, he shot at the first squad car. Two holes appeared in the windshield, one on the driver's side and one on the passenger's side. Both cops instantly were killed. The car toppled into the ditch, gouging the embankment. A pine tree jabbed the radiator.

The other squad cars blocked the driveway and the entire edge of the property along the road; police swarmed the yard, firing upon the Dodge. Watches jumped inside the driver's seat. He sat there for a second; an evil smirk arose. His fingers wiggled alongside his face, excited over the firepower at his beck and call. He ran his hand across the dashboard. He cackled, "This car was supposed to defeat me." He reviewed the buttons. "Finally, I got the Armybrats' car."

A sprinkle of rounds lit the Carsons' driveway. Squad cars shredded from weapons mounted at the front of the Bratmobile. Police dove into the ditches as they were still firing at the tank. One single pop sounded; smoke left a tube in the car's arsenal of terror. A single grenade struck ground zero where pressures of propulsion dispersed squad cars. A couple of cops burned through wrecked metal and pine needles shot to death.

Watches sped through the front lawn with his foot crammed over the gas pedal. Grass and dirt garbled the sky. Bullets tore the ground around him. A few sparked off the hood and roof as the police officers unloaded rounds of ammunition at the Dodge Charger. The rear tires fishtailed before he hopped the curb. He crashed through two squad cars; they swung sideways and nearly squashed other officers avoiding their path of destruction. One car shoved an officer's body inside a culvert; his eyelids hung on for dear life until his head rolled to the side. Blood gushed from the other end with a shotgun. Other cops jumped out of the way.

Watches continued to smoke a cigar, laughed, and fled away from Carson's house. He swerved. He forced an old couple into a ditch before he managed to straighten his erratic driving. In the rearview mirror, Ron Markesan sat in the back seat. Watches asked, "What are you doing here, boy?"

"I can't believe you killed them. You are a stone-cold murderer."

"Don't accuse me, boy. If you were me, you'd feel the same way I do."

Ron glared at him. "You almost killed my mom."

Watches lowered his head and shook it. "Nope. Actually, the refrigerator did that. That cop ruined our family, son."

Ron argued, "No, you did. You ruined our family, especially when you came home that night and almost killed mom. You killed me."

"You're not dead. You're right here."

"You think I'm here. You created me to feel better about yourself."

"No, that's not true," Watches reached over the seat and pointed a weapon at the backseat. It was empty; Ron Markesan wasn't sitting back there. Watches snarled, "That's right. Leave me alone, son." He glanced in the mirror; the reflection was of an empty backseat. He shook his head and puffed away at his cigar some more.

Watches glanced into the mirror; his reflection was Father O'Brien. He asked, "Father, what are you doing here?"

Watches puffed another drag and tilted his top hat backward. When he looked into his side mirror, the eyepatch had returned.

"You should find your inner peace and go with God," he argued.

Watches glanced in the rearview mirror; there sat Father O'Brien. Watches replied, "I am at my inner peace."

Father O'Brien appeared closer in the mirror. "You, however, have fallen victim to life's pleasures. Your adversary is God. The devil prowls around like a roaring lion. You are a lion seeking someone to devour."

Watches argued, "I don't need any lip from you, Father. You stay out of this too. This conversation is between Ron and me."

Father O'Brien interrupted, "Don't yell at him. He's your son. And no wonder, for even Satan disguises himself as an angel of light."

Watches shook his head and smoked some more. "I guess if you need something done, you have to damn well do it yourself. I'm done with you two ass clowns."

Watches shifted into drive and peeled away from the curbside.

Chapter Twenty-One

Whimsical Moment

Ambulances were on the scene. A few police crawled around with mangled legs; many officers surrounded the two dead police in the lead car. Neighbors clung to each other. Smoke billowed between houses. White shirts chased after the victims left bleeding in and around the Carson's driveway. Paramedics worked their way inside the dismal display.

More squad cars arrived. Police officers weaved in and out of bodies, burning cars and emergency personnel. Michael Anglekee and Jake Carson jumped out of another vehicle. Jake was screaming in agony. Mike tried to calm him as he frantically called for his son. Jake wandered through the mess. Mike met up with him in the center of the drive.

The smoke was thick. An officer cried from a ditch something about no feeling in his legs. A culvert collected the blood trails; an officer protruded from one end, grated like cheese. Neighbors had drawn to the Carson's home like a bad episode of Cops. The entire area had been quarantined with a yellow ribbon, keeping onlookers away.

"Oh my god! Billy!" Mike leered at a figure in the ditch, lying motionless. Jake watched him disappear through the black smoke and chased after him. "Officer Darcy, check the house. Take Jake with you." Mike hopped over his son's legs and tore his shirt open. "Oh, thank god you wore it, Billy." Mike prodded at his vest with his forefinger, pealing shredded material away from the flattened lead inside. When he withdrew his finger from a third hole, traces of blood filled his fingernail. Mike glanced at his son's face, feeling for a pulse. He screamed, "Paramedic?" He tilted his face to see the blood on his lip..

Officer Darcy and Jake returned to the driveway. Jake hollered, "There's no sign of my boy."

Mike climbed inside an ambulance after paramedics rolled Billy's body inside on a gurney. "Meet me at the hospital. Officer Darcy, get the squads together. I want all shifts standing by within the hour, got it?"

"Yes." He nodded.

The ambulance drove around burning cars. Firefighters had arrived. Water blasted the fires as they drove away from the scene. Jake glanced at Officer Darcy as he shook his head with disbelief. Two ambulances left the scene.

Mike pulled Wayne Richard's message out of his jacket pocket and a pencil. He began deciphering the letter left at Rachel Waters' residence. He scribbled what he started writing and circled capital letters in the message. There was odd capitalization throughout the body of the text. He extracted a cellphone from his pocket.

In a moment of hesitation, he wrote all capital letters in sequence from the message: NEXT ATTACK CAMPGROUND SCHOOL TRI AIR SUP NEE. His eyes lit up. "Next attack, campground school trip, air support needed!"

He bounced a bit on the seat inside the ambulance and dialed his old boss. His old boss answered, "Tony, I need your help."

Tony asked, "Let me guess, Stanley Markesan resurfaced."

"You guessed it, pal. We're sending teams north to the Upham Woods campground. We have reason to believe he has hostages in that old sawmill south of the camp. He has Gerry, Tony. He also has Julie Carson."

Tony asked, "Mike, is your family safe?"

"My wife and son are on one of those buses headed to that camp. Billy is here with me. He took two slugs to the chest and a couple more in the lower abdomen."

"Oh man. I'm sorry, Mike."

"He was wearing his vest, thank god."

"Don't worry, Mike; I will have teams standing by. We'll see you there, buddy."

"Thanks, Tony. Oh, and I need air support on this one."

"Ten four, Mike." He hung up.

Chapter Twenty-Two

Confession

A man strolled down the sidewalk, holding his head low with his hands buried deep inside the pockets of his trench coat. The Armybrats' car slid to a halt before the curb where the man had been walking. They were before a bridge on the outskirts of Verona. It was the same bridge where the boys met Watches for the first time. It was the same bridge where the Armybrats discovered their own hell.

The man seemed ecstatic. "Billy, is that you?"

The passenger window dropped inside the door and Watches hollered, "Get in, Wayne." In an outstretched hand, a pistol aimed at him.

Wayne Richards turned towards him and raised his hands. The door opened as Watches moved the pistol to his other hand, maintaining his aim. Wayne climbed inside and asked, "Watches?"

"Billy's gone. At least the worst of my problems is taken care of." Watches grunted and drove away after he shut the door. He stated, "You've done good, Wayne. We make a great team—*you and I.*"

"We have been tormenting this family for years; I think it's time to put an end to all of it."

"Those trackers you planted in those boys during training work real well." Watches laughed. Watches seemed to have a personality. He continued to explain, "I know where they are at all times. We need to catch that bus."

"I installed a GPS link to those boys in this car too. You can watch them right here on the monitor," Wayne added.

"You continue to amaze." Watches grinned.

"The school principal came through, huh?"

"Doug! Ha! He has the entire community believing that camp is safe. Even Chief Anglekee thinks Gerry is in control of his own camp. Doug was easy to pay off. Poor bastard got dusted though."

"What do you mean?"

"Billy got a whack at him. Man, that kid was a crick in my neck, a pain in my ass, and he wouldn't die. Actually, all these little Armybrats are relentless."

"You taught them well."

"Well, we both did."

"Pretty soon they'll be working for you. Isn't that what you wanted?"

"Yeah. While they're trying to save the lives of their classmates, we'll have Gerry's good fortune and the entire product. The cartel will be at the camp in a couple hours, the sheriff and his boys will be kept busy with the cartel. They'll become local heroes. Gerry will have no choice but to surrender his good fortune to help save the lives of those students. And the Armybrats may have to die trying!"

"Then what?"

"Then while the Armybrats fight their last fight, we can move the fortune and the product. We'll be out of there before anyone even knew we were gone."

"I don't know how I could ever thank you for paying my debts."

"I needed you to move Mike and his family far enough away so that I could continue operations without any interference. He was catching onto me. And you did that. You did that quite well I might add."

Wayne laughed. "They thought I was WITSEC."

"Yeah, but you died though!"

Wayne snickered.

"You played that real well, Wayne. I also like the modifications you made to this sweet ride."

Wayne glared at Watches from the corner of his eye.

"Although, I'm not too crazy about Armybrats written on the doors."

"I had to sell it somehow."

Watches smirked. "You think Mike bought that note you wrote him?"

"He should be led astray. He's probably at the House on the Rock right now trying to determine where all this activity is going on."

"Billy was more relentless than his father. I'll miss the sorry sap. But soon, I'll have his other son and his wife right where I want them."

"You gonna end them too?" Wayne asked.

"He took my family from me so I will take his. And he can go on the rest of his miserable life wondering and wishing he had done things differently. Now turn on those trackers. I wanna see the boys," he demanded.

Wayne messed with some buttons and a monitor flickered and snapped on. He zoomed out and found four significant blips on the screen. He zoomed in and questioned, "Where's the fifth one?"

Watches glanced at the screen. He suggested, "What? Billy's? I killed him!"

Wayne insisted, "Yeah, I get that. But that doesn't stop the tracker."

Watches grinned from ear to ear, "Hmm, maybe he's in a body bag already!"

The Armybrats' car flew up highway twelve toward the four blips. Wayne was paid in drug money to conceal the truth from Mike's family. He was merely a babysitter to make sure Mike remained in Verona far enough from the demon's lair in Little Rapids—the old sawmill. Billy was correct; everyone was headed straight for the demon's lair, and they didn't even know it.

Chapter Twenty-Three

Roadblock

Students were becoming restless. On the bus with the Armybrats, a few students were bundled in little balls, sleeping. Other students found other ways to pass the travel time. Many kids were listening to music. Some kids were playing cards. They've been told they were going to Upham Woods Campground, but the ugly truth was a final destination unknown.

Jerome dropped his bag. It slid to the seat in front of him. The objects inside his bag scraped across his legs; they knocked against the floor with a thunderous thud. Danny, who sat next to him, reached for the strap to lift it for him. Jerome was rubbing his legs from the scrape and brushed him away.

Danny squinted at him and wondered, "What's in the bag, Jerome?"

Jerome tucked the bag along his side, between his thigh and the window. He sighed. "Nothing."

"We're going camping, so I imagine toiletries, a few changes of clothes, and maybe some personal items such as a Discman, Gameboy, Sega Game Gear with some games. C'mon, Rome. You can tell me. What's really in the bag?"

"Exactly that."

Jerome nudged his arm. "Look, I'm not a student at the Verona Area High School. This entire trip is a hoax, Dan. The odds are not in our favor, man. There's only of you, and in the eyes of Watches and all of his men, you are expendable. So is your mom. I can help you," his voice dramatically lowered. "Your brother and I are both investigating officers in this. I'm someone you least expected, man."

"What?" Danny shot out of his seat.

"Dan, what are ya doing? Sit down, man." Jerome laughed while glancing at wandering eyes; he stood up with him and looked into his eyes, a grumble in his voice, "You'll blow my cova." Duffy stood after he noticed them face to face. Jerome looked back, smirking.

The chaperones asked for them to take their seats. Danny's head tilted to one side. Jerome's attitude changed. His eyes were a different color. He had a little secret about him—perhaps he was about to share it. Danny sensed it the whole time. Jerome placed a hand on Danny's shoulder and asked, "Listen to me unlike the way you don't listen to your fatha."

Danny whispered, "Who are you?"

Jerome released his hand and snapped his head back and forth with a smile. Students were watching. Larry Schwabenhaus stood up. He ordered, "All y'all, take your seats. Don't make me ask you twice now. We're almost to the camp. There's no reason for this now. Remember, I have Pit Bulls."

Jerome whispered, "Yo' brotha is my partna. We're investigatin' the Little Rapids p'lice department. The whole townsfolk are in on it, bro. I'm undacova, man—as yo classmate. Please don't blow m' cover. This thing is above us. It's huge. Dis . . . dis is my bag of goodies; it's a bonus. We know where Pete's mom is. If ya don't believe me, here's m' phone, call your brotha fo' yourself. Even yo dad knows my involvement in all dis."

Suddenly, rubber chunks bashed the emergency door. Both boys ducked. Smoke flooded the road; one of the tires exploded on the bus behind them. Rubber shredded away from the bead. The shell sparked the wheel with a flash of light. One busted the glass and looped around the frame, knocking the orange lever upward. The glass shattered; it fell across the aisle. The door swung open. A light lit on the panel near the bus driver as a loud buzz filled the bus to alert the emergency door was open. Larry pointed at some kids in the back seat. He thought they were fooling around; he hollered at them. The two innocent girls shrugged, shaking their heads.

Behind them, students' bodies flailed around inside the bus as it drove through the ditch. Clarice slid down the aisle and rolled into the hub of the transmission at the front of the bus. The bus whipped in different directions and tipped like a rolling pin to flour. A row of dogwood trees caught its domed roof. When the bus impacted the trees, the bus driver's body crammed the steering wheel, but the seat belt held him in place. Other students flew over seats and smashed into each other. When the door opened up, Clarice flung outside. She rolled into the woods and landed face down under some shrubs.

Everyone on the Armybrats' bus watched a glowing object whiz past the windows on the left side. A fire trail followed the fantastic glow of the object. Danny and Duffy were on the opposite side with their eyes fixated on the road. Duffy sighed. "Oh my god."

Jerome screamed, "What?"

Danny replied, "It's Watches."

Duffy glanced at him and stuttered, "And he's, ah . . . he's got our car." Duffy pointed out one of the windows as if no one could see the glowing word "Armybrats" across the doors.

The glowing object passed the lead bus and arched over the ditch. The object landed at the base of a few deciduous trees off the road. It was an artillery round launched from the Armybrats' car. The explosion cut the trunks and tossed a few trees sideways. They collapsed across the road. Dirt and rocks fanned the road as trees covered the sky and blocked the sun for a split second. Trees ripped from the soil. Watches had created a blockade.

Dust and debris from the lead bus blinded their bus driver as it enveloped them. Rubber tread grated like locusts in the wind as the bus attempted to avoid the obstacles. One tire blew out; briefly, they could see the undercarriage of the bus in front of them. Flipping sideways, the bus teetered against the trees along the road. It crashed on its side and skidded down the road, pushing the trees with it. After a sharp tug on the steering wheel, their bus driver had lost control. He regained it and drove around the fallen bus to avoid it and the trees.

The Armybrats' car parked further up the road and Watches stepped out. The bus driver glared at him. The old man smirked and carried a middle finger proudly in Watches' direction. Watches shook his head. The boys continued to holler at him, telling him to stop. They worked their way toward the front. The whiplash from the swerving jostled their straight shot down the aisle.

Watches pulled out a rifle and aimed at the bus driver. It was simple; he wanted the buses stopped. When one bus driver wouldn't give up, Watches was ready to stop him with lead. Their bus driver was toying with the devil, and he didn't even know it. Squeezing the trigger, a round left the barrel. A small hole appeared in the bus driver's window. Flesh flapped upward and pieces fell to his chest with blood and torn shirt fragments. The shoulder strap of the seat belt was torn in half.

Glass shot around the students as the side of the bus hammered the road. Students fell to the lower end of the bus. A few students were smeared across the road as the pavement rushed past them through the busted windows. Sam's mom landed in the stairwell of the bus; the bus driver fell on top of her. She could feel the cool road rush past the little square windows in the folding doors. Blood sprinkled over the door, covering the max capacity stencil. The bus's slide eased as the weight slowed it down.

Danny and Duffy latched onto seats above their heads. They held a couple of students from falling. Jerome was clinging to his bag, braced between seats at the lower end. On the other side of the ditch was a drop-off. A cliff face led to the Wisconsin River. Danny noticed it through the front windshield. His hairline caught his upper eyelids. Sam was working his way toward his mother, watching road debris pelt the seats around him. Students were screaming. A small tree carved through a window, smashed a seat backward, pinning him between seats; the trunk stabbed through both seats and nearly decapitated a girl. She screamed as her hair embedded into the seat with the trunk.

The bus climbed an uprooted tree. A broken limb protruded toward the sky. The bus tipped to its side. Rocks along the ledge shredded the front quarter panel. Pieces dropped for a mile as the starter line tore away and tapped the wheel hub. Sparks pranced along the rock ledge. A Danger Sudden Drop Off sign bent outward from the ledge. The broken limb sliced through the folding doors and carved out Sam's mom's stomach. The bus driver's body smooshed Sam's mom between the doors as waves of blood dissipated into the gully. Other droplets pumped out her mouth and sprinkled across the bus driver's white collar. Her last breath was a gurgle.

The door handle slid up the bus driver's arm and cracked under his armpit. The bar snapped out of its plastic holder; his weight yanked the bar backward, but the other end of the seatbelt kept him suspended. The door handle jammed the bus driver's seatbelt, strung to his neck, and his ankle. The folding doors smashed each other, bent downward from the extra force. All four windows cracked outward and shattered over his head as he hung through the door. Sam's mom exited the bus. Fuel splashed the rocks near the rear tires. The signpost had jabbed the tank.

All the students bunched to one side of the bus. Windows cracked. Larry rolled across the ceiling; the bus shook and slid a few inches across the rocks. Students watched stones flip from the side of the bus, bouncing off the rock face, causing gasps and a few screams.

Danny and Duffy hopped the seats to aid the bus driver. Jerome crawled across the windows trying to position students accordingly, keeping them off windows. That's when he noticed his duffel bag laying across one of the windows. He circled back for it. He lunged for it; at the last second, it busted through the glass, he caught the handle with his pinkie and ring fingers. His body slid forward. The weight yanked him until his bright white basketball shoes tapped at seat frames, holding him and his bag. Jerome swung out the window.

His shoelace rolled over the metal frame; he curled his toes trying to maintain control of the swinging bag below. A sharp sting across his cheek and arm carried his attention to a cable throwing sparks over the side of the bus. The power cable to the starter continued to tap the metal above. Then he heard a whimper echo below him. Joints at each finger lost pigmentation. Muscles tightened along his neck. This time the whimper was even louder. His fingers became lax. Those muscles in his neck receded. A seat busted through a window. The frame's leg protruded from it; a girl fell out the window next to it.

More sparks splashed across his face and neck. He blinked, rotated his neck, and glanced at the bag. He webbed his fingers and let the bag go; it fell down the rock cliff. He wrapped his arms around his waist, gripping the window frame; he forced himself to give up the rescue of his heavy duffle.

He hollered, "Damn it!"

Larry crawled to Mallory and wrapped an arm around her shoulders. He suggested, "We need to get these kids out of here."

Mallory agreed, "Yes, the emergency exit."

Larry and Mallory glanced at Jerome. Larry screamed, "Off the bus, everyone move to the rear. Do not step on the windows. Stay on the seats. Bleib weg von den Fenstern," he started yelling in German, telling them to stay off the glass.

Jerome's face still hung out a window watching his bag of guns disappear through the trees far below. A web of cracks spread through the glass. The cracks stopped at the framework; he glanced at a girl hanging upside down several windows over. He said, "Hang on and please don't let go."

Her leg held her as her body swayed back and forth. The window frame was bent outward, one leg clung to it. A metal bar hung out another window where a disconnected seat frame had busted through. It kept catching her head as it repetitively banged her swaying body. Briefly, Jerome studied how many windows she was from him—nine. Her eyes opened; she noticed him. She cried, "I don't want to die." Jerome felt the hairs on his neck stand as he tried to pull himself up.

Jerome hollered at her, "Don't panic—tighten your leg."

Jerome's body slid away from the window as it shattered more. His weight forced the vinyl to concave in the seat. His elbows dug into the frame and kept him from falling. Kids were screaming and crying. Other students hung from seats above, struggling toward the backdoor like a jungle gym of monkey bars. Underneath the bus, fuel dribbled down the branch that held a majority of the bus's weight, dampening the roots.

The tree trunk turned as the soil weakened. More pressure sprung the remaining root system that held the uprooted tree in place; the constant movement on the bus tugged at the dirt—granule by granule. A few students fell as the emergency door slipped from a kid's grip. A boulder slid down the incline and busted through the upper window on the emergency door. The kids inside tried shoving the door open as kids outside yanked at the handle. The rock blocked it.

Danny peeked over the front seat Duffy had crawled over. They drew upon the bus driver. Sam was screaming for his mother. He was blocking the aisle as the boys tried sneaking by to help save the bus driver.

Duffy tapped his shoulder. "Mind crying outside, Sam?"

Sam's watery eyes narrowed. They were red. "What?"

Danny shouted, "He said go cry outside."

Sam left them and mumbled, "Stupid Armybrats."

Jerome's footing missed a seat; his leg blew through a busted window. Glass sliced his ankle as he hugged a seat. He accidentally smeared a kid's face across the vinyl.

"Sorry, man."

"You're good. It's all good; we just don't know how to walk on sideways buses."

"Truth bro," Jerome smirked at him and nodded as he walked away. He checked the specks of blood on the glass below him. More blood soaked through his sock. "Damn, my Air Jordan's." All of a sudden, flesh ripped along his leg when Larry gripped his collar, yanking to assist him off the bus. Jerome screamed as the glass ripped at his ankle. Using one arm, he twisted Larry's wrist. Larry shared an awkward glance. Jerome bent his arm farther up the middle of his back, so his face smashed the seat next to him. "Take a good look, ass face. Does it look like I can move right now?"

Larry's scorn transformed to worry. "Sorry, son."

"Don't 'sorry son' me. Get the girl, man."

"What girl?"

"She's three windows that way—hanging upside down."

Larry's eyes narrowed. Jerome released his arm and positioned his weight against the seat. He kicked the center of the window frame with his free foot. The frame bent downward; the glass unstuck from his ankle. Glass shattered around his shoe revealing his bloody Air Jordan, "Mother . . ." he bit his lower lip in anger. "Aw man, my good shoes!"

Clarissa and Vicki were helping other people out the windows at the top of the bus. Their alternate escape since the emergency door had been pinned shut. Mallory scooted out one of the windows after her daughter. Between Larry and her, they continued to hoist kids through the windows. Kids were struggling to hang onto other kids, trying to help them through the upper windows. One boy slipped and fell to the edge of the bus. His eyes remained fixed on the Wisconsin River. Sloshing sounds snapped him out of the daze; he noticed fuel pouring from the inverted gouge of metal where the Warning sign penetrated the tank.

"Ahh, Mrs. Georgeson," he said, tapping at the bus exterior to pull away from the edge.

Kids were finally escaping the mess. Larry Schwabenhaus was lifting students to Mallory from inside the bus. Jerome finally crawled through the window. He eased past students moving toward Larry's extended hand. He brushed between a couple girls and swung around the seat where he had last seen the girl hanging upside down. The frame was bent outward from the window track; the upper tracks were missing. The entire window was gone; the girl was gone. He focused beyond the bent tracks; down by the river was a colorful dot near several black dots—probably his bag of goodies, minus the bag. Jerome knelt as a kid hopped him. He closed his eyes, wishing he had gotten to her sooner.

Danny glanced at Duffy and asked, "How do we get to him?"

The pole held the bus driver and was a few feet from the first seat. Larry crawled to the boys. He also insisted on lending a hand. The boys were still trying to decide how they were going to get to the pole without choking him on the seatbelt. The pole was too straight and too tight to budge, so that was out of the question. The ripped seatbelt above them was swaying, whipping the bar behind the driver's seat.

Duffy noticed the sound of the metal clip hitting the bar; he saw the belt. He suggested, "I know how."

Outside, Watches was gathering students. He was shooting into the air and vigorously shoving kids. Three box trucks pulled up. Several men jumped out. Fully automatic weapons were slung to their shoulders; they rounded up a few wild students and began tying them together. One of the gagged students was screaming. Tears stormed her chubby cheeks. Clarice held onto the third bus driver with the broken ankle from the door handle.

Watches dragged the bus driver by his hair. He dropped him next to the girl with the chubby cheeks. The bus driver winced, forgetting the pain in his ankle. Watches knelt beside him and exclaimed, "If you don't shut up Miss Fatty Flaps here, I will shoot her and then you, capiche?"

The bus driver shook the girl. She continued to cut the gag with sharp vocals. Watches aimed his gun at her head. The bus driver waved him off for a second attempt. Clarice scooted away. The bus driver slapped the girl; her head hung on her shoulder. He hit her so hard, he knocked the gag out. She fell down, unconscious. Watches lowered his arm.

"Wow, you're the bus driver? Crude, dude! I like that." Watches smiled.

Duffy hung upside down from the seatbelt. Danny had it tied to the bar behind the driver's seat and gently released slack. He was holding onto another end of the shoulder strap through the steering wheel, lowering him. Duffy carried the lap belt in one hand. His other hand guided him down the pole the bus driver hung from.

At the rear of the bus, Jerome tried to reason with two girls cowering in the backseat. He lent them a hand to help them away from the fear they tried to hide behind. Suddenly, the bus jerked. The girls retreated into a hugging choir of cries.

Watches stood at the corner kicking the taillight. "Do buses fly?"

Inside, Duffy's body swung on the line. Danny's footing burrowed into the bodyguard before the first seat. Watches antagonized kids to hurry off the bus by giving the uneasy students more queasiness with each kick at the bumper. Some students lay flat on top of the bus as Watches rocked the boat.

The girls cowering in the backseat dropped away from Jerome. They screamed as Watches repeatedly kicked at the taillight. Jerome glanced at a fire extinguisher hanging above them. He ripped it from the mounts and stuck the nozzle out the busted window. Popping the pin, he unleashed white clouds of sodium bicarbonate. Watches jumped away as dust rolled off his body. As much as his unexplained powers defined his inhumane character, the sodium bicarbonate outlined his true ghostly presence. He pranced about at the back of the bus like a baker losing flour from the top shelf of his grasp. A couple of female students laughed at the goon painting the grass white in a sloppy dance.

Jerome aimed the extinguisher at the girls. "Unless you wanna look like that big goon out there, you better get the hell up outta that seat and stop crying."

Both girls darted from the seat. Other kids helped them through the upper windows.

Watches stepped next to the girls laughing at him. He knelt before them. Each girl held in their laughter. Out of a poof of white clouds rolling over his flop hat, Watches lunged between them and shouted, "Boo!" Both girls dropped backward and rolled off the rock cliff. Their screams descended.

Jerome crawled along with the seats toward the front of the bus. All he could see was Duffy's feet. He also noticed the crack of Larry's butt pointing at high noon, the hairy ravine of the big German goon from Little Rapids. He helped hold the slack in the line above Duffy. Jerome heard the little boy on top of the bus shouting "fire."

The boy on top of the bus finally got Vicki's mom's attention, pointing at the bus's undercarriage. A little brush fire started along the base of the uprooted tree. The power line for the starter continued spreading sparks. She backed away from him and scooted him toward the end of the bus. "Go, Nate. OK kids, bus trip is over. Everyone crawl to the back and keep in the middle." She stopped and glanced through the windows at her feet. She could see Larry helping the Armybrats save the bus driver. She leaned over to inspect the small fire burning nature's wooden crutch holding the bus.

Duffy was making his way to the bus driver. By the time he reached him, the bus driver had come to. Duffy smiled at him while hanging upside down and said, "Morning. You like drove us off a cliff, man."

When the bus driver realized he was suspended in dead air, his eyes widened, and his pupils grew three times their normal size, like giant peppermints getting swallowed by hungry retinas. Duffy wrapped the lap belt under the bus driver's arms as he wiggled. He grasped onto his neck from the belt choking him. "Calm down, good sir," he hollered at him. "You aren't making this any easier on me, you know that, right?" With a few swift knots and loops, he managed to tie a harness.

Danny and Larry tugged on the shoulder strap; it wrapped through the steering wheel, hoisting them up. Duffy snuck the blade of the knife between the bus driver's neck and belt. He cut the line that choked him. The bus driver dropped a foot. He gave a slight wail and watched the loose belt float toward the river. Meanwhile, the color returned to his face as his mouth caught fresh air.

Duffy's foot bumped into the handle grip of the steering wheel. He gripped onto the belt. He held onto the steering wheel and told them to give slack. Larry and Danny loosened their grips as Duffy's legs swung to the bodyguard. He stood on the rail. The center console cracked and crumbled to pieces. The bar slid away from it. The handle slid along the bus driver's arm. He dropped a few more feet. Duffy grasped the lap belt, lost his footing, and fell from the rail, holding the bus driver.

All at once, two people were holding two people on one belt. By the time Duffy managed to support his own weight through the steering column, Danny and Larry were relieved from the tension. They still had the dangling bus driver to tend to. Danny reached over the stairwell and grasped the lap belt with his freehand. As he sat up, Danny and Larry helped brace the line. Duffy hung freely from the steering wheel, and together, they reeled in the bus driver.

Duffy performed an upside-down sit-up and opened the driver's side window. He climbed out of the bus. The rest of them pulled the bus driver around the bodyguard and carried him to safety. All three of them piled between the metal guard and the first seat before the stairwell to hell. The bar and handle pierced a sharp edge of rock embedded in the side of the cliff. It shot into the river.

Again, the bus turned. It slid a couple feet; pressure creased the bus wall inward, causing a few seats to fold while other seat frames broke away and smashed windows. Some windows exploded inside the bus, throwing glass across the ceiling; they scrambled for the other side to escape. Larry helped lift them to the upper seats where they climbed out upper windows. Jerome had already climbed out one of the windows after Mallory helped him save the two girls. Jerome swept the extinguisher along the undercarriage trying to battle the blazing grass.

Larry was the last one on the bus. He made an attempt to squeeze through the window; German blood flowed through those big veins with a girth wider than any passenger window. Larry had sweat on his brow and under his pectorals.

"Mallory . . ."

"Yes, Larry."

"My house is green, last one on the same side of the police station. Feed my dogs for me."

All of a sudden, he slipped, and his legs smashed through a few windows at the bottom. Duffy leaned through the window. Jerome clung onto him. The fire extinguisher fell and clanked against a rock. White puffy clouds blanketed the vision of the river. Duffy screamed for Larry to try. Larry laid there. He looked at him and said, "Duffy Felter, you take care, you little Armybrat you."

"The back door, you can make it to the emergency door. You can get out. Try!" Duffy said. Danny was waving them toward the rear of the bus.

Larry held no expression as he stared into Duffy's eyes. "Don't go in the second office on the upper mezzanine of the sawmill. You will find nothing there but painful secrets, my friend." Duffy stared into his eyes. It may have been the tone in his voice carving away at Duffy's soul that gave him an eerie cringe. The oddity was he had never met this guy before today. Duffy backed away from the window.

Everyone except Duffy stood and ran across the side of the bus. Duffy was strapped to the belt yet. The belt attachment was knotted around the steering wheel through the opened driver's window. Duffy glanced at Larry who still stared in his direction, one leg through a busted window.

Danny stopped. The bus shifted. Branches snapped. The tree's roots rolled out of the rock face. Duffy slid backward with one final vision of the helpless German stuck in a window below. The belt stretched and yanked at his waist as the bus turned and slid along the ledge. Another fire crawled along the dripping fuel tank. Jerome slid toward Duffy withdrawing a knife. The bus detached from the cliff.

Jerome flung the knife. It twirled and slit through the belt. The belt let loose from the bus; Jerome caught Duffy's fall, keeping him from sliding off. They flipped onto the underside of the bus. At one point, the bus was upside down. The boulder separated from the emergency door. The rotating bus tossed Larry onto the ceiling. He noticed the emergency door ripping away from the hinges. Sunlight crept in. He had a clean shot to the exit.

Danny's screams took them by surprise; they looked at him as he was hollering for them to run. Jerome and Duffy bolted across the transmission, desperately avoiding elbows in the exhaust system or joints in the chassis. Danny dropped to his knees, watching the sky come into view. Jerome wrapped his arms around Duffy. Together, Jerome and Duffy tackled him.

Watches was in the middle of the road, cackling at them. He watched the bus leave the ledge. The students stood in a line along the road. Fire zipped over the fuel tank and ignited. The explosion blew Jerome and Duffy over Danny's head. Yellow school bus particles flapped in the breeze and smoke. The bus plummeted onto the sandy shore near the river and flipped into the water. Smoke followed the splashes. Watches noticed Duffy and Danny rolling in the grass. He pushed a couple kids and approached the ledge. Jerome lifted Danny and walked him away from the ledge.

Bonzo followed Watches. Watches glared at the Armybrats. He hollered over his shoulder, "Start loading the little shits onto the mail carriers."

Bonzo stopped and nodded. He replied, "No problem, boss."

Watches snickered. Duffy remained seated next to the bus driver and Jerome. Watches stopped several feet from them and held up a pistol. A snap echoed through the trees. Duffy and Jerome felt a tug as the bus driver's body fell backward with them.

All that work, all the time and energy it took into saving one life. Watches finished his life in mere seconds. Now Danny and Duffy were lying over the bus driver's body, pouting. A new hole appeared in his chest. Smoke puffed away from Watches' pistol.

Watches smiled. "I didn't miss that time. Ha."

Duffy and Jerome reached across the bus driver's chest. Jerome felt for a pulse and dropped his head. Duffy cried, "You didn't miss the first time either, Watches."

Watches cackled. "Well, that bullet had more meaning than the first." He pointed at a few of his guys. "Put these whippersnappers on the first truck."

"Yes, boss," one man responded, a few men surrounded the Armybrats.

Clarice screamed, "Noooooooo!"

Watches held a gun to her. Danny pulled away from the men in fear for his mom's life. Clarice held an arm across her face. Watches lowered the gun and straddled her. He straddled her midsection, drawing her closer to his one eye. "Mrs. Anglekeeeeee." He jumped off her and walked away. Watches stopped on the road and glanced at Danny who appeared calm. Then he looked at his pistol.

Clarice buried her head into the bus driver's shoulder as he grimaced from the pain of his broken ankle. The bus ride was finally over. One bus driver was dead. Suddenly, this bus driver had driven his last bus as well. Clarice's body flew forward as the bus driver with the broken ankle flew backward. Watches shot a round while staring at Danny. He fired a single round clipping hair from Clarice's head. The bullet whistled in her ear. She flopped off his belly and rolled away with blood across her left cheek. "Why did you do this, Stanley?"

"Stanley? Ha. I'm not sure who you think I am, lady. But it's me—Watches, Watches, Watches!" White powder fanned away from his arms as he held them out like a crucifix. "Take your pretty little behind and move over there, Simon says." Watches waved his pistol at the flock of students. "Now move."

Clarice sat still. Watches' eye remained in an opened position without a blink. His head dipped. He shrugged. "Why aren't ya moving, Mrs. Anglekee?"

"Because . . . Simon didn't say."

Watches smirked and glanced at Danny who smirked as well. His eye narrowed. "You took my fun away." Watches sighed and walked away. "Simon says move."

They were hostages now—his hostages. For a moment, Danny was relieved that his mom played his game. If Simon didn't say, he could have lost his mom right then and there. The UPS trucks left the scene. There were two buses in the ditch. Trees lie in the road.

* * *

Squad cars parked in a wedge formation before the downed trees; they noticed bodies in the field along the side of the road and the overturned buses. A few cops ran toward the bodies. Other cops scrambled for their radios.

Inside another vehicle, a hand reached across the console and toggled a switch that reads *Scrambler*. Of course, this was one of the switches in the Armybrats' car. Watches was in a position out of sight, out of mind. In the absence of communication, wars have become difficult to fight. In the devil's eye, he could see the electromagnetic pulse killing any electronic systems within a substantial radius.

A cop shouted to his partner across the roof of the car, "I have nothing." His partner reflected the same thing to him.

One cop checked for pulses on each of the victims in the field. The other cop was searching for any signs of life as he approached the edge of the cliff. Suddenly, a hand slapped his boot. Larry had been scaling the rock wall. He glanced down, almost toppled over, and shrieked, "Ah, oh my God." He knelt and grasped Larry's shoulder. He hollered for his partner, "George come help."

His partner left one of the dead bus drivers and wandered to him. They both lured the big man over the ledge. Larry rolled onto his back and panted; he stared into the bright sky and praised the Lord. The cops sat away from the heavy-breathing German chaperone, trying to catch their breaths. Larry had sweat rings around each tit.

"I've been climbing," he gripped the grass and breathed in, "for an hour."

A cop leaned over to see a rock ledge about ten feet down with a bus seat clinging to the edge. "Were you on that ledge right there—with the bus seat on it?"

"Yeah, way down there." Larry panted and pointed downward.

"Sir, it's like ten feet. I could jump to it."

"Hey, look at me. Do I look like someone who climbs rock for fun?"

The other cop asked, "What the hell happened here?"

"We were ambushed—all three buses." He became animated. "They got the kids." He wrung one of the cops' uniforms with a balled fist of fabric.

"Calm down, sir. You had a traumatic experience. You climbed five feet."

"No, no, you don't understand. Armed men took the kids."

One cop took his cellphone out and mumbled, "Aw crap, wouldn't ya know it—no service."

Watches floated over the downed trees. The Dodge Charger torched branches and leaves. The cops rolled over, aiming their pistols at the car. They hesitated and removed their eyeballs from the weapons' sites to verify it was indeed a floating car. A series of rounds blasted through the squad cars. Some officers never made it out. A missile fired into one cruiser; it exploded. It lifted from the pavement and smashed overtop another squad car (upside down). The cops inside that car were trapped after the doors buckled. Cops fled the devastation. They rolled into ditches alongside the road. Rounds tore through vehicles and asphalt.

The Armybrats' car hovered. Jets continued to torch downed trees as they glowed orange toward the core. Leaves and bark immediately shriveled to black nubs. The car worked its way toward the squad cars as police had no other choice but to open fire. They were shooting at the undercarriage of the car. Watches watched a bullet stream between his legs, ricocheted from the roof, and the steering wheel. It struck the window next to his head and buried into the seat behind him.

"Whoa." The car withdrew from its forward momentum. Watches lowered to the ground. "Damn it, Wayne, you didn't put armor plating underneath. You must be all kinds of stupid." Briefly, he chewed out the former fake WITSEC handler of the Anglekees as he fumbled through the dashboard options.

Wayne replied, "It made it too heavy."

Compartments slid open alongside the fenders, on each side of the car. A series of tubes extracted from the slim openings. Flames shot out each side as the Armybrats' car drove through the squad cars, burning everything and anything along its path. Embankments caught fire as flames rolled away from the road. Cops were swimming in ditches of lava. Some cops struggled to crawl away from the heat. Larry lay there in shock and awe.

The two cops dragged him. "Come on, Larry. Move!"

Watches drove a little farther and stopped. The two cops, including Larry, knelt behind a small rock formation and watched the black Charger's taillights glow. Watches had cleared a path in the road; the car lifted. It curved left and flew higher than the trees. The two cops watched their living buddies scramble toward their dead partners. They ran for them. Larry crouched and cried out, "No, don't go out there."

A tiny object had jettison from the Armybrats' car's undercarriage. It floated toward earth like a tiny water balloon. Larry noticed it and shut his eyes. He eased behind the rock and covered his ears. The small canister struck the underside of the squad car that was upside down, lying on the rooftop of another. Light flashed and seemed as if time stood still. All standing human bodies vaporized leaving shadows. An explosion ripped asphalt from the road and shredded trees and shrubbery. Everything around the new crater was gone. Two more squad cars exploded. Flames roared across the embankments.

Shrubs were on fire. Even with his ears covered, Larry could hear the screams dissipate to a dull quiet. The smoke rolled around the rock formation as well as remnants of dirt, trees, steel, and more than likely dust from people. He kept his eyes shut through the entire flash. The debris rolled past him and dropped over the cliff. The blue sky reappeared through the smog. The smell of charred forestry crept into his vulnerable sense. He tried to avoid everything except the smells. He even felt the heat during the explosion. His eyebrows curled where they singed like the hair on his head.

When he could see, he sat in a bus seat; he realized he was ten feet down the side of the cliff, yet again. During the explosion, the force had placed him elsewhere. He remained in a stone-cold daze. He dropped his head and cried. He glanced up; then he closed his eyes, trying to catch his breath. A tear pushed dry dirt out of the corner of his eye. "I just climbed that."

Chapter Twenty-Four

Too Late

Students practically sat on top of each other, tied like cattle. Jerome was having Duffy extract his cellphone from his pocket. The truck was jam-packed full of students and boxes. The broken road didn't help as Duffy accidentally dropped Jerome's phone. Jerome glanced down as Duffy whispered, "Shit." He noticed his bars were low and the phone flashed "Low battery."

"Double shit." Jerome jerked his head in anger. "Why did you do that?"

"I bumped something."

Jerome smiled. "Well, you're the first man I've had in m' pocket."

"Disgusting," Duffy whispered.

One girl who was wedged between them tried to grasp the phone between her shoes. Once she had, she smiled and lifted her knees to her chest. Jerome cupped his hand below her heels; she released it into his palm. He tried to peer at his phone held along his thigh; it beeped one more time with a low battery indicator. He quickly texted what he could. In rapid succession, he sent letters hoping they created words since he couldn't see his phone while wedged tightly between other students; then the phone flashed low battery and began the power-off cycle. "Shit!"

Billy's phone lit as he sat in the passenger seat of his father's squad car; he explained, "We're too late." His dad snapped his head at him and rolled his eyes toward the road. Billy attempted reading the jumbled text as if Jerome swiped at guessed letters. "Bout eight men and Stanly Markesan high jack bus convoy. Tree trucks total. All bussses overturnd, som car wth army rats written on side, killed two bus drivers, some studens, Ans they wer all tied ans put into truck . . ."

Mike asked, "Yeah, keep going."

"Um, that's it. I'd hate to see his resume."

Mike suggested, "He may have been under duress—trying not to get caught."

Billy added, "Or he may have been on a bumpy road."

"Good, Billy. See if you can text mom's phone."

"Might that put her in harm's way?" Billy contested.

Mike slapped his hand on the steering wheel. "Damn it, you're probably right. Don't do that."

Jake sat in the rear seat and profiled Watches. "The group being tied together like that, to me, suggests control. He wants control over everyone. If your boys and their friends, including my son, were trained by this same lunatic, it may suggest he feels almost threatened. He created lethal weapons out of these kids. Through his training, if he used narcotics on them, then I have no doubt he was using as well. Whether it was to ease his own pains or help him get through most days, I am thinking that he might not even remember training them. If each of his sociopathic episodes resulted in the transformation of his mind, he may not have realized what he was doing as Ralph or Ron or Watches for that matter. He may actually possess four different personalities: Ralph, Ron, Watches and Stan—maybe more. Who knows?"

Mike looked at Jake through the rearview mirror and asked, "Are you suggesting that he had no idea what he was doing as he played any of those character roles?"

"What I'm saying is that the night those boys merely escaped the grips of this devil, not only were they drugged, but they were experiencing him being torn between each dissociative identity. They spent days in the woods with three or four different characters, and they didn't even know it. They weren't even sure when the days began or ended. I have interviewed the boys and not a single boy kept their story straight. Yet, every single one of them experienced tidbits of the same story. They believed what they were saying. And at one point, each of them thought it was a nightmare."

Billy agreed, "Yeah, one night I woke up in a clinic at the camp and then fell fast asleep only to wake up again in a canoe. I didn't know what to believe."

"Mike, if this villain's role is to get even with you. Who knows how far up the ladder he may go? If this is about revenge, he's suffering from the loss of his family and wants to take it out on you and yours."

Mike cut him short and finished his sentence, "Then he'll stop at nothing to kill mine."

"Whoa, dad." Billy placed his hands on the dash. Mike hammered the brakes; the squad car cut tread as it slid sideways. The side-view mirror clipped the charred side-view mirror on a blackened squad car in the middle of the road. The car's side-view mirror misted through the air as it disintegrated. There were downed trees in the road, small fires, and burnt bodies. Squad cars were smoking on the embankments. Other squad cars looked like Swiss cheese, bullet holes from nose to tail; a huge crater in the center of the road contained buckled pavement, a pair of police boots, and ashes; the car transformed to dust before their eyes.

Mike jumped out of the car.

Jake warned, "Are you sure you should go out there, Mikey?"

Just then, Billy jumped out and Jake was left in the car alone.

"OK, you two go. I'll stay right here. Thanks." He glanced out his window and watched a charred body roll toward the car. The skeletal remains clinked against his door. A gasp was heard. "OK, on second thought . . ." He slid across the seat and tried opening the door furthest from the body; it would not open. "Oh, I see. I'll just stay here." He angled his head to the window trying to peek at the body, but he could only see smoke.

Mike extracted his weapon and Billy did the same. Billy whispered, "The Armybrats' car did this."

Mike looked at the dead bodies in the ditch and scattered across the embankments. Tears soared down his cheeks. Billy asked, "Dad, what's wrong?"

Mike sighed. "Verona's gonna need more cops I think."

Billy brushed residue off lettering on a squad car's door. It read *Verona Police*. Below it, it read *We serve to protect*. This was most of the guys from Mike's unit. He dropped to his knees near the crater in the road as if his leg muscles gave way tendon by tendon. A body protruded from the smashed window. The body was upside down. To his left, another cop's body was in the road. The breastplate read *Penski* on what was left of his tattered shirt. He wore no shoes; his feet were charred to the bone. The policeman's shoes were smoking at the center of the crater. He looked at Billy and said, "This nightmare's gone on way too long."

Both of them aimed at the other side of the road as a man walked toward them with his hands in the air. It was Larry. "Don't shoot." He pleaded. Mike swiftly moved behind a squad car. Billy repeated his tactic on the opposite side of the crater. Each was drawn on this man as he approached them.

"Who are you?" Mike demanded.

"I'm just a chaperone."

Billy asked, "For the school field trip?"

"Yes, sir." He replied.

Mike and Billy holstered their weapons. Mike asked, "OK, where is everyone?"

Madison police cars vibrated the road, surrounding them. There were fire trucks and ambulances. Billy swiftly jogged to the downed trees and climbed on top of the first one. He stared at what used to be the road; instead, it was about a quarter of a mile of downed trees. He shouted, "Dad, you'll wanna see this."

Mike ran to his son and climbed on top of the trunk. He turned toward his son, "There's no other road into that camp."

"No, there isn't," Billy repeated.

Mike jumped down and pulled out his cellphone. "Tony?" he shouted into his phone.

"Yeah, Mike. It might be hard hearing you at the moment."

Mike rolled his eyes at Billy. "Are those gunshots?"

"Ahhh," Tony shrieked. The conversation was disconnected.

Mike closed his eyes. Only the worst thoughts bombarded his mind. He felt helpless. He felt stuck in the road. True statement, which the predicament they were in, precluded. His old boss's unit was left alone in a warzone. Meanwhile, firefighters and policemen cut through trees. Larry sat on the back of an ambulance where an IV bag pumped hydrates into his system. The daylight slipped away. *There had to be another way,* Mike thought.

Billy was staring at the river. He shouted, "Dad, I have an idea!"

Chapter Twenty-Five

Little Rapids

Mike walked into a police station and aimed his gun at the deputy behind the counter. The deputy sprung from his stool and raised his hands. Mike declared, "Where's the sheriff?" A couple of people vacated the back office and approached from a hall.

Sheriff Dunfri strolled out with big typhoons at his side, most likely a couple of Watches' men. His hands were held outward as if he were bracing himself for impact. Each man aimed weapons at Mike. Sheriff Dunfri shook his head and stated, "You've got some serious balls coming in here, Michael."

Mike lowered his pistol. He placed it on the counter as the deputy grabbed it and aimed it at him. Mike cried, "You had my son murdered, why?"

The old sheriff shook his head. He smirked. "Oh no, that's terrible. Did he get crushed?"

Mike cocked his head at him and asked, "Who else is in your back pocket . . . Stanley?"

"Well, all of us." The sheriff smiled. "Including the whole town. I'm sorry, pal, but you may not make it out of town tonight. You might wanna call home to the wife—tell 'er you love 'er."

Meanwhile, outside, homes were being ransacked by police and SWAT. People were being dragged outside and cuffed in their yards. The Wisconsin Army National Guard assembled on the main drag through the center of town. There were dozens of military trucks. They wore full battle rattle. Mike was entertaining the sheriff while the entire town was getting hard-pressed steel shackles to their wrists. Many houses remained unoccupied, which was seemingly odd.

Outside the small police station, two SWAT personnel aimed through a set of windows at the two guys standing alongside Sheriff Dunfri. On the other end of the building, two more SWAT guys aimed at the deputy and at the old sheriff. Red dots bounced on their shirt pockets. At the back of the sheriff station, a couple of SWAT personnel swept through offices, clearing rooms. Silencers were used to not alert those inside the main office. A few were shot as they attempted to retrieve weapons. Billy exited the sheriff's office and stood along a wall in the hall aiming at Sheriff Dunfri.

Mike smiled. "You shouldn't have made that deal with the devil, John. That was a bad move, man."

Sheriff Dunfri smirked. "It's all about business, my friend. Who can retire on a cop's salary anyway? Not you, not me."

Mike shook his head in disgust and proclaimed, "Oh, we aren't friends, trust me." Mike raised his hands as if the tension increased. John stared at him oddly. It was the cue for the men outside. Shots rang. Holes were created in the windows; the deputy, the two men beside the sheriff were shot and killed at the exact same time. John Dunfri took a few steps back; he glanced at four red dots swarming his heart.

Mike smiled. "Well, look at that—one for each ventricle. Doesn't that just eat your little heart out, John?"

In a wooden box on top of his desk was his favorite bone-handled six-shooter. Another pistol lay in his desk drawer. He was itching to go

WATCHES III - A CAMPING FIASCO

snatch one of the two. Mike kept his eye on him and walked around the counter to retrieve his pistol from the dead deputy. Then he noticed his son step out of the hallway.

That's when John Dunfri's pistol slid across the floor and bumped into his heel. "Looking for that, old boss?" He spun around. Billy was aiming his favorite gun at him. He insisted, "Go ahead, pick it up and see what happens." He smiled.

John's eyes widened, and he sighed. "Billy, it's a miracle, you're alive. Your boy's alive, Mike."

Billy said, "Yeah, I wanted to stop by and give you my official resignation."

Mike retrieved his pistol as John knelt and reached for the pistol. Mike shouted, "I wouldn't do that, John." He didn't even bother to aim his gun at the sheriff.

The police outside couldn't see him on the floor from the height of the windows. John stayed closer to the floor as he placed the weapon to his temple and pulled the trigger with a definite click. His eyes remained closed. Then he reopened them.

Billy smiled at him. "Hi, John. Welcome to hell. I'll be your spirit guide from here on out."

John stood and argued, "Of course, no bullets." He dropped his head to see the four red dots relocate each ventricle.

Billy smiled and explained, "Yeah, you thought you were getting a freebie on this. Heck no, we wanna see how long you last in prison."

John dropped any facial expressions. He looked at Billy and said, "Look, Billy. I'm sorry for what I've done." He glanced at Mike, "I needed the money and Stan gave me a ticket out. Listen, before I go, there's a tunnel under the old sawmill, but you might be too late."

Mike realized what he was going to do and lunged forward. "John, no." Mike was waving off the men outside.

John raised the empty pistol at Mike; the police outside the window had to react. Four shots. Four hits were confirmed as John flew backward over a desk. Billy lowered his aim and shook his head amongst the blood bubbles. Mike stepped away from his brief lunge and realized he succeeded in suicide by cop.

SWAT members flooded the main office from the hallway. Billy glanced at his dad and whispered. "A tunnel below the old sawmill . . . !"

"Yup, I think his final words were our clue, son."

"Dad, we must get to the marina now."

They stepped onto the front deck of the police station and waved local law enforcement and military closer. Officer Darcy stood behind Mike. "OK, here's the situation. The man we are looking for is still at large. He's in control of the old sawmill south of the Upham Woods campground across the river. There's a tractor company behind that fire station." He pointed down the road. "I want crews getting them on those military flatbeds to help clear the trees from the main road to the camp. I need about twenty more police at the marina and lots of guns. Do you boys have some?" he asked a soldier.

"Yes, sir," the sergeant replied, spun around, and shouted, "Clark, Toms, Coronado, King, we need eight M60's and two 50-Cals down to the boatyard; move! You guys over there, follow them. Mannarino, Buschke, Simmons, Orloff, work with the tractor company. Get those HEMTTs loaded. We have to clear the roads to the camp. The remainder of you report to your section sergeants, we will need river crews and road crews standing by."

Mike turned to the local law and said, "We're going fishing. Any questions?"

Chapter Twenty-Six

The Stairway

Bonzo and another muscle-bound jughead led the three groups of students up a winding stairway along a cliff. Everyone was tied together; they walked single file. Dusk was setting in; students were tired. There were three more weapon-toting monsters between the groups as they walked the winding stairway. Armed men staggered the line.

Danny listened to the many feet hit the wooden steps. He could hear them amidst the artillery in the background. Across the river, the campground twinkled like a thunderous war. Somewhere, his mom was in the same line. Duffy and Jerome were in front of him. White circles flashed from between a group of trees like whitecaps sparkling in the moonlight. Danny readjusted after a student bumped into him. The students above yanked him down; a man soon towered over him pointing his fully automatic in his direction.

"What's your problem, boy?" The man grunted, "Get up!"

Danny's shoulder was being yanked into a wooden step as the line hadn't stopped until the shout. Danny glanced into the trees; he was convinced they weren't alone. "Nothin', ankle itched." Danny withdrew a switchblade from his sock and stood up.

The man shoved him up the stairs. The groups continued marching. The daylight had slipped away. They climbed the old wooden steps in what little light the new moon provided. Woods surrounded the stairway; the only skylight was above the path they were on. Aside from coughs, sneezes, and shoes scraping wooden boards, the silhouettes of bobbing heads through the faded horizon remained dreary. With so many trees, the campground wasn't even visible or the river. The wooden steps wiggled their soles from every ordinance rocking Upham Woods behind them.

Danny lifted his head. A wiggling limb caught his attention. The man with the fully automatic stopped and turned to view the line of students. He was the tail gunman in the string of lost classmates. Within a split second of turning uphill, a black-suited ninja dropped before his face. It seemed dead silent at the moment the armed man was face-to-face with a ninja. Students gasped and veered around the two. Faithfully, Danny stared at the shivering limb overhead not noticing the black-suited man. He swore he saw a black panther or something. When he dropped his head, he noticed the ninja's back facing him. He began cutting at his rope as he walked.

Gently, the ninja lowered the gunman to the ground. A girl shrieked at the ninja's side. He hushed her and withdrew a knife from the top of the man's head. When the ninja spun around, Danny was fully prepared to fight until he saw the ninja wearing size eleven bowling shoes. When the man unmasked himself before Danny, it was Pete. "Welcome to the shit show." Pete yanked the fully automatic from the man's firm grip and kicked him over the edge. The same girl shrieked.

He said, "Pete?"

"In the flesh, Daniel, in the flesh. Are the Armybrats all here?"

Pete held the line. He whispered to the first person in line. "Very quietly, we're gonna play the Telephone Game. You turn around and tell the person behind you to turn around; the last person who turns around starts walking to the beach. Cool?"

The kid nodded, and their Telephone Game began.

Duffy looked beyond Jerome to see Danny conversing with a ninja. He smiled and whispered, "Man, how did we get so lucky?"

Jerome concentrated on his footing when Duffy stopped him. Jerome reiterated, "Lucky?" He leaned aside, noticing the rest of the group walking away. They were further up the stairway. Duffy stopped, "Yeah," and he showed him free hands. "What I'm trying to say is: how did we get so lucky to be at the end of our rope?"

"Wrong choice of words, Duffster." Jerome laughed.

Jerome and Duffy charged a man who approached them from the line of students. The man tried raising his weapon. Each boy ran him into the crook of a tree. Duffy's knife handle wedged inside the trigger guard blocking the man from a trigger pull. Jerome grunted as the man resisted. All three of them were sharing soft gasps in a desperate scuffle for superiority. The sling of the weapon yanked at the man's shoulder as Duffy bore against his fat arm. Jerome continued to rotate the fully automatic away from the man's waste. The muzzle pointed directly at Jerome's gut.

Significant clicks sounded as the man continued to tug at the trigger. Duffy maintained a grip on the knife—blocking it. The sling gouged into the man's neck as he shoved at Duffy's arm, trying to free the object blocking his ability to hose them with hot lead. Duffy's face grimaced as the knife handle backed from the trigger guard. The muzzle—still locked in Jerome's tight squeeze—aimed at his stomach.

Danny walked between them. His horse stance placed his left shoulder squarely with the crook of the tree. Jerome continued to press on the muzzle; the sling tight to the man's neck; his neck seemed wider than either tree trunk beyond his shoulders. Fighting back with his fat palms, he pressed on Duffy's arm tapping at the trigger with his other bratwurst-looking finger. With a straight-legged kick, Danny's foot hung over the crook of the tree. A snap echoed within the faint gunfire across the river. His limp head rolled over the sling. Jerome and Duffy dropped to the ground regaining their strength as the man's body nestled in the crevice of the tree.

Danny retracted his leg and glanced at Jerome. "You mind telling Pete who you are."

Jerome exhaled and noticed Pete. "I'm a cop. I work with his brotha."

Pete glared at him for a second and then smirked. He nodded and extended a hand to help him onto his feet. Danny aided Duffy from his relaxation period. Pete said, "I know."

The main camp looked like a Fourth of July had gone ballistic. Through the trees, the Bratmobile hovered, shooting at Wausau police. Those Wausau boys knew how to put up a fight. However, the flying contraption spread misery to anyone who crossed paths in its headlights or thrusters.

Jerome knelt to retrieve the weapon from the dead man. "Holy crap, I gotta gun."

"Yeah, yeah, so do I." Pete turned to walk toward the group.

"Well, I had more but they floatin' down Wisconsin Riva."

Duffy whispered, "Hey, man. Where are ya going? The party is back that way."

Pete said, "I know, but my friends are up that way, and I can't leave them."

Jerome stepped to Pete and asked, "Do you guys need my help?"

Duffy glanced at Pete, then Danny, and shook his head. "Nah, we got this."

Jerome smiled. "A'ight then, may the best man win."

Pete looked at the Armybrats' car and suggested, "You'd be a fool to challenge that tank."

"You're a fool too, bro, but I see why you Armybrats so loyal. Go get yo' buddies. Take yo' time going but hurry back. I'm thinkin' that I'm gonna need some help in dat firestorm down there." As he finished his statement, a group of trees exploded along the shoreline while pointing in the general direction.

Pete raised an eyebrow and lowered his finger. "It's bad to point."

Jerome's lips pooched. "Good point." Pete's eyebrows jumped across his forehead. Jerome jogged down the hillside. The Armybrats caught up to the other students. Pete began cutting them free one at a time. As he freed them, he instructed them to keep quiet and head in the other direction. Danny and Duffy pretended to walk in the line with the other students, chuckling.

In front of them was the next armed guard. He held his finger to his lips to signify being quiet. He noticed everyone ducking a large branch hanging over the stairway. He looked to his left at a drop-off. He waved Danny and Duffy to the other side of the staircase. They exited the stairway and crouched down.

The man turned to face them. "Hey." He snapped his head toward the rustle of the limbs on the tree branch. Pete held tension on the limb. The creak in the branch at its stress point wound tightly within his firm grip. The man stepped down a couple of steps and held his gun up. He turned on his flashlight; the dingy light shone on the students scattering away from them. He scanned right and then left. Pete's eyes revealed between a group of leaves and branches.

Pete let go of the branch. It sprung forward and bashed him across the upper chest. He tried blocking the branch, dropped his weapon, and tripped over a rock formation on his left. The flashlight flickered in the distance as he dove off the cliff. Pete leaned forward to watch his body curl against a rock ledge. Cracks were heard as he crumpled over the rock and fell another hundred feet to the sandy beach below. The beam of his flashlight disappeared. Pete cringed. "Ooh, ouch. That broke his fall!" he whispered.

Duffy leaned over, tapped his shoulder, and whispered, "That broke him too."

Pete tightened his grip on his weapon sling and pulled away. "Why do ya gotta do that, huh?"

"What?" Duffy asked.

"Sneak up on me when I'm so close to the edge."

"Sorry."

The memory of the Infinity Room dangling below their toes had struck a nerve. The House on the Rock without a floor to stand on was death-defying. Duffy had done the exact same thing to him back then.

Danny repossessed the weapon the man had dropped.

Duffy returned a smile. "So, what's the plan here?"

Pete hesitated before saying, "I'm not sure. I'm just wingin' it."

Danny asked, "I can't believe Jerome went to play war down there. There's plenty of war here."

Duffy said, "Seriously, that's nuts. He's crazy"

Danny looked at the rest of the group. "It won't be long before the last few guards figure us out."

Pete suggested, "Yup, we better hurry. I'm going to run past the entire group and get to that guard. When I'm about three people away, play a little tug of war with the rope and stop that group of kids."

"Wait, Pete. Let me advance over that hill so I can get a clear shot of the leader. I think there's a good vantage point up there. Give me about a three-minute head start. If we do this right, we'll get both of these cocksuckers at the same time."

They nodded. Duffy was left alone. He nodded. "OK, I'll just . . . whatever. I'll tug the rope. I love ropes."

Danny bolted through the trees toward a rock formation. He climbed it as Pete brushed past students and chaperones. Each person he passed he hushed as he marched forward. The first group of students entered a wider patch of grass at the top of the stairway. The leader headed toward the second guard. Pete lunged behind his shoulders hoping Danny had a bead on the leader. He wrapped his arm around his weapon, squeezed him tight, cupped his mouth, and ran a blade across his neck.

The leader stopped dead in his tracks and shot at Pete. Pete crouched behind the man bleeding from his throat. Rounds buried through the man. Mists of blood caused a girl to scream. Pete held the dying man in front of him as a human shield. Danny took a breath, kneeled, aimed, and squeezed the trigger. The leader's head split open on the backside; mist fizzled before the moon in the backdrop; he fell on top of another man; none of them had noticed the third guy. Danny veered around his sight post after verifying his target had been down.

Pete nudged the guard forward. He fell onto his face. Pete stripped his weapon away and aimed at the guy on the ground. After tugging on the rope of students, Duffy ran to his body and stripped his weapon from him. "You won't be needin' this anymore; thanks for all your support."

A hand clamped tightly to the shoulder strap; Duffy fell onto his back. Through the tall blades of grass was the ugliest beast he ever saw. It was Bonzo. Bonzo squeezed the trigger of the weapon as it lay across him. Pete dropped behind the dead man as bullets tore the man's side apart.

Danny repositioned himself on the rock and glanced through the sights to see Duffy wrestling on the ground. Danny pulled the trigger, and a significant snap was heard without a round. He locked the charging handle to the rear exposing the chamber where a round seemed to be wedged from the magazine feed. Bonzo stood with Duffy and wrapped an arm around his neck holding him in front of him. Duffy aimed his weapon at Bonzo's foot and pulled the trigger. Bonzo's bootlaces shredded as a round penetrated it; he fell in agony, releasing him.

Duffy swept the weapon in Bonzo's direction; Bonzo tripped him before he could fire his gun. Bonzo kicked him in the face. Duffy rolled onto his side holding his face. Bonzo stood up, grimaced in pain, and hobbled toward a dark building set back in the grassy field. Duffy opened his satchel and extracted a rope. He jumped to his feet. Before Bonzo passed a Bobcat parked on a rocky bed, a rope cinched his waist. Duffy yanked on it. Bonzo fell to the ground. He rolled away as Duffy took two potshots at him while he was on the ground. One round grazed his shoulder; the second round ricocheted off the bucket of the Bobcat.

"Will ya stop moving so I can shoot you?"

Bonzo hopped inside the bucket of the Bobcat. He worked at the rope.

Suddenly, the Bobcat started. The bucket lifted as he wrestled with the rope; he fell, dropping his pistol inside the bucket. Danny sat in the Bobcat, smiling. Bonzo stood and immediately fell again; the slack in the rope flopped beneath the tire of the Bobcat. Danny noticed it and jerked the vehicle; the rope kinked his neck; the wheel tensed the rope. Duffy lunged and swung on it. The swing took any slack away from Bonzo as it cut off circulation, bringing his face into the hard metal arm of the bucket. Bonzo pulled on the rope, tossing Duffy backward. Duffy flew against the engine guard and rolled across the ground. Whipping his head back and forth to clear the whiplash, he carried the slack to a small tree, knocking Bonzo over once again.

Duffy tied it to the base of the tree. Danny saw the knot and immediately tilted the bucket to dump the load. Bonzo retrieved the pistol, lost it, and reached for the lip of the bucket. Danny pushed and pulled the arms sending a harsh jolt of machinery. Briefly, the Bobcat's front end lifted upward. When Danny pressed forward, the machine dropped on its front tires. Danny reversed the motion. Bonzo dropped backward, fell from his grasp on the lip; the force on the rope caused his neck to snap as he swayed underneath the raised bucket.

Duffy stood up, walked to him, and batted him in the gut with the rifle. He hollered, "Take that, you big dumb piñata." He bashed him a couple more times. "Thanks for kicking me in the face, douchebag." He struck him again.

Danny jumped off the Bobcat. "You aren't getting any candy out of that, Duffster."

"Just thanking him for the hardware is all." Duffy smiled and held up the pistol he dropped. He tucked it in his pants and slung the rifle to his shoulder.

One of the chaperones asked, "What's going on?"

Clarissa smiled. "It's the Armybrats."

Danny walked to her. "Are you OK?" She hugged him.

His mom who stood behind him replied, "Yes, son."

Danny spun around, "I was talking to her, mom. But I'm glad you are too."

"Is that man dead?" Clarice asked.

Duffy stood next to Danny. Danny cringed as big old Bonzo swayed behind them.

Pete stepped between them. "Listen up everyone; I need you to stand in a circle so I can cut you free."

Pete's knife was shot from his hand. Bangs thumped their chest cavities. Students wildly dispersed. One of the male boys dragged their ankles, seeping blood, through the dirt. A round penetrated it; it was Shawn's ankle. Sam was tied to the rope in front of him; he tried assisting him as the kids dragged them along like rope lights, running away from the gunfire. Two men wandered from the dark building spraying automatic weapons. Muzzle flashes lit up the building's siding and shrubbery. Danny and Duffy returned fire and shot both simultaneously. When they turned around, they noticed Pete standing at the edge of the cliff. The string of students and chaperones was missing.

"Um, where did everyone go?" Duffy asked, walking toward Pete.

Pete looked over the ledge. An uprooted tree about ten feet down caught the students, teachers, and chaperones; they hung like a loose strand of Christmas lights blowing in the wind. Pete scratched his head. They were hooting and hollering dangling before the rock face of a cliff. About fifteen people hung over one end; the rest of them draped from the other side. The roots cracked spraying debris over them. A few screams were heard amongst cries.

Duffy laughed. "Woo-wee, is that ever cute."

Danny leaned over the edge. "Now how are we supposed to do this?"

Pete suggested, "If we only had the Armybrats' car." They watched their car flying around the camp firing rounds in the distance. Fires were burning near cabins. Flashes in the trees outlined small arms fire around the perimeter.

Danny shouted, "Hang tight, everyone. We'll figure this out. In the meantime, think about what you did, dumb lemmings."

Duffy raised an eyebrow. "That's tellin' 'em."

Chapter Twenty-Seven

The Sawmill

Explosions wiped cabins on the north face as the Armybrats' car swooped over Jerome and fired missiles. Jerome watched a police officer get shot head to toe from the tree line. He perched against a slanted tree and fired two shots at two different men who were shooting back. Both rounds found an eyebrow. Jerome made his way toward the main office fighting one man, hand-to-hand near an LP tank. The man pulled out a pistol; Jerome pulled his arm and yanked his face onto the lid of the tank. In a daze, the guy bounced backward; Jerome flicked his wrist upward, pulled his elbow back, aimed his pistol against his chest, and squeezed the trigger. Blood spotted a man's face lunging from the wood line.

Jerome flipped backward, landing on the tank as hot lead sparked at his feet; performing another backflip off the tank, he shot the man with the blood-speckled face. Standing up, he leaned across the tank monitoring for movement. Rounds hit the tank at his right; he lifted the lid—for force protection. Another man was running, firing at him. He peeked around the lid and shot him. The man buckled from the round, seemingly folding his body in half in mid-stride.

A long-haired fellow jumped from the brush, swiping a machete at his head; it struck the lid. Jerome used his shoulder to slam the lid on his arm. Using his weight to hold it down, Jerome angled the weapon across the lid and pulled the trigger. He shot the man through the lower jaw. A glob of black hair flapped upward from matter exiting across the grass. His head tapped the exterior of the tank producing a muffled echo. Below his limp head, one line of blood wrapped around the egg-white tank. He fell backward; the lid bounced open. The machete twirled on top of the LP tank like spin the bottle, *Who was next in this fight?* Jerome stared into the tree line. The scrape of the blade diminished to one final rotation toward the woods.

Another man jumped from behind the tank; it startled Jerome for a second until he jump kicked the handle of the machete, sending it like a shiny torpedo in the night; it was an immediate vasectomy as the man's eyes teetered over his cheekbones to see the blade buried in his pants. Jerome shot his face. His tongue hung out, gripping onto the handle of the machete. He died, kneeling before the metal tank, nailing it with a thud.

Another man shot at Jerome; the round skimmed his shoulder; he fell onto his back and scooted toward the tank for cover. The man leaned over the tank, sporadically firing at the ground in front of him. Jerome's body hugged the base of the tank; he wrapped an arm over the side, aiming his weapon upward. A flame torched his gums sending teeth and skin around his left ear; the round blew out his upper cheek, yet he was still alive.

He stepped to the side. Jerome leaped to his feet to shoot him again. The guy threw the lid into his weapon; a muzzle flash projected a lost round through the trees. The jawless man gripped his pistol's barrel as Jerome raised his foot and jammed the man's fully automatic into the side of the lid on the tank. With Jerome's free hand, he slid the machete out of the man's waste. One solid swing carved at the rotator cuff. His arm slid off his body. Jerome dropped his foot from his weapon. He opened the lid, jostling the man across the gas valve; he folded the lid over his bloody face.

"Stop trying to defeat me!" he hollered. Every syllable was another lid slam. Blood streaked across the tank and the lid. He stabbed the machete through the man's chest; the valve hissed below his back. He could hear the leak.

He squatted to retrieve his weapon. He noticed his pistol was ten pounds heavier; as he lifted it, the man's arm hung from it. He peeled the fingers away; the arm nailed the grass with a thud. "Disgusting."

He tactfully peeked over the tank. Four guys advanced on him from the left, two more from the right. He stood and shot one man on the left and sprayed rounds sporadically at each of them while running backward; he tripped on a boulder protruding from the grass about thirty feet from the tank as rounds blasted away at the rock. He leaned against his knees behind the boulder hanging onto his bloody arm. He winced and aimed at the hissing valve on the tank. There were men running around each side of the tank. Jerome shot the valve. A brilliant flash of light rocketed toward the starry sky. All fifteen men, including three more jumping from the brush on the other side, flew outward in all directions away from what used to be an LP tank.

Jerome cowered as the fire scorched the earth and blew over the rock. The rock slid a foot and pushed him backward. He screamed from the heat and raging fire, "Holy shit!"

Tony, Mike's former boss, latched onto him and hobbled with him toward the main office. Jerome reached across his chest and squeezed his collar. He said, "You can't take your men that way, fall back to the river."

Tony replied, "Why?"

Jerome explained, "There are at least fifty men closing in from south. I could see them from across the river."

Tony bit his lower lip. "Too late. There's hundreds more at the main entrance."

Jerome nodded in disbelief.

"This reminds me of Khe Sanh, Vietnam, all over again."

Jerome raised an eyebrow unsure of his reference to the war.

Tony sighed. "Well, then I suppose this is it, my friend. There are many men closing in from the north and many men from south. We don't stand a chance here."

Jerome leaned around a tree and shot a few guys approaching through the brush. Tony did the same with a couple of guys behind Jerome. They ran over the hill toward the main office. More Wausau police officers were taking cover along the main office, some near the bleachers on the baseball diamond. Police were firing in all directions.

The Upham Woods Campground suddenly became brighter. The baseball diamond, the basketball courts, the main office, the clinic, and the camp church lit from external lights. A couple more police were shot near the bleachers; other officers pulled their bodies into the dugouts for safety. The remaining survivors were caught in a circle of Watches' men. All Jerome could wonder was how in the hell did Watches' have so many bad guys. They were clearly outnumbered. The odds were stacked like poorly positioned dominos; it was about to become a camp massacre. Unbeknownst to them, this was mostly cartel, paid mercenaries, and residents from Little Rapids.

The Armybrats' car flew over the center of the baseball diamond. A raspy voice echoed off the porch of the main office. Watches spoke through a megaphone from the hovering craft. Jerome could barely see his face through the windshield. The lights beamed behind the car and the thrusters underneath cast a brilliant glow over second base. Jerome stepped out of the dugout aiming at the car. Intensely, he moved in on him.

Watches shouted, "Seize fire, seize fire. Fellas, fellas, the war ends now. As you can see, my men are bearing down on you and there's nowhere left for you to run and hide."

Jerome kept his weapon's aim toward the fuel tank. Watches shouted, "That's far enough Jerome Dawson." Heat from the thrusters threw arm hairs; he knelt on the pitcher's mound. Tony was hollering for him to return to the dugout. Quite frankly, with a flying tank above them and being surrounded, nowhere was safe. Jerome knew one man needed to go and that was the voice behind the megaphone.

On the main road, crews worked tirelessly to remove the downed trees. They finally cleared the last section and moved vehicles and ground personnel toward the main entrance of the camp. Ground troops took out armed guards at the entrance; they worked their way in. SWAT personnel fanned south through the woods and army personnel moved around the north end.

Up the riverbank, gleams of light flickered in the moonlight. Outlined silhouettes of bodies and what seemed like an endless display of boats closing in on the camp. Billy and his father were in the lead boat. More National Guard troops had weapons mounted throughout the fleet. They commandeered boats from the Little Rapids marina and private owners. Heavy weapons were mounted amongst the fleet with another two-man crew in a center boat manning the fifty-caliber machine guns. Two boats headed to the opposite side of the river where students had gathered at the bottom of the stairway.

In the distance, quiet wisps of propeller blades cut the midnight sky. Blackhawks were approaching in stealth—under night vision. Crews aboard a few different Blackhawk helicopters were hovering over the silent boats in the water. They operated in blackout mode. Door gunners were leaning over their assigned crew-served weapons. The boats on the river killed their engines upon approach holding the perimeter to the eastern edge of the campgrounds. The vehicles helped fortify the perimeter on the western side of the camp. Tanks waited, strategically positioned at the road's edge. Across the river, Danny, Duffy, and Pete watched the entire battlefield unfold.

Danny was in a Bobcat with a chain wrapped around the bucket. The chain led to the human Christmas ornaments, tugging the center of the human string. There were a few moans and cries as the ropes tightened around everyone's wrists. As they dragged up the cliff face, people were getting to know their buddies as they banged into each other. The Bobcat was pulling everyone to safety as they strung along the cliff wall.

Duffy was inside the bucket where he tied off a line to help hoist them up. The first body came rolling over the ledge. Two at a time, their classmates, teachers, and chaperones flopped over the rocks like marker buoys tied together. Danny backed the Bobcat over a small tree; it snapped and pierced the tire. Duffy fell inside the bucket. A muffled cry came from Duffy expressing the pain.

Pete glanced overhead at the bucket. As Duffy lie inside holding onto his head, he suddenly had to cup his ears from the snap that echoed inside. He shouted, "What was that?"

Pete laughed over the smoking barrel of a gun. Duffy screamed.

Danny said, "Pete shot your bucket, man."

"Why did you do that, Pete?"

"Remember the time you shot me while in body armor?" Pete stared skyward.

"Ow, still butt hurt about that, huh?"

"Paybacks are a bitch." Pete laughed. "There's two more still hanging over the ledge, Danny."

Duffy leaned over the bucket and held his weapon over a shoulder to see Sam and Shawn were the last two dangling below. He laughed. "You're good, Dan. Let 'em hang."

For a split second, all gunfire had seized. Everything was calm. The boats sat on the river. A dead silence loomed over the camp. White phosphorous flares shot over the canopy surrounding the camp. Jerome couldn't believe his eyes. At their elevation, he could see Watches had a fence like a militia. He glanced at the hill to see National Guard members launching flares, followed by heavy weapons fire from crew-served weapons controlled by buddy teams. Fifty caliber rounds mowed trees. The Armybrats' car jolted weaved and wobbled in the air.

Helicopters spread a hellfire through the tree line torching anything and everything vastly approaching the camp from the north and south. Jerome spun around and watched the Armybrats' car. Near the river, bodies were flying out of the woods; some were on fire and immediately put to rest as heavy tracer rounds speckled through them. Riverbanks lit up from the fleet of boats.

Watches clamored into the megaphone as his body was being tossed in the seat. "What the hell?"

The car dipped forward and rocked a bit; it was just enough where the lights from the power poles, surrounding the baseball diamond, flickered across the windshield; a single beam of light came through the hole in its undercarriage. Jerome could see it had gone through the floor panel. Watches spun the car, firing upon the army vehicles on the main road. Bradley tanks crushed trees entering the campgrounds. Ruts in the road became squished bad guys, soupy ditches.

Along the riverbed, lights lit the entire woods as the Madison police department with a select few service members and SWAT marched across the piers and closed the gap on the eastern side of the camp. Jerome charged the flying tank. His heart pounded. His feet pelted the ground. Watches men who surrounded the survivors found them being flanked from behind. Then the Wausau survivors cleaned house from the dugouts while they weren't paying attention anymore.

Jerome could feel the heat from the thrusters. Again, that flicker of light caught his eye. He moved left to be able to see around the flames from one of the thrusters and took a knee on the pitcher's mound as some dirt kicked up near his calves. Someone had been shooting at him; a Wausau cop sighted the shooter in and buried one temple through both eyes.

Jerome aimed for the bullet hole and moved his sight post slightly to the lead of the car, depressing the trigger. Three shots rang out. The Armybrats' car took a nosedive, scooped up first plate, and tossed some dirt from the grill before it flew straight backward. Jerome rolled aside as each thruster melted second base, the pitcher's mound, and home plate. Jerome dropped his pistol when one burned his shoulder. The rear bumper ripped the backstop from the hardened earth. Wausau police scattered away from the bleachers as the fencing dragged a few pine trees. The American flagpole slightly bent and whipped the flag, but it did not fall.

The car dragged the fencing through the parking lot busting windows on parked cars and screeched the paint; it flew erratically toward the riverbank. Watches dragged two of his men; they crashed into the sidewall of dumpsters along one end of the parking lot. Billy and Mike watched it fly past them as they fought their way toward the camp along the sandy front. Fifty caliber gunners took shots at the flying tank as it dipped out of sight.

Billy looked at his dad and insisted, "I'm following that car."

His dad glanced further up the hill toward the camp. He concurred, "OK, son. I'm right behind ya."

Billy acknowledged him with a simple nod and ran across the pier, diving into the river. His father shot a couple of men along the river and jumped in after his son. Officer Darcy crouched near a boatshed and watched the two swimming to the other side. A round buried through his shoulder. He fell backward, rotated onto his good shoulder, and shot both men shooting at Billy and his dad in the water.

Jerome was in celebratory mode, dancing with joy near the pitcher mound. It was short-lived as he was tackled by Tony yet again. "Kid, you trying to be a target?" Tony laid in the prone and shot a few guys running around a storage shack—containing sporting accessories. Jerome shook his head in disagreement with his question and shot at four men running in their direction from the parking lot. He got three before a reload.

Tony rolled and shot the fourth. More men surrounded the storage facility. Tony had to reload as well. Dirt fanned before them as the men fired at their helpless bodies, trying to reload their weapons. Tony and Jerome lay tight against each other, slapping clips into their weapons. Suddenly, the storage shack and the men disappeared like sand below a tailpipe when a tank dropped a shell over them. Tony and Jerome ducked.

"No, but I know I got him." Jerome smiled.

"Got who?"

"I think I got the devil right up th' ass."

Tony turned toward him.

"OK, dat didn't come out right," Jerome proclaimed. They both fired in opposite directions.

With so many teams fighting so many fronts, the idea of fratricide was plausible, but there seemed to be an intrinsic strategy performed at all levels of combat. The precision was directed by one man and one man alone. Michael Anglekee helped make this possible. Billy had the boat idea; between his dad and him, they concocted this plan and rolled with it. The success seemed to be delivering the outcome they had hoped for as Watches men fled from the wood line. No longer was there a pinched nerve at the remaining survivors. The beach fronts were stained red. Many bodies lined the riverbanks. Even the river water held a dark red tinge.

However, the victory was a far cry from wolf. The devil remained at large and there were still hostages to be found. A soldier crashed a boat into the sandy front and continued running across the sand toward the camp. Soldiers were painting undergrowth shades of red.

On the other side, the Armybrats' car flew vertically over the cliff face—out of sight through the many trees. Billy darted along the sandy riverbank toward the group of kids and followed military, police officers, and SWAT up the hill. His dad was behind him. Meanwhile, coming down the stairway were the rest of the chaperones, teachers, and students, finally freed. The reinforcement teams had to step aside, allowing them to pass.

At the top of the hill, a Bobcat busted through a garage door and flew inside the old sawmill. Sparks were hammering away at the metal frame. Bullets penetrated the tires and separated hydraulics. The cage where the operator would normally sit was sparking as rounds bounced off it or through the seat. The empty seat was shredded. Along the moonlit trellis of scaffolding at the top of the building, two boys swayed in the moonlight from two separate sunroofs.

Danny and Duffy slid ropes inside and perched on scaffolding. They shot at each muzzle flash from the dark aisles. As Watches' men fired upon the human-less operated Bobcat, they took them out one by one. Pete leaned in through the busted garage door and fired at them while they were redirecting fire toward Danny and Duffy.

Smoke canisters rolled in around the Bobcat and popped off flooding the corridor with smoke. SWAT and local law enforcement entered the warehouse. Pete took a knee behind some crates, and Danny and Duffy sat quietly watching for any stragglers. Outside, army personnel established points at each corner and worked their way around the building. They were being shot at from windows in the mill. Snipers ended their potshots. The military created a perimeter around the old mill.

Watches parked the Armybrats' car along a rock ledge. He opened the driver's door and fell out. He stood up to immediately fall as his chin bounced off the dirt. Blood trickled along the lap belt. Blood ran down the side of the seat. The fabric of the seat cushion at the center collected a small pool of blood that surrounded the hole. Watches crawled around the door of the car panting and groaning. He gripped the grass and wiggled his way around the car door like a wounded animal dragging its hindquarters.

The sawmill was being invaded by local law enforcement, SWAT and the military quarantined the area from the tree line to the waterbed around the backside and beyond. Watches angrily ripped grass from the roots and punched at the Armybrats door above his head. He crawled to the car like an infant spotting a toy rattle, withdrawing a black box from alongside the seat. He crawled around the opened door, heading to the front of the car.

He threw an arm over the bumper, hoisting his entire body onto the front end. He stood in front of the car with most of his weight on one leg and snarled as he watched soldiers taking positions around the entire sawmill. He fumed as the cool breeze tortured his open wound. His webbed fingers seemingly clawing at the stars, throwing punches at the moon. He placed his fist to his forehead and tried to calm the panting.

The moonlight outlined his body. His top hat appeared dark blue. He stopped breathing and scooted his ass further up the hood. He tossed the black box against the windshield and pulled out a cigar. His bloody hand transmitted dark red across the brown paper and the green matchbook as he lit it. The Armybrats' car keys jingled as they dangled from his pinky finger. His hand shook from the pain. The keys continued to jingle. His eye glowed red; his head dipped low; his lipped curled when he withdrew the cigar. Smoke flushed into the brim of his top hat and drifted away in swirls.

Inside the mill, a trapdoor slightly opened beneath a shelving unit. The trapdoor led to a deep dark hole where a ladder was affixed to a sidewall. The hole was a tunnel; it ran straight to the backside of the mill directly underneath a bed of water; further away from the pool was a waterfall pouring over the mountain. Halfway through the tunnel were metal bars barricading people inside.

Julie Carson was lying inside. Wesley Fifer was lying between her and his grandfather. A few of his grandfather's staff from the campground were lying on the floor; another man was inside as well. Above the metal bars, lining the ceilings, were shape charges. Shape charges lined throughout the entire tunnel, throughout the old sawmill. The facility was predetermined for destruction. Hostages were in a caged tub below a large bowl of water.

Danny and Duffy climbed through the scaffolding. Gunfire echoed through the mill. Danny lunged from the bottom of the scaffolding and tackled two men running below them. He stood between them as they rolled to their sides, preparing to shoot him, he stomped their muzzles in a crisscross pattern; each man shot each other's leg. Danny dropped to his butt and chopped both of their Adams' apples. Immediately, they held onto their throats. On his back, Danny kicked upward. Both weapons flipped over his chest, muzzles on either side of his face. When he slid them upward, the muzzles jammed tight to their hands cupping their throats. Danny closed his eyes and pulled the triggers. Brain matter spread across the concrete floor.

A man leaned below a shelving unit and was about to stab Danny. Pete lunged forward and released a knife above him. He rolled aside to watch it bury itself in the man's throat. Danny shot him through the head, crawled to him, and whispered, "That was a cutthroat performance huh?" The man's eyelids wiggled before they clamped shut.

Pete retrieved his knife from the man's throat and whispered, "Good one, Danny." Pete noticed the trapdoor. He suggested, "Shall we have a peek see?"

Duffy stood behind Danny and replied, "Well, why not?"

Duffy threw the door upward. A man from SWAT tossed a flare over their shoulders; bullets nailed the shelving units above their heads. Danny ducked and shot inside the tunnel. He knelt and aimed into the bright hole. No one returned fire after that. They began their descent, aiming over their shoulders.

Watches sat staring at the mill—enjoying his cigar. He puffed one last puff and tossed it at a tree. It exploded sending sparks inside a poof of orange smoke. He looked at the small black box near the windshield and reached for it. As he drew it near him, he extended an antenna from the corner. He flipped a black cover upward, revealing a single red switch. It was a detonator. As he flipped the cover back, the Dodge Charger's keys released from his bloody grip and jingled against the windshield; they rolled across the wiper blade and hung there. He leaned over still holding the black box, trying to retrieve the car keys. The keys flipped from the arm of the driver's side wiper blade. With the detonator in one hand, he crawled across the hood; his fingers protruded toward the keys. The pain in his thigh was overwhelming. Jerome had shot him.

The wiper blade pushed the keys; they rolled off the windshield. He watched the blade retract; it had repeated this a few times and stopped. As he sprawled across the hood, he found himself staring at Billy face-to-face through the pane. Billy flicked a switch on the dashboard and Watches began to glow. The electric force field jolted his entire body. He couldn't move.

Billy shouted at him through the windshield. "Yeah, I got the spare key, sucker." There seemed to be a moment where he appeared to be Ralph P. Fallway as the electricity flowed through him. Then his image fizzled away, and he became his son, Ron. After that, a grizzly image of Father O'Brien appeared. Then, of course, Stan returned as Watches glared at him with one red eye that seemed more bloodshot than ever.

His one eye rolled at the passenger seat and Michael Anglekee was staring at him. With his arm resting on his leg, he lifted the barrel of Mr. Steely and Billy shook his head at him. He reiterated, "No, this cuckoo clock spun his last hour, dad. Enjoy the moment." Mike's eyes never left Stanley's eye as his painful stare transformed into a smirk. "Is your eyepatch getting hot yet?" Billy asked.

He wiggled and squirmed on the hood. His one eye crossed inward staring at the black box. All he had to do was flip the damn switch and it would all be over. He would win. He would drown people Billy loved. Friends and loved ones would either perish in flames or suffocate.

Billy could see his left palm turning black; the box wiggled in his right hand. He could see the red button that Watches so desperately wanted to press. His thumb slightly moved upward. His eye patch smoked. His top hat rolled away from his head; his gangly teeth clamped together. His head twitched. His cheek skin wiggled; his white hair seemed bright. Billy stared the demon in his eye. He wasn't giving him an inch. He wanted his misery to drag out. The horror he had put his family and his friends through had been his lifelong mission to terminate. He wanted him to cook. He felt no remorse watching him fry above the grill of the Charger.

His right hand was wiggling; the black box tapped the windshield. The taps continued to click the glass. Skin separated along his cheeks and neck. The skin cells were breaking apart during his electric shock drowning. The muscle tissues had begun to show through the skin tears.

His white hair was frizzy. His hands tore along the backside and around his knuckles. Billy was burning him alive. Watches thought he had killed him, and as one of his front teeth cracked and his gums split, he wished he had. A few of his fingernails were turning black. His good eye glowed fine red veins from his lids to his iris.

Billy listened to the black box tapping the windshield. He counted the taps. He timed its pace. He turned the wipers on. The box tapped the glass. The wipers moved up. Again, the box tapped the window. The wiper blade swept the detonator off the windshield and the black box landed in Billy's palm as he reached out the driver's window.

Duffy never followed them inside the tunnel beneath the mill; he decided to join Special Forces to help clear rooms along the mezzanines and offices. As they entered one room, in particular, Duffy stopped dead in his tracks. The Spec Ops personnel moved through the room and cleared it and left Duffy trapped in the twilight of yesteryear. Larry Schwabenhaus mentioned this office to Duffy. His flashback reminded him. He appeared as if he dropped a warm one in his underwear. He remembered Larry mutter not to enter this room.

On the desk were three wallets, four cellphones, three passports, and a photo album. Behind the desk, three wigs draped different poles. Each pole had a square nameplate below the wig. Each nameplate held its own name. From left to right, they read *Ronald Markesan, Ralph Fallway*, and *Father O'Brien*. A chest in the corner held a black bodysuit, hanging partially from the side. Additionally, a fancy embroidered robe for the Catholic priest hung from a hook above the chest.

Duffy spun around and opened a wallet. The first wallet had a driver's license for Stanley Markesan and exactly $180 dollars in the billfold. Duffy threw the wallet and scavenged through each one. He started to comprehend the newfound discovery. The wallets matched the nameplates under the wigs. The passports mirrored the IDs in the wallets.

Duffy was digging through the chest of clothes, tossing oddities aside. Inside a photo album, he found a picture of a snowman in a field. He made a face at it. He didn't understand it. He found another picture of the office building where his mother's floral shop used to be in Verona and another picture of the church across the street from the old floral shop. Then there were pictures of the boys building a fort in the woods. There were many pictures of them when they were younger. He thumbed through the empty pages in the back. A couple sheets of paper fell. Duffy dropped the book.

He picked up the sheets of paper and turned them over. There were sketches of people on the pages. Again, one sketch was for Mr. Fallway wearing sunglasses and a baseball cap. Another sketch was of Father O'Brien. He glanced at the desk; the drawer was slightly out. He opened it and a matchbook lain inside a pen holder. A lonely, partially burnt cigar lay next to it. In the drawer was a newspaper clipping of an obituary. It read *Ronald Markesan, born June 12th, 1964, died July 16th, 1974, age ten.* The stories were true, he died at the hands of his father, Stanley Markesan. Duffy spun around and glanced at the wig with the name Ronald Markesan; he held the obituary next to the wig and compared the names. His mind backtracked to the training exercises, and Ron's face flashed in and out between memories. He remembered Ron saving him from the mud pit. He remembered the black-suited man shooting up the hill at nobody.

When they were inside the drums, Watches was outside arguing with himself. No one else was there—not Ron, not Mr. Fallway. They thought his son was arguing with his father. It wasn't true. They were young boys duped by a sociopath with psychopathic tendencies. He played many roles. Apparently, he was Father O'Brien from the church in Verona. He even acted the role of his son. In all this madness, he played the investigator who shared a bogus office with a bogus WITSEC handler, Wayne Richards, or perhaps it was Mr. Fallway. There were no names for Wayne Richards, no pictures, no wallets. Those two played two separate roles or perhaps there was a Wayne Richards.

Suddenly, the fourth cellphone rang. It seemed out of place since it wasn't in any uniform fashion like the other cellphones or the other passports and wallets. Duffy dropped the obituary; it floated to the floor beside the desk. His entire body jolted and brought him away from his nightmares. He spun around for the phone. It continued to ring; he flipped it open. He said, "Ya."

"Move to your right a little." The person hung up.

Duffy turned around; a red dot was planted on the whiteboard. He dropped to the floor, crawling to the doorway. He peeked out the door, immediately dropping to his side. Bullets flooded the office. The whiteboard cracked and chunks blew across the desk. Whoever was on the phone was trying to instruct him to walk into his own death. He threw an arm around the frame of the doorway and shot saw blades across the mill. A man perched on a mezzanine across the way fired into the office. Duffy held the weapon through the doorway, exchanging bullets. Rounds pelted the blades and created loud rings through the mill. Some rounds ricocheted and winged the man. He stopped shooting and held onto his shoulder. A SWAT guy began firing in his direction as well.

Back at camp, a tank fired a round through a van. The van crimped around a tree. However, the shell carried through the sidewall of the van, skimmed the flagpole before the main office, the pole spun the American flag as the shell arched across the river and buried through the waterbed behind the sawmill. Water gushed inside where the hostages were. Water filled the corridor pushing people to the ceiling.

Pete swam to the metal bars, gripping onto them, shouting, "Mom!" All the hostages were dehydrated and malnourished. And now they were being flooded. Special Forces scurried with chains hooked to a Bobcat. Two SWAT personnel withdrew a plasma torch from the water; the second guy struck it to get the flame roaring while the other team member blasted the metal bars. They cut a reasonable section near the ceiling and underwater. Chains looped around the bars and tensed through the trapdoor. A Spec Ops guy signaled with a thumb and directed another guy operating the beat-up old Bobcat. He backed the Bobcat up. Bubbles rose to the surface.

Men stood at the trapdoor waiting and watching. They lost visual through the water. One SWAT guy shared a glanced at his partner on the Bobcat who shook his head. Suddenly, Pete hoisted his mother from the hole. More bodies followed them.

Bodies continued popping up from the trapdoor, one at a time. Law enforcement was helping the hostages over piles of metal and rubble being flushed with water, gushing across the floor. Further ahead, a line of emergency people guided them through the busted garage door. SWAT teams shot at the mill where the man had targeted Duffy; the man rolled to his side, jumped to a lower section, and climbed down a ladder. Duffy peeked out the doorway to see them running through a corridor of crates and boxes, chasing the man. He rolled out the doorway and ran left to catch up with them. He ran across the mezzanine.

Finally, the SWAT team circled the man as he held a gun to a lady's head. About fifty feet behind him was another garage door; it remained shut. Duffy leaned against the railing and aimed at him. When he looked through the scope, the man was unrecognizable; however, he knew who the woman was. It was Danny's mom. He withdrew his face from the scope.

"Back up or this lady gets it."

Clarice shouted, "Wayne, why are you doing this?"

"Shut up, Clarice!"

"You were supposed to be our handler. You were supposed to take care of us."

"I tried. Believe me I tried."

Duffy squinted with confusion. Apparently, she had known the man. Duffy could see a shadow emerging behind a crate. A person was moving on the opposite side. Duffy leaned forward and peered through the sights trying to see if he could make out the figure. The figure peeked around the crate and Duffy saw his face. It was Danny. A streak of light caught Duffy's eye; he peered to his left through a set of windows. Outside the window, he noticed the Dodge Charger streaming straight toward the garage door. It seemed to be glowing.

Duffy readjusted his sights on the man's trigger finger and fired two shots in concession. He shouted, "Now Danny." Released from the clutches of Wayne Richards, Clarice fell to the floor; his finger dropped to the ground along with the weapon. Danny jumped kicked his face. SWAT personnel pulled Clarice out of the mill as she screamed for her son. Duffy ran down the steps toward Wayne who retrieved a pistol from an ankle pouch. Wayne flew backward as Duffy yanked on his arm and pulled the handgun away from his grip. The handgun bounced across the ground.

A black Dodge Charger slid through the garage door. Pieces of metal were stripped away from the roll tracks. A man appeared to be strapped to the hood of the car. His clothes were smoking; a corner of his trench coat was burning. His skin was riddled in tears. Blue lights shined throughout the mill. The Dodge drove at Wayne. Wayne was trying to stand when he noticed Billy and his father staring at him from the front seat. With the brakes pressed, the engine revving, feeding fuel through the drivetrain, tires spinning in the doorway. The exhaust kicked smoke like the tires ripping tread across the concrete. Duffy helped Danny up; they took off running. Outside, people were scattering.

A series of small tubes positioned along the underside of the bumper squirted oil throughout at Wayne. The concrete floor was beginning to shine with an oil slick. It was raining on Wayne's face. It was dripping alongside his bruised and bloodied neck. The wooden crates around him transformed to a reddish-brown as the substance oozed across the wood. Billy spun the tires. Smoke filled the garage entrance.

Wayne glanced at his fully automatic he dropped and retrieved it. He aimed at Billy but had to use his middle finger in the trigger housing; a significant click of the hammer was heard and no bang; he cocked the weapon to see a hole in the sidewall that rendered the weapon inoperable. That was Duffy's second shot. He threw it and retrieved a pistol lying on the ground and screamed as his middle finger rapidly yanked the trigger. Rounds were flattening against the glass. Mike's head bounced off the seat. Billy smiled at his dad's reaction. They watched rounds spark through the intrusion detection field and flatten in place; some rounds sliced through Watches burnt flesh.

Mike sighed. "Wayne Richards—you bastard."

Wayne's weapon emptied, and he looked at the empty chamber and licked his lips as the fluids ran down his face. "Real cute, Billy. Using my oil slick feature against me."

Billy dropped into drive, and the car sped through the mill. He slammed on the brakes as Wayne struggled to stand. Billy clicked the switch to shut off the *Intrusion* device which released Watches. His body sailed away from the hood and planted around Wayne. The Armybrats' car continued to slide and lifted from the concrete floor by flaming thrusters. The thrusters lit the oil slick, and flames chewed the crates and streamed toward the two bodies. Watches' body was already burning as he sailed into Wayne's, knocking him over. The two burning bodies glided through the oil slick. Wayne screamed, "Damn you, Michael Anglekee."

The thrusters that lit the mill as well as the fuel slick that doused everything helped spread the flames. Billy flew straight toward the opened garage door at the other end of the mill. They watched the two burning bodies sail through the trap door into the water pit below. His father was sitting in the passenger seat. He lifted the black box that Watches had earlier. His other hand never left Mr. Steely.

The sweet sorrow came from his own son as Billy whispered, "Do it, dad."

His dad looked at the mill and flipped the switch. The brilliant array of shape charges vibrated the hillside. Chaperones, students, and teachers watched from riverbanks as rocks rolled down the cliff. Flames scorched trees along the ridge. A line of police kept the students away as burning debris landed on the sandy front. The Armybrats' car curved around and laid fire into the hole at the center of the mill. The entire mill was engulfed in flames. Billy let go of the trigger and flew over the mill.

He clicked a button that read Big Boom and released a small cylindrical object much like the one Watches released on the squad cars earlier. Mike spun around to see the object drop toward the center of the mill. He asked, "What was that, Billy?"

Billy asked, "Ah, you got your seatbelt on, right?"

Mike watched the side-view mirror. Another flash of light illuminated the hillside. Trees seemed to disintegrate. The explosion dug a crater through the hill. The entire concrete foundation buckled and split away in chunks. The bed of water behind the mill filled the new crater. The conveyor belts in the mill detached and separated from their metal frames. Fires were burning everywhere. The explosion forced the Armybrats' car into a tailspin as the trunk hammered a tree. A twig jammed the bumper.

"Ahh, Billy!" Mike said.

Billy glanced beyond his dad and noticed about six five-foot sawblades streaming at them. Billy pressed the steering column. Nothing happened. The branch held the bumper. Meanwhile, the thrusters burned at the branches below them, yet the saw blades spun in their direction like shiny little saucers. Billy flipped on the rear camera and turned the guns mounts at the rear to target the branches below the trunk. Rounds scorched the tree trunk.

"I can't get a bead on those branches."

The muzzles glowed red. Bark and splinters flung from the trunk.

"Ah, son." Mike grew uneasy as the moonlight twinkled off the silver-toothed disks. Finally, the thrusters burned through the branches. The saw blades sliced the tree apart as the Armybrats' car broke free. They flew down the staircase toward the riverbank. The thrusters burned the wooden steps as they dashed down them in the dark. His dad shouted, "Students, students."

Billy saw the kids on the stairwell and turned the steering wheel. The car flew sideways along a rock face and whizzed past them. Some kids fell. Others were bewildered by the illuminance along the rocks. Billy flew off the rock wall at the base of the stairway, hit a button, wheels extracted; he yanked the steering wheel as they slid to a halt in the sand, pressing on the brake.

His dad sat still and glanced at his son. He smiled. "Good decision not to listen to me."

"What dad?" Billy asked.

"This car is awesome!"

Billy nodded, smirking.

Chapter Twenty-Eight

Discovery

Duffy walked to Pete who was standing on the end of a pier. The sun broke the horizon. The war lasted all night. Paramedics and other emergency personnel worked the beachfront, gathering injured, and the survivors migrated to the sandy embankments near the river. Pete spun around as Duffy wrapped an arm around his shoulder. He was watching his mom and dad hug near the basin. It was the first time they both noticed the blood-stained beaches. It appeared as if bodies hailed from the sky. Both boys stared into the bloody canal.

Duffy remembered Watches' quote: 'I see a camp where you'll once visit, is where I'll bury your souls, n' your cryin' families'll miss it. Puddles of your blood will stain the beaches in splotches, for I am your worst nightmare Watches, Watches, Watches!'

Pete sighed. "Wow, look at all that blood!"

Duffy reflected, "I guess he was right."

Pete cocked his head in his direction and asked, "About?"

"Staining the beaches in splotches and being our worst nightmare, yadda, yadda, yadda."

Pete attempted to finish the riddle, "Watches, Watches . . ."

Duffy cupped his mouth. He shook his head at him. Pete smirked behind his hand. Duffy said, "Let me tell you a story."

Pete's eyebrows raised; he mumbled, "OK!"

"There once was an investigator named Watches."

Pete stared into his eyes and asked, "Did you get into those druggy drugs in that mill, some of that ganja shit?"

Duffy said, "That's the story man. Watches was everybody."

"Huh, you're making no sense."

"No, I'm serious Pete. Watches was Mr. Fallway. He was also that crazy clown kid of his, Ron. Oh, and you're gonna love this: he was Father O'Brien!"

Pete placed his hand on his shoulder and insisted, "Duffy, that white powder, those puffy clouds pouring out of the sawmill, that wasn't smoke. It was blow, pure coke, nose candy. You need to see the paramedics. You ingested that shit. You're losing it, brother."

Duffy sighed in a failed attempt to express his findings. Jerome was whistling as he crashed a canoe into the pier behind them. He looked at them; they both were a bit jumpy and backed away from him. He wore sunglasses and lifted two beer bottles on a paddle. He said, "For my most favorite Armybrats." Duffy and Pete grabbed the bottles. Jerome dropped the paddle inside the canoe and pulled another beer out of a case. "I found these in the main office. I couldn't resist."

Pete and Duffy turned around. Gerry had beers brought to the docks across the river. Camp counselors helped deliver them. Gerry shouted across the way, "Drink. You're dehydrated. Drink up." Between the pier and boat shed, debris was still burning. It was a rather large bonfire. The smoke swirled above the flames.

When Duffy turned around, he almost fell off the pier. He did drop his bottle as Vicki crashed into him, hugging him. Jerome watched the beer splash into the water, bob, and disappear. He shouted, "Aw man, alcohol abuse, brotha."

At the end of the pier, Danny was kissing Clarissa. Clarice and Michael were hugging on the sandy shore. Another canoe tapped into the pier. Gerry dropped a case of beer onto the wooden planks and shouted, "Drink! Oh, you already are."

Truth be told, Gerry was already three sheets to the wind. He seemed pretty chipper for someone with a burning campground. He noticed Billy walking past his brother and approaching the pier. He shouted, "Hey, you Armybrats. I wanna show you something. Come on!"

Wesley was in the same canoe as his grandpa. Billy ran up and shook his hand. He laughed. "You're alive."

Wesley smiled. "Yup."

Wesley was already drinking a beer. Duffy and Pete climbed into Jerome's canoe. Billy and Danny climbed into Gerry's canoe. The girls squeezed in as well. They rowed across the river toward the camp. Emergency personnel loaded people onto boats; the same boats they had borrowed from the Little Rapids marina.

As they exited the canoes on the other side of the river, they overhead authorities discussing cartel involvement. They uncovered coffins full of drugs at the base of the old sawmill. Danny and Pete had noticed drugs inside the tunnel beneath the mill. They discovered coffins with skeletal remains as well. Everything had been unfolding. One thing was left looming; no one knew the answer to. Gerry was leading them straight to it. *What was missing from the story?*

They followed the old man toward the main office. Gerry held up a set of keys and approached the cellar. The boys surrounded him as he unlocked the padlock and released the hasp. He swung one door upward and signaled for them to enter.

Billy sighed. "You first this time, Gerry. I don't wanna be locked in."

He smirked and entered his own cellar. Everyone followed him inside.

Gerry stood at a toolbox as they walked in behind him. He stated, "When I locked you boys in here, you were in my most secure bunker. You had no clue how important this cellar is to me, but . . ." he withdrew a remote from his toolbox and clicked a button. Fluorescent lighting flickered. It almost cast a baby blue everywhere as the walls behind the shelving units gradually exposed more space. They wrapped around the side walls almost like a collapsing telescope.

Behind the walls was an entirely new section. The office above them had a bigger basement of course. The cellar they were in was just a crawl space. When the walls opened, the space quadrupled in size. There were piles of treasures, gold bullion, and some chests that held pearls and diamonds. There was wall-to-wall shelving of artifacts and piles of gold coins. Everyone lost their bottom jaw. Gerry Fifer was loaded. They walked through the room in amazement. Danny and Duffy were slipping pearl necklaces on the girls.

Gerry stood by his toolbox smiling. Jerome sighed. "Oh shit!" He raised a gold bar. His eyes seemed as though he was inside Candyland and asked, "Can I have this one?"

Gerry laughed mercifully and drank some more beer. A shadow appeared at the cellar door. A man stood at the top. Jerome dropped the gold bar and jogged to him. He stepped out of the cellar waiting for his eyes to adjust from the daylight. He made a face at his dirty robe with a torn pocket. Dried-up blood and mud cracked along the man's face when he smirked. Jerome sighed. "Pops."

His dad replied, "Son."

"Oh my God, pops," He bear-hugged his father as he crouched forward to accept his son's hug. "Wha' happened, I thought you were dead?"

"They had me in that tunnel, boy. Say, where's this Billy character? We have a sheriff's office to run-in Little Rapids. I need you and your partner to run that outfit with me so I can retire."

Jerome glanced at his breast pocket to notice his dad was Little Rapids' new sheriff. "Yes, pops," he smiled and shouted, "Billy, there's someone I'd like ya to meet." He turned to his dad and said, "We were in police school togetha."

"I know. I knew his father from way back. Good man."

Gerry walked out of the cellar and cornered his office. Mike was standing with a couple FBI agents. Gerry looked at the agents and then at Mike. He smiled. "Let's drink."

Mike explained, "Let's talk."

Gerry nodded; they followed him inside. He stammered, "We talk, then we drink. Good plan, Mike!"

Meanwhile, in Little Rapids, Madison authorities were arresting people by the dozens. The entire police station had been quarantined. Most of the town had been involved in some way, shape, or form. There were charges of possession, sale of narcotics distribution. The entire police department was in on the double-cross except for Mr. Dawson, of course. The DEA was already embedded within the community as well as other Federal agencies. The local law enforcement including the Wisconsin Army National Guard was cleansing the town of bad guys.

The mayor's cell was bombarded; people were brought to their knees behind desks. In his own office, the mayor stood from his desk as twelve guns aimed at him. He smiled and waved his hands foolishly. His political nonsense meant nothing to their itchy trigger fingers. They would have put the mayor out of his no-good, two-faced misery if they had to. No one was getting away from this.

At the camp, people were celebrating near a bonfire drinking beer. Some of the Special Forces were drinking with the Armybrats, telling of war stories. The Armybrats had worked side by side with them in and around the camp and through the old sawmill. A few guys recognized the boys from the House on the Rock incident. Danny and Clarissa were hand in hand. Duffy was standing behind Vicki with his arms around her midsection. Billy was kissing Andrea behind the boathouse.

Inside the office, Mike sat at a table with Gerry. Inside his theater room, some media expert was tinkering around with his video system. Another guy brought in a cassette; the monitors flashed behind Gerry. They were cueing a video scene of a restaurant. As Gerry was blabbing on and on about ancient Indian customs and traditions, the television sets were playing his ultimate demise behind him—in black and white.

Mike whispered, "Why would you feel it necessary to lie to me, Gerr?"

Gerry drank some more beer and set his bottle down. He closed his eyes. On the videotape in the background, the scene was set at Gerald and Nadine's restaurant. He appeared to be arguing with Stanley Markesan then a short brawl and a scuffle broke out. Stanley's brother, Jeff, dragged Nadine behind a counter. Gerry was held by a couple of Stanley's typhoons as Jeff slit his wife's throat and tossed her body onto a salad bar. Blood ran across the lettuce; of course, in shades of gray, it appeared to be a darker gray ooze more like French dressing. In the video, Gerry was falling to his knees before the salad bar. Fast-forwarding through footage, they found him collecting money from Stan's brother who also frequented his restaurant. Mike shook his head before Gerry.

Gerry spun around and noticed the video playing behind him. He cried over the chair and whispered his wife's name a few times as the video played out. The man rewound the tape to a specific point when a white-bearded fellow sat next to Stanley. They slid a briefcase across the counter and Gerry flipped through the cash inside.

Mike glanced at an FBI agent, then at the guy near the media center, and made a slit-throat gesture to stop the tape. The man paused the video with Stanley paying Gerry. Mike asked, "What was deal you made with the devil, Gerr?"

Gerry wiped his forehead and eyes and couldn't even bear to look at him and sighed. "You don't understand, Michael."

Mike smiled. "Appease me—just a smidge!"

Gerry explained, "They were gonna kill my family. They said I had no choice but to surrender that sawmill so they could continue their operations."

Mike suggested, "You couldn't talk to me. Over two decades go by, your wife was murdered, and you couldn't bring yourself in to tell me, a good friend, a cop friend nonetheless, huh, Gerry?"

"Mike, they were gonna kill my family, my son, his boy Wesley. They badly beat his brother. They did beat poor Wesley. That's why the poor kid's neck twitches. Watches tore a nerve in that boy you wouldn't believe. But his brother, their parents sent him away to military school to keep him safe."

Mike shook his head in disbelief and asked, "As wise as a Native American you once were, you once said to me, why hide, why the name change. You inspired me to drop this whole mask, Gerry. I thought you among anyone else would understand your own words, your customs. Why the hypocrisy, Gerry? Why couldn't you come to me with this?"

Gerry hollered, "They killed my wife. I had no choice. They said if I had gone to the cops, they'd kill them all!" Gerry was standing and throwing his arms in the air at this point, pointing at his monitors. The FBI agents stepped forward. Mike fanned his hand before them to stop them. He collapsed in his chair and pouted, "Oh Nadine. I love you, precious Nadine. Why did they have to kill her?"

Mike proclaimed, "Now that I can believe, Gerry!" As he said that, Tony entered the room behind him with a couple of his officers from Wausau. Mike continued explaining, "Unfortunately, it pains me to say this, in the least." Mike choked a little, "But you aided and harbored a known felon which makes you . . ."

Gerry's eyes rolled at him, and he shook his head. He sighed. "No." He didn't want to hear the words coming from his longtime friend. He didn't want to hear the truth, but he had already known the truth.

After Mike hesitated, he choked a bit more and could not finish explaining but reverted, "Damn it, Gerry. Your restaurant was a front—in my old neighborhood none-the-less. I even chipped in. Meals I paid for slowly killed us. You became them, Gerry. You're one of the reasons that made this monster plausible. You got my wife raped. I cannot tell you sorry enough about the loss of Nadine. God rest her soul. She didn't deserve that. In the same breath, damn you, Gerry. Damn you straight to hell."

Tony's officers walked around Gerry as he stood from his chair. He didn't say a word but carried both arms around his back as one officer slapped the handcuffs on him. The other officer patted him down, withdrawing a few weapons and laying them on the table. An officer was reading him his rights; they escorted him around the table toward the front door. Mike closed his eyes when a single tear drove dead skin cells toward the underside of his chin. He balled a fist inside his left fist and tapped his forehead in shock.

He heard the office door creek open as they exited the building but then an awkward silence loomed. After that, a young Wesley Fifer blatted, trying to hug his grandpa as officers refrained him. Tony stopped the officers and allowed him to hug his grandson. Mike stood and threw his chair across the table; it smashed monitors. FBI agents were between him and Tony as he followed them out the door. The media guy jumped away as pieces of glass and plastic rained down the entertainment system.

Helicopters swarmed in the distance. A news chopper shared the sky. Camera crews were taking pictures of the boy hugging his grandfather near the porch. It was a dismal scene, to say the least. Clarice walked behind Mike and placed her arm around his midsection. They watched as they pulled Gerry away from Wesley and placed him inside an SUV, tucking his head down. Officer Darcy collected Wesley's weeping soul.

There were emotions crawling through the camp that night. By the river, young kids were partying and swimming. Across the river, there were fire and rescue teams attempting to control the spread of wildfires. The Army National Guard helicopter was bringing Bambi buckets from a larger bed of water. In the background, they continued to spread water across the hillside.

There were still nearly a hundred boats in the river. People were scattered everywhere. A cameraman in the news chopper zoomed away from the camp; the aerial footage truly captured the surrealism of a story. This blossomed from the seed planted in 1974 when the devil arose from the mist of Wausau Wisconsin and rained Holy hell on the policeman's life ever since.

It was a conservation trip from hell. It was a true nightmare, a scar etched in any young kid's mind or any adult alike. The maps now printed the names of those towns because they truly made history like a war. It was truly a camping fiasco to remember.

A young man approached the porch and shook Mike's hand. "A couple of my boys over there told me you were Michael Anglekee, and I just had to shake your hand, sir."

Mike was dumbfounded. "Yup, that's me."

"Well, I'm Ronald Markesan. I've been working with this outfit over here for years. I also heard you visited my old office in DC."

For a moment, Mike was astounded by the name. The DEA agent was simply impressed by his accomplishments as a police officer. Mike nodded after accepting his outstretched hand. Although creepy as it may, the boy did not resemble the son of the devil, even if he held the same name as the Devil's dead boy. He said, "You're Ronald?" Mike asked. The man nodded. Mike's dumbfounded stare transformed to a smirk as they stood on the office porch, watching the SUV haul away Gerry Fifer. "Thanks, Ronald, for all that you do!"

"No! Thank you, sir!"

Upham Woods was a wonderful place to visit. Many thanks were owed to its camp staff, commodities, complimentary cabins, and group-think strategies. Natural settings were well maintained in the preservative of life.

Helicopters swarmed the skies. A bent flagpole towered the flowerbed. It creaked in the wind at its stress point, weakened metal. The American flag snapped outward. Salute to the Native American ancestry, their heritage, the perils of American history, and Armybrats as their stories may even scare their grandkids someday.

THE EH HMM . . .

CPSIA information can be obtained
at www.ICGtesting.com
Printed in the USA
BVHW070549140223
658412BV00014B/370